JUNE:

TRESPASSES

JAN FANCY HULL

A
TIM BROWN
MYSTERY

June: Trespasses
© 2024 Jan Fancy Hull

Cover design: Rebekah Wetmore
Editor: Andrew Wetmore

ISBN: 978-1-998149-27-8
First edition March, 2024

2475 Perotte Road
Annapolis County, NS
B0S 1A0

moosehousepress.com
info@moosehousepress.com

We live and work in Mi'kma'ki, the ancestral and unceded territory of the Mi'kmaw people. This territory is covered by the "Treaties of Peace and Friendship" which Mi'kmaw and Wolastoqiyik (Maliseet) people first signed with the British Crown in 1725. The treaties did not deal with surrender of lands and resources but in fact recognized Mi'kmaq and Wolastoqiyik (Maliseet) title and established the rules for what was to be an ongoing relationship between nations. We are all Treaty people.

Also by Jan Fancy Hull

Non-fiction

Where's Home?

Short stories

The Church of Little Bo Peep and other stories

Inquire Within

The Tim Brown Mystery Series

January: Code

February: Curious

March: Enigma

April: Sweetland

May: Façades

July: Confidence (coming in September, 2024)

Definitions

trespass, n.
> Law: entry to a person's land or property without his or her permission.
> Similar: unlawful entry, intrusion, encroachment, invasion, infringement, impingement.
> Archaic, Literary, Religious: a sin or offence.

ratiocination, n.
1. Reasoning, conscious deliberate inference; the activity or process of reasoning.
2. Thought or reasoning that is exact, valid and rational.
3. A proposition arrived at by such thought.

To those who acknowledge their trespasses

June: Trespasses

June 1, 1999: To do

Tuesday

Tim had several reasons to celebrate this morning. He had just concluded his part in steering his friend Evelyn to a successful business venture. He'd had a showdown with a nasty man, and had given as good as he got. Nasty-man's über-nice wife had flung baseless accusations at Tim, but she had received her comeuppance from a surprising source, leaving him speechless. And while he had always bemoaned South River's dull downtown, he had set big wheels in motion to beautify it.

He also was happy that there was still a good amount of wine left following his "June Eve" celebration last night, so he could greet this morning without the gritty lees of regret.

"And it's a sunny June day, too, Gloria," he said to his expensive and versatile espresso machine.

While he waited for his dark beverage to dribble from Gloria's twin spouts, he went to his little-used study to get a new notebook and to replenish the supply of leads in his Eversharp pencil. As a lifelong newspaperman, he had these tools always within reach, even though he was currently on sabbatical from his weekly newspaper, *The Times*.

Tim had traded his well-worn and familiar weekly routine for an amorphous quest: "to delve". Initially, he had been unable to explain what he meant by that, even to himself; but he had persevered, and was honing his particular definition.

With the support of his staff, led by the irreplaceable Elaine Fong as the Interim Editor, he had discovered, solved, or resolved a number of quests. One of them was even destined to become *The Times'* first *bona fide* "breaking news" story not involving quilts or country music.

He toasted and buttered a slice of whole-grain bread from the bakery and began to write a fresh To Do list in the notebook. He had skipped over a number of items during recent activities and he intended to deal with them now:

Ashes
His long-time employee, GB, and GB's wife Constance, had both died this spring, and their ashes were resting in urns in a quiet corner of Tim's study, out of sight of Robert, who was skittish about such things. Would he have the ashes interred in the cemetery, or would they be scattered somewhere?

Prince Edward Island
Robert would perform an organ recital at the Indian River Festival in PEI in July. Tim would go, too, of course, and they had briefly discussed extending the trip for a vacation. Tim was to make the travel arrangements. He had taken time away from the office only once in his life, and it also had been to Prince Edward Island, for a newspaper convention. That hadn't been a vacation: between presentations, he'd spent hours on the phone with his office back in South River. But he had loved the scenery, and he'd made a friend there.

Evan visit
Evan Robicheau was that friend. He was Editor of *The Daily*, the province's biggest newspaper, based in Halifax. Tim had recently promised to invite Evan to South River for a weekend in May, but hadn't got around to it. He'd make a plausible excuse about why he was late, and set a date.

Lawn and Gardens
A metaphorical by-product of this year off was being able to stop and smell the roses. However, his real roses were badly neglected, especially in the large back garden. He had let it all go to weeds since he'd rarely been home during daylight hours to look at it. Having just recently revived the sunroom at the back of the house, he couldn't escape seeing the overgrown goldenrod and blackberry brambles right outside the window. There once had been a path wandering around shrubs and gardens, and he hoped to restore some of that.

Woodshed
This was a small, open structure built to replace the previous shelter from his grandfather's era, which had collapsed under snow with half a year's supply of wood and garden tools inside it. This one seemed to be heading toward the same fate, with one end already sagging. The shed

was just a sloped roof to keep rain and snow off the wood, slatted walls to permit the wood to dry, and a small, enclosed tool shed at the near end. Not wanting to be trapped under another collapsing shelter, Tim had resorted to using the sunroom for temporary wood storage, and "temporary" had stretched to years.

Sunroom
Wherever he stacked his firewood didn't seem up to the task. The sunroom had begun to pull away from the back of the house, and he had seen rainwater leaking in at the top and running out at the bottom, indicating that the whole structure might be unstable.

House paint, exterior
There'd been a lot of talk recently about the exteriors of buildings on Main Street, including his own office, which Robert had accurately described as "shabby". Soon it would boast fresh paint. But his home looked neglected also, and fixing that was not going to be a simple job, it being three stories high, counting the attic. He had thought he might address one wall a year, but having scaffolding on some part of his house for four years straight wasn't appealing. He'd get a quote and then decide.

"C'mon, Gloria, I'm going to need a bigger mug of coffee to deal with all this. Oh, I know, let's make an Americano."

He found the *Libretto di istruzioni* that came with the European appliance, flipped through until he found the English instructions, and refreshed his memory. "Oh, right: espresso with hot water added. At least that's easy."

He nibbled toast crusts as he reviewed the list. A few months ago this list would have given him the willies. He had learned not to jump to conclusions as a Private Researcher (the title he used in public in lieu of Delver), and he reminded himself of that now.

"Sure," he said aloud, "the list is daunting, but that's what happens when you work eight days a week. You let things go, or things go on their own. I don't know why wood sheds fail. I thought the last one was built well enough. I didn't know the sunporch wasn't."

He sipped the Americano.

"House paint needs refreshing from time to time. There's no blame in that, as long as it's taken care of before someone complains to the Unsightly Premises officer. Especially since I've been making a big noise downtown about this very thing."

He sipped again.

Show some gratitude, Tim. You inherited this house, you inherited your business and the building it operates in. You've never had a mortgage, and the business, we are relieved to discover, is more profitable than ever.

"Sure, but I'll be spending money like water with that new advertising campaign."

That's not spending, and you know it. That's investing.

He frequently spoke aloud when alone, and his Inner Tim often argued with him. Sometimes Tim ignored both voices, but when he finally arrived at a decision, he felt the pros and cons had had a good airing.

He moved to a less disputatious item: the back lawn and gardens, all under weeds two and three feet high, and brambles arcing even higher. That was a shame, but he really hadn't had the time or know-how to do the job himself, and he hadn't seen the sense in paying someone to do it if he never saw it.

His grandfather, Ebenezer Johnson, had owned many acres of land back in the day. He built this huge house where the road leading uphill from the South River turned inland. It was a major road now, with traffic lights and a busy intersection bordering on his front yard, and a gaping parking lot, stores, strip malls and take-out food joints beyond that. He often thought how dismayed his grandfather would have been to see his grand estate in such middle-class company.

Grandfather wouldn't have approved of Mother divesting all but an acre of the estate, either. Sure, she donated a good parcel to the fairgrounds in return for the naming of the main building, but she made a rare tactical error there.

Tim's mother, Brownie Brown, née Lucinda Johnson, did cut a ribbon at the opening of "The Brown Building" and printed a photograph of that august event in her own newspaper, but since the eponymous building was later painted brown, the significance of the name was lost on the teamsters and their horses and oxen.

Later still, a much larger, metal-clad building was erected very near the back line of the remaining Johnson/Brown house lot, a big blank wall which kept Tim's house out of sight of the fairgrounds and vice versa. All this had transpired when Tim was in grade school, and he only heard of it when his mother was in her cups and chose that series of events to fuel her rants.

He went now to the parlour windows overlooking the overgrown mess behind the house, and he saw the outcome of all that: Brownie had planted a variety of deciduous and evergreen trees along the back line, probably thirty years ago. They were tall and beautiful now, almost totally obscuring the industrial grey building behind.

"That was wise, Mother. They say the best time to plant trees is twenty years ago, and here's proof. I thank you for doing that. It looks like a little forest grove back there. Robert loved the sunroom so much because he said he could hear the wind in the trees. I bet if I cleared that area he'd pitch a tent and try camping out there."

He returned to the kitchen. His cup was empty, toast crumbs gone. It was nearly lunchtime, but he wasn't hungry. He poured a tumbler of water and returned to the list.

"Let's set some priorities here," he said to the list. "Let's say we start by getting the weeds cleared away so we can see what's under all that. Didn't I call the lawn company already? Where are they?"

He took the business card from the cork board beside the refrigerator and called the number.

"Hello, it's Tim Brown calling. It's June first and my lawn hasn't been mowed yet. I know I called just last week about the back yard, but I was wondering when you planned to come."

"Oh, Tim, yes, we're so sorry, we ran into a delay. Dwayne had to go to the hospital, so we're quite a bit behind."

"Oh no, I'm sorry to hear that. I hope he'll recover soon. Is he the one who comes here?"

"Thanks. Yeah, he is, but he had an accident while he was sharpening the blades, so—"

"I don't mean to sound like I don't care about Dwayne, but do you have someone else who can come to mow? If you remember, I wanted to clear the back yard as well as my front lawn, and weeds are the main crop there."

"Dwayne's it, I'm afraid. I just...I'll call you as soon as I know, okay?"

This wasn't the positive start he'd hoped for. *Poor Dwayne, and poor Whoever-she-is on the phone. But still, when the chips are down, you're supposed to call your customers and tell them what's what, aren't you?*

Former Tim would have waited. Regardless of the inconvenience to him and his blades of grass, he would have been considerate of the obvious crisis in the Lawn Care Division of Mow 'n' Plow, which he'd privately pronounced "Mo 'n' Plo". Former Tim, in fact, had paid no attention to what was done as long as he could get in and out of his driveway in winter.

But New Tim had been dreaming about a revived back garden, and he wanted to see it happen.

New Tim reached for the Yellow Pages, found Lawn Maintenance, and was immediately drawn to the advertisement for a company in Chester Basin. What attracted him was a small colour photo of shrubbery and flowers surrounded by green grass and a bit of a path. There it was: his future oasis.

The services they listed would surely cover all his requirements. This was a real business, not just one guy with a plow truck and a mower.

Sorry, Dwayne. I hope you recover soon, but I need to get going. He dialed the new business and told the woman his front-and-back yard story and his latest reason for the late-season call.

"No problem at all," she said. "This sounds like a little more than just a quick mow. Is your front lawn mostly just lawn?"

"I guess it is, yes. A few things to mow around, but I think it's pretty straightforward."

"Good. I'll send Jake over. He'll bring a small mower and give it a lick and a promise. He'll walk around your property with you and you can point out what areas you want cleared and he'll quote you a price on the spot. Whether you decide to go ahead with us or not, whatever mowing he does that day will be on the house."

"Free? Does that happen?"

"It does with us. We like our clients to get to know us."

"Well, I'd like to get to know you too. When can Jake come over?"

"That's the big question. If Mother Nature agrees, how about, oh, lemme check...how about Saturday morning at eight?"

"You work Saturdays? Sure, I'll be here."

"We work whenever the weather allows, which isn't every day. Saturday's forecast is iffy, but let's hope the rain will hold off until we get our day's work done. Thanks for calling us, Mr Brown."

Tim dropped the Mow 'n' Plow card in the trash can. "*Sic transit gloria mundi,*" he said. "Not you, Gloria. You're a keeper."

That was a big Do taken care of. The woodshed and sunroom would follow.

I'd better call Evan and invite him down. But when? I'd like to use the sunroom when he's here, and I can't show it off before the backyard is at least cleared...the weekend of the nineteenth should be good.

"All right, Tim, take action. Dial that number now."

Old Tim would have practised this pitch for a couple hours. *I was so uncertain, wasn't I? It's just a phone call.* New Tim picked up the phone and pressed the buttons.

"Evan Robicheau."

"Hey, Evan, it's Tim Brown calling. Better late than never, I hope."

"Always happy to hear from you, buddy. Are you late? What'd I miss?"

"We talked about you coming down for a weekend in May, but that didn't happen, sorry."

"I'd forgotten. Couldn't have made it anyway. Gosh, this job never quits. Does yours? Oh, right, you're on leave for a year—a whole damn year! Must be nice, Tim."

"It's starting to be. Unhooking yourself from the mother ship isn't all it's cracked up to be at first, but I'm getting the hang of it now. Anyway, I've got my calendar out and I'm wondering if you could pull yourself away from the cares of the biggest newspaper in the land to come to bucolic South River for a relaxing weekend?"

"A weekend off? Is it possible? When?"

"How about the weekend of the nineteenth? Come Friday and leave Monday if you like."

"Three nights? That's unlikely. Saturday to Sunday might be doable."

"That'll work. Saturday supper is usually pizza, and I do make a mean one. Sunday morning, we go to church, but you may find sleeping in more appealing. I'll expect you by mid-afternoon on Saturday. You're welcome to come earlier, just phone to make sure I'll be home, okay?"

"Sounds good. Should I bring anything?"

"If you drink wine, we have lots; otherwise, name your poison or bring your own. We'll do the cooking. It'll be good to spend some time with you. And Robert will be here, of course."

"Of course. Thanks, Tim. See you then."

Another task done. So what's wrong? Evan forgot I was going to invite him? He agreed to come, but it feels like he's not really interested.

"Oh, come on, Tim, stop second-guessing. Maybe Evan's like you, not accustomed to being an overnight guest. He said he'd come. He'll show up, or he won't. You'll make pizza anyway, and it will be delicious. Move on."

The next most urgent item on the list was the PEI vacation. He hadn't done anything about that, either, and given the popularity of Island destinations, he might have delayed himself out of options.

Never having booked accommodations himself, he knew he needed professional help: the travel agency in the mall across the river from his office had agents happy to serve him.

It was past lunchtime now. He spread peanut butter on a single slice of bread, wrapped it around a banana half, sliced lengthwise, a favourite snack, and washed it down with a mug of tea.

Then he drove downtown and parked in his usual spot opposite the newspaper office, but he didn't go in because today was deadline day. He had been involved in the machinations of his weekly paper a lot recently, far more than might be good for a man supposedly on sabbatical.

Work seemed to be a sticky thing, harder to let go of than he would have imagined. While he had learned a lot and was enjoying much of the first half of his year, he was still too close to the daily routine. Time to book a holiday.

He strode across the bridge to the mall and presented himself to an agent.

~

Grilled sausages and mashed potatoes were supper, and he was grateful for the bottom half of yesterday's *Dénouement rouge*, with which he toasted today's great start to another month.

He had confirmed a week at a four-star inn in PEI, known for its capable chef. There were lots of harbours, beaches, and small towns to visit within a short drive. He was eager to share the details with Robert when he arrived on Thursday.

June 2: Stink

Wednesday

It was still spring according to the calendar, but South Riverites believed that summer began with the long weekend in May. Grass and weeds were growing, flowering things were in bud or in bloom, trees were in leaf, and the soft ground was drying out enough that heavy lawn equipment wouldn't leave ruts.

While Tim waited for Gloria to build up pressure for his morning infusion, he opened the cellar door to expose the dartboard hanging on its nail. He made three quick throws, but as he bent down to retrieve the three darts from the floor he recalled his Aunt Stella's brief instruction, and tried again from the wrist instead of the shoulders. All three stuck on the board in respectable places.

"Bingo! Okay, not Bingo. What do you say when you do well at darts? Not Goal. Bullseye, I suppose, but I'm not there yet anyway. Good, though."

Evelyn had brought them the board, but neither she nor Stella would teach them about keeping score. Perhaps one of them would when he and Robert managed to keep all the darts on the board.

As he closed the cellar door, he caught a whiff of an unpleasant odour, and that reminded him of another item to add to the To Do list.

<u>Basement smell</u>

Robert had earlier mentioned an unpleasant smell emanating from the basement. Tim hadn't noticed it until now. Was it there all the time, or just since the frozen ground had thawed?

The old house was well-built. The foundation was huge granite stones cut and fit together, and the floor was poured concrete. Undoubtedly there were cracks and fissures where water could seep in. Would water be smelly just because it leaked in? He had never noticed any water down there, and considering the house was built at the top of a hill, he thought it unlikely.

But what would raise this odour? He rarely went to the basement. The washer and dryer were there, but Mrs Aquino trudged down and up to do his laundry on Thursdays. Those appliances, which Tim had dubbed Romeo and Juliette, were quite new, and should not leak or smell.

Should leaks be expected? Why would they happen? A little rubber gasket gets stiff and cracks...but if so, I would see water, wouldn't I?

"Not if I don't look. Hold my coffee, Gloria, I'm going down."

He flipped the light switch and descended the steep stairs. As he had earlier discovered in the attic, very little was stored here. His mother had done him the great favour of having all the usual remnants of a life disposed of before her death—if there ever had been junk in this basement. Neither his parents nor grandparents had been 'handy' and neither was Tim, so there would have been few tools or leftover scraps.

The concrete floor was gritty, and the two bulbs hanging from the ceiling gave a dim light. *I'll ask whoever I get to pursue the mystery odour to add a light above the appliances, and maybe slip a piece of vinyl flooring in front of them in case Mrs A drops a freshly-cleaned item. They look good, though; no water anywhere that I can see.*

The furnace dominated the centre of the space, and galvanized air ducts radiated from the plenum in all directions. It had been changed over to a hot air furnace back in the day, so there was no boiler to leak water, and the current electric hot water heater was still within the warranty period. The old cast iron radiators were neatly lined up in a corner.

"Why would they have lugged those heavy things all the way down here," he mused, "down those steps? They'll have to be carried back up again to be disposed of. It won't be me and my back doing that job."

There was no ignoring the odour down here, though. It was difficult to describe, and he couldn't identify any corner of the basement where it was stronger or weaker, but it definitely wasn't nice.

"Well, something's rotten in the state of Denmark," he said to Gloria as he turned out the light and closed the cellar door. "Now, who do we call about that?"

There was no "Basement stink" listing in the Yellow Pages. There were multiple Contractors listed, eager to build new homes and wharves. Each of Tim's jobs was small: maybe a little electrical, a little plumbing, strengthening the sunroom and straightening the woodshed.

He looked up Handyman, and under it was "See Renovations and Home Improvements". That was helpful: at least he had the words to describe the category of service he was seeking without having to list all the tasks first.

His espresso had cooled. He poured it out and made a cappuccino to accompany a slice of toast while perusing the latest copy of his own weekly. The writing was improving, he thought. James Olsen, his photojournalist, was doing well under the strong push and pull from Elaine Fong.

He was especially interested in the campaign that he himself had devised last month, to freshen the appearance of South River's Main Street. It looked like it might be one of the paper's most successful campaigns, generating new advertising revenue, if today's paper was any indication. That new ad salesperson was a pistol.

He set out on this lovely June day to discover who was going to right all the wrongs on his property.

~

Tim's experience yesterday with the injured mower guy versus the business with multiple people and machines inspired him to seek a similar enterprise for this work.

He drove to a few building supplies stores to inquire about handymen. Most recommended Conquerall Services, so that's where he ended his search. The name sounded optimistic to Tim. Conquerall was the name of the small community near where his Aunt Stella lived.

He drove to Conquerall, trying to keep his eyes on the narrow, turny road while admiring the bright sun on the river. He slowed as he passed Stella's place in Lower Riverside, and was pleased to see that some work had begun on her own front lawn makeover.

He turned into the dirt lane leading to Conquerall Services, and parked in the yard. The building was a corrugated metal building with a nondescript front. Assorted trucks, trailers, and equipment dotted the yard.

A large and muddy white dog approached Tim as he got out of his car, big tail slowly wagging, but it didn't bark and it kept its muddy feet on the ground.

Tim went to the door, pushed it open, and the dog squeezed in beside him.

"No, Laddie, you know you can't come in," called the woman behind the counter. Tim hesitated. "Not you, sir. I mean the dog. Laddie, out you go now, g'wan!" She gestured to accompany the command, and Laddie backed out with a doleful look on his big white face.

"Sorry 'bout that. I can't have him wandering around in here, the big oaf. His tail knocked over a whole box of little doohickeys the other day, he was that happy. What can I do for ya?"

"I have a list of things that need fixing at my house, inside and outside," Tim said. "I asked around for someone who could find and fix a basement stink, add a light fixture, reattach a sagging sunroom, and reinforce a tilted woodshed. Most said I should come here."

"Right they should. We can do all that for you. What d'you want done first? What's that about a basement sink?"

"Stink. Basement stink. I went down to check this morning and it's there, can't tell where it's coming from. I can't see any water, but I can smell it upstairs sometimes. Is that something your guys are used to fixing, or do they just haul everything out until they hit it?"

"Ha-ha. Yeah, no, we get called out for basement stink more than you'd think. Could be anything. It's a sign that something's wrong, for sure. We'll send Corey up to start. When will someone be in the residence?"

"You mean today? Or weeks from today?"

"Not sure—just a minute." She reached for a microphone on a stand and pressed a button at its base. "Corey, you there?"

There was a loud static noise, and then Corey said, "Yuh."

"Got a fella here with a basement smell. Can you have a look after you finish there?"

She turned to Tim and said, "What address?" He quickly wrote it on a scrap of paper and passed it to her.

Minutes passed without a response from Corey. "He's moving a lady's toilet," she said. "He'll be back in a mo'."

More static noise alerted them that Corey was on the line. "Yuh. Where?"

"Top of town," she said. "I'll give you the address when you have your hands free."

Corey didn't respond, and she didn't wait for him. "Okay, then, that's lucky. Corey'll come have a sniff around suppertime. Now, what's your name?"

She set up an account for Tim, and they exchanged business cards.

"Nice to meet you, Amanda. Now, what do we do about my other tasks, the sunroom and such? That's more carpentry than plumbing—"

"It don't matter. Show Corey when he's there. He'll decide if it's something he wants to tackle or pass it to one of the other guys. We'll take care of you, Mr Brown. You just call us whenever anything goes wrong and we'll fix you up."

"Anything?"

"Haven't been stumped yet."

"I like that. Thanks very much, Amanda."

Laddie was waiting outside the door, and his muscular tail showed how happy he was to see Tim again so soon. He smiled at the dog but didn't speak in case that would encourage him to show more affection.

~

When he walked into the newspaper office, he was startled. Other than the fixed Reception counter, and the Editor's office and staff lunchroom, nothing was where he'd seen it last.

The dominant feature in the open space had been the file cabinet fortress which housed copies of every issue of *The Times* since its founding. There were whole copies, plus whatever and whoever had been named in the pages had a dedicated file of clippings. Inexorably, the number of cabinets had grown. They had been presided over by the late Gregory Barss, known as GB, the paper's longest-serving employee.

But the file cabinets were no longer in the configuration that had compressed the space available for staff desks, and the desks were no longer jammed in too-tight clusters.

Tim stepped to one side and watched movers in overalls and back braces wrestling with heavy-duty hand-carts. Harold, who had inherited the cabinets and their contents, was directing which cabinet would go into the space where one desk had been, and then that desk moved again, and another cabinet was shifted. It was like a three-dimensional chess game, and Tim, who did not play chess, thoroughly enjoyed watching it.

Elaine Fong came out of her office to stand beside Tim and watch the changes unfolding. "Impressive, isn't it?"

"I guess. Do they keep playing until all the pieces fit together?"

"Exactly. The more they move, the more they *can* move, I think. But you know, Tim, this wasn't just a good thing to do for better use of space. I went to the basement this morning, do you know why?"

"Can't imagine."

"To see what kind of extra reinforcement had been supporting this solid mass of filing cabinets. You know what I found?"

"Yup."

"Precisely: nothing. The building was well-built, thank goodness. But still, that was risky."

"Who knew? In my defence, there used to be heavy printing presses on this floor, so perhaps Grandfather made allowance for that when he constructed the place. Even so, it's good to have the weight moved from the centre of the floor. Where is everyone, by the way?"

"Upstairs. I don't know how much work is getting done up there, but at least we have the rooms. Not including your private room, of course. Harold is calling them down as their desks come up on the roster. He's quite the organizer. Are you going up?"

"Not now. I have to go home to meet a handyman about a few repairs. Just thought I'd come in to say hello. Today's paper looks swell. Everyone happy?"

"I am, which matters most to me. Cindy Martin is setting sales records. I think she's pulling in new advertisers every day. Not just new ads, but new advertisers. You opened the floodgates for her."

"Isn't that wonderful! I know you'll find ways to spend that new revenue."

"Yes, I will. What kind of repairs are you needing today?"

"I'm not sure, to tell the truth. Who would you call to find an odour in the basement? They're sending a plumber anyway. I bet he knows his stinky smells."

"Good luck with that." Elaine glanced at her watch. "I'm just about to go upstairs for the Project Sweetland debriefing. Just waiting for Roger— ah, here he comes now. Best wishes with your stinky project."

"Same to you with yours," Tim responded. Project Sweetland was the big news story his little paper would soon reveal. It, too, was smelly.

He watched Elaine and Roger wend their way across the floor. *They do make a nice couple. I like the way she tries not to smile at him.*

~

It was a quarter after three when Tim arrived home. He rummaged in the freezer for something to thaw for supper, and set it on the counter. He noticed the red dot on the calendar, there to remind him to check the passive humidifiers hanging inside his piano. He used a teapot to add a few tablespoons. This time of year they didn't dry out as quickly as they did in the winter, when the furnace blew hot air and the occasional fire burned in the fireplace.

He often rewarded this chore by practising the piano for an hour, but he feared he might play loudly and miss the laconic Corey when he came. Instead, he took the vacation brochures to the den to review while he waited.

The inn where he'd made their reservations was classy, as he recalled, having attended the newspaper convention there. He remembered the many references to the cuisine. If they hit it off with the chef, there'd be no telling what culinary delights they could maybe participate in making.

He'd booked two nights at a motel near the concert, followed by five nights at the inn. He hoped that would be sufficient, but as he gazed at the brochure, he thought even five weeks wouldn't be too much.

He heard a truck rumble into the driveway, and got up to greet Corey, who followed Tim down the stairs. When they reached the concrete floor, Corey said, "Uh-oh," and walked directly to the old laundry tub.

Tim followed, curious. "What's that?" he asked, looking in the tub.

"Gunk," Corey said.

"What's it from?"

Corey looked around, and pointed to the radiators stacked in the corner.

"Them, likely. Somebody prob'ly drained 'em here. I don't know why, but old water inside them rads is putrid. Too bad they didn't clean the tub after."

"So, is that the smell?"

"Nope."

He rooted in his toolkit, and brought out a plug. He inserted it in the laundry tub drain.

"That'll help."

"That's it?"

"Nope." He grasped the cold water tap, but it was seized, and so was the hot water tap. "Mm-hm," he said.

Tim watched and waited.

Corey looked beneath the tub, gently tapped on the drain pipe with a pipe wrench, and straightened up.

"You're some lucky," he said. "This here p-trap is dry as dry." Tim bent down to look at the drain pipe; it had a curve which did resemble the letter p.

"There's supposed to be water in that, to keep the sewer gases from backin' up into the home. If there was a flame or a spark—boom!"

"What do you mean, 'boom'?"

"An explosion. Sewer gas is methane and maybe other gases. I guess this space is open enough that it didn't 'cumulate. That furnace there has a flame, though, that's how some houses burn down. They blame the furnace, but it coulda been the sewer gas."

"So am I—did you say—am I in danger?"

"Not now. I put the plug in the drain, so that's it for the gas comin' up. The rest'll dissipate in your house, same as it's been doin'. Open the windows if you want, but it's not that bad," Corey said as he straightened up.

"Now what would you want me to do here? These taps are seized, and nobody's gonna use this nasty tub anyway. But a laundry tub is handy. I can replace the tub and taps, and you remind your wife to use it once in a while and this'll never be a problem. You smell that smell again, just come down and run the water to fill the p-trap. Or I can close the whole shebang and take the old tub away."

"I feel like it'd be safer taking the whole thing away, but I guess it would be handy to have the tub, as you say, if someone was doing any work down here. Or laundry. Okay, replace it, please."

"Okay. What else? Manda said you had a list."

"Yes, I do. Those old radiators: what do I do with them?"

"Call the junk metal dealer. They'll be happy to come and take 'em, and pay you. What else?"

"Can you put a light over the washer and dryer, and a piece of vinyl flooring under them, and clean the whole floor down here?"

"Okay. Something 'bout a porch?"

"Right. I guess we're done down here. A simple plug. Who knew? Follow me."

Tim led him to the sunroom to show where the rain trickled in and ran out again. Because he thought it might be useful information, he confessed to having stored most of a cord of firewood in it for a couple years.

Corey went outside and crawled underneath the structure. "They just nailed a beam across and treated it like a joist, which ain't real good. We'll jack it up level, put a good frame under it and some solid posts on cement tiles. That won't sink—unless you plan to keep puttin' your woodpile in there?"

"No, no, I learned my lesson about that. But that brings us to the woodshed over there, see. It's wonky, that's why I brought the wood inside. Besides, it was more convenient in the winter."

"Prolly do the same thing there: just jack it up and put it on some concrete blocks. We could haul it closer to your back door if that helps. We'll do that last, unless you're expectin' snow soon."

"You're funny. No, I'm expecting sunshine, and I want to be able to use the sunroom safely. Oh, one more thing: can you give me electricity in the sunroom?"

Corey found two electrical outlets on the wall between the parlour and the sunroom. "I'll just piggy-back them through the wall. You're not plannin' to plug anything heavy in them, right?"

"Right. I mean, no, just a lamp, maybe a small heater. Will that be okay?"

It was all okay with Corey. He took his tool box and drove away, promising that Amanda would call Tim tomorrow to book his return.

~

Tim was impressed that he had addressed and resolved a problem on the same day. *And it was potentially dangerous! What a disaster if my furnace had caused an explosion! The best way to learn about danger is after it's fixed with a fifty-cent plug.*

"I'll drink to that! What have we got in the locker to celebrate not having burned the house down? And soon getting the sunroom on solid footing?"

He selected a modest wine from the *Mercredi* vineyards to accompany his supper. He proposed multiple toasts, most of them containing variations on "Conquerall."

~

He was playing the piano after supper when the phone rang.

"Tim! I have a proposition for you!" It was Garland Greene, the town's gregarious mayor. "What're you doing tomorrow morning?"

"Hi, Gar. I plan to have coffee and then go to the Daisy Café as I do every Thursday. If I don't, Evelyn gets upset. She likes routine."

"Well, I hope she won't be upset, 'cause I'm inviting you to the monthly prayer breakfast tomorrow. There's a guest speaker I think you'll like. It's at the conference hotel across the highway. They put on a good spread."

"Oh, I don't know, Gar. You can't go to those things without someone thinking you're sending a signal about something, and I've already endured unintended and misunderstood signals about those paint samples on my building."

"That's what I'm talking about, Tim. You came up with such a good thing there, getting the businesses to freshen up their buildings and all that, and I was reading your smart newspaper just now, and I thought, 'Hey, why doesn't Tim come to the prayer breakfast and meet some new business owners?' Pretty good networking there."

"Gar, you're terrible. It's supposed to be about prayer, isn't it?"

"Sure, sure, you can pray, several times if you want, but there are people to see, hands to shake. Don't be shy. I'll introduce you. It starts at seven-thirty. I'll save you a seat, but don't be late. Oh, they're a little old-fashioned, so I'd recommend a shirt and tie. See ya!"

Gar hung up quickly, just like Tim's Aunt Stella, the MLA for South River and the Harbours. *Maybe politics requires them to make quick escapes.*

Tim returned to the piano bench. What he had been trying to play seemed too challenging now. Also, his delight at the day's accomplishments was alloyed with his reluctance to be dragged to the Multi-Faith Prayer Breakfast.

Multi-Faith meant that as many prayers would be offered up as denominations were represented. That would be all right, as long as they let the attendees eat their breakfast while it was hot.

What was that about a special speaker? Gar didn't say who it was. I've heard all the preachers in this town at one time or another. They're nice people, but uniformly uninspiring.

"But he wants to introduce me to people. That's about my downtown renewal project. It's going well, we're doing it without involvement from the Town, so Gar wants to get a little of my sparkle for himself. Fair enough. He's a promoter. I'll go for that reason."

June 3: Prayers

Thursday

In the bright light of early morning, Tim had misgivings. He meant what he'd said to Gar: if he showed up at the Prayer Breakfast, people might think he was a seeker, a believer, or even an evangelist. Not all who attended were any of those, he knew, but still. Why go, otherwise—because he was hungry?

He had attended in the past, of course, following his late mother's example. She went faithfully, especially in the days when women were not invited to the then-named Men's Prayer Breakfast. After her demise, he felt he had little to prove that needed proving there, and eventually stopped going. He had stopped going to a lot of things without his mother's prodding, choosing to stay cloistered in the office, allowing himself be needed by every piece of paper that had crossed his desk.

Maybe I didn't really need to take this year off to delve into things, as much as I needed to just get out and circulate. This may bear further delving.

He had no doubt that Garland Greene used the prayer event like all others: an opportunity to evangelize on his own behalf. Between elections, as they now were, Tim and his newspaper were neutral on the topic of the town's mayor; and during election campaigns, even more so. Tim believed in an independent press on topics of Garland Greene and God. He himself did sit in the tenor section of the choir at Saint John's United Church every Sunday, but that was about music.

"Come on, Tim. Just get dressed and go. You might learn something."

Expecting the hotel's coffee wouldn't be up to snuff, he made a double espresso and drank it while he put on his usual Sunday outfit.

~

He found a parking spot and entered the hotel, which was new and nice.

He had just waged a battle in favour of retaining old buildings, but new ones had their place, too. *Décor, that's what they call it. It's colourful, well-lit—*

"There you are, Tim!" Garland Greene boomed. "I have your ticket. Come on, we just have a few minutes before heads are bowed. There's a few people here who want to meet you."

Gar steered Tim by the elbow toward a knot of men who turned to look at him with some recognition but little interest until Gar said, "Here he is, the newspaperman who invented the downtown Gem District!"

Gar made introductions and hands were extended. "He's doing a great job, gents, and I hope we'll see your businesses listed as participants very soon. The Town will kick in funds according to who's in, so let's see some action."

One of the men asked Tim what the deal was.

"Don'cha get *The Times*?" Gar responded. "It's all in there. It's a great supporter of our town, and you should support it. Buy it, read it, advertise in it. I'll be watching. You support the campaign, the campaign supports South River, and, as your Mayor, I will support your business. See? Simple. C'mon, Tim, they're going to start."

Tim nodded his departure and followed Gar. Not surprisingly, their table was near the front.

What did surprise him was that there was no long buffet lineup. Uniformed servers stood on both sides of the swinging kitchen doors, waiting for the signal to bring out plates of whatever they were to serve, which smelled encouragingly of bacon with notes of toast and coffee.

The mayor introduced Tim around the table, ignoring the emcee's call for attention, which meant that nobody heard a word, but everyone nodded as they stood for the first prayer of the morning, after which the food was served.

It arrived hot, but that wasn't the only remarkable feature, Tim noted. It was Eggs Benedict with Hollandaise sauce and a side of crispy home fries. Very quickly, dozens of men tucked into their breakfast, and those who wanted something else received their special order.

Tim looked to the head table, where the clerics were seated in apparent brotherhood, and one in sisterhood, a young Lutheran minister. The guest speaker was a man he didn't recognize, but he stood out from the black-and-white crowd in his purple shirt and with the cross hanging on his chest. He had a craggy face, with overhanging eyebrows that flipped up and down as he spoke with the young female priest. He smiled a lot.

When the plates were cleared away, each member of the clergy at the head table was invited to come to the microphone to bring greetings and a prayer. When the guest speaker was offered his turn, he stood, bent down to the microphone, and said, "Almighty God, you've heard a good list of requests from my colleagues. We know you're listening. I'll leave you to it without further burden. Amen." Many laughed and applauded at this.

The chairman called for order so he could read a brief introduction of The Right Reverend Doctor Mortimer Evers, Bishop Emeritus of the Anglican Diocese of Nova Scotia and Prince Edward Island, who was about to begin a stint as summer relief in Blue Rocks and other tiny churches of that denomination along the coast. He said that just reading the man's title took up all the time he had, so without further "adieu", he vacated the podium for the guest.

The next twenty minutes passed too quickly for Tim. He was certain he had never heard such an engaging speaker, whether outside church or in. The cleric spoke simply, directly, without "churchy" language, and with a gentle humour.

His address was entitled "Why I wanted to serve in Blue Rocks this summer". His reasons were the parishioners, whether real or fictitious, one couldn't tell. But he drew clear pictures of a half-dozen people who, he claimed, would teach him many things, demonstrate grace, and might invite him and his wife to dinner, or take him out fishing.

Tim joined the lineup to greet the speaker after the final benedictions had floated heavenward. He shook Mortimer Evers' hand, and thanked him for the talk. "I'd love to be in your audience again. Is that possible?"

"Certainly, Tim. I'll be entertaining the faithful in my little churches until mid-August."

"Oh, well, I'm a member of the choir in another congregation, and the choir director would look sternly at me if I skipped out. Perhaps there's another angle. I own the local weekly paper. Could we publish some of your addresses as regular or occasional columns? This morning's was so good, it'd be a shame not to share it with a wider audience."

"That's very kind of you. Did I mention that I'm retired? I do like to keep my oar in, as it were, but I don't want to row too fast."

"I hear you. I'm supposed to be on sabbatical this year myself, but I find it hard not to stay involved. Where are you staying? Can I buy you a coffee sometime?"

"We've been loaned a little fisherman's cottage with all the mod cons, right on the water. It belongs to a parishioner who has gone abroad. It's another reason why I chose to serve the Lord in Blue Rocks...perhaps I failed to mention that perq, ha-ha. Why don't you come to us? You can meet my wife, who won't take no for an answer when it comes to sharing her baking, I warn you."

They exchanged phone numbers. "Call me Mort" said to give him a week to get settled in, and then he'd be happy to hear from Tim.

Tim looked around in the thinning crowd for the mayor, and found him in the hotel lobby in a hunched-over conversation. He called, "Thanks, Gar!" on his way out the door.

It was approaching nine o'clock. It didn't feel as though ninety minutes of time had passed. Tim felt like he'd been in a different place altogether. Mort's ability to draw word-pictures was a big part of it, bringing each person he talked about almost into view, making his audience care about them almost as much as he seemed to.

Come to think of it, did he mention God or Jesus at all? I don't think he did. Boy, that's a neat skill. He didn't say "Do unto others" or "Love thy neighbour", but that's what he talked about. There's a salesman for you. Well, I sure like what he's selling. Good call, agreeing to go this morning.

The food had been top notch, too. He hadn't had Eggs Benedict in a long time, and these were good. He didn't know what the ticket price was, but he could see that there was a benefit to serving good food at a prayer breakfast: the place had been full.

And Gar was pushing newspaper ads, too. If those fellows know what's good for them, they'll be calling Cindy Martin before noon today. Gar said he'd be watching, and he will, and they know he will.

Tim thought about the two kinds of leadership demonstrated this morning. The mayor told, and the Right Reverend showed. Both seemed to be quite hands-off, but there was a distinct difference. Gar found ways to add pressure. Mort would never pressure anyone, wouldn't even hint at what kind of eternal life one's deeds might earn. *But he does draw a fellow in.*

~

Tim went to the Daisy Café where he usually had breakfast on Thursday mornings. Evelyn had been quite upset when he'd failed to appear without notice recently, but he figured it was the stress of her business negotiations with Kenny, the cook, more than the lack of routine appearance of her favourite customer. Regardless, he thought it best to stop in.

"Not staying, Ev. I was persuaded to go to the prayer breakfast instead. Just wanted to say hi."

"You? At a prayer breakfast? I thought you'd never darken the door."

"Yeah, I did say that. But I was 'voluntold'. Great guest speaker, though. Everything good here?"

"I'm still standing, that's how I measure it. We're trying to figure out how to make improvements while operating. Kenny thinks it'll be easy, but he's back there in the kitchen all day. I'm out here with the whiners and complainers."

"Like me?"

"You never complain, Hon. You're my favourite."

~

Yesterday's hubbub in the office had settled down, but what a difference in the layout! Where possible, desks were separated by front-opening file cabinets, and others had room dividers which Tim recognized from the army surplus store.

Elaine Fong's door was open. "Would you like a guided tour?" she offered.

"No need. I'll just call out names."

"You will not. Come with me."

Elaine showed him a copy of the floor plan. "See here: James, Harold, and especially Ed, are along that side wall, as they have the most need for space and privacy. We've barely given them that, but it's better than before. Over here is Cindy; we're calling this a 'flex space' because Cindy's not permanent staff yet, but the dividers can be shifted a bit. The number of file cabinets will continue to diminish. Harold managed to free up four of the old front-facing ones, and it's his mission to sort through the rest of them quickly. In the middle, the clerical staff. Lunchroom, washrooms, and my office have to stay where they are. For now."

"Impressive. Are the staff happy?"

"Deliriously, can't you tell? As each space was set up yesterday, they got busy making it their own. It's funny. Instead of just standing and calling over the heads of everyone as they did before, they now seem to treat the spaces as though each had walls to the ceiling. With doors. Do you know of Les Nessman, or the call sign WKRP?"

"Doesn't ring a bell. Is it a TV show? My first hand knowledge about such things is nonexistent."

"It was a show. Les Nessman wanted an office, so he placed tape on the floor to indicate his walls, and insisted that people knock on his invisible door before he would recognize them. I think we've got a crew of

Les Nessmans here."

"Like the Emperor's new clothes—it works as long as everyone pretends the same story?"

"You got it."

Tim knocked on the cabinet that formed one wall of Cindy Martin's space. "Good morning, Miss Martin. How goes it?"

"Oh, Mister Brown, I can hardly tell you—but I'll tell you. This is so much fun! I love this work, you know, as long as my work has a chance of success. This Gem District project is going so well. We got a fresh batch of inquiries just now, from people who said they'd been at a conference with you?"

Tim chuckled. "Good for them. What about our neighbour, the bank?"

"In."

"Congratulations! And are you guiding the church on a colour scheme?"

"Am I ever!"

"Don't forget lights on the steeple. When will the painters do their work on our building, and should I see the colour scheme in advance?"

"Soon, and don't worry. Ed realized that the rainbow of colour samples he told the painters to start with was misconstrued, so now he wants to go conservative. I'm trying to restore his courage about that."

"I haven't said a word of complaint to him about it, and I won't. I'm trying to let the experts around me show their expertise, and you can quote me. Originally, I threatened to go all black. Pick something in between."

Tim's cell phone rang. Amanda from Conquerall Services was sending a crew to do the work in Tim's basement at one o'clock.

"That's wonderful, Amanda. I'll be there."

He was very impressed with her company and their ability to scramble their workers to take care of customers. Then he remembered today was Thursday. *Mrs A is cleaning today, and that includes floors and laundry...*

He quickly left the building, and then popped back in to say to Rachael, the receptionist, "Have a good day, Mrs Rafuse."

"Oh, good day, Mister Brown. Thank you, sir."

Long ago, he had known a Raquel Rafuse; the names Rachael and Raquel had become forever tangled in his mind, causing him to frequently call his receptionist by the wrong name. He had switched to addressing Rachael as Mrs Rafuse recently, and that seemed to have broken the link. *Can't say I don't try.*

~

Tim could see from the driveway that Mrs A was hard at work. The upstairs windows were open—that's where the vacuum cleaner sound was coming from—and the back door was, too.

He was reaching to close the door when a bundle of quilts and duvets emerged, small slippered feet propelling them forward. Tim held the door and waited. The pile leaned toward the railing, and one arm and then the other reached out to steady the bundle.

Finally, Mrs Aquino revealed herself, saw Tim behind the door, and squealed in alarm.

He was sorry to frighten her, and said so repeatedly. He held the bedding while she draped it over the clothesline for airing.

When they went inside, he asked to speak to her for a moment, in the kitchen where the sound of the unattended vacuum cleaner wasn't quite so disturbing.

"Mrs Aquino, did you ever notice a bad smell in the basement?"

"Bad smell, yeah. Bery bad sometime. No today."

"Did you? You should have told me, Mrs A. Anyway, someone's coming today to fix it. No more bad smell."

Mrs A started upstairs.

"But wait. The workers will also clean the floor downstairs, and replace the old laundry tub with a new, clean one. Which you can use, okay?"

"Okay."

"But wait. They will also put down a piece of flooring in front of the washer and dryer so you can keep it clean in case you drop something when you take it out of a machine."

"Okay."

"I hope they won't make a mess on the kitchen floor with their boots," he called as she disappeared back up the stairs, "but they might have to. Sorry."

He thought he heard her growl, but it might have been the vacuum.

Or it might have been the engine of the truck that had pulled into the driveway.

Corey and two other men got out and carried tools and supplies down the steep stairs. Tim saw a new laundry tub, a section of rolled flooring, a shop vac, and a mover's hand cart similar to the one he'd seen at work in the office yesterday.

"What's the cart for?" Tim had followed the men to the basement.

Corey pointed to the old cast iron radiators. "Manda said we might as well take these out for ya. The scrap guys won't do it, and you won't either." He nodded at Tim's shirt and tie and jacket, his prayer breakfast outfit.

"You're right about that. Will you take them away?"

"Can't today. It would tie up the truck and we've got another job after this. We'll stack 'em in the driveway and you call the scrap metal dealer. They'll come get them."

Tim noticed that the washer was just completing its cycle, and the dryer was signalling that it was keeping a dry load from wrinkling. *Uh-oh. That means Mrs A will be down here while they're working. What should I do?*

Things seemed to go better when Tim absented himself from areas of confusion, if the revised layout at the office was any indication. He acknowledged that workers would do their tasks, resolve obstacles, and appreciate him most if he was out of their way. He didn't want to leave the house in case the Conquerall men had questions, so he just sat in the kitchen and smiled at whoever passed through.

Mrs A finished first, and then the heavy-duty workers. Soon after that, Robert arrived from Halifax, ready for a quick supper before choir practice. Tim invited him to view the basement, the laundry corner, and the new tub.

"Take a deep breath, Rob. Smell anything?"

"Yes, what do they call it? Janitors use it to control dust when they're sweeping. Lemony."

"Correct: DustBane. What do you *not* smell?"

"Tell me."

~

On the drive to the church, Robert asked again about the sewer gas and the risk of explosion, however remote. "And you're sure it won't come back?"

It was unusual for Robert to speak of anything other than music on the way to the rehearsal, but he was somewhat danger-phobic, Tim had learned. While Tim felt relief when danger was averted, Robert's concern about what might have been lingered on.

"Absolutely gone forever, especially if we run water in the tub drain a few times a year. I think Mrs A will use the tub now anyway. No fear. I'm taking care of all the things I didn't even know to worry about, before they cause any harm. The front lawn is next, and then the big reveal of the backyard."

~

The choir struggled with an anthem they'd been working on for some weeks. It was in English, the text was familiar, and much of it was supposed to be sung in unison, but those advantages didn't carry them easily past the tricky time signatures and odd harmonies. "Where's the tune? What's the point?" were some of the anguished comments.

Robert persisted. He played it through on the organ, and they could almost get it. Two of the four section leads were a half-tone sharp when they arrived at the concluding "Surely, goodness and mercy shall follow me."

"All right, let's start again, just clapping. You're not feeling the rhythms. They su-su-separate and then fu-fu-fu-fall back together again. It's like waves on the beach. Expanding and contracting, like breathing. The Twenty-third Psalm paints a beautiful pastoral scene. This composer has written the very air into the music. Three beats against two. Four against three. Nature's like that. It's whimsical, changing. That's why we love it. And a-one."

This time, they mostly got the tricky rhythms, sang it again, and were better still.

"Good. Now, sing your parts lightly. Be birds. Be a flock of birds that take off in that directionless, random way you've seen birds fly, until they all come back and land on the same wire at almost the same time. Just la-la."

When they had finished rehearsing this piece, it would not have been an exaggeration to say that there were tears in the eyes of several singers. Not of joy, but tears of satisfaction, of insight, of having come so far.

As a reward for their work, Robert finished the rehearsal with a favourite hymn sung *a capella*, with the overhead lights turned off. The sun had just set, leaving a gentle light to come through the stained glass windows in the sanctuary. He said the name of the piece, played a single chord, and let them sing on their own, without direction. A few closed their eyes as they sang, voices swelling and diminishing as one, listening to each other. Some sang for the prayerful words, all sang for the music:

> Spirit of God, descend upon my heart;
> Wean it from earth; through all its pulses move.

> Stoop to my weakness, mighty as Thou art,
> And make me love Thee as I ought to love.
>
> Teach me to feel that Thou art always nigh;
> Teach me the struggles of the soul to bear,
> To check the rising doubt, the rebel sigh;
> Teach me the patience of unanswered prayer.

~

"Brilliant rehearsal tonight, Rob. You are an amazing teacher."

"Thank you. I don't choose music the choir is incapable of learning. But people do find it difficult to believe in their abilities."

"Why try? Why not just give us easy four-quarter pieces?"

"You know why. You could sing the whole Hymnary right now, but you wouldn't have stretched or learned anything worthwhile. There is so much great music out there."

"Just kidding. I think your image of a flock of birds did it. Worked for me."

"Nature is the first music. That's why I love the sunroom so much. I could hear the wind in the trees through the cracks, and it was a symphony."

"I might have bad news, then. I've got carpenters coming soon to seal up the cracks and shore up the foundation so we can be safe and dry out there. But you'll be able to open the windows for your listening pleasure."

They were nibbling nuts and olives with their post-rehearsal port.

"Oh, speaking of nature," Tim continued, "here are the brochures for our PEI vacation. I made some executive decisions, with the assistance of the travel agent. The first reservation can be changed until fourteen days prior, but the inn will retain a hefty fee if we cancel."

The pretty brochures captured their attention and they considered possible day-trips until bedtime.

After turning the light out, Tim thought about this long and lovely day. It had started with the prayer breakfast, which wasn't all that prayerful, and ended with the delight of musical insights, with all the other accomplishments in between.

And he'd met Mort Evers, a remarkable man whom he hoped would become a friend.

June 4: If nothing changes

Friday

Robert's regular Thursday commute to South River, and back to the city on Friday mornings, didn't leave time for much more than choir rehearsal during the academic year. His regular classes at university having ended, he was filling his schedule with private students and a few summer classes. He didn't teach until late morning on Fridays now, so he could relax in South River a few precious hours longer.

While telling Robert about yesterday's Prayer Breakfast, especially the impressive Eggs Benedict, Tim created mushroom omelettes for their breakfast. "I didn't want Hollandaise sauce two days in a row, but I'll make Eggs Benny for us soon—maybe for our first breakfast in the reinforced sunroom."

He talked about the mayor's overt politicking, and the engaging guest speaker. "I'm giving you time to get accustomed to the notion that I'd like to invite Mort to Sunday dinner sometime. I'm sure you'll like him."

"I'll trust your judgment on that. The only other minister I've enjoyed dining with was my organ student, Helen, but that's because she's first and foremost a musician."

"And a good one. That madrigal dinner was fun, wasn't it? We'll have another one sometime."

"Let's finish our coffee in the sunroom," Robert said. "I want to have a look at what might work in the space. Would a fold-out sofa-bed work here, Tim? Wouldn't it be nice to sleep out sometimes? This old sofa has a bit of an odour—but I know it's not sewer gas. Just old, maybe?"

"That would be nicotine and spilled scotch from twenty-plus years ago, and dampness. Sure, let's see what's in the stores. A sofa bed might weigh as much as a woodpile, but I'll ask the workers to make provision for that."

~

As he entered the rearranged newspaper office, Tim wondered how he would have coped if he'd really gone far away this year, as people had assumed he would. *I wouldn't have known how to fit in once I returned, considering just the changes to date. If I'd left orders not to change anything, then what would have been the point of the year away? Nothing changes if nothing changes.*

He paused in the reception area to record that last thought in his notebook. Had he heard it somewhere, or had he just made it up?

"How's everything going, Mrs Rafuse?"

"Really well, sir. Can I help you find anyone?"

"No need, thanks. I'll just wander around and bother everyone. Have you ever heard this phrase?" He showed her what he had written.

"Can't say I have, sir. What's it mean?"

"I'll get back to you on that."

He tapped on the frame of Elaine's open door. "How's everything going, Miss Fong?"

"Really well, thanks for asking."

"You're welcome. Here's another question: have you ever heard this before? 'Nothing changes if nothing changes.'"

"Not that I recall, but I like it. Shall we print it on the masthead?"

"Maybe. I like it, but I don't know if I made it up or read it somewhere. It's so self-evident. Next topic: I met a man yesterday who gave the most remarkable presentation. I offered to publish his text and others from time to time."

"Excellent. Who is he?"

Tim cleared his throat. "The Right Reverend Doctor Mortimer Evers. Bishop Emeritus. Of the Anglican persuasion. But he is nothing like his title might suggest. He's down to earth and charming. He has the common touch."

"Kipling."

"Beg pardon?"

"You were quoting Rudyard Kipling: 'If you can walk with the crowd and keep your virtue, or walk with Kings, nor lose the common touch' and so on. Many phrases become part of our own thoughts because they capture an idea so succinctly. Like your 'nothing changes' one."

"You impress me."

"First time?"

"First time today."

"Thanks. Send me the Right Bishop's stuff. We could use a bit of well-written wisdom with the common touch."

He continued his perambulation through the reorganized office spaces and presented his phrase to all who raised their heads. Ed Garamond didn't know it, nor did Harold Awalt nor Cindy Martin.

Jean Naugler, the shorthand-writing whiz and part-time reporter, looked up as he passed. "Looking for something, Mister Brown?"

Tim showed her.

"Oh. I know that one very well."

"You do? Can you enlighten me?"

"It's AA."

"Wha—AA? How do you know this?" Tim lowered his voice. "Oops, not the right question, sorry."

"It's okay, I don't mind. I'm seventeen years sober, coming up on eighteen."

"Oh my goodness, Mrs Naugler, I had no idea. Eighteen years sober. That's eighteen years of solid backbone. You have my admiration. So you know first-hand that nothing changes if nothing changes."

"I do."

"I may have a follow-up for you later. Thank you, Jean."

He went upstairs and unlocked the door to his private thinking room. The walls were almost bare, as he had rolled up the worksheets from last month's challenges. Now there were just a few manila sheets containing words of wisdom that had occurred to him while he had been in the throes of delving. *Start at the end and work toward the beginning* was one. *Consider everything to discover something* was another.

Now he had another, for which he used his prized red marker:

Nothing changes if nothing changes.

He put the cap back on the marker and went out into the hallway. At the far end was a door that was supposed to be an emergency exit leading to a fire escape. The door had been nailed shut. He vaguely recalled that the iron ladder on the outside had been declared unsafe years ago. The upstairs rooms were not to be occupied at all, according to the Fire Marshall.

Lots of people were coming to the second floor to work now, not only Tim in his private room. The staff were working on Project Sweetland, which was nearly ready to go public. And the advertising and art staff had been using the space to design the Gem District ad campaign.

If I don't deal with this fire escape situation before the Fire Marshall does, or before there's a fire, we'll be in big trouble. Averting an explosion in my basement was a relief. I'd better avert disaster here, too.

He descended to the basement to look for John, the caretaker, who was usually napping in his ancient recliner beside the boiler. Tim didn't see anyone, but he noticed a utility tub against one wall, and approached it to give it a sniff test. It smelled of cleaning solutions, and it looked as though it had been used recently. But because he'd learned a new trick, he ran the water in it for a moment anyway.

"Hello? What's up?"

"Oh, hi, John, there you are. I was just checking the drain. Can never be too careful about sewer gas. Remember I asked you about the second floor fire escape door? What's the story there?"

"It's okay. It's nailed shut."

"I saw that. But what?"

"What?"

"Is that the end of it, John? You found the emergency door was nailed shut and you did what, then?"

"What'm I supposed to do? I'm not a carpenter. I don't think it's safe to open that door. The ladder outside doesn't look too good."

"Did you report any of this back to me, John? No. How about anyone else?"

"You didn't ask for a report. You just asked me to see if I could open it."

"Is that why I had to send Ed Garamond after you to get a stuck window opened up there? What am I missing, John? You don't say what you don't or can't do, you just don't do it, is that it? And it's up to *me* to chase after *you*? Can you tell me what it is that you think you *do* do here? No, never mind. I'll tell you right now, John, in case it's not plain to you, I don't like this. I was just thinking about how wonderful it is that our staff are pulling their weight, not just to please me or Miss Fong, John, but because they have self-respect. I highly recommend you try it."

Tim turned and took the stairs to the main level two at a time, and again up to the second floor. He grabbed his backpack, locked his empty room, and strode out of the building toward his car, to drive where he wasn't sure, but he detoured into the Daisy and swung into an empty booth.

Evelyn was puzzled. "What's up?"

Tim shook his head. "I'm just hiding out. I thought I'd better get out of the office before somebody loses his job."

"Wow. You do look bothered." She sat down and leaned toward him. "Want me to go over there and smack somebody for ya? I'd be only too happy, y'know." She laughed.

"Ah, you're just what the doctor ordered, Ev. You always lift me up. No, thanks, no smacking. Anyway, this is a guy. You might get hurt."

"I wouldn't bother smacking a girl, but I do have experience with guys. I'm very effective, not something I'm proud of. Okay, then, how about a bowl of chowder?"

"Yes, please. With a side of poison."

Evelyn brought him a bowl of chowder, a biscuit, tea, and a slice of lemon pie. "Sorry, Hon, I'm all out of poison. Pie'll have to do."

"Thanks Ev. I'm better now, anyway. I thought I had a problem, but I'll fix it. As the saying goes, nothing changes if nothing changes, right?"

"Now don't start with the Shakespeare on me."

"How about this, then: Robert requests the pleasure of your company on the weekend. And so do I. Are you free?"

"Oh, actually…I was hoping…I was getting up the gumption to invite you guys over to my humble abode. Is that Shakespeare? Whatever. How about Sunday? That'll give me time to stir-fry some wieners or whatever I'll give ya."

"Delicious. Tell me what we can bring, besides the wine, of course."

"I don't know what I'm making yet. Just come. I'll handle it. It'll be nice to have company in the house. Come anytime after three."

Tim wondered if he should go back to the office, but decided to call Elaine instead.

"I'm calling to confess or inform you that I spoke sharply to our caretaker this morning, in case there's fallout."

"Perhaps that explains the banging going on upstairs?"

"Most likely. My third time asking him to investigate the fire escape got a little testy. I've already found a contractor to look at the ladder outside."

"*You* have? I mean, good! It's been a risk, I know, and we don't need risks, especially if they're also illegal."

"I concur. Keep your eye on John, let me know what mood he's in. I didn't fire him this morning, but I came close. I'd need just cause, but I don't have his job description, so we'll have to start there."

Elaine sighed. "Today is Friday, and if I finish what I hope to do today, I can carve out a small oasis of time for myself on the weekend. Selfish, I know, but I want it. Let's discuss John on Wednesday morning, before we start gearing up for the next edition."

"Done. Have a great weekend, Elaine—when you get to it. My regards to Roger."

~

He hadn't planned to confront John today, but he'd come close many times before for multiple reasons. Today was the straw warning the camel that the load was becoming unsupportable. *Good. Whichever way that goes, we'll get better service for what we pay.*

Having no tasks to do, and no desire to tangle with anyone else, Tim decided to take care of the weekend shopping today. *The lawn care guy is coming tomorrow morning and I don't want to miss that. It's not just watching him mow the lawn, though that'll be nice. It's witnessing another step toward achieving my Home Beautiful.*

He went home to make a grocery list, and to measure the dimensions of the sunroom for a potential hide-a-bed.

He visited the furniture outlets first. He was curious, maybe even eager. He identified a few possibilities. One model without bulky arms was especially interesting, as it was lighter, would fit, and didn't cost as much as a small car, as some nearly did. It also had a compartment underneath for storing bedding. He would give it some thought.

He loaded his groceries in the car, drove back to the furniture store, and put a deposit on the sofa he liked. When Robert arrived tomorrow afternoon they'd come over and make a final decision.

~

Tim whistled a happy tune as he put the groceries away. He hummed a hymn tune while he made a meatloaf and popped it in the oven. He sang "Food, glorious food" from the musical *Oliver* while he laid out containers to freeze leftovers in for their lunches next week. He uncorked a pungent bottle of *Petites victoires* and poured a glass to enjoy while he waited for the oven timer to tell him supper was ready.

He walked to the sunroom and peered through the dusty windows to the weedy backyard. He had paid Mrs A for the extra time it would take her to clean these windows, but it didn't look like she'd touched them. *I hope she's not becoming like John, needing several reminders.* Then he chided himself. "Tsk. Listen to you. John could never keep up with Mrs A. Let's have a closer look."

He touched the windows. They were clean and shiny on the inside. Mrs A had done as requested. He went outside and reached up to rub his finger on the glass. *As I thought. They're coated with the dirt of the ages. I wonder if I have a stepladder around here somewhere. I'm sure washing windows is in my skill set.*

The ground below the windows was uneven. "Maybe a long-handled window washer-thingy would be the better choice. I don't need to take a tumble. Broken bones are not part of better homes and gardens."

He looked around the yard. If the weeds weren't thigh-high, he'd enjoy taking a stroll around with his wine glass in hand, stopping for a sip, stooping to smell the roses, maybe checking a bird nest to see if there were eggs in it, maybe clipping some flowers or ornamental grasses to decorate the table. He could almost smell the potentiality.

He actually smelled the meatloaf, so he went in to check it. He cut it into portions, set it aside to cool, and poured another glass of wine.

He thought about the "Nothing changes" aphorism which Alcoholics Anonymous promoted. *That's a nugget of wisdom, for sure. And who knew that Jean Naugler had been an alcoholic? Still is, I guess. They say you can never let your guard down. I hope she caught it before she suffered too many miseries.*

He drank a toast to AA and their wisdom, and didn't taste the irony.

June 5: Cutting grass

Saturday

It was exciting to watch Jake from Chester Basin Property Maintenance mowing the front lawn. He was a take-charge kind of guy, and his brush-cut hair and khaki shirt and pants supported the impression. He had a clipped way of speaking which, Tim guessed, came from a military background.

Jake unloaded a semi-self-propelled mower from the back of his pickup truck, and poured gas in the tank. "I'll let the fumes dissipate before I pull the cord," he said. "No need to start your Saturday morning with an explosion."

Another disaster averted! I didn't know there were so many potential dangers lurking around!

"Let's survey the area before I put the machine on there. I'm thinkin' rocks, bottles, beer cans, things like that."

"Oh, I don't think—"

"Here's one," Jake said, holding up an empty ginger ale can. "Not saying you put this here, but your property is on a busy street, and people love to toss out stuff like this, especially if the area is overgrown the way this is. Oh, here's more."

He pulled a length of black rubber hose out of the grass, then a beer can and two empty 'airline bottles' of liquor.

Tim was chagrined. *Passers-by treat my shoddy property as a junkyard. Well, I blame Mo 'n' Plo for the neglect. I hope Jake will keep my lawn trimmed as evenly as his hair.*

Jake pulled the cord on the mower. It started immediately and ran smoothly. He quickly guided it around the lawn. He stopped and emptied the clippings on the side of the driveway, where the radiators were waiting for the salvage truck.

"I had to cut it long to start," Jake explained. "It was too high to do it all in one go. I'll run it lower now, and leave the second cut clippings on the lawn. You'll like what you see."

Tim did like it. Even though Jake had to manoeuvre around a few shrubs and stones that had framed flower gardens, he mowed in a criss-cross pattern that was very attractive.

"Nobody'll toss garbage on that," Jake said. "Tell me if I'm mistaken."

"I hope you're right. It's gorgeous!"

"Right. Now, you said there's a back yard to look at?"

As Tim led Jake to the rear of the house, he marvelled at how differ-ently people in the same business seemed to operate. *The front lawn was just a demo. If I don't want them to continue, it's free. Well, how could I not want him to continue? He just elevated my property value by some factor. I wonder what he'll be able to reveal in the back?*

Jake whistled. "This'll be fun. How come you let it go like this?"

"I was working all the time. That's not a good reason, but it's my ex-cuse. My late mother used to sit in the sunroom there and look out over this area, so she kept it mowed, and planted a nice garden. She's been gone twenty years now, and at some point I just gave it up. I don't garden, I didn't have time to come out here, so I said, 'Why pay to mow it?'"

"I guess you have a lot of memories buried here. Well, let me wade through this and see what I can see."

Jake strode into the weeds, past the unstable woodshed, around a thicket, under the tall trees at the back, and along the other side back to the house, and then down the centre and back.

"It's a nice big lot," Jake said. "Nice layout, too, from what I can tell, kind of a country garden. In the old days, they'd send a man to tackle this with a scythe, but only the grim reaper uses one now, eh? Do you want to restore the gardens, or do you want it all just bulldozed for a big flat lawn? I know what I'd do."

"What would you do?"

"I'd restore it. You've got the bones of a nice landscaped garden buried under all those weeds. The flower gardens are bordered with granite rocks, that's nice. The shrubs need pruning, but they're mature and well-situated."

"I think there was a path?"

"Hard to say. We'll know more when we can see the ground better. So, clear it or restore it?"

"Restore it, definitely. But I should have your quote first, I suppose. This sounds like a million-dollar project."

"Oh, not even half that. Let me get some measurements and then I'll give you our prices."

Jake went to his truck and returned with a measuring tape rolled inside a frame that had a handle to wind it up with. "Can you hold this end while I walk to the back corner again, please? Hold it tight 'till I say, or you'll be chasing into the bushes to find it."

Tim gripped the end firmly and Jake unrolled the tape as he walked. He called "Okay!" and Tim released it.

After he reeled the tape in, Jake returned and they repeated the procedure across the back of the house. "Good enough," Jake said. "Now for the gazindas."

Tim crossed his fingers. *I hope this won't cost so much that I won't want to go ahead. It really does have to be done. I'm only paying now after not spending anything for years and years, so—*

"Here you go." Jake handed Tim a long form listing his services. There were check marks beside some and Xs beside others, and fees neatly printed in the right-hand column.

"There's no total," Jake said, "because our work never ends, if Mother Nature does her job right. But you can see what every step costs, and you can call a halt at any time."

"Okay."

"I'll leave this with you." Jake pulled off the top copy, handed it to Tim, and placed the duplicate inside his metal clipboard. "Gotta go make more hay while the sun shines." He squinted at the sky, where the sun was not visible. "Give our office a call and book whatever you want us to do. If you delay, some of those charges might be different, depending on how much more overgrown you let it get. Either way, we'll come back to pick up those clippings I left in the driveway there, so the grass can be cut on that side of the drive after those radiators are removed. Nice meeting you."

Jake's handshake was firm, as Tim expected it to be. He stood in the driveway, paper in hand, admiring his front lawn that Jake had magically retrieved from junkyard obscurity in one delightful hour. He looked at his watch. *Less than an hour. Wow! If he had troops under his command in the military, I bet they marched and set up tents faster and straighter than anyone.*

Jake's sales strategy was brilliant, Tim thought. His property was large, and would be a valuable account. Giving the front lawn a golf-course trim wasn't a waste of his time. Jake knew that he'd want his whole property to look like that. He hadn't risked a thing.

There was still time to go downriver to the bakery to stock up on bread and muffins, and maybe stay for a sticky bun and a large coffee.

When he came back to town he'd pick up wines to take to Evelyn's to-morrow, and something Italian to go with tonight's takeout pizza. He and Robert would go to the furniture store to approve the sofa-bed, and get it delivered next week.

~

Robert gave the sofa a thorough test. He pulled cushions from other displays and stretched out lengthwise. He pronounced it to be a little firm, but not enough to induce a crick in his back. He and Tim sat upright at each end, and found that a few well-placed cushions made them comfortable.

They asked the sales clerk for permission to pull out the mattress, and moved the display of ottomans and coffee tables out of the way. Robert placed cushions on the mattress, slipped off his shoes, and lay down on the bed. He bounced and jiggled. He pointed to a decorative throw on a recliner chair, and the amused clerk brought it over and gently spread it over him.

Tim wandered over to the sales counter. "If himself decides he likes it, what delivery arrangements can we make?"

"Where to?"

"Just at the top of the street, at the lights, the big white house on the left."

"Okay, let me check. I'll be right over."

Robert was awake, but barely. Tim kicked the metal leg of the folded-out mattress and he stirred.

"Do we assume that you find it comfortable?"

Robert yawned. "Yes, quite." He stretched out his arms. "There's room for two, too."

"I'll take your word for it. Get up. Here's our helpful counsellor."

"We can deliver this to you next week. We have a big order going over Hebbville way, right past your door. I'm not sure yet what day or time, but if you want it delivered for free, maybe you'll be flexible?"

"Next week? Free? Sounds very attractive. Oh, here's a catch: this is going in a narrow sunroom, no room for two sofas. Can your guys take the old one out first?"

"Sure, they can do that."

"And take it away?"

"Where?"

"I don't know. Where do old sofas go? To the dump?"

"You'd be better off hiring a handyman truck for that. The municipal landfill site has a fee, and our trucks are too busy to make dump runs, know what I mean? If they get it outside, is there a place to leave it?"

"I guess. Okay, it's a deal. Robert, figure out how to fold this thing back together while I pay the nice lady."

~

They took their wine to the sunroom to visualize how their purchase would best be situated: across the end, or in the middle facing the back yard, where the old sofa was now. There was no other option.

"Too bad the room's not square," Robert mused.

"Forget that," Tim said. "I'm spending money every day, downtown and uptown; I have to draw the line somewhere. I hope to have this room levelled up and sealed soon, and the windows washed outside, so we can gaze out on the glorious gardens of Versailles. That'll take care of my allowance for a while. What did you think of the front lawn job?"

"It's beautiful. I noticed it right away. And the artful display of old cast iron radiators. Just kidding. I know you're working on it. Things are looking up!"

~

The evening was chilly and damp, so they had their pizza in the den. Tim hoped this was a good time to mention that he'd invited Evan Robicheau to spend the weekend, two weeks hence. He was aware that Robert's concert in PEI was just two weeks after that, but a visitor shouldn't upset his equilibrium.

"Will I like him?" Robert asked.

"That I cannot say. I like him well enough, but I invited him down so we could get to know each other better. I know he will like you."

"What does he like to do? Does he play an instrument?"

"I don't know. I'll ask. If so, shall I invite him to bring his clarinet? Or accordion?"

"Anything but those. What does he do for a living?"

"He's the Editor of *The Daily.*"

"Oh. I guess it wouldn't hurt for me to stretch a little, then. I know I'm a snob in some ways, and introverted in others, but I'll follow your lead."

June 6: Bullseye

Sunday

June's gift to the world is daylight, morning and evening. Nova Scotia's weather is variable, but the sun is predictable, and so this morning the sun rose at half-past five and wouldn't set until almost nine o'clock. Half the days in the month would be rainy, dimming the light somewhat and adding a new stress to outdoor plans, as Tim wondered if rain would delay the back yard mowing project.

He gazed out the bathroom window onto the weedy mess below. *Look on the bright side: your front yard is a lawn once again. Baby steps, Tim. It'll happen.*

He had amends to make at church this morning. The senior minister had represented all the local United Church congregations at the Prayer Breakfast, but Tim hadn't had time to greet him because the mayor had been steering him around. By the time he'd had his brief chat with Mort Evers, his minister had departed.

Given that Saint John's was a participant in the Gem District project led by *The Times*, Tim wanted to keep on the minister's good side, so he went to join the parishioners who had lined up at the front door to shake his hand after church.

"Good morning, Tim. This is a rare pleasure to see you down here."

"Ha-ha, yes, it does seem far away. Once we're down in the choir rooms, we forget the front doors. Anyway, Reverend, I just wanted to say how much I appreciate the church's participation in our street-painting project. If you have any questions or concerns, just call. Good sermon this morning, by the way, very thought-provoking."

"Thank you, Tim, I really appreciate your comment. We're happy to support the painting initiative, with your generous contribution. I've met your representative, a Miss Martin. She is very kind, and will give us the leadership we need. Choosing colours can be very divisive."

"Don't I know it. That's why we send her. I'm not brave enough!"

"You are very brave, according to what I heard a few weeks ago, Tim. Good to see you at the Prayer Breakfast, by the way. You're welcome anytime."

In the car on their drive home, Tim said to Robert, "I almost told him I didn't say hello Thursday morning because I was waiting to ask the Bishop if he'd write some columns for us. That would've put the minister's nose out of joint. You've got to be so careful sometimes."

~

Tim had picked up corned beef slices for lunch, so Robert put those on rye with Dijon mustard. They dispersed to attend to small tasks for an hour, eventually re-convening in the sunroom, where there was brightness if not direct sunshine. Even the weeds looked summery through the half-cleaned windows.

They decided to put the new sofa at the far end of the room, facing the door so they wouldn't be boxed in on the rare occasions that the mattress would be unfolded. A coffee-table and a few small armchairs could be moved to face any direction.

Robert was slowly declining toward horizontal on the old sofa, but Tim clapped his hands. "Up, up, sleepyhead. Time to go to Evelyn's. She said anytime after three, and that sounds early enough that she might unveil her dartboard, so giddyap!"

~

Tim had picked up a bouquet of garden flowers yesterday from the florist. They hid behind the bouquet when Evelyn answered the door, and held out the bag of wine. There was hugging and laughter.

Evelyn gave them a short tour of her one-storey, two-bedroom bungalow. Her furnishings were mid-century modern, tasteful and comfortable.

"I make no apologies or excuses for anything. It's here, I own it, it works for me," she said proudly. "You gents make yourselves comfortable in the front room while I put these lovelies in a vase."

Her house and the one across from it were the last two on the street, which ended in a wooded area. Her picture window looked out onto the quiet street, but the back view from the kitchen and the dining area was of tall, soft pine trees.

Suction-cupped to the window above the sink was a colourful piece of stained glass artwork, which Tim had given her last month when her nerves had begun to fray. She pointed to it and said, "This makes me happy every day."

"It's a gorgeous view out there, Ev," Robert said. "Do you own what we're looking at, if you don't mind me asking?"

"You can ask me anything, Robby. No, thank goodness, it's not mine, so I don't pay taxes on it. It's part of the town's Woodland Park, but hardly anybody knows it's here."

"Can you walk in it?"

"Sure can. The path is just over there. Did you want to go for a walk?"

Robert hesitated.

"He's become such a nature boy recently," Tim said, "ever since we opened up the sunroom. I can hardly get him to stay in the main house now. I'm going to get our backyard mowed so he can play outside. I don't mean to speak of you like you're a dog, Rob, but you spend most of your time indoors, teaching and playing, so I know getting out in fresh air matters a lot to you."

"I'm not offended. I do love nature. But...I was wondering, dear Evelyn...do you have a hidden games room somewhere in your lovely home? With a darts board?"

"I sure do. Wanna play?"

"We do! And can you keep score for us? We don't care who wins, we just want to know how we're doing."

Evelyn walked to the end of the hallway separating her bedroom from the guest room and bath, and opened the doors to what looked like a linen closet. When opened, the double doors protected both sides from errant shots, and revealed a very nice board hanging in the centre. She switched on a spotlight.

"Wow, this is fancy!"

She reached in the closet and unrolled a mat onto the hallway floor. "Now we're ready," she said. "The oche line is marked on the mat, and the floor is protected."

"The what line?"

"Oche. Rhymes with 'okey-dokey'. Don't ask me where it comes from, I just know that's what you call the line you have to stand behind. If you want to scare your opponents, start using fancy words and they'll think you're good. But then you better *be* good, 'cause they'll find out quick enough. Okay, how about some warm-up throws?"

"Me first," Robert said. The oche line was farther back than where they'd been standing in Tim's kitchen, so his first throw fell short.

He was winding up to throw harder, but Evelyn stepped in and gave him the same pointers Stella had done last month.

"Wrist, fingers, release," Robert whispered. The next two darts stayed on the board, and Evelyn counted his score as she retrieved them.

To his great surprise, Tim's three throws found the board and stayed there.

"Sure, you learned from watching me, that's why," Robert teased.

"Doesn't matter. I'm ahead. Come and get me."

Evelyn watched a few more throws until she was assured that her walls would survive, and then went to look after something in the kitchen.

"Need any help?" they called. "It smells delish."

"Nope," she called back. "I'm just frying the onions and garlic first. I suppose you'd say sautéeing. The recipe does, but it looks like frying to me."

She returned to the hallway, drying her hands on a towel and bringing the aromas with her.

"How's it going?"

"We're getting better by our standards, not your standards."

"Show me."

Both men threw three of their best, and they cheered for each good shot.

"I can't believe how nervous I feel when you're looking on, Ev," Tim said.

"I know how to fix that," she replied. "We'll play a round. Me first. Watch and learn."

This was a dream come true for both men. They hadn't even thought about darts until a couple months ago. Evelyn had brought one of her worn boards especially for Robert to use when he became fidgety as a concert approached.

They enjoyed watching her physique and technique now as she stood at the oche line and delivered three high-scoring darts to the board.

Ever-competitive, Robert performed valiantly, all throws scoring.

Tim took his stance, and, with Evelyn's voice in one ear and Stella's in the other, threw his three darts. The third one was so close to the bull-seye that Evelyn had to walk right up to the board to determine that it was outside, but only just.

"Congratulations, fellas. You are both now darts competitors. Sure, you can improve, but you don't have to fear little ol' me. If you can pull yourselves away, I'd love to sample one of those wines you brought while

I continue with the Stroganoff. It's a real treat to have nice wine with dinner—and my two favourite men, too."

Evelyn was the perfect hostess, a little too perfect when they first arrived; but once dinner was on the table, she relaxed to her usual state. She said she was nervous to cook for two accomplished chefs. Both assured her that they were her devoted friends, regardless of how the meal went.

"You should see what I eat sometimes in my bachelor pad," Robert said. "The campus is a food desert, unless you want yogurt and granola, or Mister Noodle."

"I would kill for either of those some days," Tim said. "I make peanut butter and banana roll-ups, or I just get out of sync with lunchtimes. And I don't always have the time to sit in your fine establishment, Ev, so I experiment. My most recent purchase was an energy bar that people take on their climb up Mount Everest. It keeps them alive, but I thought I'd die of sugar overload."

"We might have something better for you soon, Timmy. Our angel investor, Art Clarke, is developing a list of take-out items that we can sell for the same profit margins as our average meal, without our labour costs and dishwashing added in."

"Listen to you talking like a real merchant, Ev. Good for you! Good for me, too. I'll be there. When I find three-day-old donuts appealing, I know I need a better source of nutrition."

"I think I'd like three-day-old donuts," Robert said.

"Well, you're not getting them here. Coffee or tea with dessert?"

They both asked for tea. Evelyn turned on the oven while the kettle boiled, and slipped a tray from the fridge into it. When the tea was ready, her ice-box cookies were baked to perfection.

~

After lights-out Robert said, "Can we take the darts board to Prince Edward Island? I'd love to have it to relax me before the concert."

"Sure, but remember that Ev said too much throwing might strain your arm."

"I'll throw easy. I am so much better now than I was." He raised his arm in the dark and made throwing motions in the air. "Wrist and fingers. Just like playing the organ. Playing the organ is just like throwing darts. Whatever."

June 7: Garden potential

Monday

After their companionable breakfast, Robert left for Halifax and Tim re-turned to his ever-present To Do list. Property improvements had gone well last week, and he was eager to keep them going.

Now, who's supposed to call whom?

He was reaching for the phone when it rang.

"Good morning, Mr Brown, it's Amanda from Conquerall. Did you have a nice weekend?"

"Yes, I did, Amanda. How 'bout you?"

"I got kids, a dog, and a husband. What d'you think?" She giggled.

"I think you must've had a great time, then."

"You're right. And now I'm back in this cavern fixing other people's problems, yours included. Were you satisfied with the work we did in your basement last week?"

"Yes, very. The stink is gone, the house didn't explode, and your guys carried a ton of cast iron out of the cellar for me."

"Great. I'm gonna send them back after lunch today to prop up your sunroom, if that's okay, and I think Corey said he was going to do a little electrical work for you. It's a lot safer than extension cords tripping you and getting pinched in doorways and such. Electrical fires are still fires."

"Thanks, Amanda. I'll be here."

What's next? Right, the lawn. The hidden lawn, more like it. The Buried Lawn of Hill House. The Gardens of Pompeii. Isn't there a children's story about a hidden garden, or a prince who had no friends because his garden was always in winter?

"Never mind that," Tim said aloud. "Let's have a look at this extensive menu Jake left. Regular Mowing and Treatment, whatever 'treatment' is. Yes, please."

"Other services" included Garden beds restored; Planting annuals/perennials/shrubs; Pruning flowering shrubs/fruit trees; Pathways cut, and so on. As he considered each item, he thought he'd like to have it done, but he wasn't sure yet if he even had the beds, fruit trees or pathways. Fees for the services would add up.

Jake said I didn't have to select them all to start. Let's just get that tangled lawn cleaned up and go from there.

He phoned Chester Basin Property Maintenance and spoke with the friendly receptionist. Yes, Jake had been there to do his "free sample" mowing. Yes, he was impressed. Yes, he certainly did want regular mowing for the season, front yard to begin with, because he didn't yet know what they'd find in the backyard. He'd like to get the back yard bushwhacked as soon as possible. Once that was done and the debris cleared away, he'd know whether it was worth gardening, *per se,* whether there was an actual lawn, or whether he should just plow the whole thing under.

She asked him to hold, and returned just as he was thinking to hang up.

"Sorry for the delay, Mr Brown. I was just checking with the rental company to make sure they had a bushwhacker. Jake said you had blackberry or raspberry canes growing there, and we'd rather rent heavy equipment than beat up our own mowers."

"Yeah, it's quite a jungle. I'd love to have those berries growing, but I know blackberry thorns are vicious, so maybe not. Do they have the machine?"

"Yes, they do. I've booked it for tomorrow morning only. We'll try to get the whole area done in that time. The clippings will need to be raked away after that, and then our zero-turn should be able to chow down on the stubble. Our guy will load the 'whacker as soon as they open tomorrow at seven-thirty, and then he'll boogie on up to your place. Does that work for you?"

"It sure does. I'm excited. It feels like I'm getting a new half-acre of land without having to buy it! Will it be Jake again?"

"Jake will be there to get him started. He's sales and quality control, so he'll take off to other jobs once Dana gets going."

This was another giant step forward. He was Getting Things Done. It did feel like he had acquired new land, plus a new sunroom, with only the expense of a few repairs and upgrades.

Soon they'd reveal a garden for whatever benefits that might bring, maybe even fresh berries.

"A *potential* garden, you'd better say. But we won't have to wait long for the big reveal. And the sunroom's deficiencies will be dealt with this afternoon! I must say, I do like a little instant gratification."

~

While he waited for Corey and crew to arrive, Tim emptied the sunroom of excess furniture. That would make it easier for Corey to install the electrical outlets, and would clear the way for the transfer of sofas, whenever that would happen.

He hadn't seen anything suitable in the furniture store for side chairs. Everything was so large. *Maybe a second-hand shop would have just the right size pieces for this room. It wouldn't matter if they didn't match. Shabby chic would do.*

He was putting his plate and glass in the dishwasher when he heard Corey's truck in the driveway. He looked out a side window as the big truck passed it, going ever so slowly in reverse with only inches to spare. The crew had disembarked before the truck entered the tight squeeze, and they were already tossing planks of lumber from the back of the truck onto the ground.

He went out to the sunroom and watched. The two younger men had already crawled underneath it, thumping at various places and calling back and forth. They lifted a table saw down from the truck bed, followed by concrete slabs and blocks, which they shifted beneath the sunroom like they didn't weigh nearly as much as Tim assumed they did.

Thinking his weight might affect whatever they were doing beneath his feet, he walked through the house to the front door, and shimmied back past the big truck to observe.

The men were underneath the sunroom, and suddenly noises like gunfire erupted from there. Hammer-drills filled the air with their delightful announcements that Things Were Happening!

"Funny how they put this up," Corey said. "The roof sagged because the floor sagged, 'cause it's only tacked onto the shingles. We'll have to pull a few shingles off so we can bolt it to the studs. Then we'll caulk it all around. Shouldn't leak no more after that."

Tim leaned against the empty woodshed to watch the three men crawling and hauling. Not one of them rested for a single moment. Corey gave instructions and confirmed actions, handled the jacks, and paid very close attention to the spirit level. He moved his truck down the driveway so he could open the door at the end of the sunroom.

Tim looked around the woodshed. He was disappointed that it had sunk at one end. He remembered having it built. The carpenter had said it should stand "for a good long time", which Tim had assumed was a life-time warranty.

He'd be interested in Corey's opinion of the construction of this wood-shed, maybe built by the same carpenter who had tacked the sunroom to the shingles. Maybe he'd expected to be dead by the time his inadequacies were discovered.

One of the men was on a ladder, the other on the roof of the sunroom. The air was filled with a pungent, sour, chemical smell as they applied tubes of caulking. Corey was already loading the tools and leftover ends of building materials back on the truck.

"Packing up?" Tim said.

"Yuh. Got one more stop today. Need to fix a leak before it rains tomorrow. Your sunroom's not goin' anywhere now. We put solid supports in all four corners, doubled the support beams, and bolted it to the house. The guys are layin' the caulkin' in all around top and sides now. It'll be dry to the touch in an hour, and paintable in twenty-four hours, but it'll stay flexible. If you don't mind, don't go out there for a day, just until it cures."

"No problem."

"I fixed the door. It musta been hard to close with the buildin' outta whack like that."

"Yes, it was. That's great. And the outlets are hooked up now?"

"Nope. Once they started levelin' up I couldn't work in there, but I got the wires ready to put through from the inside. We'll come back to see about your woodshed and I'll finish the plugs then."

"Good enough. When do you expect to be back, then?"

"Dunno. Manda tells me what to do, and she'll tell you, too." He grinned.

"Do you think the woodshed will be a write-off? Or can you fix it?"

"Can't see any trouble from here. Might just need—"

They heard the two-way radio static in the truck.

"She's squawkin' at me now, so I better run. We'll take care of it in a couple days. Don't order your firewood yet. And don't stack it in that sun-room no more."

~

Tim defrosted a serving of meatloaf and peeled some vegetables to boil. He wondered if there was any leftover wine in the cupboard, then re-membered that they had been at Evelyn's for dinner yesterday. She'd be having the leftovers.

I'd better call to thank her. He glanced at the clock: he'd have to wait an hour. Evelyn took a bath every day at six o'clock sharp; she had made it plain that she would welcome his call when she was in the tub and not before. He set the kitchen timer to ring in fifty-five minutes.

He opened a bottle of *Un Bon Début* which he'd had a time or two recently. This was a good sign, celebrating multiple good starts.

"If starts be good, can greater things be far behind? Listen to you, quoting 'Peanut Butter' Shelley. It was a good day, though, with no disasters uncovered or averted. Here's to things fixed and more to come!"

The timer rang and he called Evelyn.

She had not been expecting his call, but she sounded like she liked the surprise. He expressed thanks and admiration on behalf of Robert and himself for the tour of her charming home, and for the fine dinner. "And for rolling out the carpet, literally, for our darts game. It was fun. You're a great teacher, and a great friend."

"Oh, shucks. Don't flatter me or I'll...no, do it. It's nice. Really nice."

"Good. And it sounds like you're making progress, business-wise. That makes me very happy."

"Me, too, Timmy. I'm pretty excited, when I'm not scared. Thank you so much for setting us on this...this path. Kenny's pretty happy, too. He thought he'd just work all his life and end up with a worn-out building worth less than whatever he paid for it. Me, too, except I didn't invest money into the diner, just my whole life. But now I have equity, thanks to you. Didja ever think you'd hear me say 'equity' in a sentence—and know what I was talkin' about?" Evelyn's laugh echoed in her bathroom.

"I knew you could say it if you wanted to. Have a nice time in the bath, Christopher Robin."

"Who? Oh, hey, I know that one. Winnie the Pooh, right? Thanks for the gorgeous flowers. And the leftover wine. Mmm." Her appreciation reverberated in her wine glass. "You and Robby are so dear to me. Go away now before I get sentimental."

That felt great. Tim had happy memories of yesterday, a feeling of accomplishment today—at the skilled hands of others—and excitement about tomorrow. On how many days could he say that?

Tomorrow would bring the shaving of the ragged beard of his back lot, the restoration of a country garden, with trees. He hoped his neglect hadn't ruined that option.

"Well, if it did, so be it. I'll have it graded and seeded or sodded and start over, like Aunt Stella is having to do. I'll still be ahead of her in some ways, because her fancy sods and shrubs were planted over a mere four inches of topsoil, whereas my soil goes all the way down, deep enough that it supports fully-grown trees. It'll be beautiful, if I live long enough to see it."

He wondered again about the children's story about a garden. *What was it about? Was it hidden, or secret, or something about winter? And whose garden was it? An ogre? A king? A lonely prince? A little prince?*

"Not *The Little Prince*. There is a garden in that story, but it has just one rose, no children. Hmmm. I'll ask Marlene. She knows everything."

Marlene Wentzell was the head librarian at the library on Main Street, two doors away from his newspaper office. He added her to the list of tasks to do on Wednesday, when he next had a good reason to go downtown.

June 8: Debris

"Here we go, Gloria! Our new lawn and gardens are being delivered today. Not delivered, you say? They're already here, just buried under weeds and thatch? Revealed, then. You say tomayto."

Tim was feeling light as he danced around the kitchen making breakfast, and searching the shelves in the den for a thesaurus. "We like to read the thesaurus at breakfast-time, don't we, Gloria? Yes, we doobie-doobie-do. Tum-te-tum."

He thumbed to the letter R, and paged through to *reveal*.

"Here's what's going to happen this morning right in my own backyard. I will reveal my garden, okay, and also acknowledge, admit, affirm, announce, concede, confess, declare, divulge, explain, expose, inform, publish, report, and tell. Goodness, that sounds like quite an ordeal, doesn't it? Let's try another word. How about, um, uncover?"

He flipped the pages. "R, S, T, U, uncover: bring to light, crack—how can that be?—discover, divulge, expose, unearth. Gee, that's not much better. I'm not going to *crack* my lawn. I won't *concede* my gardens. I thought synonyms meant the same thing as the root word? Context alters meanings, I guess. Maybe we'll just mow? Let's see. Mow: shear, trim, clip, crop, scythe, sickle. That's better, although scythe and sickle sound dangerous."

He closed *Roget's Thesaurus* with a dusty snap. "Well, the weeds will be mowed, the lay of the land will be uncovered, and who knows what will be revealed? Here we go, anyway."

A pickup truck emblazoned with the Chester Basin Property Management logo arrived, towing a utility trailer. By the time Tim had put on his shoes and jacket, the driver had lowered the back gate of the trailer and was hauling a heavy machine down the ramp and onto the paved drive. He replaced the ramp upright, firmly tugged on the machine's cord, and it started on the second pull.

Another CBPM truck pulled in, and Jake jumped out. "Good morning," he shouted over the roar of the machine. "Dana here's going to do as much as he can this morning." He pointed skyward where heavy clouds hung low. "It doesn't look good."

Jake led Dana and the machine to the edge of the back yard and then they cut the motor. "I'm just gonna walk Dana around to show him the obstacles I found."

He was holding a fistful of stiff wires with red triangular flags at one end, and as they walked, he and the driver stuck these into the ground to mark old garden beds or other unmowable features to avoid. They reached into the weeds on the left side of the property facing away from the house, tugged at something there, discussed it, nodded and shook their heads, and moved on. Flagging the whole area took about fifteen minutes.

Tim supposed that some features were easier to see when you were standing right next to them, but he hadn't wanted to wade in the weeds, and, very soon, he wouldn't have to. He had no useful knowledge to share with the workers, so he just waited at the corner of the house, out of the way.

"There's an old wire fence that has fallen down over there," Jake told him. "I told Dana to give it a wide berth. If that wire gets caught in the blades he'd be in all kinds of trouble. We'll cut it out by hand later. I think we found all the other obstacles. The machine is set to cut about five or six inches high, so don't be upset if it looks ragged after he's done. We'll be back with the zee-turn when the weather allows."

"How long do you think this'll take?" Tim asked. "Just curious."

"Normally, this size area wouldn't need an hour, just back and forth. But with all the dipsy-doodles around garden beds or whatever's there, it might take twice that. The good thing is that grass grows day and night this time of year, no matter what the weather. Weeds, too. Gotta run."

Tim watched Dana begin to work with the bushwhacker. He quickly cleared a straight line down the centre of the lawn and back again without encountering any obstacles, but on his third run the pace slowed as he worked around several red flags.

The machine was self-propelled, and it appeared to have the determination and strength of a team of oxen to go forward. Dana swung his weight to steer it left or right, slipping occasionally as he hauled.

Gradually, change was visible. The powerful blades chopped down old, brown goldenrod and new shoots of something , and there was now a swath from the house to the trees at the back.

Dana had worked up a sweat, but Tim had not. He went back in the house, brewed another coffee, and stood at the parlour windows to continue watching the show. This was a once-in-a-lifetime scene. He would never have to "bring to light, crack, discover, divulge, expose, or unearth" the lot again if he could help it.

I wasn't aware how much I'd neglected my house and property while I was working, working, working. If I hadn't taken this year off, the whole place might have collapsed around me. Perhaps the sagging sunroom and tilting woodshed were the warning signs of decay. The cellar could have blown up and the house would have burned and collapsed into the hole. I wouldn't have known anything about it because I would have been at work, work, work.

A loud bang from the yard brought him back from this doleful reverie. Dana tipped up the business end of the machine and shifted it into reverse to back away from something. He let the machine idle while he picked up pieces of a shredded aluminum can and tossed it toward a small pile of similar objects.

Who put that there? I certainly didn't throw pop cans or beer cans out there, or on the front lawn, either. What's the matter with people? I suppose they thought this was just a waste area, like Jake said about the front yard, but who would be back here? I don't like this.

He looked to the left, beyond where Jake had said there was a crumpled wire fence. There was a wide border of mowed grass outside of that, then the street leading to the exhibition grounds and The Brown Building.

"Look no further for the source of the junk. I should think it's hard to throw an empty aluminum can this far, but I'm glad they had good aim and didn't hit the house."

He looked to the right side of the lot. It bordered on a sort of no-man's land, once part of his grandfather's estate. Next to Tim's property was a gravelled path that was now an emergency exit from the exhibition grounds. It wasn't used as an access road because it entered the street on a sharp turn, but the risk was considered acceptable if there was a disaster to get away from.

Wonder what kind of disaster they'd need to evacuate for? Exploding cow belches? Fermented sauerkraut? Pie fights? There's a padlocked gate across the entrance to it. They'd have to plan the disaster ahead of time to make sure they had the key.

There was another series of loud bangs, and the mower motor shifted into a high-pitched whine. Dana quickly hit the "kill switch", and his shoulders slumped. Tim went outside.

"Hit a rock?" he said, hoping to sound sympathetic.

Dana had turned the machine sideways to reveal what was left of a garden shovel. The rusty blade was twisted and half-torn from the handle. "Scared the bejeebers outta me," he said. "I musta run up the handle, and when the shovel part got to the blades, I was standing on the handle and that tilted the blade up. I didn't know what was happening. Busted the mower, though. Busted it for good, maybe. Depends on what broke inside. Might just be a shear pin, designed to break when you hit something like this to save the engine. Sure hope so. Jake won't be happy about this."

Tim looked around. Dana had cut about two-thirds of the yard, and the change was remarkable. He could see the bones of the old layout. There were bumps where he assumed flowers had been planted, and shrubs which had been obscured by tall weeds now stood out in some kind of pattern. One-third remained to be cut on the woodshed side.

"Gosh, I'm sorry about the shovel, Dana. I saw all the pop cans and beer cans, too, not my beverages of choice. But who in their right mind would leave a shovel lying on the ground? Not me, I assure you. Anyone walking along here could have stepped on it and gotten a nasty surprise. Jake didn't find it, I guess? No red flag?"

"Nope. Well, I guess I'd better load this thing back on the trailer." Dana balefully assessed that task. The lot rose slightly uphill toward the paved driveway, and then slightly downhill to the street. It had been easy going when the mighty motor was running to propel itself, but pushing a machine seized in forward gear and weighing several hundred pounds was going to be impossible.

"I'll have to bring the trailer back here."

"Can I help at all? Tim offered, doubtfully. "Move my car, maybe?"

"No, it's okay. Just stand clear."

Dana drove the small pickup truck and trailer to the top of the freshly-cut back yard, and with a few quick manoeuvres, backed the trailer down to the disabled mower and lowered the ramp. With a heavy-duty tow-strap and a large ratchet he dragged the mower up the ramp and onto the trailer bed, where he strapped it down tight.

He pointed to where he'd turned the truck on the soft ground, leaving deep ruts. "Sorry 'bout the ruts. We'll fix 'em when we come back to finish the job."

"Sure. Any idea when that'll be?"

The damp morning was now turning to rain. "When it's not raining.

Would've had to stop now anyway. Just wish I wasn't taking back a dead horse. You'll hear from Jake. He'll likely come by around lunchtime."

~

Tim felt deflated as he took refuge from the rain inside the house. *Things had been going so well. But the thesaurus didn't forewarn that the mower would choke on a shovel. What synonym would have alerted me to that?*

"What was that part Dana said that he hoped was broken? Some kind of pin...a shear pin? Or a sheer pin?"

Curious and wanting to amuse himself a little, he opened the thesaurus to "mow" again.

"There it is: the first listed synonym of 'mow' is 'shear'. As the prophets foretold. And as it has always been with prophets, we hear but we don't understand, until the whatsit smites the unexpected thingy with a mighty lash. Too bad, but Jake will deal with it. He doesn't strike me as the kind of man who'd let a little incident like that set him back."

Tim had a mental image of Jake holding the mangled shovel over his head and hollering "Follow me, men!" as he disappeared into a thicket of man-eating blackberry brambles.

He wasn't far off. Jake arrived with knowledge of the incident, and a plan to finish the job. He apologized for the delay, said someone would return tomorrow or Thursday, depending on the weather, to finish the first cut, rake away the debris, and re-do all with the "zee-turn". He also said they would repair the ruts in the lawn at no cost.

Tim was amused that Jake had referred to any part of his yard as "lawn". He was also curious to learn what sort of beast a "zee-" or "zero-turn" was, but he wanted to learn for himself rather than ask the burning question.

He also thought about the damaged mower. It wasn't a horse to be shot and sent to the glue factory, but a complex metal thing to be repaired, for a little or a lot.

He wondered who was liable for the cost of repairs. He hoped he wasn't. Was there fine print about that? He hadn't signed anything on that long list of property maintenance options, so did that mean that he was responsible, or not responsible? What if it had been Dana's foot that had met the blades? He shuddered at the thought. He'd ask Jake when he returned.

~

Tim paced while he boiled some eggs. He wanted this backyard job to proceed smoothly, after years of not giving it a thought. He wasn't ready for delays yet. Delays would arise later when he started turning the soil for flower gardens, back and front.

His expectations for his flower garden were low. He had rarely, if ever, thrust his fingers into soil, and hadn't earned the right to expect things he planted to flourish. But he was looking forward to the challenge.

Jake arrived and knocked on the front door. "Sorry to come to this door. but I can stand out of the rain here and my boots are covered in mud. We apologize about the equipment malfunction. Dana will get another bushwhacker and be back to finish up as soon as possible. We'd like to let things dry out for a day first, but we can't be picky this time of year. If it's okay with you, we'll just send him whether you're home or not."

"I enjoy watching, but sure, do it when you can. I've got carpenters coming back to see if the woodshed can be fixed or if it should be hauled away. They're coming sometime this week, I hope. There could be a traffic jam."

"Don't worry, we can handle that. We won't fix the divots in your lawn until all the heavy equipment is off the premises. Gotta run."

Tim peeled the eggs and made lunch. He felt better. Everything would fall into place; perhaps not according to his schedule, but that was arbitrary anyway. He thought of looking up synonyms for "soon" in the thesaurus, but he'd played that game enough for now.

Instead, for diversion, he took his sandwich and mug of tea to the sunroom, trusting that yesterday's carpentry and caulking would handle his light step now. He sat on the old sofa and gazed through the dirty windows at what had been exposed outside.

He decided to run to the hardware store after lunch to get the necessary long-handled implements to clean the windows. That task he could do himself.

There was a sudden heavy shower. He ran his fingers over the shingled wall of the house where rain had leaked in and out on Victoria Day weekend. "Dry as a bone. Good job, Conquerall. Mother's sunroom lives on to delight another generation."

He heard a car door slam, followed by knocking on the back door. He opened the sunroom door, swinging easily now, and greeted Corey. "Come on in. I hope I'm allowed in here now. I couldn't stay away any longer. No leaks here. I'm going out soon to buy a squeegee to clean these windows so I can admire my beautiful gardens. See?"

To the non-owner's eye, the only visible change was that flattened weeds had replaced the tall weeds.

"If you say so," Corey responded. "I'll get the power put through for you now." He carried in his gear, went to the basement to disconnect electricity to the outlets inside the parlour, and proceeded with the wiring.

When he finished, he asked, "Got a lamp you want here?"

Tim brought a lamp out to test the outlets, which worked, and took it back inside the house. "I've got a new sofa coming this week," he said, "so I don't want anything in the way."

"They takin' that?" Corey indicated the old sofa.

"They'll take it out, but just out. I have to get someone to haul it away."

"Whaddya want for it?"

"What? Nothing. Do you want it? It's yours. But you have to get it out before the new one comes in, which I hope will be Friday."

"I c'n come back on my way home around suppertime. Need to get a tarp to cover it."

"And you'll need a helper, won't you? I'm sorry, but it can't be me. I had to carry a—a person in the winter, and my back's been touchy ever since. I did it to save her life, but this old sofa's already dead, so—"

"That was nice of you," Corey said. "No, I'll get one of the guys. Just leave this door unlocked and we'll get it. What's next? Something about that woodshed?"

"Yes. It's falling over, as you can see. I don't know why. It was built sometime in the last, oh, six-seven years, maybe? My old shed was rotten. It collapsed under snow with firewood still in it. So I got someone to clear it away and build a new shed—that one there. So why is it looking like it's going to topple over, too? That's why I started stacking firewood in the sunroom. I know, bad idea, but I never seemed to have the time to see about it. So, if you can salvage this one, prop it up somehow so it keeps the rain and snow off the wood, then let's do that. If we need a new one, well, I don't know, maybe. Or maybe I'll just throw a tarp over the woodpile? What do you think?"

"It looks fixable. I'll look at it when we come back. Rain should've stopped by then. No sense in getting soaked."

~

Tim felt better when he had a task or a quest, even one as simple as shopping for window washing gear. He put on a jacket and dashed to the car.

He soon returned with a sponge and squeegee on an extension pole, and a bottle of special window-wash to add to lukewarm water.

He didn't need the rain to stop for this chore, though it was just misting now. He filled his new bucket with the magic cleaning solution and took his kit to the yard. He plunged the squeegee into the bucket, applied it to the glass, and gently rubbed it up and down.

He was surprised at the dirty water that streamed down from the windows.

He scrubbed all the windows along the length of the sunroom and the southeast end, and the glass door at the northwest end. He carried out several buckets of clear water to toss against the windows for their final rinse, with hit-and-miss results. He went inside to look through the transformed windows, and was very pleased with his efforts.

The rain had let up. For the first time in so long that he couldn't remember, he walked around the yard where Dana had cut. He saw the wire fence along the perimeter between his property and the street.

Tim examined several rounded humps, still with their red flags, where flowers had once grown. Some green sprouts were already pushing their way up, some hardy perennials, he assumed, or hardy weeds, but at least they were green.

He walked all the way back to where Dana had turned around, under the grove of trees.

It seemed a magical place, as though it had been designed to provide shelter from the sun, and a place of respite from the street noise. From here, he could see his house all the way to the top, not just a nearby wall of white shingles defining the edges of the driveway and other spaces. The house seemed quite far away.

"But far away in a good way: I'm home, but not quite. I can see the sunroom, and from the sunroom, I'll be able to see—what? It'd be nice to have a focal point of some sort here. A bench, at least. Something to look at. To be determined."

He walked around, keeping an eye out for the well Jake had mentioned. *Oops, there it is. Almost stepped in it. Dana mightn't have seen that either. It would've been bad to drop that machine in there. I don't see a red flag. Jake must have forgotten about it. It's dangerous not being able to see where you're going.*

Tim walked back to the house and pulled out a board from underneath the sunroom. He carried it back to the hole in the ground and dropped it in. It went down only about two feet and leaned over.

"What the heck is that there for? Was there a decorative well there at one time?" He didn't want to go closer to investigate until he was sure that it really was that shallow and the sides wouldn't collapse.

He was drawn back amongst the trees. The ground was mostly clear of weeds; there was just pine and spruce needles and leaf litter. *If there was a bench here, I'd sit on it now, if it wasn't wet. A bird feeder would be nice, too.*

Given Dana's disaster with the unseen shovel, and Jake's forgetting to flag the well or whatever it was, Tim decided not to stray further off the beaten path. *I shouldn't even trust the beaten path yet in case there are sharp objects lying underneath the thatch. Better wait until Jake brings the 'zero-turn' and it cleans up all of this.*

He heard the sound of a vehicle in his driveway again, and saw Corey backing his truck just short of the sunroom door. He walked back to ob-serve this manoeuvre.

Corey and his two assistants carried the bulky old sofa through the doorway and onto the back of the truck in one smooth movement, and Corey applied the tarp and ties.

"Thanks for taking it away, Corey. See you again soon."

"Yuh. Thanks a lot."

~

It had been a long day, with a lot of fresh air. Tim wouldn't be staying up late tonight. He knew he would sleep peacefully, though. Things were still happening, moving toward the reclamation of his property. It would be completed soon.

When he picked up the thesaurus to put it back on the shelf, he gave in to his earlier whim to look up synonyms for 'soon'.

"'Ere long," the book suggested. "In a minute. In a second. In due time. By and by."

"I see," he said to the book. "Well, it'll likely be one of those. Or all of them."

June 9: Jobs

Wednesday

It felt odd to dress for the office today. Tim had been drawn to the back-yard. He could almost feel garden tools in his own hands. "Oh, yeah, and blisters, too. Blisters and a sore back take longer to recover from than white-collar paper cuts."

Today marked another significant milestone in his life, small though it might be: he'd been absent from the office for four days. In this year of changes, he had spent many hours outside the office pursuing his delving projects, but this was another step.

How long would it take me to stay away for a week?

"I'm not sure why I'd want to do that, but maybe the reason will appear. I never thought I'd enjoy digging in the dirt, either, so who knows what else might occur? Once I try it, I might be happy to run back to my thinking room and leave the gardening to the professionals."

~

Arrival time on most Wednesday mornings was "on your honour" for newspaper staff who had worked overtime on Tuesdays to ensure the paper was ready to print. Tim sat in the reception area and immersed himself in the voices and movements.

It was comforting to hear the staff quietly greeting each other as they arrived. *It sounds like they like each other, and like to work here. Wonder what they think they would gain by unionizing? Wonder who brought that idea up in the first place?*

Elaine was not the first to arrive this morning. When she did, she appeared happy.

"Good morning, stranger," she greeted Tim. "Finally missed us?"

"Maybe. I've been acquainting myself with carpentry and gardening and—"

"You?"

"*And* I've discovered that I love to *watch* the experts doing it. Machines break, rain falls, but problems are found, diagnosed, and fixed. The part where I actually do more than pay for all these skilled people comes later, maybe."

"We bought a hanging planter for my balcony. It's lovely, but it's not landscaping."

"I'll let you know when you can come over and plant corn on my back forty. What time would you like to meet this morning?"

"Can you give me an hour?" She glanced at her tiny wristwatch. "I'd like to get a few wheels in motion first."

"That's fine. I'll come to you."

Tim watched Elaine unlock her office door, flick on the lights, and pick up the phone almost before she was seated at the desk. She was well-qualified, not only to be editor of his small-town publication, but especially as a temporary editor, a 'sojourner', as she called herself. She knew how to move in, to manage, and to prepare for a smooth transition when she'd leave again.

Her fee was higher than he had initially expected to pay, but he knew that hiring someone for less would have resulted in him either cutting his sabbatical short or wishing he'd never embarked on it. She was worth every penny and so much more.

He also noted that it wasn't Elaine alone who'd hung the flowering planter on the balcony. "We" did that. *She and Roger are an ongoing item, I'd say. Decorating her apartment with flowers is a good sign. She deserves that happiness.*

Ed Garamond arrived and was surprised to see Tim sitting in the waiting area. "Looking for a job, boss? I don't think we have an opening here for a person of your particular qualifications."

"Oh? Why not?"

"Because you never left, ha-ha, not really. But you're carving out a new job for yourself, whatever it is. You're keeping us busy, anyhoo."

"At least you're not firing me. Got a sec, Ed?"

"Sure. Come on over to my new and improved location in the cube farm. I think I've gained multiple cubic molecules, and each one is meaningful."

Ed's workspace was still inadequate, that was evident, but it did appear to be laid out a little better; instead of having to converse with people over a divider, Ed now had a side chair for visitors. He removed a stack of papers from that chair and Tim sat.

"It's about GB," Tim began.

"The old fella's not coming back, is he? I don't think he'd know his way around now, certainly not with the digitizing that Harold's got going on."

"No, he's not coming back, though I think of him often when I'm here. Trouble is, he's not here, he's in my house, and so is his faithful wife. Both urns are in a dark corner of my study, but I don't want that to be their final resting place."

"Understood. I hadn't given it another thought after the funeral."

"Me, either, except that I'm aware they're in that corner. I know you didn't work *with* GB—nobody did—but you are likely the next-longest employee to work in the office with him, am I right?"

Ed looked at the ceiling. "Not sure about that, but I've been here a while. I don't want to take the urns to my house, though."

"Oh, gosh, no, I wasn't thinking of that. I was looking for some ideas about what to do with them. Keeping them on the floor in the dark doesn't seem respectful. We don't have a columbarium where I could have them sealed in a wall with a plaque. I could arrange for a burial plot in the cemetery, but burying cremated remains seems like overdoing it. I was wondering about scattering their ashes somewhere, and if that happened, do you think the staff would like to attend a short good-bye?"

"Are you looking for an answer today?"

"Not at all. He's been gone since—what—March? And Connie in April. Seems so long ago now. I'd like to close this chapter sometime this month. Any thoughts you have to share, I'd be grateful."

~

"You seem relaxed, Elaine. Things're going well, I take it?"

"They are this morning. Today's the day we pretend we have a week to assemble another edition, right? Next Tuesday's when we wake up and jam it all together. So, what's up with you and our caretaker?"

Tim recounted his tangles with John, his sleeping beside the furnace, needing multiple reminders before acting on requests to free up stuck windows and open the second-floor emergency exit. "I can't recall when he has ever initiated anything, like suggesting a fix. I feel—just a hunch, but I can't shake it—that we are over-paying him, or more likely that he is under-performing. But I don't know details of his job description, nor his remuneration. So I guess we should start there."

Tim sat back, then leaned forward again. "And I wonder if we should replace that whole boiler system with a new, efficient furnace. If John needs to snooze beside it to listen for sounds of its demise, then shouldn't we be proactive? Right now, he's running it because our hot water heater is oil-fired. That makes no sense. I'm glad he's cracked some windows open upstairs, otherwise we'll cook up there this summer. Not that we're supposed to be occupying the second floor, but that brings me back to the stairway access and egress issues. Whew!"

Elaine opened a file lying on her otherwise-bare desk. "Here's his personnel file. He's making Level Two salary, which is the same as clerical staff with added tasks, like Jean Naugler, for instance, who does typing but also attends town and county council meetings, and Project Sweetland debriefings, as you have seen."

"Remind me what's Level One?"

"Typing and filing, taking notices over the phone. General dogsbody stuff. We offer fifteen cents above minimum wage for that, plus benefits. I'm surprised you don't know this by heart."

"Ask me about anything else but personnel and I would dazzle you with my knowledge. I always shied away from personnel issues. I'm just not good at it; witness my outburst with John. When we hired Miss Martin, I briefly interviewed her, but I told Ed to discuss her terms with you. Minimum wage plus fifteen cents is so foreign to me that I can't negotiate it properly. For sure it doesn't sound generous. I bet you'll find some inconsistencies in our payroll."

"I have seen them. That's something that union organizers would make noise about, by the way, and they'd be right. I know you think I'm good at everything, but this is an area of specialty I didn't train for. We aren't big enough to afford a Human Resources department. There are companies that provide HR services, for a fee. We could engage one to review our jobs and remuneration and advise on any re-alignments or whatever antiseptic language they use."

"Ha-ha, that's right, that's how HR people talk, isn't it? Everything's positive, nothing's critical. Are they worth it, though?"

"I think they're worth a listen. The caveat is that the employer's sins will be exposed, too. Do we pay too little? Ask too much? Show favouritism? Pay unequally? Do the job descriptions accurately describe what staff actually do? Do we evaluate performance regularly? Do we reward good scores and discipline bad ones? If so, on what basis?"

"I think I'm getting a headache," Tim said. "May I please take the rest of the day off?"

"Not unless I can go with you. See, this isn't journalism, however you and I practise it. It's people-management, and that's a different ball of wax. Most staff here are extremely loyal to you, Tim; don't forget that. But we shouldn't let the terms of their employment be the thing that takes that down. Shall I contact an HR company to see what their services would do for us?"

Tim sighed. "Needs must. Does that mean I can't push John to do things?"

"Leave him to me for a bit, why don't you? I think we should tag-team so he's aware that we're both paying attention to him. Why don't I ask him to get a plumber to quote on switching our hot water heater to electric? It's not that I don't think this is important, but Project Sss is nearing go-time. Are you coming to our debriefing this afternoon?"

"I will—unless the sun comes out. I never thought I'd say such a thing, but my property will be the scene of men and machines if the ground has dried enough, and I want to be there in case something comes up. Yesterday it was a shovel hidden in the weeds, and it defeated a robust piece of equipment. Fortunately, the operator wasn't hurt. All I do is stand well back and drink coffee, but it's hugely entertaining. If I'm able, I'll attend your meeting."

~

He had one more visit before returning home, and this one would be fun. He walked next door to the library and asked for Marlene Wentzell, the head librarian.

"Good day, Tim. What part of your active mind has brought you here on this fine day?"

"Greetings to you, Marlene. My active mind is wondering about an old children's story about a garden that was occluded in some way, and later filled with blossoms. I must have read it in kindergarten or thereabouts. Whose garden was it? I know it wasn't *The Little Prince*. Was it an ogre? A king? A lonely prince? Was the garden hidden, or secret? Was it called *The Winter Garden*? How does the story end?"

"My goodness, Tim, your reading tastes do run the gamut—from Sherlock Holmes to Jekyll and Hyde to *Stone Soup*, and now this. I believe you are looking for *The Selfish Giant*. Just a moment."

Marlene returned with a thin book with a colourful cover. "Have a look at this. We have two copies, so you won't have to rush right back with it if you're struggling with any of the big words."

"I appreciate your thoughtfulness, Marlene. Let's see."

He flipped the illustrated pages of the book, and read the ending aloud. "'And when the children ran in that afternoon, they found the Giant lying dead under the tree, all covered with white blossoms.' Ouch. That's a tough way to end a children's story, isn't it? They wouldn't publish such a thing these days, I bet."

"You're right, they don't. It's all happy-happy now; but that's changing, too. The characters nowadays aren't necessarily dead, but authors are beginning to write about the lives children actually live. So, no giants and ogres, *per se*, but perhaps more recognizable bullies. May I inquire about your interest in this particular story?"

"The property behind my house once had gardens and shrubs and a path amongst them, thanks to my mother. I would stand in for the Selfish Giant, I guess. I would've been the only child in the garden, but I don't remember much about it. As I grew up, I was, um, encouraged to spend my time in the office while my mother worked, and I continued to do that as I gradually took over. So I let the yard go to weed and seed. Now I'm trying to reclaim the space, and this story popped into my mind. I thought it might be amusing to read it. You never know where it might lead."

"I hope you enjoy it. It's by Oscar Wilde."

Tim looked at the book's cover. "So it is. I would never have guessed that Oscar Wilde wrote a children's book. It's not the cutting wit he's known for, is it?"

"No. It's more or less an allegory, and so is *The Happy Prince*, also written by him. He was first and foremost a talented writer, and he wrote widely. He had children, and most likely wrote stories for them. The scandals are what people remember, sadly."

"Well, well. I thought I was going to read a light children's book, but I'll be reading *bona fide* literature instead. Good for me. I always learn so much from you, Marlene."

~

His downtown tasks accomplished, Tim drove home, eager to see what developments might unfold there. Nobody had called to say they would or would not arrive, but he expected to hear from someone soon.

Tim entertained himself imagining how Jake would handle John, hiding out in the basement. A court-martial, likely, and dishonourable discharge. *That may come for John, but Elaine will make sure we do it right.*

He phoned Jake. "What's the chance I'll see Dana here this afternoon? The sun's almost out."

"We had to dispatch everyone to mow a bunch of lawns that we missed because of the wet weather. It looks good for the rest of the week, so we're catching up as fast as we can. June's a four-letter word in our business."

"July's got four letters, too."

"July's not as wet, and, in a perfect world, the grass is growing at a predictable rate by then. But uncertainty is the environment we work in. If all goes well, we'll get to finish the bushwhacking at your property Friday morning. Then the guys will take away the clippings, and we'll bring the zero-turn and cut the stems right down to the roots. That's not how we normally mow lawns, but you don't have any lawn there yet. Have a look at the list I gave you. I quoted top-dressing and overseeding, which I recommend. Or you can just let nature take its course, but nature is used to growing goldenrod and other weedy things, so it'll take longer to get your soft green lawn out of that. Think it over. We'll likely load up the equipment Thursday evening, so we can start as soon as it's light enough to see Friday morning. That okay?"

"Sure. I'll be up. Not that you need me, but I'm eager to see the progress. Thanks, Jake."

He had one more call to make, to the furniture store to confirm delivery of his sofa on Friday afternoon. They said that "shouldn't be a problem", which didn't sound as solid as he wanted, but he wouldn't insist. Everything was lurching toward its conclusion.

Whether the sofa arrived Friday or Monday wouldn't matter a whole bunch. He and Robert could sit on two chairs from the dining room to admire the changes. The new sofa would still be new when it finally did arrive.

Now what? Should I go back downtown to sit in the War Room and hear the latest on Project Sweetland? Isn't there something useful to keep me here?

He went to the tools closet in the woodshed, where the rusted lawn mower still sat. He dragged it out and left it next to the cast iron radiators. There remained an old lawn rake, a rusty leaf rake, and a few lengths of rope.

He closed the door, and went back inside the house to call Amanda again, who would tell him what to do, as Corey had predicted.

"Corey wasn't going to take that stuff away," she said. "He just got the guys to carry it up and out for you. He was supposed to give you the number for the metal salvage yard to come and get it. They'll pay you for it, so that's a good thing. Got a pencil handy?"

She recited the number. "You tell them I said they'd come right over.

I'm serious. They're not doing *you* a favour, but I like them to know when I'm doing *them* a favour."

He thanked her and made the call. The salvage guy agreed to come for the cast iron radiators and one lawnmower, and would call him with the rebate amount after they weighed it. Tim urged them to come "soon", but he thought he shouldn't escalate it to "right away". Thursday and Friday might be busy days for trucks in his driveway, and he didn't want to set himself up as a traffic cop.

What was that synonym of 'soon'? 'By and by'? Sooner than that would be good.

He'd managed to avoid going to Project Sweetland, which would be half over by the time he'd get there. He'd read the report tomorrow.

Today was still Wednesday, the day to check the piano humidifiers. They needed no water added, not during these humid days. Tim's reward for remembering to check was to play the piano after supper, with a glass of *Mercredi ordinaire* to keep himself hydrated.

Apropos of learning about the elusive synonyms of "soon", he began with "In the Sweet By and By," a Gospel song rarely sung in his church; but it had a good chorus, which he sang as he played. Then he tackled something more challenging, and noted that he was getting better at it.

He saved *The Selfish Giant* for another day.

June 10: Ear training

Thursday

Breakfast-time at the Daisy Café seemed more upbeat than usual. Evelyn was smiling and laughing her infectious laugh, and Tim thought she really *was* happy, not just sounding like it.

"You look hungry, Timmy. Ready for a South River Log Jam platter today?"

"Bring me whatever you think I want."

When Evelyn returned with the platter, she slid in the booth. "It's nice to see you. Once a week doesn't seem enough. After you and Robby left on Sunday, I just felt like...like I'd like to see you more often, y'know? It isn't because"—she lowered her voice—"it isn't because I have a crush on you, which I do, but I can't help that, and I'm okay with it. It's because you are such a good friend, and I do know the difference. When you were getting our new business plan worked out, I saw you more often and you were so helpful. I don't need you to be helpful all the time, but I just like to see you. Am I making sense?"

"I hear you. I'd enjoy that as well. Got any suggestions?"

"Nope. Just wanted to get that off my chest. Enjoy."

He worked on the platter. When Evelyn returned to offer a third coffee, he declined and said, "Don't bother with a take-out box for the leftovers. Last time you did that, I discovered it in my car two days later. We'll remember to give me the kiddie portion next time."

"You know what I'd like?" Evelyn said. "I'd like you to call me sometimes, like you did on Monday. You're different on the phone. It's conversation I want, right? Or maybe connection. Nothing complicated. I say 'more coffee' a hundred times a day, and then I go home. I'm not lonely, but maybe I'm bored. Now I've said too much. Get outta here."

~

Tim stopped in the office for a copy of the transcript of yesterday's Project Sweetland debriefing.

"Almost ready," Harold said. "Ten minutes."

He walked around the bridges, slowly, stopped in at Harold's desk again, signed for a copy of the top secret report, and headed home for lunch.

~

Tim noticed right away that the cast-iron radiators plus the old lawn-mower were gone. *Vanished! That referral from Amanda worked wonders! They'll pay me something for them, too, so that's a bonus.*

This outdoor work was very interesting, and the workers were doing great things for him, but when they weren't on site doing the tasks, he wasn't sure exactly when they'd return. He was the customer, ever grateful, but at the mercy of the tradespeople.

"But they're at the mercy of the weather. And of machinery damaged by shovels and cans hidden in the weeds. Fret not, Tim, they know you're waiting for them. Other customers are likely calling and hollering at them because it rained. You don't do that. But you could just call Amanda and inquire."

That thought cheered him. Phoning was Doing Something.

"Hi, Amanda, it's Tim Brown. I just discovered the recyclers were here this morning already. They must be scared of you!"

"They should be. I send them a lot of business."

"Any word from Corey about my woodshed? I'm hoping he'll do whatever he's going to do before the weed-whacker comes back, so they can clear that whole side."

"Hang on. Corey, you going to Mister Brown's this afternoon?"

Corey's two-way radio blasted static. "Yuh."

"When?"

Tim heard the truck horn blowing in his driveway and over the phone via the two-way.

"I guess he's here now, Amanda. Gotta run. Thanks!"

Tim greeted the Jack of all trades with enthusiasm. "Glad to see you! I'm eager to get the woodshed mystery solved. Either you can repair whatever's wrong with it, or you can haul it away."

Corey said, "Mm-hmm," and walked around the structure. He pushed against it and it wobbled. Tim stepped back in case it would fall over.

Corey dropped a square of canvas on the ground at the sagged end, and lowered himself down to look underneath. He got up again, stepped inside, and rocked back and forth.

"Nothin' wrong with it," he said. "They just put it in a bad place. That end is mostly hangin' in the air. The blocks sank down in that corner until the middle fetched up on a high spot that made it rock back and forth."

"Really? The shed's still good?"

"Far as I can see right now, yuh."

"So, what's the remedy? Just fill in there with rocks?"

"Could, but it's hard to know how deep that soft spot is. We'd have to dig it out and then dump maybe a yard of gravel in it, but it might sink some more. Easier to just drag the shed a few feet closer to the driveway and then block it up proper like we did with your sunporch there."

"Drag it?"

Corey had already returned to his truck. He turned it around and backed it into the yard until the rear bumper was close to the good end of the woodshed. He tossed planks and straps to the ground, and jacked the structure up far enough for him to push the planks under it. More planks and jacking went on behind it.

He placed a long strap around the base of the woodshed and attached it to a hook on the truck's bumper. He grinned at Tim and said, "You said fix it or haul it away, right? Let's see which happens."

He started the truck and gently pressed the accelerator. The strap tightened. The transmission hummed. Nothing moved.

Then the woodshed slid ahead on the planks as the truck wheels turned. It stopped again, then jumped ahead and rocked dangerously as boards cracked somewhere underneath. Corey pulled it another foot farther and then shut off the truck.

"Something broke under there," Tim offered.

"Yuh. A joist caught on a rock. I'll brace that, easy."

The woodshed and its tiny tools storage closet were now nearer to the house, more convenient for wintertime dashes for firewood. Corey, working alone, had spent less than ninety minutes at the job.

"Better fill in that hole there," he said. "Toss in some rocks from them gardens. Funny place for a sinkhole. Was this ever a farm?"

"My grandfather likely had chickens, maybe a horse, who knows? That'd be half a century ago or more. Why?"

"Sometimes people used to bury horses on the property. The graves would sink like that years later. Or a big dog. But not so close to the house."

"We never had a dog. My mother used to say she knew where all the bodies were buried, but I'm pretty sure she was joking. There's a bunch of rocks around the garden beds out front so maybe I'll dump them here."

"That's everything, then?"

"Yes, for now."

~

Corey had fashioned a rudimentary step of leftover lumber in front of the open side of the shed. Tim stepped up on it now and stood in the structure. He envisioned getting a load of seasoned firewood from Buck, his friendly supplier. Buck would dump the load at the end of the driveway, and Tim would toss and stack it right here. The roof would keep the rain off the wood, and the open sides would allow the wind to blow through, continuing to dry it out.

No more abusing the sunroom. Robert wouldn't permit it now, nor would the ghost of Tim's mother, who had practically lived in it in her decline.

He thought about how much they'd enjoyed the painted sunroom on Victoria Day. He remembered Robert's valiant efforts as grillmaster, trying to keep the coals out of the rain while he stood in the drips.

"Hey, here's our hibachi corner, right here in the woodshed! There's room for it. I know exactly the thing for it, too. That army surplus place had heavy-duty metal cabinets. One of those will hold the woodpile in its place and make a great spot for grilling."

Robert was due to arrive soon, so he went back in the house to prepare their supper.

~

The choir was excited. The minister had invited them to sing two extra anthems of their choosing on the last Sunday in June.

"So let's make good choices," Robert said. "The minister will give short meditations on the themes of the music we choose. This is a rare opportunity to collaborate."

"I have a suggestion," said Bruce, a bass. "Everything we sing has a text. Much as we try, the congregation doesn't always grasp the words we sing, especially if the music is unusual. Why don't we just give him the texts and ask him to read them?"

"Great idea, Bruce, thank you. Barbara, our valuable librarian, has printed this list of our current repertoire. We have more in the Library, as you know, but these are ones we know well enough to sing at the drop of a hat. Take a few minutes and mark your top three. Barbara and her two assistants will tally up the votes."

~

It was too dark by the time they returned home for Robert to fully appreciate the changes in the backyard. Tim enthusiastically described the stops and starts he'd experienced in the week thus far, and potentialities to come.

"We even have a little shelter for the hibachi and the Grillmaster—that's you—so you won't be exposed to rain or hot sun. And I'm putting into use everything we learned about gardening at Stella's."

"We didn't learn anything. That Aubrey fella's doing it all. How's that going?"

"I've only glanced as I drove by. Work is happening. Perhaps we'll drive down that way on Sunday and spy on her landscaping. We have a competition now, if only in my mind."

June 11: Zero-turn

Friday

The racket that woke Tim wasn't a nightmare, but a dream come true. He jumped out of bed and quickly pulled on his sweatpants, reassuring Robert that all was well.

What he actually said was, "They're here!" as he bounded down the stairs to see the roaring, snarling machine in the backyard.

He greeted Dana in the pre-dawn light like Scrooge greeted the boy on Christmas morning.

Dana acknowledged his presence with a nod, but kept both hands on the voracious machine as he wrangled it around the marked obstacles.

He worked quickly, but he was also vigilant, frequently putting the bushwhacker in neutral to walk ahead and kick at a tuft of grass that might cover something that should not be mowed. The machine seemed to paw at the ground, eager to go forward.

Tim saw Robert in the window of the sunroom, holding up a cup of coffee, and went in to join him.

"I nearly died of fright!" Robert said. "First the racket, then you racing down the stairs, I didn't know what to think!"

"I didn't expect him to be here before sunrise. Isn't it great?"

"I'm sure it will be. It looks chewed up."

"Sure does. He's cutting high to avoid obstacles, though that didn't work with the shovel. But they're coming back to mow everything down with the zero-turn."

"What's that?"

"Haven't a clue, but I'm eager to find out. When it's all mowed and raked, they'll spread a layer of peat moss and scatter some grass seed. After that, it's a race between the sun, rain, and birds."

"There's a gamble in everything, isn't there?"

"Yes, but I'm loving it. This is so different from any other project I've been involved in, though most of my involvement is standing by and watching. Before you head back to the big city, do you want to see where your hibachi will go in the woodshed?"

"Not this morning, thanks. I won't risk my ears anywhere near that noisy machine's decibels. That fellow is wisely wearing ear protection. I'm glad you're enjoying this farming experience, though. It looks good on you—even if those clothes don't."

"What? This is my dress code for the new me—unless you'd prefer I wear the park ranger uniform like this fellow's boss. Jake must be retired from the army, but he looks like he's ready for inspection anytime."

~

The self-propelled machine easily loaded itself onto the trailer this time.

"I'm glad you didn't hit any more hidden obstacles," Tim said.

"Yeah, me too. They sure weren't happy when I took the other one back, but I told them about the shovel and why I didn't see it. They said it wasn't my fault, and Jake convinced them to let me have this machine to finish up this morning, but I gotta run back with it now because somebody else is waiting for it."

"Then…you'll be back to rake?"

"I think so. Jake is trying to get all our clients caught up by the end of this weekend, so somebody'll be here to rake, and then I'll bring the zero-turn if I can get it. We'd work ahead if we could, but you can't cut grass that hasn't come up yet."

Dana's early arrival had made Tim think it was near noon, but it was still early morning. The truck wasn't going to deliver his sofa until the afternoon, they said, and if Dana returned to trim, he'd be at it for some time.

There's just enough time to go downriver to that surplus shop to snag that cabinet.

The shop proprietor directed him to a corner where several metal cabinets were in a jumble. One that would keep the charcoal briquettes dry was his preference, and he spied just the thing, behind several other heavy pieces.

This salesman knew that a cabinet in the hand was worth two in a pile, so he made quick work of clearing the obstacles.

Tim opened the metal door beneath the metal drawer, and saw a metal shelf inside. The surface was metal, and the whole thing was painted gunmetal grey. It was perfect.

"How much for this?"

The man told him a price which Tim knew he wasn't expected to pay. He rubbed his fingers over a scratch on the side and offered twenty dollars less: immediately accepted. Both were happy with the transaction, though less happy with the work they now had to do.

They pushed and pulled the heavy cabinet through the narrow pathways around other merchandise, got it on a cart and rolled it to Tim's car.

"You think it's gonna fit in your trunk?"

"I hope so. The latch might scratch it but that won't matter."

They tipped the cabinet into the trunk opening and pushed. It cooperated better than either had expected. The trunk lid was up all the way.

Tim said he'd be fine, wasn't going far, would be careful, and drove off.

He pulled in his driveway and parked in the turn area. Whoever arrived next might help him get the thing to the woodshed.

Who arrived next was a woman in a CBPM pickup truck towing a utility trailer that was carrying a lawn tractor. She jumped out of the truck and extended her hand as Tim came out to greet her.

"Hi, Mr Brown, I'm Jocelyn. Jake sent me to do a bit of cleanup for you." Her handshake was like iron and her smile was wide. Her khaki uniform was as crisp as Jake's. *Perhaps another ex-military recruit*, Tim thought.

"Nice to meet you, Jocelyn. What's happening now? Is this the zero-turn?"

"Gosh, no. Jake let me bring the John Deere instead of just working with a wheelbarrow. Not because he's doing me a favour, he just thinks it'll be faster. I'm going to rake off all the thatch that Dana cut down."

"Anything I can do to help?"

"No, sir. If you don't get in my way, that'll be all the help I need. Oh, if you like, you could gather up those pop cans. That'll save a little time. Here's a garbage bag. Careful of your hands. Got gloves? Okay, I gotta march."

She lowered the trailer gate, started the mower and backed it down to the ground. She rolled a little wagon off, hooked it to the mower, tossed in a rake, drove to the back of the mowed area, and began to rake. She worked quickly and effectively, and soon the little wagon was full. She quickly drove it back to the truck, tossed the rakings into the truck bed with a pitchfork, and went back to where she had left off, raking piles, filling the wagon, pitching into the truck, and back again.

Tim was fascinated watching her. She was right to ask him to stay out of her way. *If there was a yard-work competition, I'd bet on Jocelyn to win. Middle-aged or not, she's in fantastic shape. She'd be almost as fast with just that wheelbarrow.*

He gathered up the cans and paper debris Dana had collected. He walked around to look for strays, but saw nothing else that would endanger the machinery.

During one of her trips to the truck, Tim offered Jocelyn a coffee, but she declined. He went in the house to make himself one, and returned with a tumbler of cold water for her. She accepted it with thanks and drank it down in one long gulp.

As entertaining as it was to watch her work, Tim thought he should do something useful. He had the Project Sweetland report, so he took a dining chair to the sunroom, where he could do both.

He tried to read the report, but wasn't taking it in. Harold used code names for people, places and things, so one had to be familiar with the context in order to follow. *I know the point of the code is to keep this info from accidentally being revealed to outsiders, but it's tricking me. I must be an outsider. I'll try again tonight. Imagine Project Sweetland, the biggest news story we've ever broken, coming second to watching an athletic woman raking hay!*

He put the chair back in the dining room and the document on his desk in the study.

Jocelyn was tying down a tarp to secure the hay-wagon load of debris in the box of the truck. Tim went out to express his admiration for her work.

"I enjoyed it," she said. "I see you have a cabinet or something in your trunk there. Would you like a hand getting it out? Your trunk probably shouldn't be open all day."

"Oh, do you—can you? That'd be great. It's going to the woodshed."

"We'll pop it in the wagon and run it over there, no problem."

They tilted the cabinet from the trunk to the wagon. Tim walked along to steady it while she manoeuvred. When the cabinet legs pointed into the shed, all it needed was a tilt-up and a turnaround.

"Perfect!" Tim said for the second time today. "It's going to be my barbecue station. Thank you so much, Jocelyn. I would've done damage to myself on my own."

"No problem. You can't hurt that cabinet, anyway. I saw lots of those in my day."

In minutes, the mower and wagon were back on the trailer. With a grin and a wave, Jocelyn was gone.

"Well, your impatience was rewarded, wasn't it?" Tim asked himself as he made a tuna sandwich. "That was quite a show! I wonder how many other properties she'll visit today. They charge by the service, not by the hour, so there's an incentive to be swift. I hope they are well-paid."

It was a lovely, late-spring day. He would have eaten his lunch outside, but there wasn't anywhere to sit, so he opened all the doors and sat in the kitchen.

I wonder who'll come in the driveway next? The movers? Or the mysterious turnaround, what's it called—the zero-turn? I really hope it's the zero-turn, because it's the machine that's supposed to make the final cut so those sharp little stumps won't puncture the soles of my shoes.

Jake came next. "Of course you're here," Tim said. "You're the quality control guy, right?"

"That I am. How'd Joce do?"

They walked to the yard.

"I've never seen such a hard worker," Tim said. "She never stopped, and hardly seemed winded."

"Retired military. She didn't want to let that hard body go soft after all the work she put into building it, so she loves this work. Let's have a look. Good, good. Okay, we're ready for the next step. We need to get the cutting done so the growing can start. Next week looks a bit damp, which would be perfect for top-dressing and overseeding with some clover. Were you wanting that service?"

"Let's. In for a penny and all that."

"Good. It looks like Joce found your flagstone path. Might as well bring it back, don't you think? It'd cost you a fortune to build it new."

Jake handed Tim a batch of red flags to mark the edges as they walked.

"That's going to be a nice feature. Good thing we found it. We're going to set the mower blade quite low next time, so we don't want it chewing on stone. And that'll save about six bags of peat and two of seed."

"Those red flags are handy little things, aren't they?" Tim said. "I always thought of 'red flag' as a metaphor for danger, but they're real warnings, too."

"If you like sayings," Jake said, "here's mine: 'Well begun is half done'. Folks are almost always happy to see some progress, even if we can't finish it on the same day. If we tried to finish one whole job before we moved on, a dozen other people would be frustrated to be kept waiting, and they might wander off to the competition."

"You have competition?"

"Not if I can help it. Okay, I better run. We're working twelve hours today and tomorrow. Somebody will be here later today. Might have to finish tomorrow. Like I say, well begun. I hope you didn't invite people over for a garden party tomorrow."

"No, but soon, whenever it's safe for people to walk on my precious grass. Can't wait to see it. I loved hearing the bushwhacker instead of the alarm this morning. Very effective."

~

With that assurance from Jake, Tim felt he could relax and let events play out as they would. The work was more than half done.

He made a second mug of tea and tried the Project Sweetland document again. This time the code names made sense, and he studied it with growing interest.

Under Elaine Fong's leadership, guided by lawyer Roger Smith, the staff had continued to pursue rumours and hunches, as Tim had insisted they do. They had found significant instances of dirty tricks by the Principal Culprit, Eric MacIntosh, the over-ambitious property developer.

They had considered looking for even more examples of his misdeeds, but had decided that what they had was sufficiently damning. Now they were working to secure irrefutable, iron-clad proof.

That was a great comfort to Tim, and made him proud. *The Times* wouldn't be guilty of yellow journalism, as Eric would undoubtedly accuse them. He would be furious that Tim's community newspaper was attempting to punch above its weight, while he himself operated however he wanted to in the county. Many people had agreed to admit their part in his tin-pot operation, as long as they could also describe the kind of pressure and threats he had applied to them.

Blackmail, Eric? Really? Extortion? Don't people go to jail for that? I hope you do. When you get out, you won't even drive an old dump truck for somebody else. I'm sure Jake wouldn't hire you. Good, honest, hard work is better than swindling, Eric. It might even pay better, too.

He was pleased to see that his Aunt Stella, the MLA for South River and The Harbours, had brought her influence to bear in the right way in this matter. She would, of course, use some aspects of the investigation to attack the government from her preferred seat in opposition. Ministers of Lands and Forest, Development, and even Tourism, were going to feel the heat of her righteous indignation when the story broke.

Tim wished he could be in the Legislature to witness this in person, but he'd likely have to settle for reading about it in the city newspaper. Stella would take good swipes at Eric MacIntosh, with whom she may have been close enough, briefly, to hear some incriminating pillow-talk.

Eric was married to Mary, but since she had attacked Tim at a church meeting last month, he was unsympathetic about her plight. She appeared to have mental health issues, so he couldn't totally fault her, but he wouldn't excuse her, either.

He put the papers away. Wheels were turning without him, that was all he needed to know. Elaine was working hard on this, not only for *The Times*, but also for her own resumé. *As she should. I will sorely miss her when she moves on. Too bad she turned out to be so good.*

~

It was Friday night, the end of a tremendous week in the life of Tim Brown. He explored the wine cabinet for a suitable vintage. He deserved a nice-ish one, he thought, since he'd finished up the heels of leftover bottles this week.

He selected a bottle of *Lastre di pietra,* an Italian red. He often picked up different wines from the stores, with varying results. The label said it was "robust", an essential part of the description. The fine print said it was named in honour of the fine flagstone workers in some district or other of Italy.

"Flagstones? Well then, *Lastre di pietra* it shall be!"

He pulled the cork, poured a serving, and took it out to sip as he strolled along his flagstone walkway, outlined by red flags.

It was nice to walk the meandering path. It inspired a meditative pace, given its layout. *No rushing here. I will literally come out here to smell the roses.* He drank a toast to the roses, and another one to flagstones.

He wandered back on the path and over to the woodshed, now ready to receive wood to burn in the fireplace, which he very much enjoyed in the cold months. And there was the grey metal cabinet, ready to support the occasional outdoor feast. He raised his glass to that, too.

He returned to the house and found something to heat for supper. He considered running out for fish and chips, but didn't feel like running anywhere, and he'd already toasted his way into a second glass of wine.

He heard yet another truck in the driveway, and went to the front door to see. *Is the Zero-turn here?*

No, it was a big moving truck, backing in from the street, its transmission whining and backup signal beeping.

Tim stood at the back corner of the house and beckoned to the driver. A man in the passenger seat jumped out and guided the truck safely past Tim's car.

"Right here's good, I think," Tim said. "It's going in there." He pointed to the sunroom.

"That's easy," the man said. "Your sofa's heavy, though."

"I'll hold the door."

The movers held the sofa at an angle to fit through the door and set it down. He signed for it, the driver handed him a copy of the delivery slip, and they were gone.

It was perfect. He quickly brought out a little bookshelf, the blue quilt that matched the ceiling, and the two decorative cushions. He set his wineglass on the shelf, and checked the time. Just five o'clock.

The sun would set at nine o'clock. Four hours of potential working time for the "zee-turn".

Evelyn would be soaking in the bathtub soon. While he waited to call her and his supper warmed, he browsed the pages of the children's book by the unexpected Oscar Wilde.

~

Tim had dozed off on the surprisingly comfortable sofa. For the second time today, a CBPM truck woke him with an industrial machine, and this time it was fired up right outside the sunroom where he was snoozing.

The racket spooked him, and then delighted him. "The zero-turn is here!"

He went out to greet Dana, who had this assignment. "Long day, Dana."

Dana nodded. "We don't mow in the winter, though. I'll get my summer then, in the Caribbean."

"Nice. So this is the famous zero-turn? Why's it called that? Funny-looking mower."

"Each of the power wheels operates independently, so one can go forward while the other one's in reverse, spinning it on a dime. It's great for cutting around irregular gardens. You'll see. I won't be able to finish tonight, maybe Jake told you, but I'll be back to wake you up in the morning. I guess you won't mind?"

"I sure won't. Carry on, Dana."

We're nearly there. Getting closer. Garden beautiful, coming right up! Tim put supper on a plate and returned to sit in the sunroom, balancing the plate on his lap.

The action outside was too good to miss. Each machine, operated by man or woman, had worked in a special way, and this one was different again. As the large machine shaved around the humps, it seemed to lower the ground.

Tim fully appreciated Jake's mow-rake-mow process now. If the previous work hadn't been done, this machine wouldn't have been as efficient.

It was now six o'clock. He served himself another splash of wine, which *was* pleasingly robust. He brought the phone to the sunroom and dialed Evelyn.

He heard the water thundering into her bathtub when she answered, so he jumped up and held the phone outside as the mower passed.

"I win," he said.

"What the hell's going on over there? Are you demolishing the house?"

"No, just all around it. Remember the desolation that was my back-yard? Well, that's going, going, gone. Soon there will be flower gardens with nymphs and satyrs dancing around fountains of, um, peppermint juice."

Evelyn laughed enthusiastically, finally getting breath to say, "You damn fool, you almost made me drop the phone! So, you're getting the back forty cut down? That'll be nice. I like my own back forty. It's a real park, but I never saw any fountains of peppermint juice, ha-ha. Zero maintenance."

"Right now my maintenance is done by Chester Basin Property Management. The work was beyond me, anyway. I do hope to plant some flowers, you know, buy a tray and stick 'em in the ground, at least. So, what're you doing this lovely evening?"

"Not a damn thing, same as always. But tomorrow night I'm going down to White Point Resort."

"White Point? Why?"

"Oh, because," she said in a sing-song voice.

"Because there's a darts tournament?"

"Mayyybeee."

"A big one?"

"Kinda."

"Tell me, Ev. Are you the defending champion?"

"Bull's eye! How'd you know?"

"It's my superior skill at wild guesses. I'd love to see that. Are there spectators?"

"Some, I guess."

"Could Robert and I go?"

"Oh, I don't know. You might make me nervous."

"We wouldn't want to do that. If we do go, we'll wear disguises, okay? And we won't cheer for you at all. Maybe just a little." He made his voice squeaky. "Yay, Evelyn, Ev's the best!"

"You silly man. I'm glad you called. I was winding myself up. Now I'm loose."

"Well, then, I've done my job. I better go now. Tonight I'm cheering on the zoom-zoom zero-turn machine. G'nite, Ev."

"G'nite, Timmy."

That was nice. Ev likes me to call her sometimes because she gets lonely. But you don't have to be lonely to want to talk with a friend. We'll do that again.

The sun hadn't officially set yet, but the shadows were long and Dana was peering ahead of the mower. A few minutes later, he disengaged the blades and drove the machine onto the trailer.

Tim leaned out the door, called his thanks and goodnight, and Dana drove the rig away.

He leafed through *The Selfish Giant*, admiring the illustrations. He would read it soon. There'd be plenty of rainy days for that.

June 12: Grave matters

Saturday

Dana was back at seven.

"Did you oversleep?" Tim teased. "I expected you at five o'clock."

"Had to pick up extra fuel. We've got a long day ahead, me and this machine."

"Well, I guess you'll rest when you get to the Dominican Republic. I used to work twelve-hour days, too, but I did most of it sitting at a desk."

"I couldn't do that."

"I didn't like it much, either. I'd rather sit and watch you work, ha-ha. So, you think you'll finish up here this morning?"

"Oh, yeah, this won't take much longer. I tried to finish last night, but I couldn't see well enough. I think Jake's coming later with the edger to cut out your stone walk, and sign off on our work so far."

"Another machine! If I'd tried to clear this lot by myself—"

"You'd never do it. It's hard work, even with the specialized machines."

"You got that right. They'd probably find me lying in the undergrowth. Well, I won't hold you up, Dana. I'm going out for groceries now, so I'll say goodbye and thanks, for now. It's been a pleasure having you work here."

They shook hands and turned to their respective tasks.

This weekend's grocery shopping wouldn't be extensive. It was Tim's turn to make pizza. Something for Sunday dinner, whatever looked good. Fresh fruits and vegetables. A supply of coffee beans and wines. Life would proceed smoothly.

The mower wasn't clattering as he got into his car. Dana was clearing around the depression left from moving the woodshed. Tim had witnessed plenty of yard-work this week, so he didn't mind missing the final minutes of it. If he did his errands quickly, perhaps he'd get back in time to have a chin-wag with Jake about what was next.

~

A month ago, Tim had begun growing his beard. It was a real beard now, a little too real for his comfort. Making an appointment for hair care, and now for beard care, had always been low on his To Do list, more often on his Drive-By list.

It occurred to him now as he drove by the salon. He dropped into the small shop where he normally received the services, and asked for his enthusiastic stylist.

She was busy, he was told, but if he would return in an hour, she'd be happy to give him a scrub and a trim. The timing was perfect. He went to the stores, quickly made his purchases, and returned at the appointed time.

He was in the stylist's chair when he thought about the groceries in the trunk. That had been of no concern in the months when the exterior temperature was colder than the interior of his fridge, but those days were behind him. He mentally reviewed what he'd bought and hoped nothing would spoil in the hour.

When he was once again "the handsomest client I have," Tim left a goodish tip for the compliment and drove home.

At first glance, he was pleased to see more vehicles in the driveway.

Then he could not comprehend what he saw.

Dana's zero-turn and its transport were still there. Jake's truck was also there, plus a police car and a brown sedan he recognized as the town police's ghost car. Bright yellow caution tape was stretched from the woodshed, across the yard, back around a tree, across to another tree, and back to the woodshed.

Standing at the top of the driveway, outside the taped area, were Dana, Jake, a uniformed South River Police Service constable, and another man, not in uniform.

"Good morning, gentlemen," Tim said as he approached. "What's going on? Is somebody hurt?"

Jake and Dana appeared very unhappy. "I tried to call you, Tim," Jake said. "The call wouldn't go through."

"No worries. What's going on? What's the tape for?"

Tim began to walk toward the taped-off area, but the police constable raised his hand toward Tim.

"Who are you, sir?"

"Timothy Brown. I live here. What's going on?"

"Is this your property?"

"Yes, it is. Excuse me, but I asked you a question, too, Constable—" he looked at the policeman's name plate—"Constable Etche-verry. We haven't met before, I don't think. I used to know most of the people on the—"

"Mr Brown, what do you know about Mr Singleton and Mr Comeau's discovery?"

"Who are they?"

"I'm Singleton," Jake said. "Dana is Comeau."

"Do you not know these men?" the constable asked Tim.

"We've met many times recently. I wasn't aware of their surnames. What did you discover, Jake?"

"I'll ask the questions, Mr Brown. Mr. Comeau and Mr Singleton, please go directly to the station now. The detective is waiting for you."

"Why are they going to the police station? What have they done? Is somebody hurt?"

Nobody answered Tim. Dana and Jake got in their respective vehicles.

Tim's car was blocking the driveway. He moved toward his car to shift it, but the constable stopped him.

"Give me your keys, please."

"No, thanks, I'll move it."

"Mr Brown, your keys."

"Seriously? Why the—?"

He shook his head and passed his keys to the constable. The plain-clothes cop stood at his elbow, his presence like a restraint to Tim.

When the trucks and trailer were gone and the remaining vehicles were rearranged, the constable returned. Tim held his hand out for his keys.

"We'll keep your keys for now, Mr Brown. We want to ask you some questions about this incident."

"Well, do ask away, Constable, and don't hesitate to share a little info in the process. I'm about to lose my patience here. Please tell me what's going on. What'd you discover, oil? There's the remnant of what might have been an old well back there, though I think it was just decorative."

"Are you saying you don't know why we're here?"

""Of course I am saying exactly that, yes. I haven't a clue. I was out getting groceries and a haircut while Dana finished cutting my grass. I come home and find you guys here occupying my property and I *do not* know why."

Another cruiser pulled into the driveway. Two uniformed police got out and conferred with Etcheverry. The plainclothes man got in the unmarked vehicle and drove off.

Tim felt two contrasting sensations invade his body simultaneously: his anxiety was rising, and his heart was sinking. Things were falling apart. He was losing control, and nobody was telling him why.

"Excuse me, gentlemen," he said, struggling to keep his voice neutral, "but I have perishables in my car, and I'd like to get them in the refriger-ator before they spoil, if it isn't too much bother. May I please have my keys so I can take care of that?"

The two new uniformed policemen looked at Etcheverry. None of them appeared willing to comply with Tim's request, which elevated his distress another notch and didn't keep his heart from pounding as it con-tinued to sink.

"We can't let you into the house at this time, sir," Etcheverry replied.

"Well, that's just ducky! I have no idea why you're here, what in hell you're after, or what any of it has to do with me, but I *really* can't under-stand why a tray of chicken breasts and two litres of milk can't go in my refrigerator, for heaven's sake! If you're afraid I'll do something illegal in the house, there are three of you here, so escort me in. Or take my stuff in yourselves, can you do that for me, at least?"

"Lower your voice, sir. We're not permitted to enter your house at this time," Etcheverry said.

Tim felt short of breath. He leaned against his car. "You may be doing your job, Constable, but I never imagined that your job would entail this bizarre invasion and occupation of my private property. And the big secrecy. Now what?"

"We need to secure the site until the Coroner gets here."

"The Coroner! The Coroner? Constable, was—is there—did someone *die* here? When? Is there a *body*? I know it wasn't Jake or Dana. Did something happen to one of their employees? Can you please tell me that, at least?" Tim attempted to peer into the yard. "Why won't you let me see?"

"I'm not at liberty to say, sir. Stay here, please."

"Bloody hell. Well, the Coroner wouldn't be coming just to have tea, so there must be a body, and it must be a human, not a raccoon or a deer, or you'd be waiting for someone from Lands and Forests. That is indeed serious, but I don't know how that leads to you locking me out of my car and house. How long will he take—the Coroner?"

"We've put in the call, and we'll guard the site until he arrives, that's all we know. Sometime tomorrow, possibly. I understand your frustra-tion, Mr Brown. I'm going to take you down to the station now. The detective will have some questions for you, and your questions will be answered then, too."

"Right *now*? How long will *that* take? This is really not—makes no sense," Tim finished lamely. Was he right to be annoyed about his own inconvenience, when someone was possibly dead in his backyard?

The two uniformed policemen came around the corner of the house, unrolling yellow CAUTION tape.

"What're they *doing*?" Tim said, riled up again. He began to walk toward the house, and then stopped. "What do you think is inside my *house*? This is *ridiculous*! You're calling attention to my home as a crime scene, for heaven's sake! You're making it look like I've committed a *crime*! People will speculate all kinds of things when they see that tape and they'll remember it for years. *Please* take that tape down. *Right now*!"

"I'm asking you to calm down, Mr Brown," Etcheverry said. "This is standard police procedure in a situation like this."

Tim took a deep breath. "Right. Calm down. If only you would tell me what you mean by 'a situation like this'. What's the point of keeping me in the dark? I'm sorry, Constable Etcheverry, but this is a shock, as I'm sure you're aware. This is not what I expected would happen today, or ever. So, please explain to me fully what's next in your crazy plan. That yellow tape means that you suspect something illegal happened in my house. What is it?"

"I'm not able to answer that question."

"Oh, that's just dandy. I'm expecting a weekend guest this afternoon. Where are we supposed to go?"

"It's standard procedure, nothing personal. We'll deal with things as expeditiously as we can. As I said, the Coroner has been informed, and we have to secure this site and all your property until he clears it."

Tim stepped closer to the policeman. "For the record, I take offence at your standard procedure. Am I a suspect in a crime, Constable Etcheverry?"

"No, sir, you are not a suspect, but we appreciate any assistance you can give us. You may be a witness."

"You're crazy. It must be clear to you by now that I haven't a sweet inkling of what happened here in my absence. I haven't witnessed anything except the crew cutting my grass."

"You may know something that will help our investigations. You may not know what you know, but it's our job to sort it out. We want you to come to the station to answer some questions, and the sooner we can get that going, the sooner this can be over."

"Do I need a lawyer? Seems like I might, since you have occupied my property and banned me from accessing it. You're treating me like I'm more than a potential witness, Constable. I don't believe this can be 'just procedure.'"

"The detective will discuss that with you."

"Right. What a mess. It sure does seem like I'm being accused of something—falsely, for the record, whatever it is. Are we—are you taking me to the station now?"

"In a moment. Does anyone else have keys to this house?"

Tim felt tidal waves of emotion. He had always respected the role of the police, and had always seen himself as one who would give them assistance. They requested his assistance now, but entirely on their terms, which included suspending his freedom, locking him out of his house, seizing his car, and stealing his happy weekend—the weekend he'd been looking forward to all week.

"Yes, my, uh, my visitor has keys."

Etcheverry asked for the name and contact information for this visitor.

"Robert Kirk. Dr Kirk is the organist and choir director at my church. He lives in the city but he usually comes here on Saturdays, so...so he won't have to drive down on Sunday morning."

"Anyone else?"

"No."

"Who else has a key to your car?"

"Nobody."

"Not Dr Kirk?"

"Asked and answered, Constable."

Constable Etcheverry consulted with the other members of South River's finest. Tim turned his back to them and looked at the now-completely-mowed-and-raked expanse of yard and gardens. It was a pleasant day to be there, but everything in view seemed colourless and dull. The weeds might as well have stood upright again.

Buck up, Tim. This is just a blip. Go with the cops. The sooner you find out what's up, the better. They're probably just doing their jobs, but it sure would help if they were a bit friendlier about it. What'll I tell Robert? I can't shield him from this. I'll just tell him. The sooner I do, the more time he'll have to calm down before church tomorrow. Me, too.

Now the two policemen were carrying a heavy canvas bag into the back yard, inside the yellow tape area. They removed the bag's contents and began to erect a blue canopy at the far end of the woodshed.

Constable Etcheverry got in his cruiser and had a radio conversation.

Then he walked back to Tim.

"What's the hold-up, Constable? I'm starving. Will you not permit me to go in the house to make a sandwich? Can I make you one?"

"No sandwich. We were waiting for instructions. I'll take you to the station now."

Etcheverry handed Tim's key ring to one of the other constables, and escorted him to the back door of the cruiser. Tim didn't want to create a scene over yet another indignity, so he got in without further comment.

On their way to the station, the constable turned into the drive-through of a nearby take-out, and said to Tim, "Burger and fries okay?"

"Sure," Tim replied. He was so off-kilter that this gesture almost brought tears of appreciation, but he stifled that response. "And a large coffee, black."

He slid to the centre of the back seat, hoping he would be less visible through the side windows. Without asking permission, he took out his cell phone and called Robert. The call went to voicemail. He said, "It's me. Call me back immediately. It's urgent."

Etcheverry looked at him in the rear-view mirror but made no comment.

The smell of the food made Tim's stomach growl. His phone rang, and he answered it before the constable had a chance to deny him the privilege, if he was going to.

"What's wrong?" Robert sounded distressed.

"Where are you?"

"I just started on the 103. Had to pull over to call you."

"Okay, listen carefully. I'm all right, okay? I'm in the back of a police cruiser on my way to the station."

"*What*? What station?"

"The police station."

"What happened? What's wrong?"

"I do not know. Wait a sec, I'm going to put you on speaker so the constable can listen if he wants."

He punched the button.

"The South River Police Service are being very secretive about something in my backyard, possibly discovered by the lawn crew. They're treating my property like a murder scene until I testify about God knows what, I have no idea. I'm being taken to the police station for questioning, as the owner of the scene of some crime. Or maybe as the criminal, I don't know."

"You? They're accusing *you* of a crime? That's the most ridiculous thing ever!"

"Ridiculous is right. I haven't been accused of anything, not yet, anyway. I don't know anything about it. I think they think I'm some kind of witness, so I'm to tell them everything I know, which is nothing, or everything I don't know, which is a lot. But listen, Rob: I don't know when they'll be done with me. The house is surrounded by yellow caution tape and there are cops on guard, so there's no point in you going there. I'm not sure when they'll let me back in the house or even my car."

"Why, though?"

"Beats me. I went for groceries and a haircut, that's all I know. I gotta go. You can either turn back and come directly to the church tomorrow morning, or you can meet me at the hotel, because that's where I'll have to go tonight."

"I'm coming. What hotel?"

"Take Exit 12 as usual, but turn right at the lights. It's just past the next lights on the left. Get a nice room. Oh, and you'd better go to the wine store on the way. I think the only wine the hotel has comes in boxes. I'll need my own bottle, for sure, whenever I do get there."

"Got it. Now, don't you worry. Remember who you are, and be him. Do you want me to call anyone for you, like—?"

"No. No, thanks, not yet, anyway. Oh, Ev's in a tournament tonight, but I guess we won't be going. If you want to spend some time practising at the church, go ahead. Keep your phone handy. I'll call you when I'm released, okay?"

"Okay, Timo."

He disconnected. The cruiser had arrived at the station. Etcheverry was waiting, evidently interested in this phone conversation. Tim wanted to ask him, "Did you catch all that? Did you hear anything incriminating?" but he simply said, "Thanks for waiting. That was important. Now let's go play your Twenty Questions."

Tim was grateful for Robert's reactions. He had sounded incredulous, which echoed his own thoughts. It felt good to be validated. Robert said to "remember who you are, and be him". He took that as an endorsement of his own sense of right and wrong, and to keep his temper. Robert had once told Tim that he was "toweringly respectful" towards people; he would try to be like that now, but it hadn't been easy so far.

Robert had called him Timo, his favourite nickname, a verbal hug, and he took that with him into the station and the interview room.

~

Tim waited for the detective in the bare interview room. He'd been very hungry, and the bag of takeout food resolved that basic need while he waited. He assumed the detective was getting up to speed on what the constable knew before he came in to question Tim.

They're probably on the other side of that glass, watching me. I sure don't like this. The constable said I wasn't a suspect, but the way they're acting, I could become a suspect at any minute and still not know how or why. I don't know how else they should do their job, but I resent this, as an upstanding and innocent citizen. I'm not under arrest, but my plans sure are, no two ways about it.

I'm glad I reached Rob. I was worried about how he'd react, and worried that I mightn't catch him before he got here. I hope the hotel has a good room. Their food is edible. If Rob goes to the church to practise, that'll keep him from worrying about me.

I wish I had my notebook.

This room is mind-numbing. I like my plain room at the office because it doesn't distract me from thinking, but this place is anti-thought. It's less than a block from here to the office as the crow flies, but very far in terms of purpose.

Or is it? I've been trying to delve into issues over there, to find answers to questions, and questions behind answers, pretty successfully, too. The police try to find answers to questions, too. They have the power of legal processes, but are they better than my delving processes? I guess being able to restrain people without apparent cause is a big help to them, but I'm not sure they're using that power correctly on me.

Maybe I'll observe something useful, after I learn whatever the hell this is all about.

Lost in these thoughts, he'd been making good use of the bare room after all. He was startled when the detective entered the room, accompanied by another policeman carrying a notebook.

"Good afternoon, Mr Brown. I'm Detective Sergeant John O'Neil. Thank you for coming in. A serious situation was discovered on your property, I'm told, and we appreciate knowing anything you can tell us about it. Before you do, it is my duty to inform you that you have the right to retain and instruct Counsel in private, without delay."

"Detective, I haven't a sweet clue what was discovered or reported or imagined on my property. Your constables have been very good at not telling me anything, which I find extremely frustrating and more than a little insulting. I'll try to answer your questions. I understand I've not been accused of a crime—if there even *was* a crime—so I'm here to help,

I guess, though I don't seem to have much free will in the matter. If this somehow takes a turn towards accusation, I will consider involving a lawyer then. But I've done nothing wrong, so let's just get on with it."

"You have not been accused of a crime, Mr Brown, and I doubt very much that we'll go there. We're sorry to inconvenience you. It does appear that someone was buried on your property, so the wheels of an ordinary day do have to stop spinning for a bit. That's appropriate, wouldn't you agree?"

"Buried?" Tim was suddenly short of breath, as though he had been hit in the chest. "Who? When? There was no grave when I left home this morning. I did think someone had died when your cops mentioned the coroner."

"Were any of your relatives buried on the property? It is unorthodox, but legal."

"No. If you look up the word 'orthodox' in the dictionary, my forebears will be listed there. They're all in the cemetery."

"Was Mr Singleton mowing in the backyard for you?"

"No, Jake supervised. Dana was mowing this morning."

"Did he make a scraped area, like something heavy was dragged on the ground?"

"No. I had other workers doing carpentry and repairs this week. The woodshed was unstable because one corner had sunk into soft ground, so it had to be moved. They dragged it, hence the scrapes."

"Did they remove a stone, such as a gravestone?"

"No."

"Do you know who is buried in the grave, Mr Brown?"

"What grave? No, I do not. I fully support having the remains removed, exhumed or whatever, and I assure you I won't get in your way while you do whatever you have to do. I don't want a grave on my property, and I most assuredly did *not* know there was one. Are you sure there is a body in it?"

"Do you think there is?"

"Do *you* think there is? I don't *think* anything, Detective. I'm desperate for a little information."

"Where on your property was the grave discovered?" The policeman accompanying the detective was busy making notes in his notepad.

"How would I know? When I left this morning to get groceries, one of the lawn care workers, Dana, was mowing. When I returned, your cops were there, treating me very much like I had committed a crime, except no handcuffs. I saw the constables setting up a tent at the far end of my woodshed. Your people had wrapped the lower half of my property in caution tape, so it's a reasonable guess that it was somewhere in that area."

"Why would you say that?"

"Now you're playing charades where I'm supposed to guess without any clues, that's why. I was not permitted to look. I wondered if maybe someone had wandered in and died there last night when they mentioned the Coroner. But they wrapped my house, too. I was the only occupant, and I'm alive. Alive and mystified."

"What caused the structure—this woodshed—to be unstable?"

"I don't know."

"When was it built?"

"I was afraid you'd ask me that—but not because it's incriminating. I just don't recall. May I tell you why?"

"Go ahead."

"I had this shed built but I was not paying attention when it was built."

"Where were you?"

"At work. Day and night, seven days of every week."

"There's no need to exaggerate. What is your work? I assume school teacher?"

"Who told you that?"

"What is your work?"

Tim sighed. "I am the publisher and editor of *The Times*, South River's marvellous community newspaper. Perhaps you've seen a copy."

"Yes, I have. That's why you looked familiar: you're *that* Timothy Brown. Your picture is in the paper a lot lately."

"Good eye, Detective. Thank you for reading *The Times*."

"Do you employ a groundskeeper?"

"Not *per se*. I've taken a sabbatical this year, so I've been home some in the daytime, finally. It's nice. I thought I'd get the backyard cleared of weeds, remove the brambles, smell the roses. I contracted with the Chester Basin Property Management company to accomplish that for me. These fellows have some powerful machines, and a great work ethic. We agreed to clear it right to the edges."

"When was the property last mowed?"

"Previous to this week? That's what I was starting to tell you. I don't recall when, not precisely. I'd have to look it up. Several years ago is my best guess. We discovered that people had been tossing empty beer and pop cans onto my property, and I'm told that happens because it looked like a vacant lot, which isn't an excuse, but that's what people do, I guess.

Dana even ran his machine over a hidden shovel. Wrecked the mower. Chewed up the shovel pretty badly, too. We were lucky that—"

"Where is it now?"

"Where is what?"

"The shovel."

"The shovel?" Tim shrugged. "I dunno. If it's not still in the yard some-where, then one of Jake's workers might have taken it away, along with the weeds."

"Where would they have taken it?"

"They would be able to answer that question, Detective."

"Who is Jake?"

"He's the man who called the police, I think. Constable Etcheverry was talking to him. I just learned that his surname is Singleton. Jake Singleton. He's the crew boss. Nice fellow."

"Why did you decide to clear the weeds right over to the edge?"

"Why not? Is it a crime to want a tidy property?" Tim held his hand up. "Sorry, strike that. The lawn crew had the machinery, they impressed me with their skill, and I chose to have the whole yard cleared. They even pulled out a crumpled wire fence on the opposite side that had fallen down and was tangled in vines."

"Who did you say lives in the house with you?"

"I didn't say. I am the only permanent resident. My—a friend from the city visits me Thursday nights and most weekends. He's the organist and choir director at the church where I sing in the choir. Dr Robert Kirk."

"Does Dr Kirk ever stay in the house when you aren't there?"

"No."

The detective examined his notes. "Do you ever leave the house overnight, or for extended periods?"

"I was away for three nights about five years ago."

"Can you recall those dates?"

"Thursday to Sunday, mid-July, 1994. I don't have the exact dates in my head. I attended a conference for newspaper publishers and editors. In Prince Edward Island."

"Any other time?"

"No. I'd remember that. I'm the least-travelled person you'll ever meet."

"Did you say someone stayed in your house while you were on that trip?"

"No, I did not say that. Nobody has stayed there in my absence since my mother died twenty years ago. I have always been there, except for those three nights. I worked long days, as I told you. The house would often be dark until late, so maybe someone thought it was vacant."

Mrs Aquino suddenly appeared in Tim's thoughts. *Please move on from the house! I don't want to even mention Mrs A. If these guys called her she'd have a conniption.*

"Detective, I don't know how many ways I can tell you that I don't know anything about what you say is a grave in my backyard. Nothing at all. I didn't hear anything. I didn't notice that the ground was disturbed or grave-like, not even when I was standing in that area, if it was near the end of the woodshed—or if it indeed caused the woodshed to become unstable. Nobody I ever knew has disappeared under mysterious circumstances, though we have reported on missing persons from time to time in the newspaper. All my ancestors are properly buried in the cemetery. If someone was murdered, it wasn't by me, not that you've asked me that question. If someone was buried on my property, it wasn't by me. I wouldn't know how to do either crime!"

Easy, Tim. Don't raise more questions.

"You said something about a shovel." The detective nodded to his assistant.

"'They ran over a shovel. Pretty chewed up,'" he read from his notes.

"Can you tell me more about that?"

"It was a shovel that Jake—Mr Singleton—didn't discover even though he walked over the whole property for the purpose of finding such obstacles before they ran the bushwhacker over it. I guess he just didn't step in the right place. So the machine chewed it up."

"What does that mean?"

"I have no idea. Those are the operator's words. I don't know how the mower cuts, with blades one assumes. It cuts heavy bushes like alders and blackberry brambles, but apparently it's not designed to cut a spade blade. The metal part looked like it had been fed into some kind of demolition machine, *ergo* chewed."

"Where did you say the shovel is now?"

"As I just told you, I have no idea. Jake or his workers may know."

While the detective reviewed his notes, Tim tried to think of something helpful to say.

"I can try to pinpoint dates for you, Detective, but right now my head is spinning. My best guess is that I had the current woodshed built seven years ago or less, and it started to lean about four years ago or less, which disappointed me a great deal, and I stopped using it two or three years ago."

"If you would clarify those dates, it might help us determine when the victim was buried there. We'll find out eventually, but we do appreciate any pointers."

"I'll see what I can do. Can you tell me when the Coroner will let me back into my house?"

"I don't know that," Detective O'Neill said. "It may take a while. Depends on where else he might be."

"What does 'awhile' mean? I can't go back into my house until that's all done?"

"That's right."

"Can I have my car?"

"I don't think so." The detective nodded to his assistant, who left the interview room. In a moment, he returned, and shook his head.

"They haven't completed the search of your car, yet, Mr Brown. We'll have to hang on to it."

"Search my *car*? What do you hope to find there, I wonder? Never mind. This whole circus is too much mystery to me. Can you tell me if either of your constables has entered or will enter my house while they have my keys, for any reason?"

"No, they haven't. We can't enter your without a search warrant."

"A search warrant: what next? That's not a question. So, I can't go home, and I can't have my car to go anywhere. What do you suggest I do now? Will you just keep me in a cell here?"

"You're free to go, Mr Brown. We can take you to the hotel where I believe you told Mr, uh, Dr Kirk that you would meet him, is that right?"

"That's correct, but I do *not* want to arrive in front of the hotel or anywhere in a police cruiser, if it's all the same to you."

Tim stood and pulled out his wallet. "Here's my card. My cellphone number is on it. Don't call the house number because I'd have to break in to answer it. Please call me as soon as I can enter my own home legally. And for the record, Detective, barring me from my home and vehicle without *any* indication of my culpability, other than that I own the property where a theoretical grave is supposedly located, is outrageous and offensive to me. It *must* be evident to you that what you are calling a grave—which I must have stood next to but did not recognize as such, remember—was *not* my doing, and the unfortunate person who you say is in it is not someone known to me. If I had done what you seem to be implying, I would have moved the woodshed to cover it, *not* to reveal it, as it seems I have done. I am not a crook, but if I were, I wouldn't be that stupid. Good day."

~

Tim left the police station and took the steep shortcut between buildings down to the Main Street level, emerging in the parking lot of Saint John's United Church. He looked for Robert's car, hoping he was inside practising, but he didn't see it anywhere.

Walking quickly, he passed out of range of the Daisy Café, not wanting to engage with Evelyn right now. She would have questions, and he had no answers. Her sympathy might turn his frustration to tears, and he wasn't ready for that to happen.

He crossed the bridge and turned right. He entered the shopping mall, and felt lightheaded. *What's wrong now? What's happening? A ton of stress, that's what.*

He walked to the coffee shop, joined the short line, and when it was his turn ordered a medium double-double and two honey crullers. It was medicine, not a treat.

He phoned Robert's mobile, but didn't get an answer. He left a message: "I'm out of jail, but I can't pass Go yet. I'll be at the hotel around"—he glanced at his watch and was shocked at how much time had passed—"around five-thirty."

He debated walking to the hotel, but feared he'd be recognized and offered rides from friends or strangers, one of the risks of small-town living. He called a cab, which the dispatcher said would be there in twenty minutes, as they were on the way back from Mahone Bay.

He sat for a moment with the comfort food, feeling steadier as soon as the caffeine and sugar got in his bloodstream. After taking a few deep breaths, he walked slowly down the mall to the pharmacy, where he picked up a few toiletries, a pocket comb, and a package of underwear.

He stood by the main entrance of the mall to wait for the cab. When it arrived, he quickly got in, relieved that he hadn't encountered anyone who would ask why he was taking a cab or—worse—offer to drive him wherever he was headed. *Good neighbours aren't always what you want, even when you're in a tight spot.*

Again, he sat in the middle of the back seat until he was out of the parking lot and out of town.

~

The hotel lobby was busy. There was a conference going on, a professional association that Tim had never heard of. The attendees were milling about with cocktails in the conference room prior to their Awards Banquet, according to the sign in the entrance.

Someone was playing the piano at the front of the room, and something about the pianist's keyboard style sounded familiar. He stepped inside the door and shuffled along the back wall to see who was playing.

Of course it was Robert, though not totally "of course". Of course Robert could play anything, including the rag-time piece he was playing just now. *But how did these people manage to snag him for this gig?*

Just then, a man entered the room and waved to Robert, who nodded and quickly wrapped up the "Maple Leaf Rag". Then he began to play Elgar's "Pomp and Circumstance" march, and the head table VIPs and guests paraded in and took their seats at the table on a dais.

Tim was shaking his head in amazement as Robert left the piano bench and came out to the lobby, where he was waiting. "While I'm languishing in the iron grip of the law, you've joined the Loyal and Splendid College of the Rhinoceros as their band leader?"

"That's not their name, but close enough. Scientists of some kind. Nice people. I got your message but I couldn't call back at the time. I was in the middle of "The Music Box Dancer." Very popular, still. Amazing."

"You played it from memory?"

"What's to remember? Let's go up."

They went to the elevator and Robert pushed the button.

"I was sitting in the little bar to have a rare apéritif while I waited for you," Robert explained, "since I was in a hotel. I overheard these people expressing dismay because their pianist had cancelled at the last minute. Naturally, I inquired about what they needed that disappointing person to do. All they wanted was a few pre-dinner cocktail tunes and a processional march. I revealed that I was not a member of the Loyal Order, but I was staying in the hotel, and I was qualified to fulfill their needs. *And* I would do their job for a simple price."

"You never cease to amaze me. What was your simple price? I know it wasn't money."

They exited the slow elevator and Robert led Tim to the end of the carpeted hallway.

"I charged them two dinners from the room service menu, delivered to Suite 310 tonight, on their tab. They were so happy! All those smart scientists down there, and not one of them knew how to play a few popular tunes for their colleagues without sheet music, imagine. They are well-educated, but not widely."

Robert unlocked the door with the card key and they entered a small suite, with a well-furnished sitting area, a small table and chairs, and a hallway leading to the bath and bedroom. It was at the end of the building, and the windows looked westward, where the sun was beginning to lower over a winding road and wooded hills. On the coffee table was a bouquet of sunflowers. On the black granite counter were a wine bottle and two glasses.

"Oh, Rob," Tim said, feeling tears rising for the second time today, "this is so nice. I had hoped to lay out something like this for you today. I didn't get cut flowers, though, just a lot of cut weeds. The cops were there when I got home from the grocery store, and then they wrapped the house in that awful tape."

"I saw it. I drove past just to check it out. How are you now?"

"I don't honestly know. They wouldn't tell me what was going on, and then they took me downtown and the detective gave me the third degree about a grave all afternoon, and after a while, you do feel like confessing to something, just so they'll quit, you know? I can't go home now until the Coroner comes and determines whatever he determines."

"So frustrating," Robert commiserated.

"It sure is. And now we're here at this oasis, a desert island at the end of a blankety-blank shipwreck day. Thank you so much for making these arrangements."

"Come here." Robert reached out and pulled Tim into a warm hug. "It'll get better soon. Why don't you have a shower and put on one of their fluffy robes. We'll sit and talk and have our free dinner sent up when you're ready for it. They have risotto."

Tim went straight to the shower, and emerged scrubbed and refreshed. Robert handed him a glass of wine and a plate of canapés he'd brought up earlier from the Loyal Rhino reception. They sat on the sofa to debrief.

Tim related random bits as they came to mind, starting with his high and rising indignation. Some things didn't make sense to Robert, but his purpose was to listen, not to interrogate. Tim said he'd had to mention Robert's name to the police because he was the expected guest and had a key to the house, but he'd managed to steer the conversations away from Stella.

"What would she have to do with any of this?"

"She grew up in that house. She might remember the lay of the land, if it's relevant. I just didn't want her name in their notebooks at all. I don't think this grave goes back that far anyway. Gosh, this wine is tasty. I've hardly had a moment to spare a thought about the poor person in the cold ground. Do you think it would be someone innocent? Or would it be a double crosser who got caught? Hard to know what to think, isn't it?"

"Absolutely. I'm not sure I could have kept my wits about me as well as you did. Here's to you, Timo, and your nice haircut. Let's order dinner."

"Imagine that—I can order dinner! This is much better than sleeping under the overpass, which is where I might have been, for all the police cared about it. I don't understand how they can just say, 'Nope, you can't come into your house until we don't know when, and you can't have your car, either.' At least homeless people can sleep in their cars—the lucky ones, anyway."

"All right now, have a look at the menu. Will it be the risotto, or...?"

June 13: Dem bones

Sunday

The light was coming in from the wrong side of the bed. The recessed bathroom lights were confession-strength bright and the white basin was undermounted beneath black granite counters. A carafe of fresh coffee and warm pastries under a silver dome had just been delivered to the sitting room.

It wasn't a dream, but it felt like one to Tim. He had slept completely, solidly, deeply, and was a bit groggy waking up.

Robert was sitting on the sofa, fully dressed, reading a music score. "Good morning, sunshine. How are you this morning?"

"Are you my jailer?" Tim responded. "Mmm, coffee actually smells good. Oh, brioche, yum."

He took a large drink of coffee. "Oh, that's good. This is no jail, that's for sure. Nice place you have here, Robert. Compact. Convenient. Can't beat room service. I should have sent my clothes to the concierge, though."

"I'm not sure this hotel offers that service. Thanks for thinking of picking up a razor for me. You don't need one, lucky you. And the deodorant. Our clothes are okay for another day. If we can't get in the house today, the stores will be open tomorrow morning."

"Oh, please tell me they'll let me in today. What a shit-show, Rob, pardon my French, sorry, French people. I was absolutely shocked. It isn't only the discovery of human remains on my property, if that's what this turns out to be, but the sudden and absolute loss of my—my world, really."

"I know, I know," Robert said. "You made that clear last night. It took nearly two bottles of wine and our tenderloin dinners—which I busked for, don't forget—to get you settled down. I think you slept well?"

"Like the dead. Am I permitted to joke about it?"

"Whatever floats your boat. But listen, now: I don't want you to dwell on police procedures and your freedoms or lack thereof today. You were definitely inconvenienced and felt very insulted, but I suggest you let that rest for a day. You work on conundrums for other people, and by your own account you've been quite successful at it. So give yourself a little space, settle your feathers, and then tackle this situation tomorrow with one of your flip chart grids, or however you do it. If this happened to you, it must happen to others who feel they're treated like they're guilty until proven innocent. Maybe you'll find something to publish, in a generic way. Meanwhile, the gendarmes do need to find out what happened. The deceased was possibly missing for a long time. Now he's found. For someone, somewhere, this discovery will solve a mystery or close a cold case or whatever they call it."

"Won't it bother you that somebody might have been buried in the garden?"

"Not if the remains are completely removed. Just don't plant vegetables there. Maybe a rosebush or something that you don't have to tend. They'll take it away, right?"

"I certainly expect so. Somebody will. I'll go over after church and check on how they're doing."

"No, you won't. Let them do their thing. If they want you there, they'll call. Is your phone charged and turned on?"

"No. I wasn't allowed in the house so I don't have the charger, and yours doesn't fit my phone. I'll just turn it on every couple of hours, I guess."

"All right, then: you don't need to do anything more. Staying away is cooperating. Now, we have half an hour before we have to leave for church."

"Oh, I don't know, Rob. I'm not really in the mood for church."

"You don't have a choice. I want to keep you in my sight and out of trouble, and anyway, it's choir, not church. Singing will be good for you. My title isn't 'doctor' for nothing. Get dressed. I'll save one of these little cinnamon twists for you."

~

They arrived early at the church, in time to don their choir gowns before the others arrived to notice they weren't wearing Sunday clothes. Several male choristers had begun wearing casual clothes, but Tim and Robert had continued with shirt and tie, which looked nice with the collarless gowns. Several lost and found ties had accumulated in the men's choir room, and they chose from these today.

Robert was right, of course. Whatever was bad became better with music, more so if one was making the music. Today's music wasn't especially challenging, but Tim enjoyed singing every note. He concentrated on his intonation, vocal production, breathing technique, and all the ways music could keep his thoughts from straying.

The sermon wasn't strong enough to keep his attention, so his mind wandered back to yesterday's craziness. Not able to organize his thoughts on a manila sheet or even a tiny notebook, he turned to reading random verses in the Hymnary. For the most part, he found it lacking on the topic of being a prisoner by exclusion, and he didn't care to read anything about anyone rising from the dead.

He came across one of his favourites, "Once To Every Man And Nation" by James Russell Lowell, and was struck by the lines:

> New occasions teach new duties,
> time makes ancient good uncouth:
> they must upward still and onward,
> who would keep abreast of truth.

Leave it to a poet to give me advice I didn't know I was looking for. I've responded to that whole mess as the victim. No wonder, the way the police treated me. I didn't even know for sure there was a grave with a body in it until I was downtown, so what was I supposed to think? That was a stupid game, to tell me I was a witness but oh, we can't tell you to what. You bet I was angry, and rightly so. I felt bullied. I don't like that game.

He read the lines again. 'New occasions teach new duties.'

Apparently, someone is dead in my backyard, likely not from natural causes. I didn't know a blinking thing about it. But I know a thing or two about detecting. I'd better set my bruised ego aside, get my Private Investigator hat on, and see what I can do for that poor person. It would be a notch in my Delver's cap to tell the cops what happened. I don't have their 'procedures' to get in my way, and I'm pretty good at what I do. Upward still and onward!

At the end of the service, Robert began to play the postlude, quietly at first, but it soon began to crescendo. He was improvising on a theme, one of his many skills. The choir found it vaguely familiar, even ethereal, as it climbed chromatically toward a robust rhythmical conclusion.

The small mid-June congregation had nearly all dispersed, so the choir was the only audience paying attention at the end when Robert dropped the disguise and played the final *forte* chords. Several choristers had caught on to the theme by now and sang along: "Now *hear* the word of the Lord."

Robert had improvised on a spiritual, based on a story from the Book of Ezekiel, known as "Dem bones, dem bones, dem *dry* bones."

No one enjoyed the joke more than Tim.

Nobody had mentioned seeing police cars or yellow tape at his house.

~

No call had come during church. Robert was adamant that they would not go to the house, not even just drive past.

"Where'll we go, then? I'd love to go to the newspaper office to look something up, but my office keys are on the ring the cops confiscated."

"Look up what?"

"Missing persons. If it was printed in *The Times* in the last century, we'd have a record of it."

"Impressive. But if you have a record of missing persons, the police would too, wouldn't they?"

"Should. Could. Might. But I wouldn't go so far as to say 'would'."

"Sounds like you're beginning to think on behalf of the victim, anyway, which is a positive move. You can do that tomorrow. Now, we can't visit Stella or Evelyn, because you'll start into the story again—not that it isn't important—but I don't want you to get riled up. We haven't checked out, so let's keep the room for another night, can we? We could go for a drive up that road that goes past the hotel, stop for lunch somewhere, go back for a snooze, swim in the pool, order room service again, and just chill."

"They don't have a pool."

"So you *were* paying attention."

"Do we have more of that delicious wine to go with supper?"

"What do you think?"

"You're the best, Rob. I'm still mad because I can't go home, but I know your plan is best. Driving somewhere unfamiliar will be like practice for our trip to PEI. Won't be long now!"

"Don't remind me, or you'll be the one doing the comforting. Take your turn."

"Okay. We're taking our chances, looking for lunch on that road. There's next to nowhere to eat up there because there are next to no communities big enough to have eateries. But it's June, so if anything's going to be open, they'll be open now."

"This is your territory, so you be our guide. It's my car, so I'll drive."

~

This inland route didn't offer dramatic coastal vistas, but the drumlin hills constantly revealed ponds and marshes and fresh green leaves everywhere. They arrived at the village of New Germany and passed by the pizza shops, but when they came to the "Home of the Road Kill Burger", Tim said, "Here! Stop here!"

"Are you sure about this?"

"Hey, where's your sense of adventure? All these cars are the equivalent of a five-star rating, locally-adjusted. C'mon, let's see how the other half lives."

Inside, they found it challenging to choose from the long list of standard, deep-fried, take-out fare. There were platters of clams and chips, scallops and chips, combo platters of clams and scallops and haddock and chips, plus hamburgers, cheeseburgers, chicken burgers, and chips. And one hamburger-chickenburger combo, "The Road Kill". The servings were huge.

"Are we going to eat here, or in the car?" Robert asked. There were two large families of small, free-range children just settling in for their meal, and similar outside on picnic tables.

"Let's share a combo platter in the car. We can nibble as we go, and savour every bite."

Whoever was at the deep fryer knew what she was doing. Everything came out crispy, neither greasy nor overcooked. Tim asked for their order to go in something that wouldn't spill in the car, and it came in a high-sided cake box.

"Perfect!"

They gathered their utensils, napkins, condiments, and two bottles of water, and took their delicacies to the car. When he wanted another bite, Robert just hovered his right hand, claw-like, over the box, and Tim guided it to the next treat.

~

"Ah, home sweet home," Tim said when they were back in the suite. "Everything's cleaned, bed made, just like Mrs A but without the racket."

"Can you snooze on a full tummy? I'm going to try."

They wasted no time letting the king-size memory foam mattress and allergens-free duvet send them to the Land of Nod.

Later, they perused the room service menu for dinner. Tim had just turned on his phone to check for messages when it rang. "Hello, Mr Brown. It's Detective Sergeant O'Neil calling. I thought you'd like to know what's happening at your property."

"I would indeed."

"The Coroner has come and gone, did that sometime last night, actually. The Pathologist is conducting tests and analysis today, and will advise us just as soon as he can. We know you're anxious to get back in your home."

"Anxious is one word."

"Understood. We should hear something tonight. I'll call you to come in as soon as I hear, possibly tomorrow. You'll be free to resume your normal life soon. There'll be a bit of a mess in your yard where our crew had to excavate and then scrape around to fill it in."

"I'll get the landscapers to cover it very quickly, believe me."

"Good. Keep your phone on. Where are you staying?"

"I'm at the new hotel. I've been keeping my phone mostly off to save the battery because your guards wouldn't even permit me to go in the house to get my charger. So, until I check out tomorrow morning, you can call me here. After that, I'll check my phone on the hour for messages. Thanks for calling, Detective."

"I think I've been absolved," Tim said to Robert. "Detective Sergeant O'Neil is friendlier today. He knows I didn't kill or bury anyone."

"Smart man. Let's go for a walk before we order dinner. That should clear our heads."

June 14: Aftermath

Monday

Because they could, they called room service one more time. And because Tim wanted a repeat of the Eggs Benedict he'd enjoyed at the Prayer Breakfast.

"Will you stay here until checkout, unless you hear from the police sooner?"

"No, but I'd appreciate a ride to the office. I have work to do and I can't think here. But I promise not to go to the house until I get the all-clear, though I don't think they'd mind."

"You'll mind if you're ordered to stay away by someone wearing a pistol."

In the street outside *The Times*, Robert said, "You take care of yourself, and call me with any developments, okay? And I mean *any*."

"Promise. Thanks for the ride, and thanks for looking after me, Rob. And for your improvisations on 'Dem Bones'".

~

Tim was surprised and delighted to see scaffolding going up on the front of his building. *The Gem District transformation has begun. Yippee! I wonder what colour the design staff have chosen for my building.*

He dodged the workers and went inside. Elaine Fong was going from one desk to another, handing out assignments or calling them in.

"Can I buy you a rare coffee, Elaine? The Daisy's coffee has been bad since 1967, but the service is friendly."

"I'm not as fussy about coffee as you are. Sure. It's a quiet Monday. Let's go next door and let all hell break loose while we're out."

"Oh, I will tell you about all hell."

Evelyn was surprised and happy to see Tim. "You know today's Monday, right?"

"I do. You remember Elaine Fong."

"Yes, I remember you, Elaine. Too bad for you he didn't really go away this year, eh? But he's welcome here any old time. Just coffee for both?"

Evelyn returned quickly with their coffees and two muffins.

"These're on the house. We're trying out some new items. We've never baked anything besides pies. We don't even make the crusts for them, sorry if that disappoints you. Let me know how you like them. My mother's recipe. Wave when you're ready for more coffee."

"Those are magic words, aren't they?" Elaine said. "'My mother's recipe' makes things taste better, somehow. Expectations, I suppose."

"You're philosophical this morning," Tim said. "How are you, by the way?"

"I'm very well, thanks for asking. Scared to death about what Roger and I are...doing, but foolishly happy. So, what's on your mind?"

"These booths have ears. Got a pen?"

Elaine retrieved a pen from her purse. Tim took a napkin and wrote A <u>GRAVE</u> WAS DISCOVERED <u>IN</u> <u>MY</u> <u>BACK</u> <u>YARD</u>. He turned it so Elaine could read it. She looked up sharply, and he turned the napkin over.

"Let's not say these words aloud or I'll have a fit. But that"—he tapped the napkin—"happened Saturday morning while I was out getting groceries. That right there is a double tragedy: mine and somebody else's."

"My God, Tim! Who—?" She tapped the napkin.

"I sure as heck don't know. I didn't even see it, thank you very much. I wasn't permitted to, by the—"

He flipped the napkin over and wrote POLICE!

"My personal urgent story: I have not been allowed into my home or on my property since Saturday. Not because I'm a suspect in that"—he tapped the notebook— "but because that's what they do, *les gendarmes*. 'Procedure.' I'm hoping to get the all-clear this morning."

"Wow, Tim, that *is* tragic. I don't think I've ever covered a story that dealt with such a discovery. Accidentally discovered? Old, like just bones, or a cadaver?"

"Shhh. Yes to accidentally, and beats me as to the state of the remains. When this is settled, I think I'll research an article about what happens when John Q Public becomes a Person Of Interest. The Police Gaze is very uncomfortable, I've discovered. The rules are not kind to the innocent, to people with plans. I can't imagine how the guilty feel, but I don't care about them. I'm not one."

"You'd want to call attention to yourself like that?"

"Why not? I did nothing wrong. Besides, my house is festooned with that damn yellow police tape, visible to all people driving past my door."

"Oh, no!"

"Not only that, but isn't somebody on our staff assigned to follow the police blotter? Every call the cops go out on is recorded, and we print the list, don't we? Jean Naugler is probably going to find out about it today."

"What do you want the newspaper to do?"

"Nothing...can we? We have to deal with this like I was John Q. Public. That's ironic. Here I am complaining that the little guy doesn't get treated fairly by the cops, while we blithely print the dirt on every poor schmuck who's had a speeding ticket or a drunken fight. Let's review that policy one day soon. Right now, we can't show favouritism by suppressing the dirt when it's about me or there'd be a hullabaloo. Anyway, I'm not the perp, so all we're discussing is my right to privacy at some level."

"I'll keep an eye out for it. We can print it below the fold and in the crease, if that helps. Unless James has seen it and submits a crime-beat photo. But he knows your house, so he'd surely consult."

Evelyn refilled their coffees wordlessly and moved on. She knew when not to interrupt.

"Don't do anything heroic, Elaine, but thanks for your consideration. If James brings a photo of my house, just do whatever we normally do. Maybe there won't be room for it? I wouldn't have thought that was possible, but things are changing in our little pages. By the way, I see the painters are getting started. Do you know what colour we'll be?"

"Yes. Do you want me to tell you?"

"I'll see it soon enough. I just hope there's no symbolism hidden in the choice."

"Can't guarantee that. Don't leave that napkin here."

"Right."

Elaine returned to the office and Tim went to the counter to pay. "Those muffins are fantastic, Ev. Are they going to be in your new take-out counter?"

"We're working on finding the right items, things you can't get in other places. What would go with a date and bran muffin, besides a pat of butter?"

"A piece of cheddar cheese. Or a muffin, cheese, and an apple in a paper bag. That'd carry me over many lunchtimes. And don't overlook my favourite, peanut butter and banana sandwiches. So, how'd you make out at the tournament Saturday night? Sorry we couldn't make it to cheer you on. We were unavoidably detained. I'll tell you about it another time. Did you win?"

"No, dammit. I came second."

"Hey, second's darn good, isn't it?"

"Second doesn't get my name on the trophy."

"Oh, sorry. Want me to break somebody's arm before the next competition?"

"No, you crazy man, but you can remind me to practise more instead of watching television in the evenings. I want to get 'Evelyn Whynot' engraved on all the trophies in the same year, if I can. A Grand Slam!"

~

Tim had been hoping Elaine or Evelyn wouldn't get too close to him in the Daisy Café. He had showered several times since early Saturday morning, but was still wearing the clothes he'd dressed in on Saturday morning, back in the time before his backyard reclamation plan had blown up into a murder mystery.

It is *a murder mystery, isn't it? I mean, why else would a person bury another person in my backyard unless they were murdered? These remains didn't dig their own grave and then lie down in it and cover themselves. I* am *curious.*

He sniffed.

"And I'm odiferous. This is ridiculous. Do the police expect me to smell homeless, too?"

He turned on his phone and saw the battery was almost depleted. It beeped to signal that there was a message. The detective was asking him to return to the police station for "just a few more questions."

Tim shut off his phone again and climbed to the police station, using the shortcut he'd taken on Saturday. It was steeply uphill, but he made it without mishap, and asked for the detective at the front desk.

~

"Why have you kept me out of my house and car, Detective?"

"In case we needed to dust for fingerprints, or search for a murder weapon, things like that."

"Interesting. So, why *didn't* you do that? You must have found some clues that absolve me. Or the pathologist did."

"I'm unable to discuss that with you, Mr Brown. We do appreciate your cooperation, though. Do you have any children?"

"No."

"Nieces? Nephews?"

"No."

"Who else rides in your car with you?"

"Rides, as in regularly, or even sometimes? Robert Kirk, on occasion."

"Think back."

"I don't need to. If you saw my car, Detective, you'd understand that nobody would volunteer to ride in it. And I don't pick up hitchhikers. Whatever was spilled in there was spilled by me."

"Why did you allow your back yard to become unkempt?"

"I told you. I was never home, didn't see the point of keeping it mowed."

"You said you built a new woodshed, but you didn't put it where the old one was. Why not?"

"Because it would save me a few steps when I was collecting wood in the winter."

"You don't sound very concerned about the grave."

"Don't I really? Don't waste your time trying to evaluate my feelings. Perhaps it's because of how I was treated from the moment I arrived in my own driveway on Saturday. I understand some of it, but it sure felt like your guys were on a big power trip. I'll set it aside for now. Whatever happened in my backyard was not recent, I know that. The ground around the woodshed post looked the same as it did everywhere in the yard, except that the post had sunk. So my guess is that it would be years old, like some old graves in the back of the cemetery."

"Did you ever see anyone in your yard who wasn't supposed to be there?"

"No."

"Did you say you let the yard go to weeds so the grave wouldn't be discovered?"

"No, I did not say that. Don't keep trying to put words in my mouth. I let it go to weeds because mowing it was a waste of money. Because I was never home to enjoy it."

The detective repeated his previous questions in several formats. Tim remained calm and focused and repeated his answers. Finally, the interview came to an end.

"You've been very helpful, Mr Brown. We'll be in touch if we have more questions."

"Are you permitting me to go home now, Detective? May I have my keys, if so?"

"Yes, all clear. You can sign for your keys at the front desk. Do you need a ride home?"

"I'll take care of that myself, thanks."

~

The taxi drove away. Tim was back where he had stood on Saturday. He was not nearly as anxious as he had been then, but the latest encounter with the detective had brought his frustration level back up a notch.

He tugged at the yellow tape around his house until it broke. He pulled it down, bundled it up, and stuffed it into a garbage can.

He unlocked the car to retrieve his backpack, and was repelled by the stink of food that had been spoiling in the trunk for two warm days. He opened the trunk and took out the bags, reeking of rotting chicken breasts. He couldn't recall what else was in the bags, and didn't care. Carefully, he carried them to the shed, where he placed them gently into a garbage bag, closed it tightly, and gingerly lowered it into another can.

He left the trunk lid up and rolled down the windows.

Finally, he unlocked the door and entered his house.

It's over. Have a shower and put on some fresh clothes, make lunch, have some tea. Do normal things to take your mind off the cops. Charge your phone.

Backyard planning didn't appeal today. That was disappointing, but he knew it would come back. Was there someone he should call? *Yes! Poor Rob will be as frustrated with me as I've been with the detective!*

If Rob was teaching and unable to answer, he would see that the call was coming from home, the most important information. "I'm back in the house, Rob. Free to come and go. I'm going to change my clothes and get back on track. Talk later."

In fresh clothes and with a hot double espresso from the ever-empathetic Gloria at his elbow, he followed up on his Sunday-morning meditation about new occasions teaching new duties. He was a Private Investigator, armed with Delving Principles. He had honed them on investigations which were of interest to his living clients.

Now here was a different challenge: his client—if he could call him that—was very dead, and also unknown. How could he even begin to investigate that?

"Delving Principles state that we must start at the end and work toward the beginning. We examine everything in order to find something. Whatever I can find might be the missing piece that the police couldn't find. Our first task is to establish what kind of dead this person is. Was he murdered? Or did someone find him dead, of natural or unnatural causes, and decide to bury him hastily on my property?"

He went to his study to get sheets of foolscap. This line of thinking needed to be recorded.

"I know I don't know the answers to these questions, but that's no problem. It's my job to ask all the questions. The unanswered questions that remain will be the ones the police will want. Unanswered questions are signposts that say, 'Look here. Ask about this.'"

He hastily wrote these sage observations on the paper.

"We have two people of interest to consider: one who died, and one who buried him." He tapped his pencil on the foolscap. "But how many people know about this? Only one knew about the grave before Saturday, that's plain. *Unless* the gravedigger told someone, which is unlikely. But the grave contained a person, and nobody lives and dies in complete isolation, do they? There's that hermit on the North Shore who lives totally isolated in the woods, but people still know he's there. So, did this deceased person have a family? Do they know he's dead? Or do they still think he's missing? A runaway?"

He made another coffee to fuel these thoughts. The subject matter wasn't comforting, but delving into the possibilities was a familiar process, if imperfectly practised.

He drew three boxes on the paper, and wrote VICTIM in one, DIGGER in the middle, and FAMILY in the third.

"No matter what the victim's parting words were, this middle person came between him and his family. He might have said he was going out for a bag of milk, or he might have said he was going to hitch-hike to Montreal. But he never came back, that's likely all they know. Even if they yelled 'Good riddance!' and slammed the door. Unless they hired someone to murder him. But let's not get ahead of ourselves. Let's do what we can to identify our victim first."

He phoned the newspaper office and asked for Harold, who was the caretaker of *The Times'* archives.

"Harold, it's Tim Brown. I have an assignment for you."

"Interesting. To which of my extensive list of cares does this pertain?"

"Today it's the archives. I need a listing of all missing or murdered people reported in *The Times* in the past decade. Is this possible? I know we have files by name and topic, but I've never wondered about that particular category until now."

"My predecessor was remarkably inventive when it came to categorizing newspaper stories, I'll give him that. He didn't always make separate files, but I've come across lists."

"Such as?"

"Oh, things as innocuous as birthdays, for instance. Those would be filed by name, perhaps, but I found a listing of every day of the year and every person born on each date. Pretty interesting. I don't know if we'll keep that up, but—"

"Don't stop yet. Can you give us an idea of some of those lists sometime? If we knew we had them, we might be able to make use of them. But right now I need missing and murdered, 1991 to present. Call me on my mobile when you have them, or when you know you don't, please."

There. Positive step taken.

Tim checked his pocket calendar to see what plans he might have made. It was easy to forget when one had been dislocated from normal life.

One notation caught his eye: Mortimer Evers, the guest speaker at the Prayer Breakfast. The bishop had asked him to wait a week and then to get in touch. *It's been eleven days, so I can make that call today. That's exactly what I want to do. Talking to him will be interesting, and a good change from the weekend.*

"Reverend Evers, good day. This is Tim Brown calling, we met at the —"

"Hello, Tim! I've been expecting you. Are you calling to say you're going to visit us here in Blue Rocks? My dear wife is in the habit of baking something every morning, and I would sincerely appreciate the assistance of a younger man to help reduce the supply. If you like that sort of thing, of course. I recall that you are of quite a slender build, if I may say, so perhaps you don't indulge?"

"Indeed I do, Rev—"

"Please call me Mort. And my wife is Martha."

"Thanks; I did wonder. Yes, I do indulge in the occasional pastry, especially if it's right out of the oven. I would love to visit you, that's why I'm calling. I have some time tomorrow."

"What day is that? Oh, Tuesday. Martha!" He partially covered the phone. "Martha, dear, remind me, where am I supposed to go on Tuesdays?"

Tim heard her sweetly reminding Mort of his duties.

"I have a meeting at two o'clock. Can you make it in the morning, Tim? Around—what, dear? Nine? Ten? Yes, around ten? We'll have our devotions then. I call it devotions. You will, too, when you get one of her biscuits on your plate."

"I'd be honoured to come for devotions, then. Just give me the house number and I'll find you. Thanks so much, Mort."

Tim went to the sunroom to get acquainted with his new sofa, delivered Friday afternoon and forgotten in the ensuing disturbance.

"No two ways about it. I'm going to have to buy some side tables and a couple small armchairs for this room. We need a place to set our drinks and papers. I didn't see anything suitable in the furniture store. Everything's so big and bulky. Maybe a second-hand or vintage store? We shall keep our eyes open."

Thinking about this helped to pass the time. The big wall clock in the kitchen told him it was time to make supper and that reminded him of the wasted chicken breasts in the garbage can.

Rob called. "So I don't have to spring for your bail? I hope you didn't sass the nice detective. He's just doing his job. I hope."

"No bail, but thanks for the offer. The detective did say I could go home after I went in for more inane questions, so that wasted a few more hours of my life. But I didn't confess. I'll get over it, but I'm not finished with this little drama. Our Sunday dinner was rotting in the trunk, and is now in the garbage, such unnecessary waste. Thanks for your thoughtfulness and support, Rob."

~

Dinner was a box of Kraft Dinner with lots of grated parmesan and fresh ground pepper, accompanied by a glass of a chilled and buttery *Récupérer*.

Then Tim phoned Stella at home, hoping she'd be there and on his side. The call went to voicemail, so he left a brief message: "I'd really appreciate hearing from you this evening."

She called back within minutes. "I was on one of the other phones."

"You have two phones? What're you, a drug dealer?"

"No. I'm saving that for my retirement. What brings you to my *third* phone this evening?"

"I have a story to tell, and knowing how much you prefer to be the first to know rather than last, I called to update you."

He knew if he began with the many and wonderful mowing machines, she'd bark at him and rightly so. He started by telling her about taking down the police tape today, and told the rest of the story backwards, newspaper-style. She was engaged, evidenced by her frequent questions such as "When was this?" and "What was his name?" and, of course,

"How did Robert handle it?"

It was a long phone call, perhaps the longest ever with Stella. He heard her other phones ringing from time to time, but she let them all go. He was impressed and grateful.

"So, that's it in a nutshell, Aunt Stella. Thanks for listening. I wanted you to know in case someone mentions me and police and murder in the same breath."

"Exactly right. Thank you for that. What an awful time you've had. Do you think there will be repercussions?"

"Like being accused of hosting an illegal graveyard? Or murder? I doubt it, though as I've learned, anything can go wrong. You know, I was tempted a few times to quote Mother to the cops, but I didn't figure I'd risk it."

"What would Lucia have said that would possibly be relevant?" Tim's mother had claimed the nickname Brownie as soon as she married Ford Brown, so it always sounded strange to Tim when Stella referred to her by her given name.

"Mother often said she knew where all the bodies were buried. Maybe she missed one. Or—ha-ha—or maybe the yard is full of them!"

It wasn't that funny, but funny enough for Tim to release a load of tension with someone he trusted. He laughed until he ran out of breath, blew his nose, and wiped his eyes.

He picked up the phone again, expecting that Stella had chosen to sit this one out. "Hello?"

"I'm still here. Feeling better now?"

"Sorry about that. Yes, I'm okay now."

"Good. Please don't take that show on the road, not with the police. They are notoriously not amused. Their work makes them like that. Some people they apprehend are guilty as hell of heinous crimes."

He took a deep breath. "I know. But I bet Mother would have enjoyed the irony. Speaking of olden days, I have a question for you relating to all this. Can you think back to when you were growing up in this house, what structures were in the backyard?"

"I'm the only person permitted to say this, but that *was* a long time ago. There was a small barn, back where the exhibition buildings are now. Any animals were long gone when we were children. We weren't allowed in the barn, which was a rule to be obeyed, to me, and a rule to be broken, to your mother."

"Quite a girl, my mother. There was an old shed, too. I used it as a woodshed until it collapsed, then I had another one built. Do you have any recollection of when that happened?"

"About when an old shed fell down and you built another one?"

"Yes."

"Why would I know anything about that? Until this year, my visits to the old homestead were mostly formal and focused around your fine dining table. I can't even dredge up an image of the back garden now. Why?"

"I thought I'd try to be helpful to the police. They might think I'm hiding something because I can't remember when the new shed was built. It matters because one end of it was resting directly on this grave, which must have seemed solid enough at the time it was constructed. But then it collapsed, presumably because the body in it had decomposed, ugh. The date those things happened would give the cops a clue as to when to look for a missing person."

"I see. Well, you'll have to go into your own records for that. I do recall one Christmas that you went out to your mother's sunroom for firewood, and you said that was the first time."

"I did? When, though?"

"I'll think about it. Timothy, I must go attend to these other petitioners who think their urgencies should be mine. Is there anything you'd like me to do on your behalf? Put in a good word with the executioner, perhaps?"

"If it comes to that, please do. But I'm okay. I was shocked and indignant and displaced, and it takes a while to recover from that. Thank you for listening, Aunt Stella. It means a lot."

Stella said goodnight and was gone. Tim poured another glass of the *Récupérer*, which seemed to be working, spurred by supportive conversations with his nearest and dearest.

He owed Evelyn a call, too. She would have sensed that something was up this morning even if she hadn't heard the details. She wouldn't like it if she heard about his experiences from the grapevine.

"It's way after six o'clock," Evelyn said by way of greeting.

"I know. Please excuse. Did you have a good practice session?"

"Just finished. How did you know?"

"I think coming second in that tournament was a wake-up call for you, and when the mighty Evelyn is awakened, look out!"

"You're absolutely right, Timmy. I'm workin' on it. So, what was going on with you today?"

"Who's saying anything was going on?"

"Oh, come on. You bring your lady editor over, which doesn't happen every day. You huddle, which I told you before is a red flag that you're talking about something secret, so of course I listen more. I don't snoop, Timmy, it's just my habit to listen. Most of what I hear there is stupid stuff, mothers-in-law, kids, husbands, women problems, the usual. But once in a while, it's interesting. Like I told you before, nobody sees the waitress."

"I see you. You're hard to miss."

"I know you do, Hon. I wasn't listening in. But the expressions on your lady-friend's face were pretty interesting."

"Yeah? Like what?"

"Like surprise. Or sadness or, oh, like you were telling her about something awful, anyway. I don't know, and I don't need to know. It was just different, that's all, so I noticed. But you liked my muffins, right?"

"I sure did. Your mother had a winner there."

"You kidding? My mother couldn't make a can of soup. It's my recipe, but people like it if they think some dumpy lady covered in flour has just pulled them out of her oven, right?"

"You are a marketing genius and a wonderful baker. Keep it up."

He took a deep breath. "I want to tell you a bit of what we were talking about today. It doesn't involve you at all, but it did upset my applecart, and as friends, we share our spilled apples, right?"

He briefly and lightheartedly related the weekend's events, called it the "bare bones", said the police had to "dig into it" so he and Robert had taken refuge in the hotel suite. He did his best to find the humour in the tale, and Evelyn rewarded him by laughing at his jokes, after she was convinced that he was all right.

"So, m'dear, that's my excuse for not going to watch you *not* win the trophy Saturday night. A feeble excuse, but effective, don't you think?"

"Jaysus, Timmy, if that happened to me I wouldn't be laughing about it. I'da been freaking out! They cleaned it all up, right?"

"Yup, all gone. Anyway, it's not a secret, but the less said about it better, please. And besides, I'd rather talk about my new lawn and garden."

"Thanks for telling me, Tim. It's a shitty thing to happen to a wonderful guy. I really appreciate knowing."

~

He was pleased with how the day had played out. This morning at the hotel seemed like days ago and miles away. But he had started an investigation, a delving chart, and had shared his misery with people close to him who had been uniformly kind and caring. He could feel his Humpty-Dumpty life putting itself back together as he prepared for bed in his old fashioned bathroom with familiar things in their ordinary places.

And he was looking forward to his visit with the Very Titled Mort Evers and his baker-wife. Eager anticipation was a dreamy cloud to fall asleep on.

June 15: Blue Rocks

Tuesday

"If you were a dog, Gloria, I'd take you with me, especially to places where a smart coffee might be appreciated. Everybody'd love you. Alas, you don't travel well. So let's have a latté to get me started, there's a good girl."

Tim felt so buoyed by this bright morning that he devoted the time before visiting Mort to opening his mail and paying bills. "When the grass is green and flowers are blooming, it will be worth it. The garden will give me pleasure long after the money's cleared the bank."

He took this serene outlook with him on the half-hour drive past Lunenburg to the craggy fishing village of Blue Rocks, named for the outcroppings of blue slate. Houses and fish shacks were perched impossibly on the stone, and fishing boats were anchored in the protection of pocket-sized coves of slate.

Mort's summer parsonage was a yellow cottage that appeared too tiny for the tall man Tim had met. It was an optical illusion, as the house next door was built on top of a huge rock, and this cottage was built a few feet below the road in a rare grassy vale.

Tim was grateful there was room in the driveway for parking, as the narrow shoulders of the narrow road dropped steeply to salt water. He knocked on the door and a voice invited him to enter.

The side door opened directly into the kitchen, where Martha Evers was bending over the open oven door to pull out a tray of cinnamon rolls. She placed them safely on the counter, straight-ened up, turned to Tim and smiled warmly.

"Hello, Tim, I'm Martha. Welcome to our happy hideaway. Mort will be down in just a moment. I hope you like cinnamon rolls. Would you prefer tea or coffee? Coffee's on, but tea's no problem. Why don't you make yourself comfortable over there on the sofa? Oh, watch your head in the archway. Mort's always banging his noggin on it, poor man. The house was built for short people like me, not you long drinks of water. It was a fisherman's house, though I don't know if all fishermen are short. Mort! Tim's here, love."

"Coming!" Mort called from the top of the stairs. "Good morning, Tim. I don't run on the stairs any more, certainly not in this house, but I smell cinnamon rolls, so you know I'll get there soon."

He appeared on the landing, bent low, and straightened up when he reached the floor.

Tim stood to shake hands, minding his own head as he did so. Both men were inches over six feet tall. They sat again as Martha quickly set a plate of rolls on the coffee table and served their drinks.

"Coffee, please, just black," Tim said.

"I really enjoyed your presentation at the prayer breakfast," he said to Mort. "I don't think I know anyone here in Blue Rocks or Stonehurst, but I felt like I did after you spoke about them. You made them quite real, like painting them in colour."

"You're very kind, Tim. However, I have a confession to make. They are fictional people, or fictionalized, you might say. I used an amalgam of different folk for each one, and changed the names to protect the innocent. What I wished to convey was not individuals, *per se,* but the character of the good people who live here. I might end up in Davy Jones' locker if I were to reveal the true private lives of my parishioners. With slight alterations, I have given that speech many times, with different titles, right, my dear?"

"About fourteen times and counting."

"Martha's my editor and archivist, you see. I'd be lost without her. She's been with me every step of our career, so she knows the people as well as I do, and often suggests improvements, thank goodness. If you're ever tempted to quote my best lines, you likely have Martha to thank."

"A tag-team, then. That's wonderful. You're fortunate, Mort, that your editor is such a fine baker as well."

"Indeed I am!" he said. "Martha keeps the flour mills in business. I try not to have more than my allotment of daily bread, so we enjoy them fresh and quickly send the rest home with whoever's visiting."

"They're my mother's recipe," Martha added. "Yours are cooling on the counter, Tim." A kraft paper bag was open at the top. "I leave it open so the rolls will cool without getting soggy."

Tim laughed at Martha's "mother's recipe" remark. He told them about his friend Evelyn at the Daisy Café, and her "mother's muffin" recipe.

Mort and Martha appeared interested to hear more about Evelyn, asking questions about her background and her interests. He wasn't gossiping. He was celebrating her, sharing a dear friend with these new friends.

The conversation moved smoothly and swiftly, as Mort and sometimes Martha talked about people they had met, and then back to Tim as the conversation went on.

"Lunch is ready," Martha announced, and Tim looked at his watch with dismay. "What have I done? I'm so sorry, I had no idea of the time. I didn't intend to stay for lunch. I must go."

"No, no, we want you to stay, don't we, dear? There's always a bone, so there's always soup. Today's is beef barley. Soup makes itself. The washroom is by the back door. Would you like a glass of milk, Tim?"

"Just water, please and thank you."

When they were seated at the table, Mort told Tim he would ask the blessing, but not to be alarmed. He and Martha bowed their heads and Mort said, "May the Lord know how sincerely grateful we are for this food. Amen."

"Amen," Tim said politely. "I *am* sincerely grateful. This soup smells delicious. Why did you tell me not to be alarmed?"

"Oh, I wasn't sure what your experience may have been with the small prayer commonly known as 'grace'. Some use it as an opportunity to settle family arguments, or to show guests how pious they are."

"Yes, and meanwhile the fat is congealing on the gravy or the soup has gone cold," Martha said.

"I've had little experience with saying grace. When my late mother invited the minister to dinner, it was said for show. One time, she sprang it on me to ask the blessing, and I said I didn't know what the heck that was, and then I was loudly invited to leave the table."

They talked about meals, where they'd had them, what they ate, who was at the table. The Evers talked about places they'd been, and Tim revealed that he was about to embark on the second trip of his life to the same destination, to PEI.

"Nowhere else?"

"No. It's a long story, a lifetime long, and I won't burden you with the details today. Robert and I are very much looking forward to going."

"What is the nature of your pilgrimage, may I ask? Of course, PEI is beautiful. We've served there a few times, haven't we, Martha?"

Tim explained that Robert was giving an organ concert at the festival in Indian River, and that they would extend the trip to stay where Tim had stayed before, where the accommodations were lovely, the view spectacular, and the cuisine was hauled fresh out of the Gulf of Saint Lawrence daily for their dining pleasure.

"A worthy trip!" Mort said enthusiastically. "We are hired to attend to the souls of our congregations, but we do tend to select the coastal communities when we can, hoping for some fresh seafood. Sometimes we've misjudged it. Remember that place, Martha, down the Eastern Shore, wasn't it? All the fishing boats had been hauled up years ago—"

"Yes, and they kept feeding us 'preacher food,'" Martha added, "which was an inventive array of casseroles."

"The common ingredient in all of them was cream of mushroom soup," Mort lamented. "Before our sojourn there was over, I was tempted to get a line and rod and try my luck at catching something fresh myself. The ocean was *right there.*"

"Yes, right across the road from us. Like here. But we survived."

"We did. That's where I learned to appreciate the brief blessing. No need to overdo it. 'Thou knowest, Lord, the secrets of our hearts,' I'd say, inwardly. We are grateful to have food to eat. But we are even more grateful for fine food." Mort and Martha laughed unabashedly.

"That's Henry Purcell, right?" Tim said.

"Beg pardon?"

"'Thou knowest, Lord' is an anthem by Henry Purcell. We sing it at least once a year."

"Your United Church choir does? That's remarkable. It's from the Anglican Book of Common Prayer. Have we heard it sung, Martha?"

"I don't recall, Mort."

"It's not terribly difficult to sing," Tim said, "but it's difficult to sing well. Perhaps choirs in small churches don't tackle it."

"Perhaps not. Many small congregations have no choir, especially in the summer, which may be a blessing in disguise. Martha has a lovely voice, so she sometimes offers a solo. Please ask your Minister of Music to send word to us when he has your choir singing that Purcell, would you? We'd come to hear it."

"I'd be happy to do that, but wouldn't you be leading your own services?"

"I hope not. Retirement gives us choices. I pinch-hit sometimes, and I counsel other clergy sometimes, but I try not to have regular duties. We're reviewing my half-century of sermons to see if enough of them are worthy of publishing. That's fun, isn't it, Martha? We kept good records of the Old and New Testament Scriptures and the hymns we used with each one, and what season of the Church Calendar it was, so a priest might find the book handy should they experience writer's block when Saturday night sermon-writing time comes 'round."

"That sounds like a great idea. And that brings me back to printing some of your homilies in *The Times*. I still think the one about the made-up characters would play well. You could call it, 'Why I like to serve in communities *like* Blue Rocks.' That would be safe. We could add a disclaimer that characters are drawn from real life, but are fictional. Think about it, please."

Tim helped clear the table, and then said, "I really must be going. I had no intention of staying so long, but I've enjoyed every minute. I'll invite you to my house, too. Both Robert and I can do wonders with a can of cream of mushroom soup, ha-ha."

He expected handshakes, but both Mort and Martha insisted on warm hugs. Martha said, "Please come back anytime and often, Tim. Mort takes a walk in the afternoons, weather permitting. I worry about him on these narrow roads, and he forgets to pay attention to cars if he's in deep thought. I'd feel better if he had a walking companion; and I think you would, too, wouldn't you, Mort?"

"I would! Come join me on the Camino de Blue Rocks. Just call ahead to avoid a wasted trip, if such can be said about coming here. I do have to make pastoral visits sometimes."

"That's a deal! I can take you to other trails as well, some without vehicles, some as foggy and miserable as can be out here. Bye-bye!"

"Oh, Tim," Martha called as Tim left the house. "Your rolls. Please take them."

~

How long have I been away? How far was I? It feels very long and very far, but not in a bad way. When have I ever been in someone's tiny home for cinnamon rolls and coffee—good coffee, too—and then sat at their kitchen table for soup? And such conversation! Did I talk too much? Did I listen attentively? They certainly are warm people, both of them. I felt an affinity right away. I wonder what that is. Mort wants a walking companion? Maybe we'd go for drives sometimes...

He stopped in the middle of his kitchen. There was an echo in his thoughts. *An affinity...go for drives...*

"That's what I hoped would happen with dear old GB. Connie was dying, and I thought I'd take him for drives after she passed away, as my honorary uncle. But he died first and we never got to do the uncle thing.

Looks like I still want elders. Fortunately, they don't appear to be facing their demise."

He wrapped the cinnamon rolls and froze them to share on Sunday morning.

I do have a real aunt, but Martha and Stella are as different as chalk and cheese. Martha's very astute, though. She has the advantage of being overlooked a lot, I bet. Not fun if you want to be noticed, but like Evelyn, if people ignore you, they won't notice you watching and listening.

There was a serving of *Récupérer* remaining from yesterday, and he made it do for supper. He did feel restored, though many issues were still unresolved.

He was ready to jump back in the stream.

June 16: Three sheets

Wednesday

The dream from last night flitted through Tim's mind. He had been gripping a shovel. That was all there was. *Why would I dream of a shovel? That's nuts.*

Tim and Elaine arrived at the office at the same early time. "It's Wednesday morning," he said to her. "Why are you here so early?"

"It's 1999," she replied. "I have no better reason. Why are you here at all?"

"Habit. Silly dream. Let's go for breakfast and call it a meeting."

"Tongues will wag," Elaine giggled.

"I'd love to hear that. Let's go downriver to the bakery by the ferry. But can we take your car? Mine still stinks."

On the way, Tim said, "I read the Sweetland updates. Things are coming together there?"

"Yes."

"When is go-time?"

"I'm not sure. Since it's a weekly, the possible publication dates do seem too soon, but may be too late. This project is like peeling an onion. We uncover something that reveals something else, and so on."

"Do you think you're digging too deep? I thought the original injury to the flora and fauna, plus stealing crown land and swindling rich Americans, were plenty."

"It did seem like that, but it isn't just Eric and Mary MacIntosh. They had helpers, some staff in the provincial department of Lands and Forests, and some politicians. We're making sure that when we lay it out, the charges will be well-founded."

"Charges, eh?"

"I hope. It's not just ignorance and stupidity. There's been a good bit of breaking the law."

"Are you relying entirely on Roger for legal advice, or—?"

"Not at all. Roger's specialty is land use law. He's not a criminal lawyer. We've had to dip into the cookie jar for that expertise."

"That's good. I'd rather be bankrupt from doing it right than from losing a lawsuit."

~

On the return trip upriver, Tim asked Elaine to turn into Stella's driveway. He wanted to examine the new flowering shrubs and garden beds her horticulturist had arranged.

"Who lives here?" Elaine asked.

"Your good friend, the MLA for South River and the Harbours."

"Oh, wow, I didn't know she owned this place. It's lovely. She's done well for herself. Perhaps we should investigate her."

"Good luck with that. Aunt Stella has always had money, I don't know where from, and I value my relationship with her too much to ask."

"I was kidding. Nice place, though." Elaine sighed. "I'd like to have a nice home someday, you know, rose-covered white picket fence and all that. I love my independent career, don't get me wrong, being well-paid to see the country one year at a time, but it's quite rootless."

She turned the car around and continued driving to the office.

"To get the picket fence, you'd have to stay at one job in one community. Would that suit you?"

"I don't honestly know. I've been like the Littlest Hobo, trotting into a town, righting all the wrongs or holding things together, and then trotting down the rail line to the next needy place."

"That's a dog?"

"Yes, a very smart TV dog."

"Did you find us needy?"

"Sure, but not in a bad way. You needed to take a year off, and you needed a damn good person to take over as editor and publisher for a year. Lucky for both of us, you chose me, and I love it. People are depending on me to do something I know how to do. Fail-safe. In this case, you didn't go away-away, and that's a comfort, though I worried at first that you might be an interference. Instead, you're challenging me with award-worthy journalism."

"But you'll get bored and move on, like the dog in the TV show."

"I don't need to get bored, but our contract does specify an end. I'm usually ready to move on by then. Thanks for the breakfast and the chat, Tim."

"My pleasure. By the way, where's Harold? I asked him for a report from our archives on Monday, and haven't heard boo from him since."

"He's under the weather."

"Uh-oh. Serious?"

"It's always serious when someone who has three jobs is knocked down. It's something fixable. An abscessed tooth, I think."

"Ow, that's no fun. Hmm. Do we have backups for Harold?"

"Harold *was* the backup for GB, and for me when I was backing up what you used to do. We're tight. He'll be back Friday, I think."

~

Tim felt a tug when he unlocked his room, a pull to get back in there, working on a project. Like Elaine, he loved the challenge of solving a problem.

He did have a problem: the big one that had been unearthed in his backyard mere days ago. As a Delver, his first challenge was to identify which aspect of the problem required solving first and he had begun that line of thinking at home.

He pulled out sheets of manila paper from the cabinet, and taped them to the walls. Referring to his notes from home, he wrote VICTIM in a box on the first sheet, DIGGER in the second box, and in the third, FAM-ILY.

I felt like a helpless victim, so frustrated. I don't know what I could have done about it, if anything. The timing was terrible, that's for sure. I was excited about the backyard improvements, Robert was coming, we would celebrate the big reveal—then boom! You're darn right I was frustrated.

On the second sheet he wrote ME vs POLICE.

"Why wouldn't they let me go into my own house, not even escorted? I wasn't being accused of murder, wasn't even a suspect, so why the seizure of my home? Dusting for fingerprints? Searching for a weapon? It sounds made-up to me. The constable acted like he was doing me a big favour to get me a burger, when I could have just made a quick sandwich. It was stupid not to let me put the milk and chicken in the fridge."

Tim paused to look out the window and reflect. He had been hearing, but not paying attention to, the scraping on shingles on the outside of the building. As he looked, a pair of feet in work boots moved in front of the window, and flakes of paint drifted past like snow.

"Are the police good at their jobs? Did they treat me according to the rule book, or did they make mistakes? I could put on my Press hat and interview the Chief, but I bet he'll stonewall me. He'd never admit that his cops were wrong, not if it's going in the newspaper. Maybe I'll get their rule book. I wonder how Jake is coping. He's the one who had to call the police."

He found Jake's number in his phone and called. "Hi, Jake, it's Tim Brown. How're you doing?"

"Hi, Tim. I'm good. How're you? That was a bit of a surprise there, on Saturday."

"For you and me both. I'm sorry you guys had to discover that. Are you okay about it all?"

"Oh, yeah, this was just bones. I've seen much, much worse, serving overseas. I thought cutting grass and clipping rose bushes would be good therapy for me, and it is, but you never know what you'll find in the weeds, right?"

"I guess. Have you finished at my place, now? Or maybe you don't want to come back there?"

"No problem at all. I've been waiting for the all-clear from you. Will you be there late this afternoon?"

"I sure will. See you then. Thanks, Jake."

He blew out a big breath. *That's good. I shouldn't have waited so long to check in on him, but we all deal in our own way, I guess.*

He carried on listing his grievances. He didn't record the unexpected enjoyments of the hotel experience, Robert's "busking" at the piano for the conference, the surprisingly good room service food, the modern décor of the suite, and the serendipity of the delicately deep-fried seafood at the home of the "Road Kill Burger". These pleasant experiences occurred because he was forced to leave his home for two days, not because he chose to give himself a holiday weekend. *Who pays for that? Is there compensation for being locked out?*

He left the office at half-past two, having filled the sheets with notes. Now he wouldn't need to carry them around in his head. When he next looked at them, he'd begin to sort them out, and he had no doubt he'd uncover something worth delving into.

~

Tim was standing on the flagstone pathway with a mug of tea when Jake arrived.

"Nice to have this path uncovered, Jake. This is a bonus."

"It's well made. This was a nice area at one time. We've brought it back pretty well, and the shrubs are established now, just a bit overgrown. The rest is up to Mother Nature."

"I guess the berry crop didn't survive?"

"You can't kill blackberries and raspberries that easily. We'll watch for them when they start to come up again, and red flag them."

"I'm sorry again about the grave. I have no idea how it got there, but I'm looking into it. As are the police, of course. Did they question you and Dana for long?"

"Not really. I told them it's normal for Dana to check the ground before running the machines, and that spot looked sketchy, so he checked it out, found what looked like human remains, and called me. I did try to call you but the call wouldn't go through for some reason. I couldn't just walk away, so I called the police. They seemed satisfied with that."

"That's good. I know you likely lost valuable work-time, and I'm sorry about that. They kept me downtown for hours and locked me out of my house and car for two days. I think they were hoping I would confess that a family member had gone missing or something. But people don't put themselves in shallow graves, do they? Anyway, that's not your concern. I guess we're on a regular lawn care schedule now?"

"We'd be happy to do that for you. Oh, what about that other hole in the back? Do you plan to do something with it?"

"Fill it in—please! I'm not a decorative-well kinda guy and I'm rather nervous about holes in the ground at the moment. You were saying something about top-dressing and seeding here? The front has real grass already, but goldenrod and every other weed is likely to come up again here, right?"

"Grass will take over eventually, with regular mowing, but clover will work faster. I'll get someone over here to take care of that as soon as possible. I think the next few days are going to be damp, not the best for mowing, so we'll do jobs like that then."

They shook hands and Jake left.

Tim sat on the open floor of the woodshed. It was the only place to sit in the whole yard, but he'd remedy that.

~

After supper, he topped up the humidifiers, and then entertained himself at the piano. Wanting a break from more challenging pieces, he opened a book of Gospel songs and looked up "Dem Bones".

It was fun to sing about the knee bone being connected to the thigh bone, but wasn't at all easy to play, with all the chromatic key changes.

June 17: Needle in the red

Thursday

"Good morning, Mrs A!"

Tim was cheerful because it was a damp morning, which could mean that Jake could get the lawn seeding underway. He went to the Daisy and waggled the door a few times to make the bell over the door ring loudly.

"I hear ya, ya big goof. Everybody hears ya," Evelyn called to him from behind the counter.

He sat in his usual booth and opened his copy of yesterday's *The Times*. He was hoping not to see that James had taken a photo of his house wrapped in police tape. He slowly leafed through the pages and noted a small item under "Police Blotter":

> Members of the South River Police Service were called to a home in Top of Town on the weekend to investigate items revealed following the removal of an outbuilding. No further action reported.

Wow, Elaine, that is masterful. Or was that the official police wording? Very kind of them, if so. I suppose all the fol-de-rol after the cops showed up wouldn't have changed the generically-worded original dispatch. At least she didn't write "Prominent Citizen Victim of Unreasonable Detainment".

Evelyn brought coffee and stood by for his order. "There's nothing in it about you, Hon," she said quietly, nodding at the paper. "I already checked."

"Thanks, Ev, it's nice to know you're riding shotgun for me."

"An-ee time. What'll it be this morning?"

"Why do you always ask me? You bring what you want anyway."

"I dunno. Maybe I'll surprise you by not surprising you today."

"How about scrambled eggs, with a toasted English muffin, and bacon?"

She vanished, and Tim resumed his perusal of the newspaper. He turned the pages without dread now. His private bodyguard had already scanned it for disturbances. She hadn't mentioned the old name for his neighbourhood, Top of Town, rarely used these days. He was safe.

~

The paint scrapers were now working below his window. Soon they'd complete that stage and the staid old Johnson Building would step out in its new summer outfit. Tim rather enjoyed the sound of someone labouring outside his window, a kind of rhythmic white noise.

He turned to the sheets on the walls and began delving into the events of last weekend. His Rules of Delving would be very helpful here, to "Look at Everything to Find Something" and "Start at the End and Work Towards the Beginning."

But where was the end? What was the Something? Were yesterday's topics his interests today? He reminded himself that uncertainty was the Delver's hallmark. Jumping to a conclusion at the get-go could hide the real story.

Below *Victim?* he wrote WHO | WHAT | WHEN | WHERE | WHY | HOW, and left spaces below each time-honoured question. He was confident that he would put something interesting in these spaces, guided by these essential questions. His job was to look at everything to find something. Depending on what Harold found, he might be able to point the police to someone, sometime.

The same *W* categories applied to the DIGGER column. This was a topic about which he had no knowledge. and none for FAMILY either. Maybe Harold's report would identify a Person whose Family had reported them Missing, and the Family would point fingers at a likely Digger.

He put the cap on the pungent marker and went for a walk around the two downtown bridges crossing the South River. He had left home wearing a long-sleeved plaid shirt, no jacket. It wasn't raining, which was a frequent definition of a nice day along Nova Scotia's south coast, or probably any coast.

While he walked, he thought more about the person who had been buried in a shallow grave in his garden. *One, I don't know if it's an adult or a child, if that matters. A child would be most tragic, because a child would be innocent; an adult, not necessarily. Two, he might have been a nasty person. Three, were they local or were they transported here from away?*

He walked twice around the loop. At the end of the second lap, he was facing the church, his building, and the Daisy Café. The scraping was almost down to street level now, and primer would go on soon, weather permitting.

He noticed a small sign in the window of the café, and walked over to see what it said.

> Today's Snack Special:
> Muffin and Cheese

He walked in and saw a basket on the counter beside the cash register. Grinning, he went back to purchase his healthy lunch.

"What're you smiling at?" Evelyn asked.

"I'm smiling because I'm hungry and here's the solution. I've been wishing you would do something like this forever. Good job, Ev."

"Thanks. Just the raisin bran left. The banana ones were gone in a flash."

Tim made a cup of tea in the staff room to go with the muffin and cheese. It sustained him as he filled in blank spaces on the manila sheet until it was time to wrap it up for the day.

~

Robert was delighted to see the new sofa bed in the sunroom. "We can camp out here now! This is so exciting, Tim, you have no idea. I don't know what it is, there's just something about this room. I'm inside, but I'm outdoors. You're making a beautiful scene outside. What's that brown stuff?"

Tim had stayed in the kitchen to get their supper underway. Now he rushed to the sunroom to see what Robert was talking about, hoping it wasn't something sinister.

He was relieved to see that Chester Basin Property Management had been there.

"It's peat moss top-dressing, overseeded with clover. Don't I sound knowledgeable? That'll get the green growing faster than just waiting for the weeds to come up. Though I think it'll be a race between nature and the birds coming to feast on the seeds."

"I like birds, too."

~

After choir, although it was dark outside, they had their glasses of port in the sunroom, sitting on the new sofa, a plate of assorted nibbles resting between them. At Robert's prompting, Tim related more details of his time at the police station.

"I said to the detective that I hadn't decided if I'd get new fences put up, but now I thought I would. He said 'Why do you say that?' I said, 'To keep trespassers out would be a good reason, don't you think?'"

"That was a little impertinent, Tim," Robert said.

"Was it? He asked me what kind of trespassers I meant, and I said 'The kind who would come onto my property without my permission or invitation, I guess.' Geez. He wouldn't let up. 'Such as?' he says. 'I don't follow where you're going with this line of questioning,' I said. 'D'you mean the trespasser whose remains are reportedly buried there, is that where you're going? But I suppose he isn't the trespasser, is he? The trespasser would be whoever brought him there.' I think he was just trying to wind me up."

"Maybe he just wanted to see if your story remained consistent. It did, because you have only one story. It's good to be innocent."

"I'm as innocent as the driven snow, but I wasn't getting any credit for it. Then he asked about you, like did you ever stay in this house alone. I guess he was hoping that you were a suspect, to make his job easier."

"I'm also 'driven snow'."

"Precisely. I said no, you hadn't. He said, 'Never?' and I said, 'Never.' He asked if you have a key, and I said you do, but you've never stayed here alone overnight. He said I sounded very certain of that and could I explain why. You can see why I was frustrated: he was poking, poking, relentlessly. I said because I'd never been away from home, except for three nights about five years ago. And I said you wouldn't stay here if I wasn't here. I told him you're easily spooked, sorry. It's true, though. You wouldn't choose to be alone in this big old house, would you?"

"I would if I had to, but you're right, I wouldn't prefer it. Maybe we'll get a priest to exorcise the ghosts someday. Just in case. Did you tell me how he knew about me?"

"The constable asked who else had a key to the house. I gave your name and I said you were Doctor Robert Kirk, that your title was from a DMus. I felt like he thought I was lying."

Robert sighed. "Thanks for filling me in, Tim. You don't have to keep all this silliness in your head now. Let's let sleep knit up the 'ravelled sleeve of care.'"

After lights out, Tim said, "I was so stressed about how you would react to the whole grave thing. I worried that you'd never want to be in the sunroom again, let alone the garden."

"You're very thoughtful about me, Timo. I really appreciate it. Ordinarily, I would've said you were right to worry about me freaking out. But *your* needle was already far in the red, and we can't afford for both of us to be freaking at the same time, so I had to act cool about it all. Funny thing is, acting cool made me cool. I still am, because how *you* feel about it is all that matters."

Tim was silent as he absorbed this sentiment.

Then Robert added, "As long as nobody takes my sunroom away."

June 18: Camino

Friday

"I almost forgot, Rob: Evan's coming down this weekend. I sort of wish he wasn't, considering all the upset, but it's too late to cancel now. Anyway, that trouble's behind us, over and done with. I'd rather not mention the police or the grave to him at all. Do you agree?"

"You won't catch me bringing it up. When's he coming?"

"Tomorrow afternoon—same time as you, come to think of it. Would you like me to set up a carpool for you both? You could get to know each other on the ride down."

Robert declined that offer with a side glance.

"Gotcha. Don't worry, Evan won't be a burden. We need to relax this weekend, and we will."

~

Tim wanted to spend some time with the manila sheets this foggy morning, to see if any of the spaces had filled themselves in since yesterday. He decided to add another question because he'd dreamed briefly about it again last night: it was a long-handled shovel this time, and he'd been gripping it as before, but not actually digging. *Sure, the gravedigger would have needed a shovel, but the dream is about* me *holding it. That's not helpful.*

He wrote SHOVEL?? on the ME & POLICE sheet where there was room. If it had any relevance, it might reveal itself to him later.

His curtailed rights and freedoms seemed more interesting this morning. He began to fill in the spaces.

> WHO: Timothy Brown, property owner.
> WHAT:

He paused. Of all the indignities he felt he had endured, was there a line crossed or a rule broken from which everything else had unfolded? He put down the marker and sat to look out the window and think.

This is a good question. Is my quarrel with the police actions, or was it how I felt about the police actions? If it's the latter, why did I feel that way? I was detained: could I have refused to cooperate? They didn't act as though I could. They sure weren't kidding about me not being able to enter my own house. Why wasn't I allowed to look at the grave? Poor Dana, he was probably digging in there with his hands, yuck. But they didn't say gruesome, they just said remains. I guess the gruesomeness had decomposed a long time ago, that's why the grave collapsed, especially with the weight of the woodshed on top, ick. I only ever went to the shed in the winter, when the ground was frozen, to get firewood. Good thing. The guys who delivered the wood in the fall didn't mention any stink, but the body was underground. You don't suppose the fellow who built the shed put it there on purpose, because he had buried someone there and this would hide it?

"Don't be silly," he said aloud. "Let's not get carried away. The shed-builder would not have left a time-bomb like that. The remains would never have been discovered if the new shed had been built just a couple feet one way or the other. Both of us are blameless."

He considered what was near the site. The emergency exit from the fairgrounds, then a strip of weeds growing through gravel, never mowed, but that wasn't his property. Then more weeds, not in gravel, which was his property. At least he assumed it was.

Come to think of it, I don't recall seeing surveyors' markers anywhere. No wonder, with those weeds. I suppose there'd be one at the street end of the lot, and one at the back, under the trees, so there wouldn't be one in the middle anyway. I'm curious, though. I should see what the deed says.

He made a note in his notebook to find the property deed. Then he looked at the sheets of paper. "We're not getting very far delving into rights and freedoms. What upset my applecart the most?"

He thought back to last Saturday morning. He had run for groceries, hoping to watch the final passes of the zero-turn. He even managed to squeeze himself in for a haircut. *And wasn't that fortunate! If you're going to have your plans suddenly come to a halt, you might as well look your best when it happens.*

"Perhaps the real WHAT that happened wasn't the loss of my rights. Perhaps it was the suddenness of the disruption of my plans, my life.

Dana didn't intend to find the bones, then or later. Jake knew he had to call the police right away. And the cops did what they do best, I guess: stop everything! Still seems heavy-handed to me. But it was all so *sudden*. That's what knocked me for a loop. I came home happy and—*bam*—I was plucked out of my life and dropped into a play I didn't want to act in."

He had paced while he spoke aloud, and now he stopped to face the big pages.

"I don't think the police are the Big Issue," he said. "It's me. Is this my 'What'? That it was *sudden*? That seems a bit selfish. Okay, let's set the victim aside for a moment. Let's pretend it was a—what?—an accident, like a car accident. *Discovery* of the remains was my accident, not the fact that they exist. If I had run over somebody, that'd be sudden. If he died...I don't know for sure, but I doubt the police would just let me drive home with a wave and a promise to be a good boy until they called me, would they? Or would they? They'd hold up the traffic, which would interrupt plans for a whole lot of people—suspending *their* rights and freedoms— and they'd ask me to blow into a breathalyzer if they had the least suspicion, which is only right, and then what? Assuming my car was driveable, could I just drive it home? I don't know. It would likely be impounded as evidence, wouldn't it? What if I didn't admit my guilt, or came up with some story that cast doubt on how the accident happened? They'd tow my car...but my insurance would give me a rental, wouldn't they? I can't be forbidden to drive without a trial, can I?"

He sat again.

"But I can be police-taped out of my home without a trial. Without even being a suspect. That's confusing."

He pondered this as he looked out his window, now speckled with paint flecks.

"I think these categories need a bit of rearranging. I'm sure I'll get delving like a house afire once I see my path."

This had not been a productive morning by most standards, but he knew not to expect results at the start of investigations.

He put on his shoes and headed outdoors for his lunchtime walk around the bridges, stopping to ask the receptionist if she had heard from Harold.

"He's having dental work, sir, but he called to say he would be in on the weekend. He mentioned that he had to finish a report for you, and a bunch of other things."

"It's bad, I guess."

"Dental surgery, sir."

"Yikes! No wonder he hasn't been in. Next question: can you tell me why painters aren't at work on the building today?"

"They're painting interiors somewhere today, sir. Wet days inside, dry days outside."

"How do you know this?"

"They come in to use our washroom, and they stop to chat. Nice fellas."

"Good to know. Let's hope for dry weather soon."

He strode along and swung his arms. He thought about taking a walk with Mort in Blue Rocks this afternoon. He stopped halfway across the new bridge and called Mort's number.

"Hello-o?" Martha Evers answered cheerily.

"Hello Martha, it's Tim Brown. Thank you so much for your hospitality the other day. I know I stayed an unforgivably long time, but I really enjoyed meeting you both. And your delicious food."

"You are most welcome anytime, Tim. You didn't stay long enough. Mort has been talking about you ever since. If you hurry you can come for lunch today."

"You're so kind. Not for lunch this time, but I was calling to see if Mort would like a walk on the Camino de Blue Rocks this afternoon?"

"Just a moment, Tim, I'll ask him. He's upstairs."

He heard a muffled conversation, and then she was back.

"He's delighted, Tim, and so am I. What time?"

"You tell me."

"After three would be very good. He's working on something, but he expects to be finished by then. He never finishes, but you know what I mean. It sounds like you're standing in traffic. Be careful, Tim."

They disconnected, and Tim smiled. This would be a terrific way to end the work-week. Maybe they'd chat as they walked about sudden interruptions to one's rights and freedoms and weekend plans.

After one lap around the bridges, he popped into the Daisy for a couple banana muffins. He had a thought. "Do you have gift certificates, Ev?"

"You know we don't. What for?"

"Well, the painters are working to make my building pretty, and I'd like to give them a little treat. If you had five-dollar certificates I'd buy a bunch and hand them out. You'd have the cash, so when they come in for a muffin and coffee, they'd just hand in the certificate and you stick it on this pointy stick, same as your other receipts. Cash won't compel them to come here. Money wanders off. But if they never bring the certificates in, you keep the money and the muffins."

"That could work. These muffins sure are selling. Who knew?"

"Hand food, Ev. It's the way of the future, and the future is now."

"Hand food sounds weird, but I get your point. How would we get the certificates?"

"I have an office full of 'how' next door. Want me to ask my design guy to take a crack at it?"

"We're watching our expenditures, you know."

"Ex-pen-dit-ures, is it, Miz Business Tycoon? Good for you. Let me see what I can come up with."

Tim ducked carefully under the painters' scaffolding. He went directly to Ed Garamond's cubicle and knocked on the card that read, "Visitors Please Knock Before Entering!"

"He's not in," Ed said. "Come back later."

"Wrong answer. I have a tiny freelance design project for you," Tim said to Ed's back. "You'll be paid in muffins."

"Well, why didn't you *say*?" Ed swivelled around with a grin. "Whatcha got?"

Tim handed him a muffin. "They're trying out new snack items next door, low-cost, handy, take out, sort of like 'I-forgot-my-lunch', or maybe that's just me. I think a muffin and coffee would come in at five dollars, tax and tip in. I want gift certificates to give to people like the painters outside, or even to you hard labourers inside. If you design them, you'll likely get free muffins for a week. Printing's on us."

"Five muffins? I'm speechless! I've won the lottery! Hang on." Ed opened the wrapping on the muffin and took a bite. "Mmm! This tastes like my Mom's."

"Evelyn claims they're *her* mother's recipe. Maybe that should be on the certificate, but talk to her about that. You may keep that muffin, compliments of the management."

Tim stopped at Elaine's office. "Did I dream that we're to have a conflab about HR issues and such? Are we to be enduring—I mean, enjoying—the personnel pros and their clipboards? I'm sure I won't be qualified to continue as editor when they've finished with us, so you'll have to stay to run the ship."

"Yes."

"Yes what?"

"And no."

"Come again?"

"Yes: we did discuss HR, and I did contact a company. They're very busy. They will come with their clipboards next week, not to do anything, of course, but to discuss doing something. And, no: you won't be qualified to be the editor, nor will I, but maybe we never were. I'm sure 'winging it' is not in the HR lexicon. But we manage."

"You're a hoot, Miz Fong. Have a very nice weekend."

He didn't want to revisit the sheets upstairs. Left alone, they could shuffle their positions on the wall, words leaping from one sheet to another. Or maybe they would all jump to one sheet. He'd let them slither and slide for the weekend.

~

"Won't you come in, Tim?"

"No, thank you, Martha, not today. If I come inside, you'll offer me something to eat and I won't be able to refuse. I'll wait out here for my walking companion. Nice to see you, though."

Mort emerged from the little cottage, and shook Tim's hand when he extended it, but he clapped him on the back as well. "Let's not be formal, my friend. Now, which way?"

"Doesn't matter to me, Mort. If we go left today, we'll go right the next time. Let's see." Tim pulled a coin from his pocket. "Heads or tails?"

"Heads," Mort said, and Tim flipped the penny.

"Heads it is," he announced. "But what does that tell us? You still have to decide which way is heads. They should mark our coins Left and Right, or Go and Stay. They'd be more useful."

"Oh boy," Mort said. "You sound just like me. So many angels dance upon the head of every pin that I am often rooted to the spot, discussing the dance steps. Come, my young friend, let us go left. There's my decision-making done for the day."

They walked side-by-side when there were no cars, and stood aside, smiling and nodding, when an occasional car passed. They talked about anything, both choosing to ask questions rather than debate, and found laughter wherever possible.

"Martha said you were working on something this afternoon," Tim said. "May I ask what it was?"

"Oh, it's an open secret. My beloved and our children have been pressing me to write my memoirs. I've just begun. I'm not convinced that I will live long enough to complete it. Distilling fifty-plus years of wearing my collar backwards will take a very long time."

"Interesting. Can you remember details from the early years?"

"Pretty well, especially aided by my wife's archives. My name's been on the paycheques, small as they've been, but we've always approached my ministry as a team. To be sure, just naming the year doesn't bring any memories to the fore, but Martha will open that file and mention a name or place, and—behold—I'm there. Or I will recall something we did, and she'll say I have it wrong, because this or that was happening behind the scenes. So it may take a while."

"Do you think the chronological approach is best, then? Have you considered going by topic? Like choirs, suppers, parsonages, church boards, burials, weddings, social issues, that sort of thing? For readers who don't know you, topics might be more interesting than reciting year after year. For you, too. Just a thought."

Mort stopped walking to consider this. "I think you have an idea! As you named those topics, images of people and places were flashing by. It wouldn't matter if I left some items out, would it? Or got them out of order? Martha loves order, and I suppose she does it to make some sense out of me, poor dear, but I will propose this to her. I like it."

They stopped multiple times to admire the stark scenery of dark rocks poking through the surface of the water, waves breaking against them, colourful boats swinging at their moorings. When they reached the end of the narrow road they turned around. The return scenery was just as beautiful.

Tim had noticed that Mort's pace was more like a stroll than a hike. "May I ask you a personal question, Mort?"

"Anything."

"Are you in good health?"

"I will answer you, but may I inquire why you ask?"

"Well, you're as tall as I am, so we both can cover a lot of distance in a few steps. But you're being very careful of yourself."

"You are very perceptive. I am recovering from a recent hernia operation. My physician encourages me to walk, and I enjoy it, but my wife is very protective of me, and doesn't want me to go alone. Our strides are normally quite different, hers and mine, so she struggles to keep up with me, but right now, I'm at her pace. She was thrilled to know that you'd be walking with me today. Am I too slow for you?"

"Not at all. I'm here for the conversation, not a walkathon. Stroll as you wish."

"Thank you. Now, my turn. What were you working on today?"

"I'm trying to...something happened last weekend, and I'm trying to work out what it was. I mean, I know what happened, but I wonder what it means, you know? Here's the analogy I was considering: say I was driving my car, and I accidentally, inadvertently, and unintentionally killed someone—I didn't, it's just an analogy—and say it was the victim's fault, though that sounds harsh, but it happens. So, what's the real story here? It's about the deceased, but isn't it also about me, the hapless participant in this terrible event? Isn't it about what this sudden and unexpected event does to *my* plans, *my* hopes, my *life*? I might sound like a sociopath because I'm not sparing much sympathy for the deceased, but strictly speaking, the dead can't be disappointed. The living can."

Mort burst into laughter. They were standing on the crest of a rise in the narrow road, between the ocean view and a fish shack built on a pier. "Of all the thousands of times in my career that I have asked someone what's on their mind, this has to be the best response! And here I was wrestling with whether to mention lime jelly salads at the church socials! Oh, that is rich!"

He sobered suddenly. "But these questions are theoretical, you said? You didn't kill someone?"

"I didn't kill anyone. Someone *was* killed, quite a long time ago, and the remains were discovered recently. The discovery interfered with my plans. And now that I've put it that way, it seems petty and selfish. That's helpful, thank you. Let's turn back here or Martha will be hunting for us."

They turned toward the cottage, and Tim asked, "Do you preach the parable of building your house on sand and rock here?"

"No, I don't. Every house around here, with few exceptions, is built on rock. Knowing this, my parishioners could say they already have a firm foundation and need no further support. I don't tell them to be fishers of men, either, nor to cast their nets on the other side, or any other salt-water parables. I stick with stories like Zacchaeus the tax collector, or Lazarus who was four days dead. The wedding at Cana is always good for a laugh."

They were passing a small church with a steep roof and tall, narrow, stained-glass windows. "I'm preaching here on Sunday. You're welcome to attend."

"I'd love to, but our choir has two more Sundays of anthems before the summer break. And we are expecting a weekend guest."

"And then you and your organist are off to PEI."

"Yes. We're looking forward to it."

~

Back home, with a takeout order of fish and chips crisping in the oven, Tim opened a bottle of *Inattendu*, a mid-priced white, and poured a generous serving in a balloon glass. It was unexpectedly good.

He took it outdoors and walked on the flagstones to the bottom of the garden and back again. The flagstones had been unexpected. Mort Evers had been unexpected. *These good things deserve to be considered along with the unexpected discovery of last week. I'll celebrate the good things, and the bad things will eventually fall to the bottom, like lees in wine.*

He hoped that his weekend visitor would be another of the good things.

June 19: Houseguest

Saturday

Tim was looking forward to the diversion of hosting a guest, someone he wanted to know better, and also, he admitted, someone to proudly show his house and garden to. That was something new. He had never taken anyone to the parlour windows, pulled back the drapes, and gestured expansively toward the overgrown field.

He took his first espresso outdoors. The morning was dewy, fresh. He inhaled the scent of green, growing things. "Come on, tiny clover seeds, you can do it. Put down your roots before the starlings peck you all for breakfast."

Reviewing his plans for the day, Tim hesitated as he recalled last Saturday's fiasco. "Nothing I can do about that, though, is there? The anvil falls from the sky and Wile E Coyote is flattened beneath it, but he rises, snout bent a little, to chase the Roadrunner once again."

Checking that his phone was in his pocket, he embarked on his errands. First stop was the roadside emporium in town, displaying on the sidewalk a jumble of old furniture which a tattered sign referred to as "antiques".

He settled on a kitschy set of wobbly metal folding tables, with Olde Englande scenes on the trays. The proprietor "threw in" the storage rack.

In another store selling new patio furnishings, he picked up an assortment of lightweight and brightly-coloured folding chairs that they could use in the sunroom or the garden.

In the grocery store, he knew where the homemade pizza ingredients were located, so that part of shopping went quickly. He selected three well-marbled ribeye steaks for tomorrow, knowing Robert would agree to be the grillmaster. A real Caesar salad would go nicely: he selected anchovies, pine nuts, a block of Parmesan, and a head of romaine.

He wasn't sure about dessert. There might still be coals glowing in the little hibachi after dinner, but he didn't think of Evan as a toasted marshmallow sort of person. He compromised with a bag of chocolate-covered marshmallow cookies.

After the essential stop for wines, he took his finds home, noting that no police cars were in his driveway this time, nobody forbidding him to take his purchases into the house. Last Saturday's memory still rankled.

Tim knew the expression "retail therapy", but he hadn't known there could be so much enjoyment gained from spending so little. The bright chairs gave a party vibe to the sunroom, the barbecue station and, fifty steps away, the grove of trees.

On impulse, he went to the basement for the can of sky-blue paint he'd used on the sunroom ceiling, and took it, a stir-stick and a new brush to the woodshed. The label said it was interior/exterior paint. He hoped that was true, though if it flaked or faded, that would only add to the rustic charm.

He wrestled the grey metal cabinet away from the wall far enough that he could reach the spaced slats behind it, and slathered on the paint. It dried almost instantly, soaked into the untreated boards.

He pushed the cabinet back in place, and brushed a very light coat on the doors and drawer. It would be dry by tomorrow, when Robert would hold court there.

"Quit now, Tim. You've done enough."

After a quick lunch, he brought the electric fireplace and a lamp to the sunroom. He wiped down the metal tray tables and set up one to hold glasses and ice, and one for bottles. He had bought a bag of ice in case Evan wanted some with a cocktail. He cleaned the kitchen island, where he would perform his amazing feat of dough-tossing. He opened the guest-room window for the first time this year.

He liked the look of the blue hibachi cabinet and the multi-coloured chair in the woodshed. He took a bright towel from the kitchen linen drawer, and barbecue mitts and tools, added them to the station, and put lighter fluid and the bag of briquettes inside the cabinet.

Eventually there was nothing else to do but wait for Robert and Evan to arrive. He took the library book about the selfish giant to the chair in the woodshed, where he could keep an eye on the driveway.

~

Robert was the first to appear. "I thought I was late. Where's our guest?"

"I told him mid-afternoon, so when's that, three or four o'clock? It's after four now, so I expect him any minute. Get yourself settled and let me show you the latest improvements."

Robert was amused by the rattling tray tables, and the painted cooking corner and accoutrements. "It's great, Tim. You've accomplished a lot since you started reclaiming this area on Victoria Day."

At four forty-five, Tim phoned Evan's cell phone, but it went to voicemail. "He's likely on the highway and can't answer."

Tim and Robert sat in the sunroom. They always talked easily, but talking to fill in time felt a bit tedious. Finally, at a quarter past five, they heard a car in the driveway, and Tim went out to greet his guest.

"Hi, Evan! Welcome to my humble abode. Come on in. Pop your trunk and I'll get your bag. Robert's inside. I'll soon make my famous pizza."

"Hi, Tim. Thanks for inviting me," Evan said. He reached into the back seat to retrieve a small sports bag and a carton full of groceries. "Can we get these in the fridge?"

"Sure. Follow me. Robert, Evan's here!"

Tim cleared a space in the fridge, and stepped aside so Evan could take care of the items. "What you got there, Evan? You didn't need to—"

"Oh, I know, but I thought I'd like to make something, give you guys a break, okay?"

"Well...but...I'm making pizza...I have everything ready, we've just been waiting for you. It won't take long—"

"It's no problem. I'd really like to do it. This'll be something different. You fellas can just relax. It's all here, I just have to put it together. I'm sure you have lots of pans."

"If you insist." Tim struggled to sound lighthearted, but he didn't feel it. *Shake it off, Tim. It's only supper.*

"Let me show you to your room, Evan. Then we'll get this party started."

"We can do that later."

"Okay. Will you come out to meet Robert, then?"

Robert had remained in the sunroom. He smiled and stood to shake Evan's hand when Tim introduced them. "Nice to meet you, Evan. We're glad to have you here. Overnight visitors are rare."

"Thanks," Evan said. "I've heard good things about you."

"Let me show you around so you'll know where things are," Robert said. "We want you to feel at home. You saw the kitchen, of course, and the powder room is just over there. Your room is upstairs. Come on."

Evan followed Robert as he led the way to the stairs. "There's only one bathroom upstairs, but we'll likely be up and gone before you in the morning anyway, unless you're a dedicated churchgoer."

"You never know," Evan said.

"Either way is fine. Here's your room, these are your towels. Come on back down to the sunroom when you're ready and we'll have a glass of wine. We're dying of thirst!"

Robert went back down the stairs. Evan was right behind, holding a quart of scotch. "Mind if I have this?"

"Hey, whatever floats your boat," Tim said. "I'll get some ice. Do you take water as well?"

"Neat, thanks. No ice, no water."

"You're brave. Oh, wait, I have just the thing for that. Hang on."

Tim selected a glass from the china cupboard, rinsed and dried it in the kitchen, and brought it to the sunroom. "It's a Glencairn glass, designed to enhance your Scotch experience, I'm told; holds in the fumes or whatever they're called. It was a gift from someone who mistook me for a Scotch drinker."

Robert poured their wine, and when Evan had poured enough liquor in the glass to eliminate the chance of any fumes accumulating, Tim toasted: "Welcome, Evan. To good health."

They all quenched their thirsts.

"Evan has brought something to cook for our supper, Rob. Instead of pizza."

"Really? But I—you don't have to do that, Evan. We always have pizza on Saturdays." Robert was doing his best to change gears, seeing that he was going to lose his favourite Saturday treat. "But...what's on your mind?"

"You guys save your pizza. I'll make you my specialty. It's a seafood dish. I hope you like shrimp?"

Tim and Robert exchanged glances, but they were careful not to convey any signals, given that Evan was right there, and insistent. His offer to cook was an odd imposition, but neither of them could think of a way around it.

"We love shrimp," Robert said. "You haven't started the dough yet, have you, Tim?"

"It'll keep," diplomatic Tim replied. He knew they'd lost this round. "I'll help you find the pans you need, Evan. How long will it take?"

"Oh, not long at all. Let's relax first."

"Good plan. Excuse me for a moment."

Tim went to the kitchen and quickly cut up a plate of pepperoni, olives, and cheese, and brought it back to the sunroom with a container of toothpicks. "This'll tide us over till supper's ready."

The appetizers were a bad call. Evan was apparently in no hurry to cook, and the plate of bites took the edge off their hunger. It also increased Evan's thirst. His hosts kept up with him for a while, except they were drinking wine and Evan was downing a large quantity of straight Scotch.

The conversation was interesting enough, but Tim and Robert were on edge, and each could tell that the other was 'trying', not the way they liked to spend their social time.

It was approaching seven o'clock when Tim said, "Listen, Evan, I don't mean to be rude, but I really need to eat something. If you'd rather keep your seafood until tomorrow, that's okay: I can pop a pizza in the oven in no time."

"Oh, sorry, I forgot we're in the country now. Country-time. Not city-time. We eat at nine or later in the big city."

"Really?" Robert said with feigned surprise. "I live in the city. I hadn't heard that."

Evan stood, picked up the bottle of Scotch and his glass, and aimed himself through the door toward the kitchen. Tim and Robert stood and followed him.

"Mind if we watch?" Tim said. "We can help you find things. Let's play 'Just Ask Me'. Tell me the name of this dish, and we'll guess what pan or dish you need."

Robert rolled his eyes at Tim, taking advantage of being behind Evan's back for a moment.

"Creamy Shrimp Pasta."

Robert opened a cupboard door and produced a pot for the pasta, while Tim brought out a casserole dish. "This size good?"

Robert put the butter, which Evan had forgotten, on the counter. He had brought a partial bottle of Chardonnay for the sauce, and lots of cream and garlic. The kitchen filled with delicious aromas.

The wine drinkers had been enjoying an Italian Chianti, assuming they would have pizza. Knowing it would overwhelm the seafood, Tim selected an Italian white from the cupboard and stuck it in the freezer.

"What've you got there?" Robert asked.

"Another new one to try: *Qualcosa di sospetto.* It's supposed to pair well with seafood. Don't anyone let me forget it in the freezer."

"Evan, come outside for a moment," Tim said when the casserole had finally gone in the hot oven. "I want to show you my back garden, recently exhumed from years of neglect."

Robert gave Tim a warning glance at the 'exhumed' comment, and looked sidelong as Evan paused to top up his drink.

"Nice glass, isn't it?" Robert said when he saw Evan looking at him. "Interesting shape."

Evan displayed no interest in the bare backyard, nor in hearing about all the machinery that had recently been employed on it. He was unsteady on his feet, though less so than his hosts feared.

They came in and sat for dinner at the dining table. The crisp wine paired perfectly with the over-creamy and buttery shrimp dish.

The evening carried on well enough, though both Robert and Tim remained on edge. Aside from Evan's odd insistence on cooking, and his alarming thirst, he was polite, curious, and funny by times. But quite drunk.

Tim and Robert expected this evening might not end well, and they worried in advance. However, they were the hosts, and they did their best to draw their guest out by asking him questions about himself, his Shelburne roots, his career path, his interests.

He didn't want to discuss his roots, scorned his work at the newspaper, and couldn't name an interest outside of his job. His hosts joined in conversationally when they could.

Tim couldn't help but think of the first time they'd hosted Evelyn to a silly costume dinner and a movie. They'd laughed at themselves and the stiff actors in the movie, and had become fast friends.

This isn't like that, that's for sure. I wonder if Evan is drinking like this during the week? Was he fortified at our lunch in April? I didn't notice, and I didn't think to smell his breath. I hope he stays upright. I haven't had to put a drunk to bed since Mother's creepy gentlemen callers were around.

"You don't play a musical instrument, Evan?" Robert said.

"No, not me. I can't even play the field, ha-ha. But you play—music, I mean, ha-ha, no hanky-panky for you two, must be nice."

Robert cut Evan off. "Yes, we play the piano. Shall we, Tim?"

Tim went along with Robert's redirect. They moved to the parlour and Robert insisted that Tim join him on the bench. They attacked a few pieces for four hands, not well, but it was noisy and Evan applauded as they played and when they stopped.

"I must ask to be excused now" Robert said. "Tomorrow's a work day for me and I need my rest. You two carry on, don't worry about disturbing me. Thanks for dinner, Evan."

Tim played another piece, something easy, then abandoned the piano bench. He sat in the armchair opposite the sofa.

Evan left to go to the powder room and returned with another full glass. "You guys are lucky," he said.

"Yes, we are. Very lucky." Tim meant it wholeheartedly, but was unwilling to discuss his luck with Evan in his condition. "So, what do you think, Evan? Coming to church with us tomorrow?"

"What time?"

"It's from eleven to twelve. We'll leave here about ten or ten-fifteen. The big white church on Main Street at the bridge, right next door to *The Times* office."

"That's your newspaper, right? You're still on leave?"

"Yup, until January first. My year is nearly half gone already. I must say, it's going far better than I expected when I started out. Though I didn't expect much."

"In what way?"

"Oh, lots of ways, big and small. I've disconnected myself from the daily grind a bit, lifted my head to look around and smell the roses, and learned how to uncover some good stories."

"Yeah? Good for you. Will you go right back to it, then, next January? Or do you think you could use a highly skilled, well-educated editor like myself? I could run the paper and you could continue smelling those roses. I'm sure I'd like it better than what I'm doing now. You could make life easier for me, and I would make life easy for you."

"You're kidding, right? Dailies and weeklies are more different than alike, you know that. I know for sure I couldn't make the transition to your job: too many people, for starters—and too many papers. A new issue every day? Gaah! And you—you'd find our little community paper had too few people. We don't have departments, *per se*, we just have Ed, and James, and Jean, and Harold, you know?"

"That's risky."

"How so?"

"If one of them quits, that whole function is screwed."

"That's always a risk. It's happening right now, actually: one abscessed tooth is affecting several functions. Back in the day, I used to be able to fill in most of the positions because I'd done them all, but now they've gotten smart and techy with computer programs and digital cameras and the like, and I'll soon be left in the dust. Might be there already. Where do you go when you become irrelevant? To management!"

Tim found this quite funny. Evan managed a wan smile.

"I've been learning, leading, motivating. If I'm successful, my staff will love their jobs and stay as long as I keep out of their way. You're better off where you are, Evan. Keep your eye on your pension."

Evan excused himself to go upstairs. Tim removed their dishes from the dining table, and rinsed and loaded them in the dishwasher. Evan returned and retrieved his empty glass from the washer. He reached for the bottle to pour another.

"Easy there, buddy. Can I get you some water to thin that out a bit? Or make you a coffee?"

"Nope, thanks. I'm good. Do you have cable?"

"Cable? What's that? Just kidding. Sure, there's a TV in the den. I pay for cable every month but never watch it. Something you're interested in?" Tim glanced at the clock. "Late news?"

"Whatever's on. The late shows are good sometimes."

"Okay, let's wiggle the rabbit ears and see if we can tune them in."

Tim pressed buttons on the remote controls, but couldn't get the television to play.

"Let me," Evan said, and took the devices from him. The cable playlist appeared, and Evan scrolled through it to find a channel he wanted.

"D'you mind if we watch this for a bit?" he said, pushing a button. "Where's the sound?"

"Oh. I watch movies on the DVD player, but I often turn the sound way down. I don't care what they're saying most of the time. I listen to the theme music, and then watch horses galloping if it's a Western. Here, is that better?"

"Yup, thanks. Join me?"

"I think I'll call it a night, Evan. Those late shows don't help me sleep, but you stay up as long as you like. I'll leave the bathroom light on so you can find your way upstairs. Good night."

"Good night, Tim. Thanks for inviting me. Your house and property are really nice, and Robert is a super guy. You're both very lucky."

Robert stirred when Tim came into the bedroom. "Everything okay?"

"I guess so." Tim sighed. "Why couldn't it be easier?"

"Because it's people. That white wine was lovely. We'll get it again if we ever decide to serve cream and butter with a little bit of shrimp tossed in."

"Be nice, now."

"Oh, but I am. You said the label mentioned fish? Fish in Italian is *pescare*. What's it really mean?"

"You find the craziest things to keep you awake. *Qualcosa di sospetto* translates as 'something fishy'. Close enough."

June 20: Writing on the wall

Sunday

Tim heard the television blaring for a second or two sometime in the wee hours, and then it was off. He thought he heard Evan moving about downstairs, but sleep reclaimed his attention.

The guest room door was closed when they got up in the morning. They prepared for church as usual, except to keep their upstairs banter *sotto voce.* They were certain that Evan would be under the weather this morning, and chose to let him sleep it off.

"I'll make him dry toast and coffee," Tim whispered to Rob. "He can warm it in the microwave. I'll leave him a note."

"I'd like to burst a paper bag behind his rude head," Robert said in a regular voice, which didn't matter since Tim had closed the swinging kitchen doors. "That man is a danger to himself, and could have been to us, too, wandering around drunk."

"I was freaking out. That was a lot of booze."

"He must have been close to alcohol poisoning. If he comes back another time, we should get a stomach pump just in case. Living near the university campus, I see a lot of this sort of thing. It's sad. Something heavy is on his mind."

"You're right about that. He asked me for a job after you went to bed. I bet he's going to lose his. Probably saw the writing on the wall."

"*Mene, mene, tekel, upharsin.*"

"Beg pardon?"

"The writing on the wall. From the Old Testament Book of Daniel."

"Aren't you the biblical scholar this morning. How do you come by this knowledge, rabbi?"

"I probably sang it in a university choir. I don't remember the composer. Forgettable setting, as I recall."

"Do you also recall what the words mean?"

"'Numbered, numbered, weighed, divided'. Daniel said it meant that

God would destroy the Kingdom of Belshazzar, but how he arrived at that interpretation is not clear to me."

"Interesting. It would be frightening to have that written on your wall."

"Let's get to church, or I'll find out."

~

In the men's choir room, Spencer, the other regular volunteer tenor, sidled up to Tim and leaned in so close that Tim began to back away.

"What's up, Spencer? Do I have dandruff on my collar or something?"

"I don't mean to pry, Tim, but I was just wondering if everything is all right up at your house."

"It was when I left. Why do you ask?"

"The police report said they went up there to investigate something. I saw the yellow tape. I don't mean to be nosy. Just remember, if you ever need any help, you just call on me, okay?"

"Thanks. It was nothing. Somebody thought they found a—a noxious substance, and called the cops. I wasn't home at the time and didn't see it myself. Might have been a manure pile from the old farm. I was having the weeds cut. That exposed a lot of trash, most of which people threw there."

"Oh, I'm so glad to hear that, Tim."

"Thanks for caring, Spence."

During the sermon, Tim decided that if his fib to Spencer got him banished to hell, it would surely be at the outermost fringes, where he might have to clear weeds with a chewed-up shovel for eternity. There could be worse punishments. Like trying to deal with a headstrong yet deflated man like Evan.

I'm not a very good friend, though. When Robert mentioned alcohol poisoning I didn't run upstairs to check that Evan was still alive, did I? He'd better not be dead in the guest room. I do not want another interrogation with South River's finest.

~

"Okay, Rob, let's go home, if we must."

"You're not very charitable toward your friend."

"Maybe that irritating Father's Day sermon ticked me off. Either way, I'm entitled to my attitude. It's going to be a long afternoon."

He needn't have worried. Evan's car was not in the driveway. The toast and coffee were still on the island, untouched.

Tim went upstairs to look for Evan's body. The door to the guest room was open, and the bed had not been slept in.

A greeting card lay on the pillow: *Thanks for your great hospitality* was pre-printed on it in fancy script. It was not signed.

"No sign of him," Tim called down to Robert.

"I know where he spent the night," Robert called back from the sun-room. "Come on down."

The blue quilt on the sofa was scrunched up and the cushions were at one end, crumpled.

"He slept out here, the cheeky interloper. This sunroom is *my* territory and he didn't ask my permission, which I would have denied. I don't think he puked though, so that's something."

"Uh-oh. I better check the powder room." Tim rushed to the foyer and cautiously opened the door. "No sign of gastric distress. All clear!"

They met in the kitchen. "He's vanished without a trace. I'm grateful for that. I'm sorry, Rob. I could not have predicted that Evan's visit would start or end like it did."

"Don't be sorry on my account. I admit, last evening was a bit of a strain, and his insistence on cooking that artery-clogging thing was bizarre. I knew we'd lost the battle when we tried to entertain him on the piano. He's gone now, so we have this lovely sunny afternoon to ourselves. I'd call that a win, wouldn't you?"

"I guess," Tim said. "I got some lovely steaks for you to barbecue, and I plan to make a real Caesar salad. Is there anybody you'd like to invite for this feast?"

"Sure, how about...no. You know what? Let's not tempt fate. We tried, and we're none the worse for the experience. I will go for a walk or a drive wherever you say, and I will turn your juicy steaks into a taste of heaven while you make your salad. Let's continue to enjoy our sunroom and back garden on this beautiful day. It's the final day of Spring, so that's something to celebrate."

"Deal. Let's go to that nursery over Chester way. They have a great garden shop. I feel we need some whirligigs, don't you? Something to add motion or reflect the light, to attract the eye."

~

They found several items at the garden shop. The woodshed was awarded a tin star, which Tim nailed to the door of the tiny tool shed.

"Look! He was out here, too!" Robert exclaimed. Resting on the hibachi cabinet was the empty bottle of scotch and the Glencairn glass, none the worse for its travels.

Tim dropped the bottle in the recycle bin, then carried the delicate glass to the kitchen for later washing. There was no further discussion about Evan, though his odd behaviour stayed on Tim's mind.

They stuck new, brightly-painted wooden flowers on long bamboo stems into the raised garden beds. They had found a tiny chime with solid rods, a cheap import, which had a pleasant tinkle. Tim tacked it to the end of the woodshed closest to the former grave site.

There," he said. "This'll scatter any bad mojo and put an end to The Curse of the Wobbly Woodshed!"

The message light was flashing on the kitchen phone. Harold had called from the newspaper office to say that he had the list Tim had requested, he didn't know how useful it would be to him, but he had put it in a sealed envelope and slid it under Tim's upstairs door.

I hope he's gone home and has the right kind of antibiotics and painkillers. Poor fellow sounds miserable.

The warm salad and perfectly seared steaks were top notch, and the tray tables were adequate because the steaks were so tender. They were glad that they didn't have to share the meal with someone who was not in control of his taste buds.

"Not to complain unduly," Tim said, "but I would like to have a weekend go the way I envisioned it. Or less wrong, at least. I think I've earned the right to ask for that."

June 21: Equinox

Monday

They sat in the sunroom with morning cappuccinos and a basket of Martha Evers' reheated cinnamon rolls, and watched the rays of the sun —already up—move down from the treetops. The fresh morning air smelled of summer and cut grass.

"Happy Vernal Equinox, Rob." They clinked their mugs.

"Mm-hmm," Robert responded enthusiastically. He had a mouthful of one of the baked delicacies. "These are magic. Who'd you say made them?"

"Martha Evers. Her husband is Mort, the speaker at that prayer breakfast the mayor made me go to. The Right Reverend Doctor Mortimer Evers. I went out to Blue Rocks on Friday afternoon to join him for a walk. What a delightful man he is. No guff, straight talker. Such a great listener. Even when he's talking, you feel he's listening."

"That's quite a feat. Now *they* sound like people I'd like to meet. Why not invite them over sometime? After you've recovered from our recent guest, of course."

"Evan? I've recovered. I wanted to expand my circle of friends, but he's more a liability than a friend. He has a problem, but I'm not his fixer. I did notice one very odd thing, though."

"Odder than his behaviour? What could that be?"

"He didn't mention my beard. I wasn't looking for compliments, but it is a major change in my façade, and he didn't even blink. Definitely something wrong there, but I'll leave that to him."

"Maybe your handsomeness shocked him."

"I'll ignore that. I have more important mysteries to delve into. And I'm ready for summer. Today's the longest day, daylight-wise. I'm going to spend as much of it outdoors as I can. Can you?"

"It's unlikely. Lessons. Rehearsing. Arrangements for the Festival."

"Oh, yes, PEI. Do you realize we're going there next week? I can hardly wait."

"I'm eager to perform, and wound up as hell. I don't like the little im-pediments that get tossed in my way. As of Saturday noon they still hadn't located a page-turner, and they're obliged to provide one for me. Stuff like that."

"It'll be resolved."

"It better be, or else you'll be turning pages and pulling stops."

"What? Don't wind *me* up, now! Get on the horn to them and tell them they *must* do what you want! Just be outdoors when you call them. This day is a gift to all of us."

Robert tooted his horn from the driveway. "Don't forget about the choir's potluck thingy this Thursday. It's our final rehearsal, remember? I wasn't sure if you were paying attention when they discussed it last night."

~

Tim made an Americano and strolled in his yard with the mug of coffee in one hand and the last roll in the other. He admired the new leaves on the shrubs, and looked for buds that would be flowers soon. He leaned down to examine the evolution of the clover seeds, and thought he saw a tiny green sprout in the dark peat moss.

He thought about PEI. It would be a lovely time, especially after Robert's concert. Getting there, getting Robert there, hoping the accom-modations were as advertised, finding edible food at the right times, those were concerns but not worries, just steps to be taken with care.

His present life came to mind. *Harold's report is waiting for me: missing and murdered people in the past ten years. I'm not sure what I'll do with that info, but it will be a start. It's sad that there's even one name on the list.*

~

On the way downtown he remembered a vague dream detail from last night, again about a shovel. He couldn't tell what kind of shovel it was, but he saw his hands gripping it to dig in rocky ground. It was annoying.

~

As he approached the newspaper's building, he saw the surprise he'd been waiting for. The lower courses of shingles already bore the new colour, a creamy yellow. Tim breathed a sigh of relief. *They could have gone with any colour in the rainbow, or the whole rainbow again, and I wouldn't have said a word about it, but this is the* best! *I don't know what colour they plan for the trim, but I trust the art department, especially now.*

Everyone in the office seemed cheerful, and he smiled and waved as he strode past and up the stairs. Summer was a mood as well as a season.

Eagerly, he picked up Harold's large brown envelope from the floor and was about to tear it open when he heard footsteps on the stairs and Elaine Fong calling, "Tim, are you there?"

He opened the door to see Elaine, with James Olsen behind her, standing in the hallway, both wearing expressions he couldn't recall seeing before. Elaine said, "Baker Street," and proceeded to the room at the end of the hall by that name, followed meekly by James, who did not make eye contact with Tim.

Mystified, he followed them. Elaine closed the door behind them and indicated they should sit. She appeared close to tears, though James seemed closer, with red blotches on his freckled cheeks.

"What's—?" Tim began, but Elaine interrupted.

"Project Sweetland. After all our care and diligence to get the story right and guard our intel, it seems James here has just gone right up to the central figure and discussed the whole thing. We won't have a 'breaking news story' because it's broken already."

James had been resting his head on his folded arms on the table, but now he lifted his head to say, "I thought I was doing what I was supposed to do. I'm a reporter. I ask questions, right, Mister Brown? You told me in February to be curious, right? How'm I supposed to know what leads to follow and what not to—?"

"You had only to ask, James."

"Hold on," Tim interjected. "Can someone tell me what happen-ed, please? From the beginning?"

Elaine glanced at James and then looked away, and James took this as his signal to explain or defend himself.

"Remember last month when the developer, Eric MacIntosh, barged into this building and you guys had a shouting match?"

"Well..." Tim was about to defend the volume of his voice in that encounter, but decided that wasn't relevant at this moment. "Go on."

"He said that he was going to start his own newspaper to give you some competition, remember? And we all joked about it afterwards, me, Harold, Ed, even you, Miss Fong. We said we'd sign up to work there if he was going to take over. So anyway, I was wandering around one day, being curious like you told me to be, and I saw some carpenters working in a little building on the road upriver, an old storefront. I poked my head in the door, and there was Eric MacIntosh. At least I thought it was him, so I asked him if he was him."

"What did he say?"

"He said he was, and who was I? I said I was a freelance reporter—well, I might be soon if you fire me—looking for a story, and thought renovation of that old storefront might be interesting."

"What did he say?"

"He invited me to sit down right then and there. I was gob-smacked! He told me nearly everything we've been working so hard to discover—right from closing off public access to the old swimming hole on Crater Lake, moving the sharp turn in the road, clear-cutting the woods, surveying the lots and selling them to rich Americans! And he wasn't one bit shy about it!"

"Did you write this down?"

"You bet I did!"

Elaine nodded, sombrely. "He did. I've read his notes."

"And the thing is," James carried on, gaining enthusiasm, "he wasn't one bit ashamed! He didn't try to hide or excuse anything he did. In fact, I asked him a few times, 'Did you get permission?' and 'Was that legal?'"

"What'd he say?"

"He just laughed." James put a sneer on his face in imitation of Eric MacIntosh and said, "'Who's gonna stop me, boy? I'm on the county council, the town mayor's busy selling cars, the local newspaper's nothing but an advertising flyer. I'm bringing progress to this area, and the best way to do it is to do it. People will fall in line when they see what I'm doing.'"

"He said that?"

"Yup," James said.

"It's in his notes," Elaine said.

Tim stood and paced. "Why the long faces, then? Doesn't this prove our allegations? Along with the municipal and provincial employees who are willing to testify about coercion and fudged or missing records, having the perpetrator crow about his malfeasance pretty much locks it up, doesn't it?"

"Not quite," Elaine said. "I believe the information was obtained under false pretenses."

"What? Explain, please."

"You heard him. James introduced himself as a freelancer, which he was not. It was a lie."

"Did you tell him who you worked for, James?"

"N-not exactly. He asked me, 'Who'd you say you work for?' after he'd bragged all that stuff, kinda careless, and I said I'd heard rumours about a new newspaper starting up in the area and that's why I was freelancing; I changed it from 'a freelancer' to 'freelancing' so it wouldn't be a fib, see?"

"Very thin ice," Elaine said.

"Fine line," Tim said. "What did he say?"

"He said he had business connections with a newspaper, and he'd be interested in seeing my story. In fact, he said he was sure I'd be paid double if I'd give him an exclusive, which I took to mean that he was the new newspaper's owner. Isn't that a hoot? He wants to break the news story on our breaking news story!"

"Hilarious, James. What are your concerns, Miss Fong? False pretenses?"

"And misrepresentation. I don't think we can use a word of it. And I don't know how to move forward around this."

Elaine looked frightened, which Tim found especially disturbing since she had never exhibited any doubts since she had arrived as interim editor last winter. *What is wrong here? Why can't Elaine figure this out, and why must I? I know it's my newspaper, but I'm on sabbatical. And I don't have any experience or training in how to handle a big news story. I thought we were on the right track. What do we do now?*

"What do we do now? I'm asking both of you. James, you go first."

James sighed and shook his head. "I dunno. I didn't think I was doing anything wrong. I wasn't trespassing; he invited me in. He was happy to blab everything to me, I didn't have to say a word to encourage him. He thinks he's the best thing ever. I guess I shouldn't have said I was a freelancer at the beginning, but I didn't think he'd talk to me if I said I was with *The Times*, right?"

"That's the point, James—" Elaine began, but James interrupted her.

"Yeah, but when I said I was freelancing, he just asked if he could have the exclusive. He didn't care: I think he wanted to get his side of the story out, and he likely assumed that *The Times* would never give him the ink. Maybe that's why he was talking about starting his own rag. I think we'd be doing him a favour. It won't be the kind of favour he thinks he's going to get, not with the accusations of wrong-doing we're printing. I just don't think I did anything wrong. I guess I sound just like MacIntosh," James finished lamely.

"Okay, thank you, James. You believed you were doing the right thing, after you walked into the shop not expecting to find our Number One Crook inside. I hear you. Miss Fong has your notes? Will you leave them in her custody for a day or two, please?"

"Sure."

"Thank you, James. That'll be all for now."

James left the room, the red spots on his cheeks only slightly less bright.

Tim turned to Elaine. "Next steps?"

"I'm sorry, Tim. I don't really know what's next. I've never faced this before."

Tim nodded, and they both sat in silence for a moment.

Then he said, "Elaine, I've never faced this before either. If I make a decision, it'll be my best guess, but it won't be an educated guess, which is what we need now. You went to Journalism School: did any of your classes cover this situation, and if they didn't, shouldn't they have done? Why don't you call a friend for some advice? One of your colleagues, or a former prof? You may have forgotten about it in your excellent career of temporary assignments at community papers where the fine points of reportage don't come up very often. To me, this is more about good journalistic practice than the letter of the law. We can consult our lawyers, but let's get advice from the trenches first. Agreed?"

Slowly, Elaine nodded her assent, thanked Tim, and left the room.

He remained in Baker Street to gather his thoughts about what he had just seen and heard. *It does look like James stepped in doo-doo, but what bothers me just as much, or more, is Elaine's reaction. She's knocked right off her pins! I've never seen her like that. Is there something else going on there, I wonder.*

He sat and contemplated a while longer, then said to the empty room, "Well, I have nothing new to think about or with, so I might as well get back to my other challenge, where facts and hunches can flock together and nobody gets sued."

He walked back up the hall to his private office, and opened the envelope Harold had left for him.

The top page was a list of people who had been reported missing in the pages of *The Times* in the current decade: two in one year, none in another, one in another, and so on. Harold had noted where their files were located.

The rest of the pages appeared to have been copied from a federal government document. The preamble began with a daunting statement to the effect that tens of thousands of Canadians were reported missing every year in Canada, many were found within days, and many more joined the growing list of missing or murdered Canadians. Harold had printed a sample page, and on it he had written, "Let me know if you'd like me to try to print this off, as it could be too large a file to download. Better to request a copy sent?"

Look at that! If GB were still here, he'd no doubt get me the report from our own pages, but with no inkling about what was happening in the world outside our jurisdiction. Computers and the world wide web do have their advantages, I can see that.

He flipped back to the listing of people reported missing locally.

"They could have come from anywhere before they went missing here, and local people could disappear anywhere, not just here. If there truly are thousands of missing persons in the country, the police sure do have their work cut out for them, to try to match one of thousands to the remains discovered on my property. No wonder they were treating me as a potential murderer. If I were, and they'd let me slip through their fingers, they'd likely never find clues later to convict me, or even to identify the deceased. I see their motivation. I don't like how they went about it, but I can see why."

There were eleven entries on Harold's list in the decade from 1990 to present. The burial would have occurred sometime in there, but for a deep dive into the stats, more precise timing would be a valuable aid to the police.

"I can help there. I didn't think the precise date was necessary, but I do now. A little patience, please, whoever you are: I'll find out when you were buried, or close enough. With that info, the police can marshal national forces to find out who you were."

~

When Tim returned from a washroom break, his attention went immediately to the chart and line he realized he should have been working on all along. He grabbed the marker, sat in his chair and rolled to sit in front of the VICTIM column.

"That is the wrong question. I'm not the police. They'll search the records of missing persons and unsolved murders. That's beyond my jurisdiction. That body didn't do anything wrong, not to me. Who dug the grave, that's what I want to know. Who was out there on my property? Who dug that hole in my back garden? Who placed the body in the hole and then covered it up? Find that person, then you'll find your victim."

He focused on the DIGGER column and quickly sketched in the five Ws.

Tim sat back and considered the shovel that had disabled the powerful mower. "Was that the shovel our Digger used to do the dirty deed? It was well-hidden under years of weeds. Did he bring it with him? He didn't leave it on top of the grave, that'd defeat the purpose of burying a body if you wanted to hide it. And he wouldn't have run away carrying it."

In the WHAT line, he wrote *Shovel**. The asterisk was to denote uncertainty about whether the Shovel of Interest was the recently-mangled one, or whether that was just a coincidence.

WHEN came next. "If the ran-over shovel loses its asterisk of uncertainty and becomes the Shovel of Interest, that narrows down the timing, doesn't it? If the shovel had landed on my lawn when the 'Mow 'n' Plo' folks were cutting the grass, it would have stuck out like a—like a shovel —*on* the grass, not under thatch. They did not mow over it because it was not there then. Good point, Tim, keep going. Now, how long would the grass have to be un-mowed to hide a shovel? I know a little about a lot of things, but the rate of growth of grass is not one of them. Let's say two years, okay?"

He got up and paced.

"Two years from when, though? I know of three events that took place out there. Event One, the old woodshed collapsed under snow. Were they still mowing in the summers around then?"

He closed his eyes to visualize, but all he saw was deep snow.

"Let's say they were. So that's not when the shovel would've been tossed. Event Two: I had the new woodshed built, which turned out to be resting on some poor soul who never intended that as his final resting place. Was I paying for mowing then? I don't remember. Event Three: the new woodshed began to tilt, which seemed dangerous, so I began stacking wood in the sunporch, shame on me. Were they mowing then? No, they weren't. I do know that one. We were knee-deep in weeds by that time, and I was up to my ears in work here."

He sighed. *I know where the answers to these date questions are: in my cheque records. I always pay my personal bills sooner or later, and never in cash. I can't avoid it any longer. I'll have to dig in the file drawers for my bank records.*

Next was WHERE. "On my private property, that's where. Mister Gravedigger not only disposed of a person in a highly irregular manner, he did it while trespassing!" He wrote *Ppty of TB** on the line.

"Didn't I write myself a note to find the deed and look for the surveyor's pins? Why do I write things down if I don't follow up? Better put another asterisk here. I have no reason to doubt that it's my property, but the original parcel of land was sold in bits and pieces, so there might have been a jog somewhere. Maybe it belongs to the Exhibition and *I'm* the trespasser. Wouldn't that be fun?"

He left WHY alone, as he wasn't sure what this question was aiming for. "Why dig the grave, or why use the shovel, or why on my property, or why at that particular time, whenever it turns out to be? The only answer I'm sure of right now is that someone was dead, but why he was dead is not for me to say. *Why* is a good question, and there may be multiple answers, but first I have to look up my financial records, and the deed."

This was the most progress he'd made yet, and he was happy to leave it there for the day. He was surprised that it was early afternoon already. He'd worked right through lunch. Martha's cinnamon rolls had kept him alive since the early morning.

~

Once home, Tim spread peanut butter on a plate of saltines while the kettle boiled for tea. Thus fortified, he bravely ventured into the deepest, darkest recesses of the filing cabinet in his study, a room he rarely used.

He had evidently run out of file tabs some years ago. Records since the late eighties were just one long, compressed wodge of papers, shoved in as they arrived, not by subject, but hopefully chronologically, back to front.

The deed, however, wasn't a tax bill or any other kind of regular transaction. *I would have received the deed when the title was transferred from Mother to me. I removed her documents from this cabinet after her estate was finally settled. They're in a box somewhere, possibly in the attic. So, would the deed with my name on it be at the back of the drawer? Which drawer?*

He discovered the deed after an hour of searching. The property was his, bequeathed to him by the estate of Lucia Linda (Johnson) Brown.

"Thank you, Mother," he murmured.

The description in Appendix A had the standard wording, 'beginning at a stake at such-and-such a spot or marker, thence continuing in a compass direction so many feet or yards or chains or furlongs to another marker, and thence...'

He straightened his back. The sun was still high in the sky. It was still the first day of summer outside. *I'd better heed the advice I gave Rob and get outdoors.*

He took the deed and rummaged through the kitchen junk drawer for a tape measure. It was only eight feet long. *I'll be at it all night if I use that. What else do I have?*

Hanging on a nail in the basement stairway was a plastic bag containing a fifty-foot length of rope he'd once bought for a reason long forgotten. The bag had never been opened, so he was reassured that it was an accurate-enough measure.

First challenge was to find the starting point, a surveyor's mark at the sidewalk. He started looking at the edge of his paved driveway. *It has to be somewhere between here and the gatepost of the emergency exit road.* He couldn't see anything other than gravel and the weeds that grew in gravel despite being showered with salt in the winter.

This could take forever, since I don't have the surveying skills, nor a compass. But if there's a jog in the property line of concern to me, it wouldn't be out here anyway, it would be back along the area currently known to me as the burial site. There would be surveyor's marks.

Tim stepped around the gatepost and the Do Not Enter sign, and walked up the exhibition grounds' emergency exit lane. He couldn't recall ever being on this side of the line, having obeyed the sign and having no reason not to.

He walked along, half-heartedly looking for a survey marker, until he was parallel with the industrial building which his grove of trees camouflaged.

"If I was here, needing to bury a body..."

He looked around. Trees, grass, and topsoil had been scraped away in preparation for some industrial purpose Tim was not aware of. The exposed ground was hard and the opposite of fertile.

"I wouldn't think of digging over there without a backhoe, and that wouldn't be very surreptitious."

He swivelled around to face his property. "Over there would have looked like a field of weeds, indicating soft ground, much more inviting for digging. Also the last chance, as the lane ends in a locked gate."

Good work, Captain Obvious. I already know where the grave was. I don't have to prove that. I came out here looking for a property marker, but that's not one of my delving skills. I'll have to get a land surveyor for that job.

~

Tender bites of steak leftover from yesterday, and some of the Caesar salad, not as crisp now but still delicious, were his supper. He opened a bottle of "We're Always First, Mate!", a cheeky Australian red he'd bought solely for the label, to observe this first day of seasons all around the globe.

He took supper to the sunroom to meditate on his theories until the twilight finally faded to dark.

As Tim brushed his teeth in the upstairs bathroom, he peered out the tiny window overlooking the yard. All he could see was his own face, re-flected back.

Someone could be out there right now, quietly digging. I'd never know.

Then he said, "Oh, for heaven's sake."

Then he said, "Let's go see!"

Tim rushed down the stairs, grabbed a jacket without turning on the light in the foyer, and dashed into the unlit back yard. The sky was over-cast, but rather than increasing the night-time darkness, the cloud cover actually reflected light from the tall standards in the nearby parking lot.

He walked to the end of the woodshed and—more carefully now—re-traced his earlier path across the invisible property line to the evacu-ation lane, and turned around to face his property.

It was dark, but it wasn't pitch dark. He waited a few moments to al-low his eyes to adjust to the indirect light, and was soon able to see everything around him surprisingly clearly.

Looking out at night, it seems so black because I have the lights on in-side the house. Out here, it's dark enough to hide me and what I'm doing from anyone in the house, but light enough for me to see what I'm doing.

He was imagining the old woodshed that had been there that night when somebody had stood right where he was standing now, desperate to hide a body.

Yes, desperate, because nobody casually lugs a dead person around, do they? No, they're in a hurry. They see that old shed, looking very un-used. For sure nobody from the house had ever gone behind it. And the way it's angled, they can't see behind it from the house.

"I'll bury this body back here."

There was no fence to keep him out. He crossed onto his property as the trespasser would have done. In the dark-not-dark night, Tim became the trespasser.

Step by step, one action logically following another, he reasoned how, why, when, and what had transpired that fateful night, out behind the old woodshed.

When he came back inside the house, squinting against the light, he was certain that he knew everything but the names of those involved.

He'd done his job. He was quite willing to leave the rest to the police to discover, once they knew what he had deduced tonight.

June 22: Longest day

Tuesday

The sun rose at half-past five this morning, its budding light having blossomed over the sky even earlier.

Tim didn't want to miss a minute of this day, at least not at this end of it. He was up before five, writing and rewriting his discovery of *What* had happened behind the woodshed, and *How*, and *By Whom*. He was soon ready to copy it again, this time with a sheet of carbon paper in the foolscap to make a duplicate. He'd give the original to Detective Sergeant O'Neill and keep a copy for himself.

But before he did that, he wanted to see if he could get his hands on the mangled shovel, if it hadn't gone to the landfill to be ground to wood chips. He wasn't particularly interested in the business end of the shovel, just the handle, but he hoped the damaged blade would be attached in order to identify the handle.

He also wanted to narrow down the dates when the scenario he'd worked out last night would have happened. That wasn't as long a shot as he'd first feared. If he found the year, he'd get the weather reports for that summer, and find out when it had rained heavily.

He had convinced himself last night that whoever had trespassed onto his property and buried a body had done so in summer. Tim hadn't been permitted to look into the grave, but the police would know what kind of clothes the body had been wearing, if it came to that. There might be shoes, from which the age and sex of the victim should be easy to guess —if they hadn't been lost in whatever fatal event went before. There would be remnants of pants and a shirt, or a dress, he supposed.

He was willing to stake his reputation as a Delver and Private Researcher that there were no insulated boots, no heavy coat, no gloves or knitted hat.

Anyway, they couldn't have dug when the ground was frozen, December to February for sure, maybe another month on either side. I'll focus on the warm months of May to September, and I'll know what year when I find when I stopped paying for mowing.

Tim phoned Jake at Chester Basin Property Maintenance at six thirty. He didn't want to delay beyond then, for fear that Jake would out be pulling the starter cord on some machine after that.

"Jake."

"Good morning, Jake. Happy summer! It's Tim Brown calling you."

"Happy summer to you, too, Tim. It's a great day. We'll do a week's work today, if all goes well. I think Dana is heading to your front lawn. I'm checking everyone's assignments now."

"Great! Two quick questions, arising from events in my backyard. One is about the shovel that disabled the bushwhacker. Do you know where it went, where it is now?"

"The shovel? Gosh, I don't know, Tim. One of the guys likely picked it up with the garbage. Maybe Jocelyn? She raked up the cut stuff. Were you wanting it back? You'd be better off buying a whole new one."

"No—yes, I want it back if possible, but not to use. I want to show it to the cops. I'll ask Dana when he comes. One more quick question: you saw the remains, I believe?"

"A bit."

"Were there clothes? Can you describe what you saw?"

"A piece of a shirt, I think. Something plaid, maybe? Not much left of it, but I didn't dig around."

"I'm glad you didn't. You've been very helpful, Jake. I'll let you go to run the day. I'll look for Dana. The front lawn has grown so fast!"

~

Tim brought some empty wine cartons from the basement to the study. He loaded them with the contents of the top file drawer and carried the boxes to the sunroom. It didn't take as long as he'd feared to find the little cheque registers, four or five for each year.

Cheques paid to Mow 'n' Plow were what he was looking for, and he found some in the first bundle. He noted the amounts. The next bundle contained several stubs to the same company, for a slightly higher amount, and ditto the next.

He heard a truck in the driveway and went out to greet Dana.

"Good morning! How are you this bright morning?"

"Good, 'n' you?"

"Great, thanks. I have a question about the shovel you ran over here.

Do you know where it is now? I'm curious about something. Nothing to do with you."

"Yeah. I took it with me to the rental place when I returned the bush-whacker, to show them what I hit."

"Do you think they still have it?"

"Sure do. I was there the other day and they had it mounted on the wall."

"No kidding! On the wall?"

"Yeah. They got a sign under it that says 'Check before you Wreck' or something like that. Pretty funny."

"I must drop in to take a look at that. But you would save me a trip right now if you can answer this question: what kind of handle did it have? D-shaped, or a long, straight handle?"

"Not D-shaped. No, it was long-handled. Made it easier to miss, maybe."

"Thanks for your help, Dana. Carry on."

Tim returned to the sunroom and continued to sift through the bank records until he found what he wanted. He took another sheet of foolscap and began a list. He already knew what he believed, but he needed actual facts to encourage the detective to pay attention to him. Police weren't familiar with his work with hunches, and would scoff.

The foundation of his theory was the weather. That was why the grave hadn't been discovered. Why the digger had a raincoat. Why there had been no witnesses around.

To bolster that conjecture, Tim needed weather reports for the summer months in the years indicated by his bank records, when cheque amounts written to Mow 'n' Plow reduced because they ceased working in the back of the property.

He made a tuna sandwich and tea for lunch, and reviewed everything again, chronologically:

- ceased backyard mowing: spring 1992 onward
- old shed collapses: winter 1994
- new shed built: summer1995
  (have cq paying carpenter)
- new shed dangerous wobble: spring 1996-97
  (remaining wood at far end)
- wood stored in the sunroom: Stella recalls first time
  Xmas 1997
- new shed moved: June 1999

He had paid for backyard mowing only once in 1991, in late May, after which he had cancelled the service. So his theory about weeds hiding the shovel and the grave would be most plausible in 1993.

He dialed the library and asked to speak to Marlene Wentzell.

"Good afternoon, Marlene, it's Tim Brown. Happy Summer!"

"Same to you, Tim. It's a gorgeous day, too. How may I help you?"

"That's my favourite question, and here's my answer: how can I find on what days it rained, and how much, in the period of May to September, 1993?"

"Well, that certainly is a different request. I appreciate variety. Precipitation reports for that period would be in an almanac or weather archives. We have them here in the reference section. I can't let you take them out, but you are welcome to come down and have a look."

"I'm on my way! Oh, if I find what I'm looking for, can I make photocopies of the pertinent pages?"

"Absolutely, Tim. You're coming now? I'll put them out for you."

~

Tim told Marlene he'd been working on an old case he'd read about, to see if he could solve it. He said he had first attempted to guess and assume, getting nowhere. But once he began to put himself in the shoes of the person he sought, things started to make sense.

"People mostly do what people ordinarily do, don't they, Marlene? I mean, committing a crime isn't ordinary, but if you were going to, say, smother someone, you would likely grab a pillow and hold it, wouldn't you? Or a plastic bag?"

"Yes, I would, definitely," Marlene replied with a smile. "I would be an ordinary murderer. And I would surely be nabbed by you, because you seem to be practising ratiocination."

"Ratty-o what?"

The librarian reached for a well-worn dictionary, opened it to the word and turned the book so Tim could read it.

"'The process of exact thinking; a reasoned train of thought.' I did not know that word, but I like it! I'll use it as my guide henceforth. I was harassing myself in the winter with Oliver Wendell Holmes's advice to set my sails and not drift. But he didn't say what I was supposed to do after I got moving. I've crashed and bashed around, arriving at conclusions eventually, but this ratiocination is methodology gold! Thanks for the new word, Marlene, and for the weather data. Very helpful."

~

Tim now had weather conditions for the summer of 1993, copied from the almanac. He took the photocopied pages to the sunroom, where files were piled on two folding chairs, four of the wobbly tin tables, and the part of the sofa he hadn't been sitting on.

He was eager for this next stage, looking for the wettest periods in the five warmest months of 1993. According to his 'reasoned train of thought', one of those periods would reveal when the grave was dug.

When the sun finally set, he had his notes and recollections, he had the pertinent cheque books in order, he had the almanac with three likely and four less-likely dates circled. He had Harold's list of *The Times'* missing people, all in duplicate. He was ready to hand the pile over to the detective, who he hoped would be grateful for his help in solving the case. Maybe he'd even apologize for wrapping his house in yellow caution tape for no good reason.

If Tim was expecting gratitude from the detective, he wouldn't get it if he phoned him at this hour. He knew the police worked long hours and bored themselves silly following dead ends all the time. His revelation could wait until morning.

~

Tim knew he would sleep well. Soon, he could begin the process of forgetting the whole distressing affair. Gratitude from the police would come second after his own feelings of pride for having worked out the major clue: WHO buried the body.

"I've spent precious time supposing and considering all kinds of possibilities, but isn't that what all good detectives and Private Researchers and Delvers do? Sherlock Holmes' clients told him their troubles, then he'd sit in his Baker Street quarters, quietly supposing, with Doctor Watson sitting nearby."

But I misunderstood the nature of Sherlock's supposing: he was actually deep in ratiocination.

June 23: Ratiocination

Wednesday

"Good morning, Aunt Stella. Sorry for the early call, but I know you'll be up and away soon and I wanted to catch—"

"I'll be gone before you finish your preamble if you don't speed it up. What is it?"

"Do you have my shovel?"

"I beg your pardon?"

"My shovel. When Rob and I came to look at your shrubs in May, I took a short-handled shovel to dig out a little piece of root. I haven't seen it since. I wondered if I left it there somewhere."

"I wouldn't know. I'm never outside…well, I did go out to greet Aubrey a few times when he came with his crew. Come to think of it, there was a shovel leaning against the house near the garage door. I assumed it was Aubrey's."

"Where is it now?"

"Inside the garage. I didn't want to leave a weapon outside my house. Someone could use it to break in."

"Very wise of you. Shovels can be very dangerous, I hear. I apologize for leaving it. Would you mind putting it outside the garage door again? I'll come down for it right away. I want to dig a little."

"All right. Any repercussions from the recent events at your house?"

"No repercussions, thanks for asking, but I've been delving into it, and I believe I've discovered something the police will find very useful."

"I might have known. Be careful, Timothy. The police services want assistance from the public, but they don't look kindly on interference."

"Duly noted. Has Aubrey finished transforming your property into a horticultural showpiece?"

"Yes, quite. It's up to Mother Nature now, he says. Lovely man."

"I've been doing some transforming of my own here. I think you'll enjoy seeing it."

"You're cutting the weeds?"

"Yes, that's it. The weeds are gone. Thanks for the chat."

He had another very important phone call to make now, and he was pleased as Punch to be doing it.

"Good morning, Detective, I hope I'm not calling too early? It's Timothy Brown."

"Good morning, Mr Brown. What can I do for you?"

"I have some valuable information about the origin of the, ah, the grave in my backyard, which I want to share with you."

"Go ahead."

"It's more complicated than I can cover in a quick phone call. I have some personal records to show you, and a theory."

"A theory, eh? What's it based on?"

"I will tell you, Detective, but I'd like you to come to my place so I can walk you through it. I assume that you have not resolved the case yet."

"We have not."

"Then I'm certain that what I have to show and tell you will be very helpful. Would you be available this afternoon? Around two o'clock?"

The detective sighed. "Okay, Mr Brown. Unless something urgent comes up."

Tim punched the air like a boxer in the gym. *Bam-bam-bam. Boom! This is going to be such fun! I've got all the clues for them, clues I know they don't have.*

He made a double-shot cappuccino and took it to the sunroom to review yesterday's work. It was all there, step-by-step, if the detective would suspend disbelief until Tim completed his presentation. That was a big if, but he'd do his best to sell it.

He had slept well last night following his discoveries in the back garden. When he woke this morning, the puzzling dream of a shovel in his hands came to mind again. He'd been digging, but what caught his post-dream attention was where his hands had been placed—on a D-shaped handle, like the shovel he had taken to Stella's in early May.

He didn't think this shovel was involved in the case at hand, but he'd like to have it back to establish that there once had been a set of tools. The other shovel in the set, long missing, was now on the wall of the machine rental shop, serving as a warning.

He called *The Times'* photojournalist. "Good morning, James. How're you feeling today??"

"Not great, Mister Brown. I still don't think I—"

"Not to worry, James. We'll work it out. Miss Fong is consulting some people who can advise us. I like what you got from Eric MacIntosh, but I agree with her that we need to do it right or not use it. Hang in there. Right now, I need you to take a picture for me. I hear the noisy tires of your Jeep in the background, so I know you're on the prowl. Are you any-where near the rentals shop at Westhaver's Elbow?"

"Not far, actually. Why?"

"There's a broken shovel mounted on the wall behind the counter there, with a sign saying 'Don't Let This Be You' or something like that. I need a picture of it. Are you heading to the office?"

"I can be, yeah."

"Excellent. I'll come down to pick up an eight by ten print in about an hour. Thanks a bunch, James."

He boxed the air again.

He used the errand to Stella's as an excuse to pick up some fresh items at the bakery. It was impossible to tell if Stella was home as he drove past, as her double garage door was always down, but when he turned into her drive on the way back, his shovel was leaning against the door.

He admired the landscaping work on her property. The new shrubs were looking healthy, and the garden beds were showing green things and flowers.

He put the shovel in the trunk and drove back to town.

The newspaper office was in the usual Wednesday lull. Tim had no reason to engage with anyone there except James, who was just pulling his photo out of the printer.

"How's this, Mister Brown? That's a sad sight, isn't it?"

Tim examined the photo. "It certainly is, James. I'm glad it was only a machine that was injured. Thanks for your quick work on this."

Elaine Fong was in and her door was open. "How goes the battle?"

"I don't know yet. I was on the horn late into the evening. Thank good-ness the West is hours behind us."

"Yes, good. I was making phone calls by the dawn's early light this morning, and my attention to newspaper business was diverted. Is this week's issue good, though?"

"I think so. School graduation photos compensate for a lack of other items due to the resources we're giving to Project *Sss—if it hasn't been derailed, that is*. Will you attend the briefing this afternoon? Please?"

"Oh right, today is Wednesday. I have an important meeting at my house at two o'clock...but sure, I'll come. Might be late, but I'll be here."

Tim took two clipboards from the supply cabinet, and went home to wait.

~

Detective Sergeant O'Neil pulled up in a cruiser at ten past two. Tim met him in the driveway, carrying the clipboards. He found himself feeling resentful again at the sight of the uniform, so he didn't offer to shake hands.

"Thanks for coming, Detective. I won't tell you what I've discovered. I'd rather show you, okay? Just follow me over here and behind this gate. Watch your step, there's a little drainage ditch there."

They walked along the exhibition grounds' gravel lane until they were parallel to the recent grave site where Tim had begun his discoveries Monday night in the dark.

"So, my focus has been mostly on the gravedigger, how he came to dig a grave on my property, what tool he used, what the weather was like, and why the grave was discovered on the twelfth of June of this year. I don't know who was in the grave or how they became deceased. That's your territory, but I do have some records that may tell you where not to look."

The Detective's expression didn't change. *He's listening. He's looking around. That's good.*

"For starters, he came from this direction."

"Who did?"

"The gravedigger."

"Why from there?"

"Because the only other access to my backyard would be up my driveway, and that's unlikely when you're carrying a body. My hunch—and it's pretty much all hunches—is that he was driving a vehicle along this lane, likely searching for a place to dispose of the body. You can see how difficult that would be in the hard ground over there. But over here is a nice, soft, weedy spot behind a shed. Perfect, right?"

The detective looked across the lane, and back to where Tim was pointing.

"There's no fence to climb, no obstacle to a trespasser. But this body needs to be buried, not just dumped. Why? Well, my hunch is that nobody knows this victim is dead. They might know he's missing, but not dead. And as long as a death is not confirmed, you follows wouldn't look for it, right? Or not for a long time? It'd remain a missing person, possibly a runaway. It's evidently important that the body remain undiscoverable. So he needs to dig a hole."

"We already know there was a grave, right there."

"Let me continue, please. I need to show you the big picture."

Tim walked through the border of weeds to where the body had been buried.

"At that time—which I have determined was the summer of 1993, by the way, and I can show you the records I used to determine that—my grandfather's old woodshed was right here. It collapsed under snow that winter. It was similar to this one. Here, behind it, would be a perfect place to dig a quick grave. It was hidden from view from the house, and if the body was in the trunk of a vehicle, it wouldn't be too far to drag it. I came out here Monday night to walk through how it happened, and it was plenty dark and secluded. Now, how one unexpectedly acquires a body is your department, but a car accident comes to mind, like a hit and run, except in this case the driver scooped up the body before running off. Or maybe it wasn't accidental, but again, beyond the scope of my work. I do expect the pathologist found broken bones. Whatever led up to the death, a grave became essential, otherwise there would soon be an unholy stink, and flies. But I do know it was *not* premeditated. Why? Because he didn't bring a shovel. Now, come over here."

Tim led Detective O'Neill to the tool storage closet at the end of his woodshed and opened the door with the metal star nailed to it.

"This woodshed is a replica of the one that was there then, including this little tool closet. We even reproduced the rack for holding the shovels and rakes. Our suspect was in luck: here were shovels. I'll show you the shovel that he used in a moment."

Tim led O'Neill back to the burial site.

"As I was saying, the perp is busy now, digging with *my* shovel. But he's not an ignoramus when it comes to matters of turf, no sir. First, he takes the sod off in, well, in sods, and lays them aside, upside down, so he can put them neatly back on top when the deed is done, right? But what about the excess dirt when the body's filling in the cavity, huh? A heap of dirt piled up next to a sod-covered grave would be a dead giveaway, pardon the pun, so he has to get rid of the excess soil. I can attest and will swear that I never noticed a bare pile of extra soil anywhere when I came out to get an armload of wood for my fireplace. You with me?"

"Continue," the detective said.

"So, our digger could've just flung dirt over there into the lane as he dug, but that'd be risky, because what if he flung too much and didn't keep enough to fill it in level? The grave must be undetectable, no dip, no hump. He's in a hurry, too, naturally. He needs to get this done and get away *pronto*. So a person who knows to keep top sods for a lid also knows to put a cloth or a tarp down to hold the dirt. When he's finished the job, he scatters the remainder out there, shakes off the tarp, and floofs the weeds around the grave so it will look normal."

As he spoke, Tim mimed tossing the ground from the shovel, shaking out the tarp, and fluffing up the weeds.

"You may be wondering who goes around with no shovel, but with a tarp? Or a raincoat? You likely have a raincoat in your cruiser, don't you, Detective? Don't worry, I'm not accusing you. But I don't have a tarp or raincoat in my car. Men don't wear raincoats, generally speaking, but many women do. The more I think about it, the more I believe it was a raincoat, because I believe it was raining that night, and quite heavily, too. Rain would cause a person to be wearing a raincoat if he or she owned one, personally or as part of their work attire. It would come in very handy as a ground cover should one be needed unexpectedly. Pouring rain would help to wash away the dirt. A downpour could also contribute to accidentally hitting someone with your vehicle. We know how hard it is to see a person walking on our backroads and dark streets in the daytime, let alone on a rainy night."

"You're not kidding."

He's still with me. I'm amazed.

"You've been very kind to hang in while I spin my tale, Detective. I just have a few more points to suggest, resulting from my ratiocinations."

"Ratty old what?"

"Sorry. It's a new word I picked up. It means 'a reasoned train of thought' among other things. You do it, I'm sure, but you may not know the word. Anyway, the final detail: that shovel. Our suspect did a tidy job of planting the poor victim in the ground in the pouring rain, but the muddy shovel didn't go back in the tool shed, which might have been a dead giveaway if I'd been looking to use it. In fact, the shovel was just over there in my yard, lying face down under progressive years of thatch, lost to me and the world since 1993 until two weeks ago when my lawn contractors mowed over it."

Tim pointed to a red flag he'd stuck in the ground where the mower had met the shovel.

"We had two long-handled rakes but just one shorty shovel. Now I know where the matching long handled shovel had gotten to. This is that shovel now."

He handed O'Neil a clipboard and turned the pages to the photo James had taken just this morning.

"So, we have our shovel. Now—"

"Just a minute. The shovel in the photo came from that shed, you say?"

"From the old shed, yes."

"What if I say that you knew this shovel was there, and *you* came out here to get it to dig the grave?"

"Me? Please. You know darn well I'm not your digger, Detective. If I were, I wouldn't call you over to prove that the shovel used to dig the grave belonged to me, would I!"

"You might. Guilty people always try to act innocent."

"I'll ignore that. If you charge me, I'll respond to it then. Now, you may wonder why the shovel was way over there. I certainly did. I believe someone or something surprised the digger. Someone was coming. It was dark, so I'd guess there were headlights from an approaching vehicle. As you can see, this emergency evacuation lane curves around from the exhibition parking lot. A vehicle can get around the gate at that end even when it's closed. So, our digger is just finishing up, maybe even has wiped off the raincoat on the grass and put it on because it's raining cats and dogs, when he sees lights coming around the corner. He panics. It might be a cop car. *Biff* goes the shovel, right? A hasty javelin toss. He wipes his hands on the grass if they're muddy, and scrambles to get back in his vehicle before the intruder comes around the corner. *No time to lose!*"

Tim mimed the actions as he spoke these words, and the detective finally allowed a smile.

"This is where my trail runs cold, Detective. *Was* it a patrol car coming? Did the cop roll down the window and have a chat with the soaking-wet digger, who was by this time turning his vehicle around in the lane? Did he tell the cop he mistakenly thought he could drive to the street this way, didn't know there was a gate? Did the constable ask to see his licence? No, because it was pouring, the cop didn't want to get out, and our perp wasn't doing anything wrong that he could see except harmlessly trespassing on the evacuation route. The cop just told him to drive carefully and then followed him out to the exhibition grounds. If the digger's headlights were working as normal, the cop didn't have a reason to look for dents or damage to the front of the vehicle. Did the cop make a note of the vehicle's plate number? I don't know that. Perhaps you can find out. I wish I could be more helpful."

Tim lowered his arms to his side and waited, expectantly.

The detective gave him a wry smile. "That's quite a story, Mr Brown. But it's a story. It's possible, maybe even plausible, but it's all conjecture, a needle in a haystack. A car, on a dark road, on a rainy night, back in—

when did you say—eighty-seven?"

"Ninety-three. Oh, I forgot to show you this: on this clipboard are pages from the ninety-three weather almanac, showing when it rained between May and October that year; and by rain, I mean enough to wash away any dirt that might have called attention to a grave. There were plenty of rainy days, but not too many downpours like that for you to check out."

"And you think that I'm going to arrest someone for knowing how to dig a hole and keep the sods to put back on top? All the gardeners? Do you have their names, while you're making things up?"

"Isn't building a case like making things up, Detective? I don't have access to local and national police records, but I know you do. You are looking for two people: one is dead, and the other knows why. I wish I had found that someone was reported missing during one of those periods that year, but my newspaper's records don't show that. Our archival report is here on this page, see here. So, my hunch is whoever was in that grave is likely not missing from our jurisdiction. That might leave thousands of names for you to search, but perhaps a reasonable few for those dates in that year. Easier than searching for all people in all recorded time."

Tim was pleased to see the detective raise his eyebrows at Harold's neat report.

"We can produce a report like that for you anytime, by the way; you just have to ask. Now, there's a chance that my 'made up' patrol car might have reported a 'made up' licence plate in that same time period, who knows? You can look for that needle in your records haystack, or you can ignore it. I've done all I can do with the resources I have. You have all my notes and documents in that clipboard. My phone numbers are there, too, and I do expect to hear from you. Now, if you'll excuse me, I'm late for a meeting downtown. Thanks for coming, Detective."

As Tim drove away, he glanced back to see the detective flipping through the pages on the clipboard and walking through the weeds at the edge of the evacuation lane.

~

It was three-twenty when he knocked on the War Room door.

James opened it a crack, then wider when he saw it was Tim. He looked relieved.

"Timothy Brown has entered the room," Elaine said to Jean Naugler, who was shorthanding the proceedings.

"I apologize for my tardiness. Couldn't be helped."

He sat in an empty chair against the wall. All chairs at the table were occupied. "I do solemnly swear that I will keep everything confidential."

"Thank you, Tim. There are a few non-staff folks here whom you haven't met. You know Roger, our legal advisor, of course."

They nodded to each other.

"And this is Bruce Akerley, from the municipality, and Samantha Agger, from the provincial Department of Lands and Forests."

Tim nodded to each. "I'm surprised that we have these new guests, Madam Chair. You folks aren't officially representing your employers, I assume?"

"They are quietly observing on behalf of their employers," Elaine said. "Their role is to make certain that we don't make a false statement or imply anything that isn't a matter of public record, which we appreciate so very much, and I know you do, too. We've had privileged access to a number of conversations and documents, with the municipality and with the province. We will refer to "anonymous sources" but won't reveal our sources, of course."

"Sounds well thought out, Elaine. Please pretend I'm not here."

"And yet you are. So now, I must announce a change in expectations, mine, anyway. I was going to announce that next week's edition would carry our historic Breaking News story."

"Say what? Next Wednesday? You're ready?"

Several people sat up straight, especially *The Times*' staff.

"I thought we would be," Elaine said. "But something has come to light, some information and actions, which absolutely must be cleared and vetted before we can proceed. I have sent feelers out to...to everyone I can think of who can guide us to the best plan of action. But until I hear from them, I cannot proceed in confidence."

This landed like a brick around the table. Elaine didn't wait for the questions or discussion. "So, until I receive that information, I must adjourn this meeting now, and ask you to clear your schedules to re-convene tomorrow at the same time. Good day."

Elaine abruptly left the room, followed by James Olsen. Tim cleared his throat and stood to address the silent group.

"I'm sorry, everyone, this comes as almost as much of a surprise to me as it does to you. I say 'almost' because I am aware of the concern Miss Fong is referencing, and I respect her dedication to the highest journalistic standards. I have every confidence that we will have a decision on

Monday, so please carry on as though we are still on track; in the unlikely possibility that I'm wrong, we'll postpone until we can do this right. Thank you for coming today, and I hope to see you all here tomorrow."

~

Tim returned to his house with relief. The day had offered him several different kinds of tension, and as each was released, he felt lighter—and something else.

"I'm proud! I'm proud of myself. I figured out the gravedigger scenario and I know I'm right, or right enough that the cops should be able to stumble across the right clues. And I mean 'stumble' kindly. I know enough about trying to figure out a puzzle to know that the only people who really know what happened are the victim and the digger, but they're not talking. So everybody else has to narrow down their guesses until they're close enough. Then they'll arrest somebody with probable cause and try to prove their case in court. I've done the same thing, without the court. But today was the first time I was confident enough to tell my hunches to a real detective."

A chilled bottle of *Très Fier* seemed appropriate to drink a toast to himself in the sunroom.

I fully expect the Detective to solve the case using at least one of my clues. Though I wish he'd been into my scenario a little more.

Then there was that fierce and loyal team at the newspaper. He raised his glass again. "God love and protect you all. Go big or go home, indeed. I can talk brave because they're brave. What a team! What a newspaper! It has changed so much since I stepped away."

He thought about this statement for a moment, but it didn't lead where he wanted to follow, so he left it.

He boiled water in a saucepan to make Kraft Dinner again. He added a handful of frozen peas as a nod to nutrition, and a few shavings of parmesan cheese for flavour. It was delicious enough.

He finished the day at the piano, playing only pieces he knew well, so he could be his own appreciative audience, not a struggling amateur or a nervous presenter.

June 24: Pot luck

Thursday

Taking first coffee to the sunroom was now part of Tim's morning routine, even on a damp and dreary day like today. The back garden was greening at such a pace, he could almost see the tender shoots growing. He was tempted to stay and watch them do it, but he wanted to tie up as many loose ends as possible so he could go on vacation with an empty slate.

He heard Mrs Aquino pulling her cleaning tools in the back door, and his reverie ended.

"Good morning, Mrs A, how are you today?"

He didn't always wait for her response, and she didn't always give one, but today she smiled, and placed both hands on her chest to indicate the dress she was wearing underneath her two-tier apron. "New dress from home. Warm like Philippines now. Not cold."

"You look lovely, Mrs Aquino. Is this from your family?"

She smiled wider, and nodded. He knew she sent all of her excess earnings back home to her family. He was pleased to see that they showed their gratitude.

"Mrs A, I won't be here next Thursday or the week after. I'm going on vacation. I will need you to come next week, because I'll likely leave things in a mess. But the week after, there won't be anything different here except dust, so I don't know what you want to do. You certainly don't have to come early, but I'd like you to come in for an hour or so, just to be in the house, to check that everything's okay. I've written your cheque for two weeks, and I've left my phone number in case there's a problem. Okay?"

The tiny woman nodded and proceeded to her chores, still smiling.

~

Tim was looking forward to breakfast at the Daisy Café this morning. The table for two in the front window was unoccupied when he entered, and he stood beside it until Evelyn deigned to notice him. "You lost this morning, Hon? Your regular booth is over there."

"You're funny. If you don't have a reservation for this table, may I sit here today, just so I can look at my pretty yellow building, sparkling in the fog?"

"Let me clear these things away." She peered out the big window at the building next door. "You can't really see it from here, can you? Are you going to paint around the corners?"

"The corner trim, I guess. We'll leave the rest until I win the lottery. Do you know what colour you're going to paint the Daisy, yet?"

"We do, but we're not going to tell you."

"Why not?"

"Your Cindy Martin, now there's a barrel of laughs. She's got everyone on the street sworn to secrecy about their colours, to increase interest, she says. So, you'll see it when you see it. I think we're next, after they finish up with your place. They'll just shift the scaffolding over and go again."

The bell at the counter was summoning Evelyn. "What'll it be for you this morning?"

"The usual."

When Tim went to pay his bill, he was pleased to see the basket with fresh muffins, and a little display promoting Ed Garamond's gift certificates next to it. He took two muffins and paid the bill, then asked for twenty certificates.

"Twenty? They're five dollars each, Tim."

"Indeed. So here's a fresh hundred dollar bill, hardly used. Nice doing business with ya, ma'am."

In the office, Tim handed ten certificates to the receptionist. "Please make sure the painters get one each, Mrs Rafuse."

"Oh, I will, sir. That's very generous of you. I'll tell them they're from you."

"I'd rather you just give them out on behalf of *The Times*. They'd like that better, I think."

He went to Ed Garamond's cubicle and thanked him for the design work. "You may have printed yourself a lifetime supply of muffins so I won't give you one of mine, but do ask me for one if you get hungry."

Elaine Fong's door was ajar, so he poked his head in. "Are we being visited by the HR people tomorrow morning?"

"Yes, darn it—oops, that was unguarded, sorry. But sincere. It's just that Project *Sss* is taking all my brain power. We will be entertaining Mademoiselle Stephanie Duplessis-Lachance."

"Can you repeat that?"

"I doubt it. She's coming at eleven, and I really, really will appreciate your attendance. I know you're on sabbatical, but I would personally pay to have you helicoptered back from the Sahara or the Aztec ruins for this. I support HR principles, but their careful language makes me itchy."

"I shall direct my pilot to drop me off at eleven tomorrow morning for the express purpose of helping you hold your tongue, if you'll do the same for me. Next: what is my role with regard to the Big Story? When can I read the columns before they go to print?"

"You should plan to hang around here on Monday afternoon or evening. Pick up your copy of the records from Harold and have a good review of them before Monday so you're not asking questions we answered long ago."

"Will do. That is all. Oh, here: please accept this gift certificate for a muffin from next door, with my compliments. I gave a bunch to Mrs Rafuse to give to the workers outside. It would be a very nice gesture if the newspaper's interim editor purchased certificates for each of our staff, and gave them out on Tuesday or Wednesday. On your expense account, of course. Up to you. I'm going upstairs now. Cheerio."

~

Tim looked at the sheets on the walls that chronicled his quandary following the discovery of human remains almost two weeks ago. He had felt so offended.

"It was obvious that I wasn't guilty. Damn right I was offended. Locked out of my own home for two nights. Yellow tape all over the place. I know people saw it. I'm surprised nobody said anything about it, only Spencer. Maybe they were waiting to read about it in the paper. They surely will, just as soon as the detective follows my hunches and finds that trespassing gravedigger."

He was tempted to take the sheets off the wall and roll them up right now, but he hesitated. There wasn't anything that he could circle with a red marker to indicate a conclusion. He'd wait until the detective agreed that he was right.

He earnestly hoped that Elaine had secured a conclusion to the new wrinkle in the Project Sweetland case. He knew which way he was leaning, but he also knew he was a lifetime amateur when it came to the finer points of journalism.

Hearing footsteps on the stairs, Tim left his room to join the throng assembling again in the War Room. As far as he could tell, everyone from yesterday had returned.

James Olsen was still glum, but also carried an air of belligerence rather than defeat. Elaine Fong looked like she had spent the night fully-clothed, likely on the phone across the country, while replacing her red blood cells with caffeine.

"Good afternoon, everyone. I'm sorry I had to ask you to reschedule, and I thank you for returning today. Regrettably, I don't have an iron-clad decision to share with you yet, but I am prepared to share the broad strokes of what has caused my concern and this delay."

Elaine began to re-tell James' account of his encounter with the Developer In Question.

"Miss Fong, can I tell it, please?"

Elaine nodded, and James carried on. His story was consistent, Tim noted, and his storytelling was succinct. *He's come a long way this year. I hope we can hold on to him.*

The people assembled around the table were incredulous as the story unfolded.

"He confessed! He's made our case! Congratulations, James!"

"No, no, not congratulations, I'm afraid," Elaine overruled. Tim noticed her hands were shaking. "There is a strong possibility that none of what James has recorded will be admissible.

Hear me out," she said against rising voices from staff and guests alike. "If it can be determined that James misrepresented himself or misled Mr MacIntosh—inadvertently, to be sure—then we would be the target of a lawsuit that would ultimately hand our asses to him on a silver platter."

"I can't afford to lose my job. I already have nightmares about MacIntosh threatening me if I didn't do his dirty work. This is nuts! I'm outta here." This from one of the civil servants who had been persuaded to "lose" some paperwork for the developer. He hastily left the room. Elaine called to him in the hallway, but he didn't stop and she didn't pursue.

"I'm so sorry, everyone," Elaine said after she had closed the door again, her voice shaky. "I want to tell you…I contacted a number of experts in this area of journalism, and they couldn't give me their approval to proceed right away. I insisted that we need the facts, not just opinions. I have been assured that we will hear within a day or two. Until then—"

"Until then, everyone, please continue working as you were." Tim stood and shuffled around the table to stand beside Elaine. "James, that includes you: write up your encounter with Mr MacIntosh, and make it your best ever. Find a photograph of him. I suggest his County Council election campaign; don't try for a stealth shot of him. Talk with Layout to determine how many column inches you can have. We—I mean you all— have worked too hard for too long for us to toss this story aside. We were good to go before James's encounter came to light, so I see no reason why we can't continue on that track. If we can add James' interview, so much the better. Right, Miss Fong?"

Elaine had the demeanour of one climbing to the gallows. "Not quite right, Mister Brown. My advisors have informed me that we owe the subject of our revelations an opportunity to comment, repudiate, defend himself, and should print that in the same issue. We didn't do that, and I take full responsibility for that serious omission."

"So we can use my story, then?"

"No, James, or I should say I don't know, or I doubt it. The harmless little ruse you used about being a freelancer might have thrown the whole encounter into the dumpster or worse, since that was a falsehood. We can't go back and try again, above-board this time."

"Okay, let's adjourn for today," Tim said. "Everyone, please carry on, as I said. Miss Fong, when do you anticipate we will have a ruling from your advisors? Tomorrow? Monday? Let's say Monday; that should be plenty of time. This is simply an attempt at good journalism smelling like a ruse. We need to be on the right side of all that, and I'm sure we will be. Adjourned until Monday at three."

He grasped Elaine's hand as though in a handshake, pulled her in close, and leaned down to whisper, "Courage, my friend. You are still our leader, and you will not lead us astray."

He quickly returned to his room to lock the door, and made a hasty exit to his car.

~

Tim made a quick stop at the store to get something for supper and a few packs of flowers. He wanted to use that shovel with the D-handle to plant them in one of the garden beds out front.

Suddenly, out of the blue, he remembered about the choir's potluck dinner.

It's tonight! What am I supposed to take? Why didn't I pay attention? I suppose I was still preoccupied with my rights and freedoms. What'll I make? There'll be plenty of food there anyway, there always is. But I can't show up with nothing.

At this moment, he was passing through the aisle with boxes of pasta, and looked no farther. He picked up the ingredients for his dish, and a small container of cooked chicken drumsticks as their supper to hold them through tonight's short rehearsal.

At home, he set the flowers on the garden plot in their containers. "No time to fuss with you today," he told them, "but I assure you, you will be planted tomorrow." They looked nice there already.

When Robert arrived, Tim's dish was bubbling in the oven. "What delicious dinner is that I smell?" Robert asked.

"One of your favourites, according to you."

Robert turned on the oven light to see. "Macaroni and cheese? Oh, I'm looking forward to this! Wait—you're not taking this to the potluck, are you?"

"I certainly am. Why?"

"I don't want to share it, that's why. I want it all for myself. What are these things? Can't we take these drumsticks instead?"

"No, we cannot, silly man. Now you sit right there and gnaw on that cold chicken and count your blessings. Stick close to me and be ready to get your serving when I set it out tonight. I'll take a couple bottles of wine, too, and I hope the church roof won't fall in. We need wine to toast the end of a fabulous season of music, thanks to you."

~

Tim's macaroni dish was excellent. Many choir members knew how to make it, of course, having been raised on some version of it. Tim hadn't skimped on the cream and Parmesan cheese, which gave it an extra kick along with the paprika. Others had brought wine as well.

The minister dropped by for a moment, shared a small glass with them, and praised their fine ministry of music under the leadership of Dr Kirk. The choir president presented Robert with a salt and pepper shaker set with a musical motif, made by a local ceramicist. Robert thanked the choir for their devotion to musical excellence, adding that it was the most rewarding pursuit he could think of in life.

He asked the choristers to be kind and helpful to the summer student organist, who would make an appearance this Sunday morning and whenever he was required to be elsewhere this summer. She was quick on the uptake, he said, and would be looking to the choir members for signals. There were no Thursday rehearsals in July and August, but he encouraged the most faithful of the choir to come to church a half hour earlier than usual to help choose an anthem if enough of them were there to perform one.

The church's dishes were washed and put away, tables and chairs were stacked, and the last group to leave turned out the lights. It had been a big commitment to attend rehearsals and church services every week all year, plus concerts. Nobody would deny having wished for a night or morning off once in a while, but now that they would be separated from their chosen musical expression for two months, they were a little sad.

~

"That went well, Rob, didn't you think?" Tim meant the rehearsal, the social time, the food, the speeches, the evening.

"Humph. I got *one* scoop of your mac 'n' cheese. I wanted more."

"Your powers of concentration are amazing, Dr Kirk, but sometimes you concentrate on the wrong things!"

"Macaroni and cheese is never wrong. It was delicious, and now that I know you can make it so well, I will concentrate on it until you make it again."

"And the rest of the evening?"

"It was good. The choir is singing well, and they like the music I present to them, so I find the time worthwhile. I'd keep on going all summer, but I know they want a break. It'll be good for me, too."

As they were preparing for bed, Robert asked, "Any word from our elusive guest?"

"None. Maybe Evan didn't think his behaviour was rude. I'm not fussing, but a word of apology or amends would be nice. He did bring food, so he possibly thought he was generous and we were ingrates—if he has any memory of it at all. I don't like icky situations like that."

"Any word from the men in uniform about the back garden mystery?"

"No, but *they* heard from *me*. I determined when it *could* have happened, what kind of person *might* have done it, even got it down to *likely* weather conditions at the time. I had the detective over here yesterday to walk him through it. All he has to do now is look for a person reported missing during certain rainy periods in 1993."

"That's impressive. Was he impressed?"

"Couldn't tell. But I fully expect to hear from him soon. Or I'll keep asking."

"One last question: you forgot about the pot luck, didn't you?"

"Uh, yes, nearly. What tipped you off?"

"You looked so guilty when I came in this afternoon. When you're guilty, you're so transparent. When you're not guilty, you're wonderfully indignant. The detective should just ask me."

June 25: Getting and doing

Friday

Robert, the barista on duty this morning, delivered their decorated lattés to the colourful tin tables in the sunroom. Their eyes were on the fresh green backyard in the early morning light, and their minds were on their trip to the 'Garden of the Gulf'.

"Next week, Rob! My first ever real vacation starts in six days, not counting today. The timing couldn't be worse, to tell you the truth. I've been lighting little candles in the past weeks and months, and they're going to burst into one great conflagration next week."

"Sounds like a great time to skip town. Let your staff handle it, Tim. You're on leave, remember? You're up the Orinoco with a broken paddle and can't get back. You'll really enjoy it, including a stellar concert by an almost-famous organist a week from tomorrow. You know I don't like this period very much, leading up to a concert. I know the works, I've memorized the devil out of them, I know the fingerings and the stops and all that—so much so that now they're playing all the time in my head. I'm hearing the Sweelinck fugue right now. It's madness!"

"It seems wonky, doesn't it? We're so looking forward to going, but we each have misgivings."

They sipped their coffees.

"We're going, of course. Just for the record."

Robert nodded. It would be unthinkable for him to cancel a concert for any reason other than his own death.

"Say, Rob, would you like me to invite—?"

"People for dinner on Sunday? I'd love it. That'd change my mental channel, I'm sure. Is that what you were going to say?"

"You read my mind, but only after I read yours. I don't know who's available on short notice, but I'll go door-to-door, if need be. All you want is bodies, right?"

"Preferably interesting ones, nobody pushy or too thirsty, if you know what I mean."

"I sure do."

"Let me know what you get in terms of fish, flesh, or fowl, and I will make my plan of attack for Sunday. I like it!"

"Happy to aid and abet you. I'll pick up party drinks. Canada Day is next Thursday. We could observe it in advance, if that interests you?"

"Sure! Strawberry shortcake? And maple syrup drizzled over ribs on the grill. That hibachi is small for any volume of food. Do you think you could pick up another one? Just the same size. Two will fit on that cabinet. I can keep two cooking surfaces going at different stages. Okay, I have a vision now. Get fresh greens, too, for a little side-salady thing. And some bamboo skewers. Scallops, if they're fresh. And limes."

After Robert set out on his commute, Tim went out to the front lawn to plant the flowers he'd bought yesterday. He alternated marigolds with pansies in a semi-circle facing the street. These were to tell passers-by that this house was occupied, not abandoned.

He dug a shallow trench with the shovel, a too-large tool for the job, but that was all he had. Once the soft plugs were placed in their trench and covered, the flowers looked quite attractive, if a bit droopy. They needed water.

"'With what shall I fetch it, dear Liza, dear Liza?'" he sang. "'With a bucket, dear Henry, dear Henry, dear Henry, with a bucket.'"

He filled a bucket with water and dipped it out with a saucepan. It was a bit sloppy. "I must buy a watering can."

He continued to hum and sing the Harry Belafonte song as he scrubbed his hands in the kitchen sink. He made another coffee and sat to write a GET/ DO list:

GET
- watering can - soon
- small garden tools - ditto
- hibachi - today (before Sunday)
- Canada Day decorations
- bamboo skewers
- maple syrup
- paper plates
- groceries

DO
- read Project Sweetland reports - tonight
- proofread Breaking News - Tuesday
- invite guests - TODAY!!
- clean out car - Monday
- wash/clean car - ditto
- get gas/check oil - Tues
- plan clothes for trip - Sat

Not so bad. I can do this. I have five days. I just have to pay attention to this list so the right things get done at the right time.

Tim put his phone in his pocket and set out to get a second hibachi and the bamboo skewers. *Check and check.* He picked up a spare bag of charcoal as well.

He selected a bright green watering can, a set of hand tools, a foam rubber mat for kneeling, and a can of bug repellent. *Check and check and then some.*

He drove downtown. Evelyn's hand was in the window of the Daisy Café, removing the muffins sign.

He opened the door. "Why are you taking that sign in?"

"Because we sold out, that's why, thanks to you and your gift certificates. I've got another batch in the oven now. I told them I'd put the sign out when they're ready."

"Who them?"

"Everybody, you silly bugger. The painters, your staff, not to mention my regular customers. They're going like—you know."

"Hotcakes? Ha! I mean, is that good? What's Kenny think?"

"Kenny's happy. We both are, but I gotta figure out a better way to do this. I can't be making a single batch from scratch all the time, or even a double batch. I'm going to work on it on the weekend. I want to make a bucket of batter so I can just scoop out what I need."

"I knew you were smart. Are they priced right? Are you making money?"

"I think so. Our idea was that the muffins would sell themselves without me waiting table. We don't want to run out and don't want leftovers, so we're learning how many to make. I think the scoop and bucket will work."

"Excellent. I'll get out of your hair. May I call you tonight?"

"Sure can. Gotta run now."

Tim went one building to his own front door, stopping for a moment to admire the glow of fresh yellow paint. The atmosphere inside the office was quiet, focused. Heads lifted when he entered the building, and then lowered again when they saw it was him.

"People seem nervous today, Mrs Rafuse."

"Yes, sir. They're working on something special. I've been instructed not to permit visitors to wander in without an appointment today."

"Excellent! I have an appointment."

"Yes, you're on my list. With Miss Fong at eleven. And two others? I can't say their names. They're French."

"May I see your list, please? Ah, yes, it's just one person, Mademoiselle Duplessis-Lachance. Just call her 'Miss' and you'll be safe."

"Oh, thank you, sir. I'll do that."

Elaine's door was closed. He would wait, taking the opportunity to observe the bees in the hive.

A fashionably-dressed woman entered the front door: their guest with the double-barrelled surname. He tapped on Elaine's door, opened it and said, "She's here."

In the moment it took for this woman to be met by the receptionist and escorted toward him, Tim saw the heads in the hive lift and remain lifted. This visitor was drop-dead gorgeous.

Her bearing was worthy of a runway model; she simply glided across the floor on her four-inch black heels. She wore a fitted, two-piece grey suit and white vee-necked blouse, and her dark hair was pulled into a tight bun. It was a conservative outfit, but there was nothing conservative about her or the bright red lipstick on her full lips.

After introductions and handshakes, Elaine said, "Thank you for coming, Miss Duplessis-Lachance. We don't have a Human Resources office or officer, but we acknowledge that formal HR processes would be good for the firm. We are mindful of how our employees are treated, by each other and by management. We may not conform to all current procedures, but we would like to be aware of them so we can make any reasonable and necessary accommodations. Your firm was recommended to help us."

"*Merçi*, madame, monsieur. I am very pleased to present our resources to you today. Our clients are often unaware of what they 'ave overlooked, especially older, family-owned firms. Times change, and what was acceptable in the past may be unfair, offensive, or even illegal in the present. Our services should not be considered an expense, but rather the avoidance of harm and related penalties, which will always be more expensive and very uncomfortable."

"You're referring to matters of racism, sexism, that sort of thing?" Elaine asked.

"*Bien sûr*. Also of religion, ethnicity, sexuality, disability, gender equality, matters of dress, personal safety and so on. Coming to work to earn a living should not require an employee to sacrifice personal rights, freedoms or dignity."

"Of course," Tim said, "though sometimes we ask for extra effort or overtime from some employees. Nobody has objected so far."

"Then you are very fortunate, *monsieur*, but your employees are not, if their only option is to agree. If they earn more pay, but not extra pay, then they are not rewarded for their effort on your behalf. If their employment contract describes the conditions that must be met—on both sides—then everyone can operate accordingly. I'm sure what you've been doing is done in good faith, but what you 'ave *not* been doing is what will give you grief. Your employees are not unionized?"

"Correct," Elaine responded, "but we've heard rumours."

"And behind rumours are conversations. Perhaps you called me just in time."

Tim sighed. "Do you work for everyone, Miss Duplessis-Lachance, or just management, or—?"

"We work for whomever pays our retainer. That would be you in this case, as the employees are not organized at this time. We can guide you through that process so that it is the least painful for everyone. Unionizing, at its worst, is done to punish a bad employer."

"And at best—if there is a best?"

"Working *ensemble* is always best for everyone. A strong union would strengthen your workforce, perhaps even give you pride. Newspapers share a long history with unions. We can guide management *and* labour to ensure that the relationship is the best it can be. And, of course, if we are proactive with HR measures, union talk may subside. That does happen sometimes."

"It does? Well, there's an incentive. Do you have some literature to leave with us, an outline of what services you provide, and your retainer? We will give it attention, I assure you."

"Our services are outlined in these documents. After you've read them, please invite me to return, and we will discuss our retainer when we understand what you want to accomplish."

"Given an employer's cooperation," Elaine said, "are you always successful?"

"Ah, that is a popular question. Human Resources, if done properly, does not work in binary ways such as success and failure, good and bad. We are dealing with humans, and humans are emotional creatures with endless variety. I will guarantee that our work will always result in a better work experience for all parties, if all parties engage honestly."

Tim escorted their guest back to the foyer and returned to Elaine's office. Both were glum.

"I will read these pretty brochures, but I'm not taking them on vacation with me."

"We can't do anything right now, anyway. We'll be inundated with the response to Project *Sss*."

"She's a persuasive salesperson," Tim said. "She kind of reminds me of the mafia: 'Pay us to keep da bad guys away, or we'll be da bad guys.'"

"I agree, but we do have to investigate what she's talking about. If anybody complains about working conditions, we can now say we're working on it, right?"

"Only just, but sure, use it if you're cornered. By the way, we discussed hiring a security guard whenever the story breaks, we hope next week. I'm reluctantly in favour. But no guns."

"I booked security for two weeks starting next Wednesday. I stipulated no weapons."

"Thanks, Elaine. I'll leave you to do your above-and-beyond-the-contract tasks now. Oh, one last question: are you and Roger, uh, open to the public yet? To the staff, in particular?"

"Not at the moment. Why?"

"I'm having an early Canada Day gathering Sunday afternoon. Robert's doing the grilling, so it'll be good. I'd love to have you and Roger there, or just you."

"I'd love to come, Tim, but not at this time. Thanks anyway.."

"Next time. I wanted to commend you on the high-placed resources you pulled in for Sweetland."

"I approached them because I wanted to get it right. Then they wanted to help us get it right. As you have seen, James' sleuthing may have tossed it all away, but why, oh, why didn't I send him out in the first place to do it right?"

"Water under the bridge. You've got people on it and I'm betting on them to make it right."

He went to Harold's cubicle. "Agent Double-oh Brown reporting for any dispatches, sir."

"Stand by for printing," Harold responded.

While the printer hummed and chugged, Tim said, "I've been thinking about scattering GB's ashes. In the river this weekend seems like the right place and time. Do you think any of the staff who knew him would be interested?"

"Gosh, I don't know. I've never been to anything like that. What's involved?"

"Opening the urn and turning it upside down? That's all I plan to do. We've had the funeral already. It was a good one."

"What time? Where?"

"I like the idea of going at sunrise to the old bridge, because it's close to here where he worked for so many years. That seems like enough ceremony. Five-thirty tomorrow morning."

"Do you want me to tell you now?"

"Not at all. Come or stay home, as you wish."

"I'll pass the word. I just might come."

Ed Garamond's cubicle wasn't far away. "Ed, next door greatly appreciates your certificates. They're selling out of muffins."

Ed pointed to a brown paper bag under his desk. "I've got my supply to take home. My wife insists."

"I came over for another reason. You recall I mentioned GB's ashes?"

"Oh, right. I didn't—"

"No worries. I'm just letting you know that I'm going to scatter them in the waters of the South River tomorrow morning at sunrise, which is five-thirty. From the old bridge, right over there. No ceremony, just goodbye. You're welcome to join me and whoever else might like to come. I'll put a note in the lunchroom to that effect, though I don't expect anyone to come at that hour."

"That's a good idea. Let me make a poster, will you? I'd like to do that."

"Thank you, Ed. Just be sure to say it's optional. Rain or shine."

~

Tim went upstairs, but not to work with the wall of notes. He called his walking companion.

"Can Mort come out to play, Martha? It's a decent day for a walk."

"Mort, it's Tim. He wants to know—he's nodding yes, Tim. Around three, Mort? Yes, Tim at three. It's wonderful how much he enjoys walking with you."

Now, to Sunday's garden party guest list. Evelyn would likely accept, if she wasn't busy tweaking muffin recipes. He didn't know if the Everses could attend, given some congregations' propensity to invite the minister for Sunday dinner, but he'd ask. Who else? If he invited some of the newspaper staff, would he have to invite all? He didn't think Robert was up for that.

Cindy Martin came to mind. She was new, lived alone in Martin's River, and was turning out to be a hot-shot advertising salesperson since starting last month. He hadn't seen much of her lately, because she was out calling on clients, as she should be. He'd invite her tonight at home, after he called Evelyn.

Who else? Art Clarke, the accountant who was guiding Evelyn and her business partner, Kenny? Art had a wife and young children whom Tim had not met. They'd provide a nice family vibe. He'd ask Evelyn about that.

On his way to the car, he saw the Muffins sign in the window again, so he went in to get two to take home. They were still warm.

At home, he put the new gardening tools in the little tool closet, the new hibachi on the barbecuing cabinet and the briquettes inside it. The woodshed was quite an all-purpose structure now.

He placed the reading material from the office in the sunroom, looking forward to reading it tonight. *Is that weird, that I'm happy to read business material at home on a Friday night? Probably, but it matters to me, and I also want to get it out of the way before I leave for our holiday-y-y!*

He placed the *Selfish Giant* book on top, so the breeze coming in the screened windows wouldn't blow the papers away.

~

Tim changed his footwear to sneakers for walking, and drove to Blue Rocks. These visits with Mort were a valued addition to his life, simply walking and talking with a friend. Mort was in his seventies, not a contemporary, but his mind seemed ageless. Tim wondered what they would talk about today. Maybe they wouldn't talk at all.

"Are you sure you won't come in, Tim?"

"Not this time, thank you, Martha, but I will. I'm not avoiding you, please don't think that. As a matter of fact, I'd like to invite you both to my house this Sunday afternoon, for an early Canada Day gathering. Come when you can, anytime after two, and leave when you like. There will be excellent food, I assure you, and fine wines. Scallops, too. You can let me know when we return from our walk."

"We'll come!" Mort said. "Martha, would you please call that committee, whatever it was, and tell them I am unable to attend their meeting Sunday afternoon? Something has come up. I'll go Saturday afternoon if they want. I don't want to discuss linen altar cloths versus synthetics and miss a good social event."

"They ask you to attend meetings about that?"

"They would have me attend every meeting, but I've heard and seen it for decades on end. I go when I can, to be with the people, not their agendas. That's my ministry. But seafood and a glass of fine wine calls to me like Gabriel's trumpet. I can observe people at your gathering just as well."

"Some of my friends and a co-worker or two will be there. I hope it will be interesting for you and Martha."

They strolled along the curved road coming from Lunenburg, where it was wider, the traffic more frequent, and faster.

"Tell me what's on your mind today, my friend?"

"I'm going on vacation next week. How many shirts to pack is on my mind. And I'm going to scatter an old friend's ashes tomorrow morning."

"Both of those concerns are familiar to me, and both can be upsetting if you get it wrong. May I ask you about the ashes?"

Tim described GB and Connie, and what they had meant to him. Mort asked about the scattering, and Tim told him where and when.

"Now it's my turn. What's been entertaining your great mind, Mort?"

"Martha and I are revising our approach to our memoirs, as you so wisely suggested. Martha was skeptical at first, but once she saw how it could work, she got behind it. We pick a topic, and then she finds the events we recall the best, and then we go on to another. We work well together when she gets it, as the kids say. Aside from that, I've been reading the Psalms, looking for stories to tell from the pulpit. The Old Testament's pretty raunchy, you know, when it isn't just plain bloody. But I like a challenge."

"We'd better turn back here, Mort, or Martha will be out looking for us. How are you feeling, by the way? Healing?"

"Better by the day, thank you. I'm keeping up with you better today, don't you think?"

"You are. I forgot to slow down, but I don't think you were lagging behind."

"Good. Has your hit and run situation been resolved?"

"My hit and run?" Tim was astonished. "What—who told you about that?"

"I didn't mean to intrude. *You* told me. When you were here last week you said you were struggling to figure out something complex, and you used a hit and run to illustrate. That's what I meant."

"Gosh, I forgot I'd said that, Mort. Did I really? Wow. You know, the real story must have been developing in my subconscious. Or perhaps I'm psychic, is that a thing? Sorry, I'm babbling. I've been working to solve a crime. I was involved only peripherally, as a witness—no, a spectator—no, a bystander, if that. I'll explain later. What surprised me just now is that I think it likely *was* a hit and run."

"A fatality?"

"Very. I got tangled up in it because someone involved in it trespassed onto my property years ago, but it was just recently discovered. It's not resolved yet, but I am feeling better about it all than I was a week ago."

"Why is that?"

"Because I know now that I'm not the victim in the situation, or not the most aggrieved one, anyway. Well, here we are, home again. Thank you so much, Mort. I do enjoy our wanderings."

"Wait," Mort said. "I want to check about Sunday." He opened the cottage door. "Martha, what's the verdict about Sunday afternoon?"

She came to the door and said with a broad smile, "We're free to go to Tim's event, but you're not off the hook entirely. They moved the meeting to Monday evening so you wouldn't miss anything."

~

While Tim waited at the take-out for fries and two pieces of battered haddock, his phone rang. It was Rachael Rafuse from the office.

"Do you want to know how many of us will be attending, sir?"

"How many attending...where?" For a moment he thought she was referring to the Sunday garden party.

"The ashes, sir. We really appreciate being invited to see Mister GB off. And Mrs Barss."

"Right, the ashes. How many?"

"I have twelve so far, sir. At sunrise, that's a really nice touch, even if we don't see the sun. I'm looking forward to it."

~

At home, he put supper in the oven to crisp up. He had calls to make and papers to read and was happy to conduct this business in the sunroom while nibbling on the salty fried food and watching the grass grow.

His food and work were enhanced by glasses of *Une Longue Journée,* which tasted very familiar, but this was a superior vintage.

June 26: On the bridge

Saturday

Initially, the only people who saw the gathering on the old bridge spanning the South River were those who came to join in. They had left home with their headlights on, but the brightening sky quickly made them unnecessary.

Muffled car doors closing and people quietly calling greetings sounded beautiful to Tim, along with their footsteps on the wooden sidewalk. Those who had dressed for the warm day ahead pulled their sweaters and light jackets close to them against the nighttime chill lingering over the river that flowed quietly below the bridge on which they gathered.

Sunrise was fast approaching. Out of the corner of his eye, Tim saw the interior lights go on in the Daisy Café.

He stepped out into the centre of the bridge and addressed the gathering, making eye contact with each staff member and some family members as he spoke.

"Good morning, everyone. It's a beautiful morning to bid farewell to our dear friend GB and his beloved wife, Connie. We fondly remember GB as a man of few words. He wouldn't have said much if he were here this morning—and perhaps he *is* here—but you know his heart would be glad to see each of you. Here's what I intend to do now: I will remove the cap from his urn and tip it over to pour out a little of the ashes. I'll hand it off to the next person, who will pour some ashes, just a little bit, and so on until we come to the end. Connie will follow. If you don't wish to hold the urn, just step back so the next person can take it. Take care at the handover, and hold tight."

He looked at his watch. "Three minutes to sunrise."

He went to the far end of the line, where he had left the two urns in a cardboard box. Now he removed the lids from each.

There wasn't a breath of wind. The river flowed quietly to the sea.

"Okay?" he said quietly to Rachael Rafuse, standing on his right. She nodded.

Tim tipped the urn and began to pour. "Farewell, old friend," he murmured.

The ashes streamed straight down at first, but then an air current under the bridge made them swirl a little bit, as dust will do.

From hand to careful hand, the urn travelled along the bridge rail until it was emptied. Tim lifted Connie's urn and handed it to the next person in line, who continued the process.

An ash cloud drifted over the river and down into the water. The rays of the rising sun shone through some particles that had floated upward.

The group was silent while this was going on, except for some quiet words of goodbye. When all was done, someone began to applaud, and everyone joined in.

A few early-morning delivery trucks had waited at both ends of the bridge, their drivers trying to figure out what the holdup was. They now tooted their horns to join the applause.

Elaine Fong urged the group to leave the bridge quickly for their safety, and the trucks waited until they had cleared the area.

Tim picked up the empty carton and walked along to retrieve the two empty urns.

Standing next to them was the very tall Mortimer Evers in his purple clerical shirt, with crucifix hanging on his chest. "I hope I haven't intruded," Mort said to the astonished Tim. "You mentioned that you would be here at this time, and I was intrigued to see how it went. I am often asked to officiate at such events, some of them unorthodox, as this was, and it's good to see what works. Were you satisfied?"

"Very much so. I expected to be doing it alone, and just mentioned it to the staff yesterday. They are always great people, but they outdid themselves this morning."

They put the urns in the box and Tim carried them to his car.

"Someone's calling to you, Tim," Mort said, and pointed toward the café.

James Olsen was at the door, waving him over. He could see people milling about inside.

"Come over, Mort, let's see what's going on."

Tim felt he had stepped on stage in a play about happy times. The lights were on over just one aisle of booths and tables, giving the scene a cosy ambience. Ed Garamond was carrying a large metal tray loaded with coffee mugs, and a woman Tim didn't know was following behind him with two pots of coffee. A tray of cream and sugar was on a table where people could serve themselves.

Elaine saw Tim and Mort come in, and waved them to the back of the restaurant. "I know you'll want to wash the ash off your hands, fellas," she said, pointing to the washroom. "Everyone else has."

While he waited his turn, Tim surveyed the small crowd. No funeral sadness here; this was a party atmosphere. "How did this come about?" he asked Elaine.

"Don't look at me. I assumed you arranged it with Evelyn."

"I didn't arrange anything with anyone. I just mentioned the ashes to a few people."

"Do I hear the voice of Tim Brown out there?" Evelyn called from the kitchen. "Get in here and help me with these muffins!"

"I can do it," Elaine said. "Tim hasn't washed his hands yet."

"There's a sink in here."

"Okay, let me see what's going on, as if my nose hasn't given me a hint."

Tim pushed the swinging doors and slipped into the kitchen, where Evelyn was lifting two large pans of muffins out of the oven.

"Don't touch a thing until you scrub, Tim. I don't want ashy thumbprints on my dishes."

He went to the sink, soaped up, rinsed in hot water, and dried his hands on a handful of paper towels. "Okay, reporting for duty, boss."

"They're hot out of the oven, so just warn everybody. These are strawberry. Set them on a table. Here's the butter and jams. You, sir, would you follow him with these, please?"

Mort, who had just emerged from the washroom holding his hands up like a surgeon ready to perform an operation, was tickled to do as instructed.

He and Tim held their wares aloft and called out, "Hot muffins! Strawberry muffins!" "Jams! Jams and butter!"

The second pan of muffins was ready, and Harold Awalt sang, "Banana chocolate chip muffins! Oh, have you seen the muffin-man, the muffin-man, the muffin-man?"

Evelyn had baked two dozen fresh muffins and brewed four pots of coffee, and in half an hour it was all gone. Tim took her hand and led her from the kitchen to thank her for her generosity and support of the staff of *The Times*. They responded with cheers and whistles, and she appeared genuinely touched.

"You're welcome back for more, anytime," she said.

Tim also thanked everyone who had come today, said he understood and missed those who couldn't make it, and especially missed those who had departed for good, forever in the river.

People were leaving to start their day or to go back to bed. Mort was chatting randomly with the staff and their family members. Tim observed him, apparently so interested in each person he met. He overheard several people thanking Mort for being there, that it "meant a lot to have someone like you" with them at this event.

Mort signalled that he, too, was leaving. Tim went to the door to thank him for coming, and mentioned what he had overheard. "Maybe I should have asked you to say a prayer or something," he said.

"Not at all, though you may hear that I did, maybe even that I tossed a little incense. The collar has that effect on people. I must be gone now. Someone really is waiting for me to pray with them. See you tomorrow."

Some of the staff stayed behind in the diner to tidy up and stack dishes in the dishwasher, under Evelyn's watchful eye. She scooped more muffin batter into the pans for her regular Saturday customers.

"What do I owe you for all this?" Tim asked her.

"Nothing. It's not seven o'clock yet. I don't turn on the cash register until seven, so whatever happens before then has to be free. It was good practice for me, if we ever decide to cater. You better scram now. Here comes Kenny and he doesn't want anyone in the way when he fires up the grill."

Tim shook his head in wonder, gave her a big hug, and waved to Kenny. As he left, he heard her say to Kenny, "Of course I saved ya one. Whaddya think?"

~

Tim was very happy with the event. *That Evelyn, my goodness, putting on a reception all on her own. And Mort, showing up. I sure do have good friends.*

Home again, he allowed Gloria to make him a cappuccino while he organized his GET and DO lists. He'd covered invitations for the Canada Day party by phone last evening. *Check.* It would be a small group with the right balance of friends who would forgive anything he'd overlooked, and lesser-knowns who should ditto. Entertaining inside the house was old hat, but the out-of-doors was a whole new game.

He needed to get party items and food ready for Robert's inspection by mid-afternoon. It was a warm day; perishables would perish if left for long in the car today, and the traumatic memory of that pungent chicken two weeks ago was still strong. He added ice to the GET list, put two coolers in the car, and started out.

The afterglow of the early morning stayed with Tim on his rounds. The morning light on the river. The quiet. Staff who came. Staff who brought family. Mort, whose presence implied sanctification to those who might have wondered if it was needed. Evelyn's huge generosity. Staff who pitched in to serve and clean up.

I can't imagine this group mounting a union drive against us. We'll do the things, and ask the questions, as Ms Duplessis-Lachance suggests. She should have been on the bridge this morning; she'd have seen a work-team that likes to spend time together.

He drove to Lunenburg for fresh seafood. Grocery stores in South River supplied everything else on his list. Then he dashed home, the car's air conditioner struggling to cool the interior, though it didn't reach items in the trunk. The house was cool, a benefit of having a big house with two floors between him and the hot sun.

Tim took his lunch to the grove of trees at the back of the garden. It was pleasantly cooler in the shade. The flagstones made a solid path, and he hoped people wouldn't tread on the fresh clover, still getting established. The mowing crew had left a number of red flags in the woodshed, which he now placed along the path, hoping their meaning would be understood.

He found that holding a sandwich in one hand and tea in the other was awkward. He drove back to the second-hand shop where he'd bought the tin tray tables, and found two wooden tables with good legs and damaged tops, and a big coffee table. He brought them home with the trunk lid up, purchases jammed in the gap. He set one table on the ground next to the hibachis, so Robert could serve cooked items there. He dragged the others under the trees and placed the folding chairs next to them. They were in poor enough shape that leaving them out in the weather wouldn't do them more harm, and plastic tablecloths would make them look festive.

He was cooling down in the sunroom with a fan blowing gently, and the opera on the radio, when Robert arrived.

"Come on out, Rob," he called. "I made some iced tea to cool us off. Turn down *La Bohème* if you want. It just started. Mimi won't die for a couple hours yet."

They assessed the food in stock for tomorrow, placed their pizza order, then took cool drinks outdoors to try out various areas for serving and sitting. All seemed ready, and soon the pizza was delivered.

They savoured every bite, and treasured being able to enjoy this weekly tradition without the misguided interference of a guest who didn't know how to read the room.

June 27: Summer garden

Sunday

Robert's hands and feet were busy through the night, playing through his concert repertoire. Tim woke him in the morning with a tiny espresso and said, "You had better get your mind off the concert or we'll both have a nervous breakdown."

They went to the church earlier than usual to greet Robert's organ student, who would be filling in for him next Sunday and other Sundays through the summer. She was waiting beside her car in the church parking lot, and Robert took her immediately into the church.

Tim took a moment to stroll over to the bridge where that special event had taken place so early yesterday morning. He breathed in the fresh morning air and again felt gratitude.

~

The choir loved today's church service. The minister had invited them to select three of their favourite anthems to sing, interspersed by his reading of the texts. He added his own comments, but didn't wander too far astray, and the service went along seamlessly.

Robert shared the organ bench with his student at first, to show her where to look for the ushers' signals in the rear-view mirror. Being familiar with the order of service of the United Church, she caught on quickly. She selected different stops, held notes for the sung *Amens* longer than the congregation was accustomed to, played hymns at different tempi from Robert, but everyone followed. Nobody wanted her to fail.

Other than when Robert was conducting the choir, she played the whole service, including a strong postlude. The choir stayed in the loft to hear it, and applauded when she finished. The summer season was off to a good start.

~

Yesterday, Robert hadn't paid much attention to the menu or guest list for today's garden party. As they returned home from church close to one o'clock, he suddenly realized that a dozen guests would arrive between two and five, to eat a variety of walkabout food he had barely thought about.

These were perfect conditions, Tim knew, to mute the station that had been broadcasting in Robert's head for many days. They were also challenging for Tim, as Robert called on him to answer his urgent questions, mostly beginning with "Where is...?"

Shrimp and scallops were in the fridge. Ice was in the freezer. Wines were here and here. Ribs were there. Bamboo skewers were out there. Ingredients for sauces were right here. Tim had opted for ice cream in bowls rather than strawberry shortcake. It might melt, but it was easy.

With the second hibachi, Robert could do all the grilling at his station. Tim produced a cast iron griddle pan from the drawer beneath the stove, which fitted perfectly on one hibachi.

Things do work out the way we envision them, eventually. That was Tim's happy thought as he watched his guests navigate the flagstone path leading to the shady grove, while clouds of aromatic smoke wafted from the grill station. *Sometimes even better.*

Bright tablecloths with red and white napkins for Canada Day looked festive on the outdoor tables. To prevent them from blowing away in the light breeze, he had brought out paperback books as anchors, including the thesaurus which had entertained him weeks ago. The ground was soft, so Tim risked using glass tumblers for the drinks rather than plastic cups, saving those for any children who might arrive.

He had found an apron sporting the title "King of Coals". Robert proudly wore it as he kept a steady supply of food on the serving table behind him, which the grateful guests quickly took up.

And such guests!

The newspaper's advertising maven, Cindy Martin, arrived with Ed Garamond and his wife. The Garamonds' teenagers had remained at Cindy's century home in Martin's River rather than hang with grownups.

Evelyn came early and stepped right into the hostess rôle, setting plates and glasses and napkins in places where guests might look for them. She found aprons and tied on two like gun holsters, carrying drinks in her hands and glasses in the apron pockets.

Evelyn's business partner, Kenny Sutherland, made a shy appearance, and was happy to find bottles of beer on ice in Tim's window-washing bucket. Kenny chatted with James Olsen and his girlfriend Stacy, who were pleased as punch to be there, and to be sipping wine.

Art Clarke arrived with his wife and two small children. Stacy was drawn to the little ones and attempted to entertain them while their parents got food. To her dismay, the little boy managed to find something to bump his knee on, and the shrill crying couldn't be soothed by anyone, so the Clarke family soon departed. Art had told Tim that they sometimes went for drives "until everyone cries" and then they'd go home, so this was just another Sunday outing for them.

Tim was sorry Art had to leave, but was relieved when the squalling children were gone. Then he wondered if that was the story behind *The Selfish Giant.* He would read the book carefully.

Mort and Martha Evers arrived at the back garden at the same time as Stella. Stella's face registered total surprise at the changes Tim had wrought in the backyard where she and his mother had played as children. "But it was never like this," she told anyone who inquired. "No flagstone path, no grove of trees to shade us."

"Those features were added by your sister years ago," Tim said, "and the trees have grown wonderfully since then. Mother has given us the gift of shade today. Somebody will find a seat for you back there, Aunt Stella. I haven't needed to introduce anyone yet, so you're on your own. I'm enjoying being a greeter, and sampling whatever Robert is setting out, of course. You must get a plate before you go to the grove."

Evelyn approached them shyly.

"Oh, I *will* make this introduction. Aunt Stella, this is Evelyn Whynot, my oldest and dearest friend. Ev, this is my, um, youngest and dearest Aunt Stella."

Robert turned around in his station and exclaimed, "Oh my God, my two favourite ladies together in one place!" He blew kisses to both. "Hold out your plates, darlings." He served grilled tiger shrimp and sweet peppers on skewers, and huge seared scallops. "Help yourselves to the riblets and salad."

"You go find yourself a seat, Stella," Evelyn said. "Be careful in those spike heels. I'll bring you a glass of wine. Red or white or both?"

Mort's opening line was simply, "Hello, this is Martha and I'm Mortimer. Have we met?"

From James Olsen and Evelyn Whynot, the response to him was, "Yes, yesterday morning on the bridge!" James proudly introduced Stacy as his fiancée.

Having greeted most everyone, the Everses presented themselves at the grill.

"Behind that cloud of smoke is Robert, whom you've heard me mention," Tim said. "Rob, this is the Right Reverend Doctor Mortimer Evers, whom I told you about, the prayer breakfast guest speaker and now my walking companion, though we talk more than we walk. And Martha Evers, who made those killer cinnamon rolls I so generously shared with you."

Robert leaned down from his station to shake their hands. "Are these the folk you said were so keen on fresh seafood?"

"We are! At least, I hope he meant us!" Mort laughed gleefully. "What do you have there, Robert?"

"There are sirloin bits drizzled with maple syrup, and these enormous grilled shrimp and those, seared scallops on a little bed of greens. And hidden back here, I have improvised a little ceviche made with bay scallops, not enough to offer to everyone, but a taste for people who know how to make heavenly cinnamon rolls."

Mort and Martha gratefully accepted the treats on their plates. Evelyn came along to make her beverages offer.

The sun was high in the sky and only the occasional cloud drifted by to bring temporary relief. Tim signalled to Kenny to give him a hand carrying chairs from the sunroom and stools from the kitchen to the shade under the trees.

Tim and Robert carried trays of food from the grill to serve the group. Finally, Robert settled, or teetered, on a kitchen stool, happily exhausted.

Stella wasn't first to leave the party. Evelyn told Tim she heard Stella say she really enjoyed returning to the place where she had played as a little girl.

Mort and Martha asked Tim and Robert to promise to invite them back again, for conversation and exquisite food. "And those delicious wines, too," Mort said, which prompted Martha to extend her hand for the car keys.

~

Tim and Robert relaxed with wine and ice cream under the trees. The day had been a bit hot, but the trees had provided cooler shelter than umbrellas or canopies would have done. A few biting insects were about, but Tim had left the can of bug spray on a table for guests to use, and he sprayed himself now. After spending his whole life indoors, he wasn't going to let a bug chase him today.

He brought out the children's book, and began to read the story of *The Selfish Giant* to Robert. He didn't care for the ending, so he edited as he went.

> The children loved to play in the grass, beneath fruit trees, listening to the birds, but then the giant came home after a seven-year visit with his friend, the ogre, and chased the children away.
>
> He posted a sign: TRESPASSERS WILL BE PROSECUTED
>
> The pretty flowers and the singing birds did not return to the garden next spring. It was all winter, all the time. Then one day, the giant heard a bird singing, and when he looked out, the garden was in bloom again. Why? The children had broken through the fence and were playing in the garden. Everything was lovely again, except in one corner where it was still winter because one little boy couldn't reach up to climb in a tree. The giant saw it all...and rushed out to lift the child up into the tree. At first, the other children were afraid, but soon they returned.
>
> For many years the giant loved to watch the children playing. He even loved winter now, because he knew it would pass and bring summer again. Eventually he died, but the children lived happily ever after in the garden.

"That's not how it ends," Robert said.

"It is when I'm reading it. You know the story?"

"I do, and you're right to amend the ending. I don't like it when a religious lesson is so obviously jammed onto the end, especially for children. Even Aesop finished the fables first, then added 'the Moral of the Story' at the end, so you could take it or leave it without ruining the tale."

"Right."

"I like the sign the giant posted, though. I wonder if the Winnie The Pooh stories were quoting this one?"

"For sure I do not know what you mean now."

"Owl had a broken sign on his tree, which said 'Trespassers Will'. There was a lot of chatter about what this meant. Piglet claimed it was his uncle's name, Trespassers William."

Tim burst out laughing. "Trespassers Will is the name of a pig? I love it! I'm going to get those words on a sign to warn people away from my secret garden. I will get a fence put up to keep it from becoming a cemetery again, and I'll post 'Trespassers Will' on the fence."

"You do that. You will either cause winter to return to your garden all year 'round, or else fans of *Winnie The Pooh* will invade it."

"Some risks to keep a watchful eye out for. But I'll never again stay away for seven years, visiting my friend the ogre. I'll keep an eye on developments."

~

As they were clearing the kitchen counter, Tim noticed the message light flashing on his home phone. Quickly punching the buttons, he listened to the message.

"Hi Tim, it's Elaine. I know you're outside being the ever-gracious host, and I'm glad I'm not disturbing you. In fact, I'm calling to un-disturb you somewhat. I heard from my J-school prof, who chastised me for overlooking the obligation to provide balanced reporting, though I said in my defence that I thought our reporting was very balanced, but he sees it differently. Anyway, he thinks that James' approach wasn't as reprehensible as I had made it out to be. He is checking with a legal source, a retired judge, and will get back to me, possibly in the middle of the night, since this judge lives on Vancouver Island. No need to call me back today. Thank you so much for being at my back. This all hit at a bad time for me personally, but I'll recover. 'Bye.'"

June 28: Preparations

Monday

Robert was no longer distracted by his internal playlist. Tim waved two fingers in front of him and said, "How many fingers do you see?"

"Two up, two down, and one thumb."

"Good. Welcome back. Let's coordinate our actions for the next three days. I will be cleaning and fuelling the car, and packing beach chairs and towels and sunscreen. Whatever clothes you will want from here for performing or for relaxing, please leave them out upstairs. Have whatever else ready to put in the car when I arrive Thursday morning. *Ja*?

"*Jawohl*! Should we take some wines to have in our hotel room? I wouldn't want to rely on the local outlets—if there even are any where we're going."

"I'm ahead of you there. The Inn will have some good choices, but I thought we might want to take some on a picnic. I can hardly believe I'm saying these words. A picnic! On a beach! In PEI!"

"Tim, I'm grateful that you put up with me and my laser-beam focus on my music, but I still have the temerity to ask you not to bring *your* work with you. You booked a so-called year off, and when it's over I want you to have fond memories of at least one week of vacation, okay?"

"I'll do my best. The biggest story ever seen in the pages of *The Times* will hit the streets this Wednesday, and we expect the manure to hit the fan. That's why Elaine couldn't come to the party yesterday. She's a lot like you, checking, double-checking, triple-checking. She won't lose her business and family fortune if we're wrong, though. I might."

"No, you won't...will you?"

"We could be sued for defamation. I can afford the defence, but I can't afford a penalty if we lose. I'll be reading every word today and tomorrow myself, to prevent that from happening. Our approach is to call attention to the travesties and injustices that we know have happened, and to name the people we know who did them. We don't say they *knew* they did wrong, so they have a tiny bit of wiggle-room for a defence. It's up to their employers and the voters to fire them or toss them out of office. The man at the centre of it all will hate me more than he does now. It'll be good if he can't find me for a while. We've hired a security guard at the office for a couple weeks, just in case he flips his lid."

"What a thrill! I guess I'll allow you to take your phone, then, but I do hope you won't be on it all the time. I want to listen to the ocean waves."

"Me, too, pal."

~

Next on Tim's mind was his car. He rarely gave it a thought unless it was low on gas, but he was going on a long road trip, depending on the car to carry them over the Confederation Bridge and back on the Northumberland Ferry without low oil, brake failure, flat tire, overheating radiator, or whatever else went wrong with cars. It was short notice, but he knew where he could get the checkup and cleaning done right away, if he was willing to put up with some ribbing.

He drove to Greene Motors, hoping the owner was on the premises and not in his mayoral office in Town Hall. Garland Greene's big SUV, with his name painted on the door, was in the parking lot.

Tim parked and went inside.

"End of the month," Gar said. "Big deals available today only. Take your pick and you can drive one of these beauties away in an hour!"

"Keep trying, Gar. I've been spending money like water, and I know these buggies cost something thicker. Before I forget, thanks for persuading me to go to that prayer breakfast. I've been visiting with the guest speaker, and enjoying him very much."

"Knew you would."

"I am here to ask a favour, though. I'm driving to PEI this Thursday morning early, but I overlooked the need to ensure my transportation was ship-shape. Can you squeeze me in your service bay for a tune-up and cleaning?"

"I don't know, Tim," Gar said, looking over his shoulder at Tim's vehicle parked outside. "If we clean the dirt off it, it might fall apart."

"It's naturally dirt-coloured. Tires, oil, brakes—"

"That's hilarious, you telling me what to check on a vehicle. Tell you what. Gimme the keys and we'll do what we can for ya. I'll give you a courtesy vehicle. Yours'll be ready by suppertime. Please bring mine back in one piece—or buy it. We'd give you the best trade-in."

Gar led him outside to a deep blue, late-model sedan, with lime green figures two feet high on both sides, the price on one and the rate of financing on the other. "Thanks for the free advertising, Tim," he said, clapping him on the back. "I'll expect you to sell it by day's end."

Tim drove the nearly-new car gingerly at first, getting the feel of the gas and brake pedals. The brakes caught sooner than he was accustomed to. The seat was higher than in his own car, giving great visibility and lumbar support. The suspension was smooth, and there were no clunks when he drove over bumps. It still had the new car smell.

When he parked outside the newspaper office, he admired the sparkly flecks embedded in the dark blue paint. The car was classy, yet modest.

Snap out of it, Tim. Every time you leave the house lately, you spend money. Your vacation at that nice Inn will cost thousands. You haven't paid for all that landscaping yet, and you thought you would start painting your house. Where's that all coming from?

"From my bank account, that's where. Those rickety old tables at the second-hand store only cost a hundred dollars. I spend more than that on wine every month, sorry to say. If expenses like that put a strain on my piggy-bank, I have other problems."

He strode into the offices of what he hoped was a soon-to-be-famous newspaper. Heads lifted and hands waved and then their owners went back to work. Today and tomorrow were do-or-die days.

He knocked on Elaine's door and let himself in when she beckoned through the glass.

"Got your message, thanks. Any updates?"

"Any minute now. I'm looking forward to that. I've been so stressed about this story, Tim. I hope things will settle down soon after."

"Is it staff issues?"

"Not for ordinary times. It's the secrecy and the potential liability that required such meticulous preparation, and anxiety goes with that territory. But I'm loving it."

"You didn't appear so last week. Hang in. Your use of the word 'meticulous' is a great comfort to me. Are we still on for three this afternoon? When'll you be ready for me to review the galleys—if we proceed this week?"

"Yes, three o'clock is still on. In addition, we're all writing to a deadline of tonight at seven o'clock. Someone's bringing in burgers and sandwiches, on the company tab, so come hungry if you wish. We'll have twenty-four hours after that to proof it, find more disasters, correct errors. Leave me now."

Elaine turned to the work on her desk.

Feeling relieved that Elaine had become herself again, Tim dropped in at the Daisy. Evelyn was serving a full house.

At the counter, he bought a fresh muffin.

"Thanks for your help yesterday, Ev."

"You know me, I like to be busy at things like that. I really enjoyed myself. Your newspaper staff already came over to buy their muffins this morning, so my little reception for them on Saturday morning has paid off, though I didn't do it for that reason, you know that. 'Scuse me, Hon. Strangers at the door. That's happening a lot lately."

A party of four had just come in the front door and Kenny was tapping on the bell in the kitchen.

Tim drove home and began to lay out his clothes for the trip. Robert's duffle bag was at the foot of the bed, and he carried it downstairs to the den, from where he would load the car when it was ready.

~

He had just come in from watering his small flower patch when the phone rang.

"Tim, it's Gar. Can you wait until tomorrow morning to get your car? Your vehicle inspection is three months overdue."

"Oh."

"It's okay. Good thing we caught it before the cops saw it. But your brakes are shot, so we have to replace some pads and rotors. Do you know you're still running on winter tires? Do you have summers?"

"Gosh, I forgot that, too. Yeah, I have them. Should I bring them over?"

"You better. Just drop them off outside and let the girls at the desk know. We'll switch them while it's on the hoist. Should be ready tomorrow at lunchtime, okay? How're you liking the loaner? Pretty smooth ride, eh?"

"Very nice. But I need to pack for my trip, Gar, so tomorrow noon it will have to be; hope that's okay?"

Tim went out to the metal shed where the garbage and recycling bins were kept. The rest of the space was taken up by the four tires, wrapped in white plastic bags. He backed the loaner car up to the shed and popped the trunk from a handy lever inside the vehicle. It was easy to load the four tires in the large opening.

The tin shed reminded him about the woodshed, still empty except for the grill station at one end. Robert had demonstrated its usefulness on

Sunday, but it reduced the space available for stacking wood by about one quarter. He couldn't use the sunroom as backup any more, so he'd either buy less wood or find another place to put it. He decided he needed to consult with his firewood supplier, Buck.

He was really just looking for an excuse to take the almost-new car for a drive, and this would be a good drive to take. He dropped off the tires as Garland had instructed, and then headed out to visit the woodsman.

Buck's place was about twenty minutes outside of South River town limits. The road was narrow, potholed, and had many sharp turns, but it felt newly-paved in this vehicle.

Buck was in his yard when Tim pulled in, scattering a nattering cloud of hens. He watched with the quizzical expression people wear when they don't recognize the fancy vehicle in their yard and weren't expecting visitors.

Tim got out of the car and Buck's expression turned to a grin. "Thought the Preemyer was comin' to visit," he said. "New car?"

"New for the day, Buck. Mine's in the shop. Nice, though."

They walked around the car, admiring the hubcaps, the big trunk, the interior carpet that was nicer than either of them had in their homes, the stereo radio.

"What's the horn sound like?" Buck asked. Tim tapped the button and a deep, two-tone sound startled more cackles in the yard.

"That's some nice. Good price, too." Buck gestured at the fluorescent green figures along the car's flank.

"Is it? You can buy it after I take it back tomorrow."

"Not me. But your old car was lookin' kinda saggy. This one looks more like you."

"Thanks, I guess. What I came to ask is how much firewood I should get for the winter." Tim showed him the dimensions on a rough sketch of the woodshed, now standing upright but with a portion devoted to out-door cooking.

"I'd say it'll hold a cord. More'n what we got in that sunporch. If there's leftovers, we could put some on your front porch, it's big enough. Or in the trunk of this car." He grinned. "Prob'ly get half a cord in there."

"That's not going to happen. Reserve a cord of hardwood for me then, please, nice and dry like always. We'll talk about delivery in September. Right now, I'm getting ready to go to PEI for a seaside holiday." He liked the way that sounded.

"It's some nice over there," Buck responded. "Wife's family's there. If you like lobster, go to one of those dinners on the wharf. Best feast I ever had."

Having the car and the time, Tim left and turned onto the highway heading toward Yarmouth. That town was two hours away, not his destination today. Long drives were coming. He just wanted to enjoy handling this car at the top legal speed, plus five percent. He adjusted the air conditioning by setting the temperature rather than adjusting fan speed. He found the classical music station on the radio and appreciated the brand-name speakers.

In no time, he came to the exit for Port Medway, and turned left. The road out to the village was narrow and sinuous, but it was a pleasure to navigate with this suspension. He turned around at the government wharf, and got out for a minute to smell the fresh air.

He quickly returned to the filtered atmosphere in the vehicle, as he was downwind of a very pungent container of fish guts.

~

Tim returned to the War Room at three o'clock. Elaine, her equilibrium apparently restored, stood and steered the meeting through the usual formalities.

Then she drew a big breath and delivered her news. "I am pleased to inform you that John L. Arbour, retired Justice of the Supreme Court of British Columbia, advised me this morning that we are safe to proceed with printing James' interview in its entirety, including what he interprets as the subject's attempt to purchase the interview from James, which he considers an attempt to silence the press, or a bribe. In fact, he wants me to fax it out to him for his review. He says it is immaterial that James described himself as a freelancer, or freelancing: he declared himself as a reporter, and MacIntosh indicated he understood that by offering his bribe. We're on! Full speed ahead!"

Everyone in the room applauded. James was grinning from ear to ear, but didn't appear surprised. Elaine gave him the courtesy of letting him know first. That's good. She probably apologized to him, too. I hope they'll be okay.

"Madam Chair," Tim said, "may I ask the good people here two questions?"

"Go ahead."

"Do you feel that we have the facts we need? That we won't malign or besmirch any innocent party through our carelessness?"

Heads nodded. Several people said, "Yup."

"And do you feel this story must be told?"

"Absolutely!" This from Roger, the land use lawyer. "If *The Times* hadn't come along with the resources and the means of bringing this travesty to the attention of the public, I'd have tried to do it myself. There have been many instances of government departments showing favouritism to developers, developers using land for unapproved purposes, and logging companies operating on a scorched-earth basis. From time to time, politicians at all levels have ignored or assisted these crimes, supported by some rotten apples in the civil service. But this travesty surrounding little Crater Lake in Sweetland has them all. Everyone was too cocky, too confident that nobody would bother with one little body of water, barely bigger than a pond. But you did, Mr Brown, and you gave us your newspaper to get the word out. I applaud you."

Everyone in the room was standing, applauding Tim.

He was surprised. Had he done all this? What Roger had said sounded big, very big. This wasn't Evan's big-city *The Daily*, with its own staff lawyers and experts. This was South River's *The Times*, the community paper begun by his grandfather and kicked along by his mother. Wednesday's could be its final issue, but it would be great to go down swinging for a good cause, if it came to that.

"Thank you, Roger, and everyone. I've trusted you all along to do this right, especially with the stewardship of Elaine Fong, and I know I'll be impressed when I proof the galleys. The future of this enterprise depends on the veracity of this story, and your jobs do, too. It's too big a story and we're too small to survive the kind of lawsuit we'd be threatened with, if we're wrong. I guess it's good to have something on the line. Risk encourages accuracy. So, I thank you for your courage, each and every one of you—and for your ability to keep this story under wraps for so long. I was just now thinking about my forebears, my mother and grandfather, who built this newspaper. I can't think of anything they said that pertains to this moment in our history, so you can quote me later: Go big or go home!"

Tim was proud, and salt water stung his eyes.

Elaine and Roger betrayed no affection or connection between them. They were there for business, and that was the vibe they gave. Tim knew how that went.

~

It was all Project Sweetland now. Staff who were not directly involved were sent home, having signed a promise of confidentiality which would expire at six o'clock Wednesday morning. Elaine didn't want the local radio station to scoop their big story. Folding tables were carried down from upstairs so everyone could read and consult within a few steps of each other.

Tim sat behind the receptionist's desk and began to read the final drafts as they were rotated to him, red pencil at the ready.

The sandwiches and burgers and cold drinks gave a party atmosphere to their work, but there was little talking. When Tim had finished reading and marking an article, he took it to Elaine, who noted any red circles and personally carried it to the person or people who could defend or make changes. He wouldn't see it again until he reviewed the final draft tomorrow, unless he marked a big red X somewhere.

He didn't find anything to reject, nothing that seemed unfounded, sensational, or likely to trigger a lawsuit. He finally stood up to stretch, and walked over to Elaine at the table. "It's all good," he said. "Very well written."

"No concerns?"

"None, except…it's a little dull, perhaps? Not that I want the *National Enquirer* hype, but we do want our readers to read it and not fall asleep."

Elaine nodded. "Gosh, after the excitement we've just gone through, I'd welcome some dullness, but I think we've got that covered, too, with bullet points and 'explainers' in sidebars. You'll see those tomorrow when Ed does the layout, with MacIntosh's photo and bragging on the front page."

"What time?"

"Mid-late afternoon, I hope, if nothing goes wrong and every-thing goes right. Thanks for your help always, Tim. It's a comfort to me to have you here, back from your world cruise just for this."

"It's been my pleasure. I wouldn't have missed this for anything, though I'm sorry you found it so stressful there. I'm excited for my next adventure, though. Someone mentioned they have lobster dinners on a wharf somewhere in PEI. I promised Robert I wouldn't be on the phone all the time—if there even is a signal there—so, after six months of me hanging around to confuse things you'll finally have the place to yourself. With a security guard. Probably not the best time for me to skip town, sorry."

"I think it's good that you'll be away. If that crook tries to storm in here to threaten you or any of us, he'll learn that you're away, and the guard can quickly call the police. We'll shut him down."

~

Tim was still in the car in the parking lot when Ed Garamond came out of the building.

"Lose something, boss? Nice car."

"It's a loaner. I can't figure out how to turn the headlights on in this fancy thing, Ed."

"They're already on, boss. They're automatic. Have a good night."

June 29: Trespassers will

Tuesday

"I'll miss you," Tim said to Gloria while he waited for her to build up steam for a double latté. "I'm sure they have good coffee over there, but is it *this* good?"

He toasted slices of his favourite bakery bread, and wondered the same about toast. *I'm such a homebody. But I like what I like, nothing wrong with that. I'm eager to see new places and all that. Maybe I'll even find something I like better on the Island. Anyway, it's not about the same or better, it's about different. It's hard to anticipate what I don't know about.*

He didn't know anything about beach wear, never having owned any. He called Robert.

"Do you have shorts?"

"What?"

"For the beach."

"Oh. I have shorts to wear on land and swimming trunks in the water. Don't you?"

"No. I don't think I want my skinny white legs on display. Will I need them?"

"I sincerely hope so. Pick up one pair of each. There'll be shops over there if you want more. When in doubt, bring it. That's my travel rule, though it's a lot easier to do travelling with a car. We wouldn't get much in my little car, but yours is good."

"Okay. Will do. I'm excited. See you in two days."

His head was in a closet upstairs when the phone rang.

"Mr Brown? It's Detective Sergeant O'Neill. How are you this morning?"

"Detective! I was hoping to hear from you. What's up?"

"Can we meet somewhere?"

"I'm home, packing for a trip. Can you come here?"

"I'll be there in about half an hour."

Is he coming to poke holes in my theory? Or is he back with more questions? Or is he going to bring up that shovel or…No. Stop it, Tim. You want him to have an open mind. You should open yours, too.

When the doorbell rang, he invited O'Neill to the kitchen.

"Coffee, Detective? This machine makes the best, whatever you like. I'm having a latté. What'll it be? Cappuccino, latté, espresso, Americano?" It went against the grain not to be hospitable.

"Is any of that a plain coffee, with milk and sugar?"

"The Americano can be. Coming right up. What's on your mind this morning?"

"I want to bring you up to date on our search for the victim who was buried in your backyard."

"I'm eager to hear all about that. Did you discover who did it?"

"First, I want to review the story you related to me the last time I was here. You suggested a person had entered your property by way of that emergency exit lane, correct?"

"That was my suggestion, yes."

"Driving a vehicle."

"I assume so. He was transporting a body somehow. Wouldn't be on a bicycle or motorbike."

"And the place he chose to dig was behind your former woodshed."

"That's where it was discovered. Here's your coffee, help yourself to milk and sugar. It's too rocky anywhere else. Toast?"

"No, thanks. He got the shovel from that woodshed, correct?"

"Well, somebody did. If I may add another conjecture, Detective, if he had brought his own shovel, that would suggest premeditation, wouldn't it? If he'd taken a moment to premeditate, he wouldn't have come here to bury a body at all. There must be more receptive places, surely."

"Then you said it must have been raining, to wash the dirt away."

"I admit that's a bit of a fiction, but it's plausible. I thought the almanac would give you some dates, anyway, to narrow your search for a missing person. I made up the scene where a patrol car came along and surprised him, too. I wouldn't insist on that, but somebody likely did. It would explain why he tossed the shovel in the middle of the yard. So, did any of this check out at all?"

"I will tell you that I was sure you were blowing smoke, Mr Brown. Your whole story was based on conjecture, so I set it aside for a couple days. But I didn't have anything else to go on, so I decided it wouldn't hurt to play your game. I looked for missing persons reported that summer. There were none locally, as your newspaper listing showed, very helpful; we'll talk about that resource another time. There were many across the country, of course, as you also pointed out. Some have been located since that time, alive or dead, but some are still missing."

"That's too bad. I was hoping it would be a help."

"It was. We're awaiting final verification, but we're pretty sure we know who was in that grave. Thanks to you."

"What? Oh, that's great! Wow! Glad I could be of assistance, then."

Tim was high-fiving himself inside. *I helped them find the victim. Me, the Delving Private Researcher!*

"The pathologist's report said several bones were broken," O'Neill said, "consistent with being struck or run over by a vehicle. He indicated that internal injuries were likely, and likely fatal."

"Hit and run, then?"

"It appears to be, except someone scooped up the alleged victim, as you proposed in your story. I even followed your fiction about a person with gardening skills, rainy night, rain slicker, patrol car and so on."

"Was any of it helpful?"

"I started with the patrol car coming around the corner. If one of our members saw a vehicle come down this lane, they might have driven in, and *may* have asked to see the driver's licence, but not necessarily. But we're hard-wired to make note of licence plates on vehicles we see in odd places, and we'd include that in our shift report: just the plate, vehicle make and model, and location. In case it comes up later."

"A lot of reports to search through, then."

"A bit, because this victim wasn't reported missing until some weeks *after* his disappearance. The family aren't suspects and some are deceased now. Anyway, I scanned those old patrol reports, looking for a late evening mention of a licence plate on Exhibition Grounds Emergency Evac Route on and around your suggested dates."

"And?"

"And we have a suspect—"

"You're kidding!"

"—currently in another jurisdiction, so we're doing the necessary things to get them here and in court."

"You're not kidding!" Tim just had to stand up. "The story I told you— pure conjecture, based on logic—my story helped you to find the victim *and* the grave digger?"

"It did. You reasoned it out very well. What was that funny word you used?"

"Um—ratiocination? I find it hard to say myself. Let's just call it rational thinking. It just made sense when I walked it through on location, especially at night. I mightn't have thought about headlights otherwise. I thought, it's not just what a person might do, but what a person would see and do *there* and *then*. So, Detective, when will this information be released to the public?"

"Well, that's what I came here to discuss with you, Mr Brown. I know you own the local paper, and I expect you'd normally print this story in your paper, wouldn't you?"

"Most assuredly. Reporting local news is our mandate."

"Well, I'm asking you to hold off reporting anything about this story until there's an arrest. You'll get it eventually, I promise, but it's a delicate matter right now, and we need to get our ducks in a row before we, uh, pull the trigger. Does that make sense?"

"Maybe. I thought it was a pretty delicate matter when I was prevented from going into my own house, and taken to the station in the back of a cruiser. I know you had your reasons, but I'm still upset about it."

"It sometimes takes a while to get the information we need. We initially thought this case was linked to a different event two years ago that also took place back there behind the exhibition grounds. We didn't know what you might have seen or known about it. I apologize for disrupting your plans."

"I'll accept that. Thank you. Anyway, *The Times* is about to release a significant story of our own in tomorrow's edition, and we're confident of it because we kept it under wraps until we could verify the facts. So I understand your request."

"Good. We have an agreement, then?"

"Can you tell me more about why this isn't public now?"

"I can't explain much without telling you too much, but remember, I'm relying on you to keep this all quiet until I say. It's not just one bad actor involved."

"A crime ring? A gang?"

"You wouldn't want to get tangled up with them."

"No doubt. I don't want to get tangled up with anyone, not even you fellows. It gives me the willies to think that some murderous crook was trespassing in my backyard."

The detective shifted on the stool. It was a small seat for such a big man. "You can rest easy about that, Mr Brown. The person who dug the grave was not a member of a crime syndicate, and the event in question happened, remarkably, very much as you described it. However, there was another factor that was very bad luck for the gravedigger that night, and that's why we have to be very careful drawing the strings together. That's all I can say."

O'Neill stood. "I strongly suggest you put a fence around your back-yard, Mr Brown. You're on the edge of an unlit waste area, essentially a gravel pit, and places like that appeal to people who prefer to conduct their business unseen."

"Yes, sure, will do. The Exhibition people should tighten up access at their end, too. Keep in touch, Detective. We do like a good Breaking News story, whenever you can tell us about it. We want it before the radio station or the provincial daily, too. I won't ask you to promise, but you know I'm expecting that favour."

"Sounds like a plan. Thanks for the coffee. It's pretty strong."

Tim walked O'Neill to the door.

"About our breaking news story at the newspaper. We've hired a uni-formed security guard for a few weeks, unarmed, because we don't trust the person at the centre of the story. We've already seen his temper, and he stands to lose a lot from our exposé. He'll even be featured on the front page, making what amounts to a confession, which he recklessly but freely gave to our reporter. Bad timing, but I'm going on holiday Thursday morning for ten days or so. If they tell him at the office that I'm away, he might come looking for me here. My housekeeper comes on Thursdays, but I wouldn't want him banging on the door when she's here alone. And I don't want another creep trespassing in my backyard."

"Got it. I'll alert the patrol cars, and drive by myself when I can. Who is your story about?"

"It's confidential until the paper is delivered tomorrow morning at six. Eric MacIntosh. County Councillor, and a crooked wannabe developer."

"Duly noted."

"Thanks, Detective. This has been very exciting for me—about catch-ing bad people, but especially that I got it mostly right. And that you'll keep an eye out for me."

They shook hands, and the detective went to his car.

In the driveway, he turned and said, "Nice car. You should wash that green stuff off, though, unless Gar is paying you to advertise for Greene Motors." He grinned and drove away.

~

Tim checked the time. Surely his car was ready by now. He wanted to start putting things in it, and maybe he'd pick up swim trunks before joining the staff.

His car was out of the service bay, but Tim was surprised and disappointed to see it hadn't been washed. He was sure Gar heard him say he wanted that done. *Darn. Now I'll have to do that myself. Whenever I wash the windshield it just gets streaky. Phooey.*

The bombastic businessman was on the phone at his paper-filled desk. He saw Tim. "Gotta run," he said to whomever was on the other end, and came out.

"Whaddya think, Tim? Isn't that the nicest set of wheels you've ever driven?"

"It certainly is a nice car, Gar. I'm disappointed you didn't clean mine, though. Did they vacuum the interior at all? I'm going on holiday and I wanted to go in a clean car."

"Come on in, Tim. I want to talk to you. Gimme the keys to that midnight blue beauty."

Tim gave him the keys, and Garland handed them to someone. He gestured toward his office, and closed the door behind them. "Have a seat, buddy. Now let me tell you what we found. I mentioned the brakes. We had to replace pads and a frozen caliper. There's rust everywhere, but we don't do body work. We'll have to send it out for that. Also, the rad's got a tiny leak, and the manifold is crusty. We can't fix all that today. But, for the life of me, I don't know why you're hanging on to it. Some kid'll think it's a cream puff because the miles are so low, but it's not for you, Tim, not for a man of your position."

Tim took a breath to respond, but Garland held up his meaty hands.

"I know, I know, you don't want to flaunt your wealth and position, not like I do, but I need to get elected now and then, so I like to keep my success in the public eye. But what does that rust-bucket say about you? It says, 'Gee, Tim Brown can't be doing very well, business-wise. Look at the heap he's driving.' Right?"

Tim sighed and dropped his head.

"And it stinks to high heaven, man. Did something die in there?"

"I, uh, forgot a bag of groceries in the trunk. Chicken."

"Figures. It's nine, ten years old, Tim. The only good feature about it is the mileage, but they rust faster parked than driven. Don't you just love the way that classy number handles? Six cylinders. I drove it for a day and was mighty tempted to use it myself."

Tim knew he had lost the battle. "How much?"

"I painted the price right on the side of it for ya."

"Did you? I don't get my news from the sides of cars. That car, minus my trade-in and the winter tires, taxes and all that stuff, over five years: what's the number?"

"I don't want you to buy it. Since you're a business owner, and a low-mileage driver, you should lease the vehicle in your company's name for a three-year term. At the end of three years, you bring it back and we'll lease you another one, also less than a year old, gently used. If I let you buy this one, you'll try to hang on to it forever. I'll be too old by that time to chase you for as long as I had to this time. With a lease arrangement, we look after all the servicing. We'll call to remind you, and give you a courtesy car, without the advertising on it. But they'll never be brown."

"Why not? It's my name. My mother always drove a brown car. A brown Caddy."

"Well, the one you've been driving looks like your name is mud. This one looks sharp, like you."

"A business lease? Monthly payments? No money down?"

"Right. You can deduct any business travel, and you'd be surprised how many business trips you make in the run of a week. They add up. You can't count driving to and from work, but everything else in the day is fair game. Here's the sales agreement, Tim. If you have the time, we can get this done today, or you can come back in the morning with a cancelled cheque for banking information. Or you can leave it here and take your car, but we had to put a reject safety sticker on it. It expires in ten days."

~

The keys to the shiny blue car were at the reception counter, along with a bag of pencils, notebooks and sunglasses from his soon-to-be former vehicle. The cars were parked side-by-side on the lot, and it was easy for him to see which one he preferred. The lime-green numbers had been washed off the blue car while he had been inside, revealing a thin green line detailing the contours from front to back. It added a little fun to the formal style.

Gar sure is a salesman. But he really has done me a favour. I can just see Rob and me in my old car, halfway across Confederation Bridge, smoke coming out from under the hood...I like the idea of a lease, especially the part where they'll remind me about oil changes, which I haven't done regularly. Three years; that's not forever. We can give it a try. I'll ask Harold to remind me to use mileage forms for deductions.

By the time he pulled into his driveway again, he had embraced his fate. He had a nice new car. Robert would love it, too.

He wanted to pack something today, so he carried two folding chairs and an empty cooler to the driveway and opened the capacious trunk. There was room for them and a good deal more in the carpeted compartment. Packing would be a cinch.

In the kitchen freezer he found a container of overlooked leftovers. He left it out on the counter to thaw for supper whenever he returned home this evening, after the big hand-over to the printers. Roger and Elaine had volunteered to go to the printing facility to stand guard until the presses were running. Other newspaper staff had volunteered to take two-hour shifts from midnight to six. Only the essential staff were permitted to work on the printing, until the issue was bundled and in the trucks for distribution.

He stopped in the wine store for some bubbly, but decided against offering it tonight. People who were working late wouldn't want alcohol. He'd take it in tomorrow at noon, chilled.

At the sports equipment store, he said "beachwear," and was shown the colourful essentials. He declined the display of shockingly skimpy swimming briefs, instead selecting two conservative pairs of baggy swim trunks with liners, along with a jaunty cotton hat, some sunscreen, and a pair of rubber-soled beach sandals.

This'll get me on the beach or around a pool without wanting to wrap myself in a car blanket.

~

The first thing Tim noticed when he entered the building was the table positioned to block entry to the general office. On it was a tent sign:

Visitors Please Report To Reception

"Does this include me?" he asked the receptionist, pointing to the sign.

"Yes, sir. Miss Fong has already added you to the list. Here's your Identification tag. Please wear it on your shirt pocket, and return it when you leave."

"Wow, this is real security, Mrs Rafuse. I suppose we should have been doing something like this all along, or put up a gate of some kind to keep strangers from just wandering about. When is the security guard coming?"

"Tomorrow morning at seven. Sometimes people come in early and forget to lock the door behind them, so Miss Fong thought it best to have security here early."

"How will they get in tomorrow?"

"Miss Fong will be here."

He looked around the office. Few staff were in sight. "Where is every-body now?"

"Upstairs, sir."

"That's...that's a lot of people up there. Please don't let's have a fire today."

For all the people there, the "War Room" was very quiet. Elaine was wearing her usual Tuesday face, her eyes down on the table where mock-ups were lying, or searching the ceiling as she read her mental image of the newspaper, looking for gaps and opportunities.

Two staff members leaned over each two-page spread to review it to-gether. They initialled each page when they were satisfied, and then slid it along to the next pair when they had finished their pages. Tim caught Elaine's attention and said, "I'll be in mine when you want me."

The room opposite his, "Give Peace A Chance", was occupied by Ed Garamond, Cindy Martin, and two "runners". They marked changes as the spreads were carefully brought to them from the other room.

Tim opened his room and locked the door behind him. He had no fur-ther need for the manila sheets. The mystery of the backyard grave was all but solved.

"I did a lot of this work 'in the field', not just walking around, but thinking, too. Maybe I don't need this room and these sheets as much as I did. Maybe I'm getting the hang of delving. Or maybe it depends on the case. Anyway, let's roll it up."

O'Neill wasn't as effusive in his gratitude as I'd hoped, but it's not over for him, and he hinted that I led them to some nasty people. I can drop my delving projects anytime, but the police can't.

"That's not true. I can't drop Project Sweetland. My staff are working through the night and we've hired security because of nasty Eric MacIn-tosh at the centre of our big news story. He deserves whatever he gets, and I'm proud that we're giving it to him. I suppose the cops feel the same way about their cases. But with guns."

He rolled up the papers, wrote TRESPASSES in red marker so it would show on the outside, added the month, and put the roll in the cabinet with the others.

The walls were bare again, except for the sheets containing motivational aphorisms, some from Sherlock Holmes or Oliver Wendell Holmes, some from himself. He wrote RATIOCINATION on one sheet, then put the markers in the drawer on his table.

He unlocked the door, left it wide open and crossed the hall. "Miss Martin, would you like to use the table in my room today? Our extra table is in use downstairs, I realized, to repel uninvited guests."

Cindy and Ed both smiled at this offer, and she moved to his room immediately.

Tim wandered down to "War" again. Elaine's focus was back to normal, and she smiled as he entered.

"A word?" he said, and indicated "Baker Street" across the hall.

"Should I close the door?" she asked.

"No need. I just have a few questions. How are you doing?"

"I'm elated. This story is a dream come true. I was talking yesterday to a friend at a small paper in a land far, far away, and I could hear his envy. He's gearing up for his community's annual historic reenactment and bluegrass festival."

She laughed harder than the statement warranted, but Tim understood completely. Until today, *The Times* had relied for excitement on the same local cultural delights. *The Times* would revert to that soon and be grateful for it; but not constantly, he hoped.

"Wonderful. Rub it in while you can. This will look great on your CV. Unless, of course, you apply to work at your friend's paper sometime. They mightn't want your rabble-rousing experience there."

"Too late. I already did a sojourn there. Yay, bluegrass!" She laughed again. "Did you want to ask me something else?"

"Yes. I understand you and Roger will do the midnight shift at the printer, and that's wonderful. But why don't I come in at seven to let the security guard in, instead of you? You'll be cross-eyed."

"Oh, that's not—are you sure you don't mind? You're getting ready for your vacation."

"I sure am, so I know I'll be up for two hours by seven o'clock. I just let him in and then what?"

"Her. I asked for a woman, hoping she'd be less likely to escalate things should Mister Rotten Apple come in, looking for a fight. Let her in and give her the spare key. Don't forget to get it from me before you go."

"Excellent strategy! Next: how's the final scrutiny going?"

"Really well. No blank spaces. Cindy Martin's ad sales are filling them up. She's sure shaking the money tree, that one."

"Music to my ears. Next question: what's the plan, celebration-wise?

Want some bubbly? I could set that up tomorrow afternoon, when we have the real paper in our hands, rather than tonight?"

"Great idea. Nothing expensive, just something for the staff to toast themselves with. And some juice, of course. In the lunchroom?"

"How about in your office? Not everyone drinks alcohol, so we shouldn't set it up where they'd have to sit with it. You won't be working hard tomorrow afternoon. I forbid it."

"Okay. Otherwise, I think we're nearly done. Do you want a final review?"

"You know what, Elaine? I thought I would, but I don't. Not after all the scrutiny that's going on across the hall—plus the esteemed opinion of a Supreme Court Justice. The staff have been more engaged and involved in this story than I have. I found it, but you led the development. My interest was to make sure it was true and fair, so I wouldn't get my shirt and pants sued off. Anything I would do now would be counterproductive. I tend to second-guess myself, as you well know, so keep me away from doing it to other people."

He paused and took a deep breath. "Carry on. You have my blessing."

~

Driving home, Tim felt as though his newspaper was embarking on a voyage across an ocean while he remained on the dock. *Fair winds to all of us.*

His sense of separation was natural. It was a turbulent time, but the best time. The staff, led by Elaine Fong, backed up by her secret paramour, would lean into challenges, with or without him. As it was supposed to be when he began his sabbatical six months ago.

~

He permitted himself a top-shelf bottle of *Travaille en équipe,* a very enjoyable and robust red with multiple flavours. The leftovers turned out to be Chinese food, not the best match with the wine, but it didn't matter. He raised a glass in the air.

"Congratulations, Timothy Brown. You're finally cutting those apron strings. It's not your mother's newspaper now, not for the remainder of this year, and hopefully never."

He had most of tomorrow for packing. He kept a notebook handy and wrote in it when he thought of yet more items to take along. He could take anything and everything in his new car, even odd things like the dartboard and darts. *Won't Rob be delighted!*

He put the empty plate in the sink, and took a glass of wine outdoors while he walked around his estate, front and back. He watered the flowers in front. Either they would survive on their own in the next ten days, or they wouldn't. Gardens, he knew, were needy.

He admired the new clover, filling in nicely. Only twice had anyone stepped off the flagstones on Sunday, but no damage was done. He was sorry but relieved when Art Clarke had left with his squalling children, as they would have been capable of undoing the whole tender field of clover. The grass would soon be long enough to mow, and Jake or Dana or someone would come and take care of that whenever the time was right.

Tim chuckled when he remembered tugging on the seized cord of his old gas mower. *Was that only four weeks ago? Boy, have I learned a lot since then. Not all of it was something I thought I'd ever learn, or want to, but now we have clover, woodshed with grill station, flagstone path, shady grove. Maybe berries in a year or two; roses, flowers. I'll get that fence put up soon, too, and a sign.*

He strolled over to the edge of the lot, stepped through to the evacuation route, and turned to look back at his property. It looked too manicured, too lived-in, to appeal as a burial ground or garbage toss now. *Parties only from now on. And quiet contemplation.*

He was delighted with how his delving had worked out. He hadn't hesitated to tell his entirely-made-up story to the detective. He was gaining skills as a Private Researcher, and gaining confidence in himself.

He glanced at his watch. The printers were starting to run his first big news story just about now. He hoped there'd be more, perhaps not so sensational, but solid news stories.

The happy giant stepped back into his yard and went into the house. He had returned from visiting the ogre, and vowed that he would share the garden with all the children henceforth. By invitation.

Trespassers not welcome.

June 30: Breaking News

Wednesday

Tim hadn't exaggerated. He was awake at five, and out of bed soon after. Today was a Big Day, and he didn't want to miss a moment of it.

First, a double espresso, a laudatory gift from Gloria.

Then, the auspicious stepping-out to the box on his front porch, the lifting of the lid, and the retrieving of the latest edition of his very own hefty newspaper.

There it was, above the masthead:

BREAKING NEWS! COLLUSION IN THE COUNTY!
Greedy land grab! Forest destroyed! Lake polluted!
[See inside for student grad photos!]

The lead story was a summary of all the transgressions the staff had uncovered, involving all the actors in the departments of the municipal and provincial governments in cahoots with Eric and Mary MacIntosh, operating through several named and numbered companies. Each paragraph raising a new point contained a note to 'See Article on Page xx'.

Eric MacIntosh's smiling face was there, below the fold, with the headline "Developer Proud of His Work"

James Olsen had returned to the scene of the crimes against nature several times since he and Tim had first discovered it in April. Each of his photographs told a dramatic story by itself, and the captions directed the reader to 'See Article on Page xx'. James got photo credits; his work deserved it.

Tim had proofread it all already, but it was a different thing to see it in print. He'd certainly smuggle a copy or two across the Confederation Bridge to review in detail while Robert was rehearsing in Indian River.

The colourful advertising insert caught his attention, too. This edition featured the Johnson Building, home of *The Times*, resplendent in its new yellow façade with royal blue trim. Another photo showed the scaffolding going up at the Daisy Cafe next door, with the caption, "What colours will the diner be wearing?" and "Will your business be next?" It made him proud.

He glanced at the clock. It was nearly time to open the office for the security guard. *Oh, that's no problem. I'll just float downtown in my new car.*

He sang as he drove, noting how quiet it was in the car.

> Go, tell it on the mountain, over the hills and everywhere.
> Go, tell it on the mountain, la la-la la-la la!

He whistled the song as he approached the office building. The security guard was waiting.

"Good morning, come on in. I'm Tim Brown, and you are?"

"I'm Tammy Oickle, sir. I'm your security guard." She was wearing a black uniform with "Safety" shoulder patches. She wasn't muscular or tall, but she filled out her uniform snugly, and wore thick-soled boots. He assumed she knew a thing or two about stopping intruders.

"Well, Miss Oickle, we appreciate you coming here to keep an eye on our front door for a while."

He picked up the clipboard which Elaine had left on the table at the entrance, and pointed to the box of ID tags. "These people may be admitted. Throughout the day, when someone makes an appointment, their name will be added to the list. Name not on list, no trespassing, unless Reception verifies, got it?"

"Yes, sir."

"Good. Everyone worked late yesterday, so I doubt if they will come in early. If they do, they'll have their own key. Just make sure they lock the door behind them, until eight-thirty when Mrs Rafuse, our receptionist, comes in. After that, it's just this list and the tags. Any questions?"

"No, sir."

"You can leave your bag behind the counter there. Just tell Mrs Rafuse it's yours or she'll have it in the Lost & Found. I think that's everything. Thanks again, Miss Oickle, and good luck."

~

Tim returned home for that second coffee, and made his list for the day.

To Do
- Greene Auto - banking info for pmts
- Bank - get cash
- Pack bags
- Champagne/juice; ice; cups
- Flowers/streamers/balloons
- Pack car

To Call or See:
- Rob
- Ev
- Mort?
- Stella
- Piano

He appreciated two things: none of this felt like work, and he was eager to do it all.

It was time to go and make the new car his own.

Tim pulled into Greene Auto and parked. His old car was still where he'd left it. It seemed closer to the ground than it had been yesterday. *Thanks for your service, old jalopy.*

Garland Greene was waiting for him.

"Did you forget that you're the mayor of this town, Gar? Seems you're always here."

"I start every morning here, Tim. I say hello to my customers as they get checked in, and sell whatever isn't nailed down. Then I go over to the Tower of Power. Congratulations on the big story, by the way. Boy, I had no idea Eric was in that deep. He's going to take you off his Christmas card list, that's for sure. You didn't pull any punches."

"You read the paper already? Yeah, our new motto is 'Go big or stay home'. We had to go big. Hinting at it wouldn't get people upset enough to call their elected representatives to demand action."

"They're not going to call me, are they? I didn't see anything about the town in it. Didn't Eric tangle with you about a development on Main Street?"

"Yes, he did, but I stopped his nefarious scheme in its tracks. It's not a crime to be stupid, unfortunately, or even to make vaguely threatening suggestions. He doesn't like you, Gar, but we kept that comment for another day. Anyway, Main Street's Gem District is looking pretty pretty, don't you agree? That's my revenge. I assume our Miss Martin has come to see you about the town sponsorship?"

"She sure has. I'm trying to hire her over here. She'd sell every car on the lot, three times a day."

"You can't have her, but you can be on the lookout for something affordable and reliable for her to drive. I don't know why, but she doesn't have a lot of money at the moment, so she's driving something worse than my old car. But she sure will have more money soon."

"I'll keep that in mind. Now, let's make you the honest owner of this vehicle. I allowed you too much for your old heap, and didn't charge you enough for this one. Do you want to see the details?"

"Ha-ha. I appreciate you looking after me so quickly, Gar, but I know you'd never make a deal that wasn't good for you, too. I don't need to review the details. I already agreed to take it, so I have no bargaining position. Besides, I like it. Here's the banking info, and my insurance."

"Good. Give me the keys again. Be right back."

A few minutes later, Gar returned with a fistful of papers. "For heaven's sake, you know you have to put gas in the car, don't you? Gee whiz, we just turned the key to get the mileage. The warning light was lit on the dash and the low gas chime was chiming. Are you deaf *and* blind?"

"I was singing, Gar. I'm happy."

"You wouldn't be happy if you ran out of gas. We put a gallon in to get you to the station. It's not good for them to go dry. Sign here, and here, and here. Oh, and initial here. That's it."

He shook Tim's hand. "Welcome to the Greene Auto family, Tim. We'll take care of you. But you gotta put gas in it yourself sometimes. Do it now."

~

After filling up the gas tank, Tim really did need to go to the bank. The tank was huge, good for a long trip. He made sure the balance on his credit card was cleared, and he withdrew cash for holiday places that didn't take plastic.

Next was the florist. He selected a big bouquet of flowers for the staff room, and a smaller one for Elaine. Both carried arched plastic *CONGRATULATIONS!* signs. He had considered streamers or balloons, but decided against them in light of the seriousness of the news topic. A muted celebration, not visible through the front windows, would be more appropriate.

He went home for the champagne and juice, put them in a cooler, stopped again at the gas station for ice, and drove to the office.

It was close to lunchtime now. Everyone was in, including uniformed Tammy Oickle, who stepped out when Tim entered, and said, "Welcome to *The Times*, sir. May I have your name, please?" She wasn't going to make any mistakes.

The receptionist smiled as she watched Tammy Oickle check the list for Tim's name, hand him a GUEST badge, and mark down the number.

"I'm glad someone was expecting me," he said, "or else we would've had to drink this ourselves in the foyer. Any calls, Mrs Rafuse, good or bad?"

"Yes, sir, lots of calls. No complaints. Quite a few new subscribers."

He set flowers in the lunchroom, and took Elaine's bouquet and the beverages to her office.

"That's sweet of you, Tim, thanks very much! You are very thoughtful. And supportive"

"I am very grateful. Any unusual calls this morning?"

"None from MacIntosh. A number of folk calling to say 'Well done'. A few said it was about time somebody blew the whistle on that you-know-what. That feels good."

"Nice. How do you want to do this? Just leave the drinks here, or call everybody in?"

"Let's call them in. I think most everyone is here now. I've heard a lot of congratulating going on already. Will you round them up?"

"My pleasure."

Tim waved everyone toward the editor's office, where Elaine was setting out drink glasses. She handed one bottle to James to pop the cork, and another to Ed Garamond.

There were several calls of "We did it!" and multiple "Woo-hoo!"s. They squeezed inside or stood just outside the door.

Tim toasted "the best staff this community newspaper ever had," and Elaine echoed that.

"We couldn't have done it without you guys," someone responded.

"Well, you will now," Tim said. "Me, anyway. I've supposedly been 'off' all year, but as of tomorrow, I'll really be 'off', gone away for ten days."

"Tomorrow's a holiday for some of us, too," Jean Naugler said, "because it's Canada Day. Some picked Thursday, and some picked Friday. We'll catch up later if we need to. You know we know how to work!"

"I certainly do. Miss Fong is in charge, but so are all of you. My goodness, I'm proud of you all. Now, if you'll excuse me, I must go and work on my tan. Cheerio!"

~

Tim stood in the door of the Daisy Café. When Evelyn looked up, he mimed that he would phone her at six this evening, and she nodded enthusiastically. He didn't want to go in. They could talk more freely on the phone later, when they were both relaxed.

He started the car and pushed the button for the A/C to come on. It blew cool air quickly and gently. He took out his phone and dialed Mort Evers.

"Hello, is that you, Tim?" Martha answered. "The telephone says it is."

"I am me. How are you today, Martha?"

"I'm very well, thank you. Are you coming out for a bowl of soup? We're late getting to our lunch, but there's lots and it's ready now."

"I'll be there in an instant!"

He was, too, transported by his new magic carpet. He knocked and entered, and was immediately invited to sit at the table. They had waited for him. Mort asked the blessing, and then the conversation began.

"Your house, Tim! The grove of trees! The exquisite food! I never expected ceviche! That Robert! Your friends! Your aunt!"

Tim felt as though he had joined his parents for lunch, but not the parents he'd once had. The Evers were family and friends at the same time. He was glad he'd come.

"Do you fellows plan to go for a walk this afternoon?"

"I have a different suggestion, Martha. Would you both like to come for a short, scenic drive with me? I have a newish car, and I think it would glide over the bumps on that narrow road out to Stonehurst. You can sit back and digest your lunch while enjoying the view. Then I must go home to pack."

The ride was fun. Mort joined Tim in the front, and Martha took the back seat, where she would have rolled around without the welcome restraint of the seatbelt and the drop-down armrest.

The car seemed as wide as the road was narrow, and Tim slowed to carefully avoid walkers. It was a spectacular part of the coast, though, and they both thanked him enthusiastically when he delivered them back to their cottage.

"I'm happy to be going on vacation and hearing Robert's concert, but I do feel a teeny bit sad to be leaving. I never thought I would, but so many good things have happened for me recently, including meeting you folks. We'll catch up when I return. We'll have you over for a sit-down dinner, too, without the crowd, or not as many."

"Before you go," Mort said, "may I ask if you've resolved your "hit-and-run" yet?"

"I have, or mostly. My theoretical account of events steered the police toward finding the victim *and* the perpetrator. I'm very proud of that. It's very hush-hush, but we'll write about it eventually. I still don't know how I feel about my involvement, though. I felt I was treated unfairly. I'll figure it out, I guess, or get over it."

"I was thinking about that, too," Mort said. "There were trespasses against you. We are taught to ask for forgiveness when *we* trespass, in the same way 'as we forgive those who trespass against us'. That is difficult. Sometimes we just walk away. Some events in life don't end in balance, even though the Lord's Prayer implies that there should be. It's disconcerting, to have such an important life moment left up to us to resolve."

"I hadn't thought about it like that, not being a biblical scholar. I appreciate that you've phrased it succinctly for me."

Mort laughed. "Nobody's ever accused me of being succinct before!"

Martha had gone inside the cottage, and returned with a now-familiar paper bag of this morning's baking. "For you and Robert. You'll need a bite on the road."

Tim glided home, feeling so fortunate.

Finally, it was time to put his clothes in the suitcase. He'd leave the lid open until the morning so things wouldn't be creased too much.

~

Tim had discovered a frosty pork chop in the freezer, inspiring him to put a note on the fridge to defrost the freezer when he returned. He put the chop in the frying pan and made a single portion of instant rice. It was a simple supper, but he'd be dining well very soon. The wine was a serviceable *Plonk de Mercredi.* He had lots to celebrate today, it seemed, but *vin ordinaire* didn't dampen the elation he felt about all the good things happening.

At six, he phoned Evelyn.

"I'm not in the tub yet." she said. "I had a business meeting. Is this how it goes when you're a tycoon?"

"Yup. No tub-time for tycoons. Things going okay?"

"Seem to be. Art said he was sorry to leave early on Sunday. His kids are little hellions. He didn't say that, but I do."

"They'll grow out of it eventually, won't they? I hope Art survives. I'm just calling to say bye-bye. Ten days seems like a long time."

"I won't notice you're gone. I'm working twice as hard, thanks to you."

"Making any money, though? That's why you do it."

"Is it? Yes, actually the extra money is nice."

"Good. Well, you take care, my friend. Robert says I'm not to be on the phone all the time. I don't think I'll need to be anyway, but I will have my mobile phone with me, and you are welcome to call me anytime. I mean it. He'd be happy to hear from you, too."

"Give him a hug from me and a rub on the head for good luck about his concert. I wish I could hear it. Drive carefully, you. Love you."

"Love you, too."

~

He called Robert next. "All set?"

"I think so. I'm packing now. How much room do we have? I can't decide which jacket to take. Do I have room for two? What about my tux? I'd like to lay it out in the back seat. I don't want to have to press it in the hotel room, that makes it shiny."

"Don't worry. Take whatever you want. I got—I had the car cleaned. It's good. There's room for everything."

"Really? That makes it a lot easier."

"Anything for you, maestro. Did the garden party help to break your fixations about the concert?"

"It sure did, thank you so much for doing that. All I needed was to be distracted for a couple hours. I'm settled now. I'll be nervous, of course, but not wound up so tight I can't play. What time will you be here?"

"Whenever you say. I said all my goodbyes today, so I'm obliged to leave now."

"Want to come in tonight?"

"Gosh, I hadn't thought of that. I've been drinking wine already."

"I'd have thought you'd have something more celebratory?"

"I had a sip of bubbly at the office at noon to celebrate our excellent breaking new story. I've got a copy of the paper for you to read sometime."

"I will, too. Bring champers for after the concert, okay?"

"Done. See you in the morning. Nine o'clock okay? Eight?"

"Nine's probably good. I'm going to try to sleep in. Wish me luck."

"Good luck, and good night. Love you."

"Love you."

That was everyone except Stella. He called and got her voice mail. He reminded her that they would be "overseas" until the following weekend —overseas meaning across the Northumberland Strait. She was welcome to call on his cellphone anytime, and he'd call her back when there was a signal. He hoped she was well, and thanked her for coming on Sunday and being so charming.

He phoned Elaine, but she didn't answer. *She's likely celebrating with Roger.* He left a short message of gratitude and congrats and hello to Roger.

Whew! Going away is exhausting! But I'm fortunate to have people I care about to go away from and with.

The last unchecked item on his list was the piano humidifiers. He topped them up with a tablespoon of water, and then played happy music until the month was over.

Jan Fancy Hull

Tim's June wine list

Tim continues to drink wine nearly every day. The names of the vintages he selects are often in a language other than English. Their meanings (as we intend them) might mystify even those who actually understand the languages. We have provided a handy translation to assist the puzzled.

Chapter 4: *Petites Victoires*: little victories
Chapter 7: *Un bon début*: a good start
Chapter 11: *Lastre di Pietra*: flagstone
Chapter 14: *Récupérer*: to recuperate
Chapter 18: *Inattendu*: unexpected
Chapter 19: *Qualcosa di sospetto*: something fishy
Chapter 23: *Très fier*: very proud
Chapter 25: *Une longue journée*: a long day
Chapter 29: *Travaille en équipe*: teamwork

Acknowledgements

I rely on my imagination for story ideas, but I needed outside help this time, since I have no experience with the police in the way that Tim Brown does in this novel. I needed real facts about police procedures, and I am grateful to Chris Trites, a retired policeman and author of many novels himself, for providing them. While he was clear about what he would have done in the situation I describe, I'm sure I blurred the facts in places; any errors or omissions are mine.

My Dear Readers continue to be my guardrails, guiding me when Tim's behaviour seems out of character for him as they've come to know him, and I am deeply grateful to Cynthia French, Janet Barkhouse, Judi McDonald, Eric Hustvedt; and Margaret MacDonald Trites for picking grammatical nits.

My editor, Andrew Wetmore, is a mighty guardrail, too, and his gentle but firm suggestions always make my good stories better.

As we embark on the second half of Tim Brown's year of discovery, my gratitude continues for Moose House Publications—Editor Andrew, Publisher Brenda Thompson, and illustrator Rebekah Wetmore—for their enduring support.

And to you, my enthusiastic readers: share your thoughts at info@-moosehousepress.com.

In Memoriam: Cynthia French, 1953-2023

One of my Dear Readers, Cynthia French, died from a fast-moving cancer not four months after handing me her valuable notes on this manuscript.

She was so enthusiastic about Tim Brown, taking special delight in his dinner table and his kindness toward everyone.

In writing that, I see I have described Cynthia, too. All who knew her have lost a dear friend.

About the author

Jan Fancy Hull lives in a log chalet beside a quiet lake in Lunenburg County, Nova Scotia, where she has written non-fiction, award-winning poetry, short stories, and novels.

In former lives, she worked as a radio broadcaster, arts administrator, sailing tours skipper, and employee benefits broker.

During the winter, Jan watches snowflakes fall as she writes. In warm months, she carves Nova Scotia sandstone into sculptures. She enjoys the occasional round of golf, and drifting on the lake in her little boat, which she claims is a great place to edit.

In 2022, Jan received the Rita Joe Poetry Prize for her poem, "Moss Meditations."

Sneak peek into *July: Confidence*

Here is chapter 5 from *July: Confidence*, the seventh book in the Tim Brown Mysteries series. It is due out in September, 2024.

~

July 5: Clamouring

Monday

They had eaten well since arriving in Kensington, but sporadically, so they had tucked into last night's dinner with gusto. Mussels were on the menu, but they'd had an abundance of that delicacy already. They leaned toward more standard fare, though they would not have described their salads, salmon (Robert) and rack of lamb (Tim), as standard.

"It was superb, wasn't it, Rob? Absolutely see-you-perb!"

Robert groaned from under his fluffy pillow. "I'm still full. Do we live like this, now? Tall Dan asks us for our every wish, and then grants it?"

"That's it exactly: we live like this now. But only now. Not forever. It's been a long while since I dined in a place like this—and it was likely right here! Someone to take our orders—no, to discuss our preferences, right down to which side of the green hill the lambs were raised on—and someone else to bring water and bread, and change the cutlery, and the sommelier who picked a perfect wine to complement both our choices…"

"The *amuse-bouches*, too. We should have sorbet sometimes at home between courses."

"Sure, if we have multiple courses, but who would serve it to us? Hey, I have an idea, Rob: let's do a dinner party on a posh theme! For sure, real posh people wouldn't dream of doing it, but it's like a play here, isn't it, with the staff all playing roles? I wonder who Master Dan is when he's at home? Does he slurp soup in his slippers, alone in a drafty garret?"

"That sounds more like a Gothic novel. Or a murder mystery; I think you can get scripts for those. Might be fun. I wonder who we'd murder?"

"I can think of someone, ha-ha, but that wouldn't work: he'd have to be invited to be murdered, and that'll never happen. This inn right here would be a great place to stage a murder mystery."

He adopted a sepulchral voice. "The guests were trapped inside by the dismal weather, no chance of escape because every narrow road twisted back to the old inn. They had nothing to do but nosh their way through the wonderful menu, drinking flaming cocktails at the bar and playing endless games of cribbage in front of the fireplaces, and then—"

Tim jumped up, wringing his hands melodramatically. His voice raised a couple octaves. "Eek! Old Dan's dead! He's been stabbed to death with seventeen fish forks! Ew. Oh! Oh! Who will attend to our every wish and whim now? Alas and alack!"

"Poor old Dan," Robert said with a giggle. "The nicest of them all. He didn't deserve it. We didn't mean to do it, we were just bored, and once you start with the fish forks, it's hard to stop. Thank goodness it wasn't Angelique—we can't kill the bartender, or the story will fall apart."

They were talking and laughing a bit noisily for the early hour when there came a knock on the door.

"Uh-oh. Maybe that's Inspector Fumble."

Tim peered through the peep-hole, then opened the door quickly to admit room service. Before ending his shift last evening, Dan had inquired about their pre-breakfast preferences, and they had asked for strong dark roast coffee, of course.

The beverage arrived in an insulated carafe, their cups were wrapped in hot towels, and a dish of bite-sized oatcakes was on the tray.

Tim gave the attendant some folding money and closed the door. The coffee smelled delicious in the room.

"Dear old Dan," Robert said, still chuckling. "Thank goodness he survived. Shall I pour?"

~

Tim and Robert took their time getting ready for breakfast and whatever the day might present, first taking full advantage of the surprisingly-modern bath in this century-old establishment to soak away the residue of previous anxieties.

They dressed in clothes appropriate for the surroundings if not the season, and again descended the grand staircase.

Looking out the dining room's wrap-around windows, they wondered whether any attire was appropriate for what was going on outside. Rain was streaming down the windows, and what trees they could see beyond the manicured croquet lawns were waving their branches in strong winds.

"On the bright side," Tim said, "we don't have to worry about getting a sunburn. I could have booked a room with an ocean view for more money, but now I know why I didn't. We haven't even seen the ocean since we left Cavendish."

"This place could be called 'More Money Inn'," Robert said. "It was built by oil barons, I was reading, and it has continued to cater to that money class for a century. Good for them, I say. Barons need a place to spend their money. So how come we're here? I know you're well-to-do, but you work to earn your money. The oil barons' money works to earn their money. What I earn at the university hardly buys a salad here. Did you see the bar prices last night?"

"Sure, but you enjoyed yourself, didn't you? This is my first vacation and second trip of my whole life. Many of my employees fly all over the world for vacations every year, so how much is that, maybe a thousand per? I'm due a little fun, too, and it wouldn't be fun without you. Nobody else has their own concert organist for company."

As if on cue, a waiter approached their table to say, "Excuse me, is one of you gentlemen a Dr Kirk?"

Robert said, "Yes, I am he."

"Sorry to interrupt, Dr Kirk. A couple who are guests of the inn thought they recognized you. They asked if they might be introduced to you."

Robert was facing the dining room entrance and naturally looked around to locate a pair of eager faces, but didn't see any.

"They're outside in the Great Room, sir. They didn't want to disturb you while you're dining, but they'd be pleased if you and your companion would join them afterwards for a coffee or other beverage. No rush. Or shall I tell them you're not available at this time?"

"I don't know about more coffee, but I can say hello, at least. Sure. We won't be much longer here. Thanks."

"Look at you, Rob. Your fans are clamouring to meet you!"

"You work with words, Tim; you know 'clamouring' doesn't mean two people asking shyly via a third party. But I can practice for future clamourers by being gracious with these strangers."

"Let me check them out for you first," Tim said. "I'll go to the loo, and cast my eye around discreetly on the way. Excuse me."

The concourse was moderately busy. A convention was in session somewhere on the grounds, but families and couples who hadn't wanted to brave the foul weather were milling about undecidedly.

Tim located the washroom sign beside the registration desk and kept his eyes on it, but concentrated on his peripheral vision. He didn't identify any couple on the way in whom he judged to be interested in Robert, who wouldn't just walk right up to him without an intermediary —but he did on the return.

If the inn were hiring models for a photo-shoot for their promotional brochures, they couldn't do better than these two: mid-fifties, well-acquainted with skin and hair care, slender, tastefully dressed, small but expensive bits of jewellery on both. All of this Tim took in as he glanced disinterestedly along their side of the room before he re-entered the dining room.

He relayed the description to Robert. "Know them?"

"Can't say any of that rings a bell, though I'd like it to. Maybe they're potential sponsors like Jeremy hosted on Saturday night. I didn't ask for their name, but I don't think it matters. Thanks for checking them out. They sound safe; not boorish, at least. Shall we say hello?"

The couple who'd asked to meet Robert—the very ones Tim had picked out—turned out to be really nice people, friendly, classy, and easy talkers. Equally important, they claimed to be great fans of 'good music', especially pipe organ music. They said they had been in the audience for Robert's performance on Saturday, had returned for yesterday's concert by the string quartet, and were now at this inn by happy coincidence.

They hoped he didn't think they were too forward.

"Of course not," Robert said magnanimously. "Organists rarely attract fans, with the notable exceptions of the late E. Power Biggs, or Virgil Fox, also gone, or Diane Bish, the old dear, still going strong in her gold shoes with crystals on the heels. Maybe that's how one gets famous. I should get a pair of sparkly organ shoes. I could wear them for that pedal encore I played Saturday night!"

That broke the ice. The fans were Gunter and Maria Schmidt, and they were smooth hosts at this impromptu kaffeeklatsch. Although Tim and Robert had just eaten and were well-coffeed, they agreed to join them in the armchairs in front of the fire for a small fortified caffé mocha.

"We really don't know much about music, I'm afraid," Gunter confessed, "so we can't describe your performance as the reviewer does in today's newspaper, but we feel it in the heart, as we say. Music uplifts us, doesn't it, Maria?"

"Oh, yes, very much so. That's why we support the arts at home and abroad: so we'll have performances, and galleries, for all to enjoy."

"Where's home?" Robert asked politely.

"Manitoba," Maria answered. "Near Winnipeg,"

"That's so far. You didn't drive all the way here, did you? I find navigating even just around here rather tedious, and we're a long way from Manitoba. I'd never make it."

"Oh, goodness, no. We flew. We fly everywhere for business and so forth."

Tim nodded. "I understand. I flew over here for a conference several years ago, thinking I couldn't spare the time away from work to drive. But we're touring around this time."

"From where, may I ask?"

"From South River, Nova Scotia. Just a small town. I'm not here for a conference now, though; this is my vacation, our vacation, I should say, now that Robert's concert is over. He has certainly earned some R&R after that, I'm sure you'd agree. So many notes! All from memory!"

"It was phenomenal! Dr Kirk, may I inquire the name of your management company?" Gunter asked.

"I don't have one."

"What? Pardon me, that was rude, but how do you get seen—what do they call it, Maria?"

"Get on the circuit?"

"Yes, yes. How do impresarios find you without representation? Must they read this?" He waved his manicured hand at the Charlottetown paper, which suddenly seemed small and unworldly.

"I'm not on any circuit, not yet. I work hard to get noticed by people who know people, which resulted in last weekend's very nice booking. Not every university organ prof gets there. I'm confident it will lead to more engagements, but it's baby steps all the way. I'll send a copy of this review—if it's good—to my contacts, and they—"

Gunter shook his head dismissively. "In Europe, they do not rely on reviews from small town Canadian papers. One must have a publicist who has the ear of the great impresarios in order to get on the truly big stages with the great organs."

Robert shrugged, ever so slightly. "In Canada it may be different—"

"With respect, Dr Kirk—" Gunter interjected.

"No, Gunter." Maria reached toward her husband. "Forgive us, Dr Kirk, we're not here to argue. Gunter and I simply want to express our admiration and gratitude for your performance, and wish the best of success for you, however you choose to approach it. We mustn't keep you from your R&R, both of you. You've been very kind to let us meet you and learn a little about you. Are you beach people? We prefer somewhere more tropical for that, but we'll stay indoors today anyway because of this beastly weather. I so dislike hob-nobbing with conventioneers, but such is our work. Gunter is always keeping the wheels turning here and on the continent."

"I don't know if we're 'beach people' or not," Tim said, "but we won't find out today either. I'm going to check with Dan, the concierge. Have you met him yet? I hope he'll recommend some nearby indoor diversion for us."

Gunter handed his business card to Robert and Tim. It displayed his name, an international phone number, and a website.

"'People Wealth' sounds intriguing. What business are they in?"

"It's our management company. It is involved in many areas of endeavour."

Tim fished out one of his cards from his wallet. "No clues on my card, I'm afraid, just my phone numbers. I'm on sabbatical now, so I'm downplaying my work connection this year. My card is useless really. The bottom number will ring at my house, where I'm not, and the other one's in my pocket."

"I admire a man who protects his energy," Gunter said, no longer argumentative. "You are fortunate, or perhaps wise is the word I should use. May I inquire what your work is when you are not on leave?"

"I, uh, I work for a community newspaper. In South River."

"And may I ask what kind of management your company does, here or on the continent?" Robert asked Gunter. "'On the continent' sounds a bit like Noël Coward."

"Does it? I'm not familiar with him. So many great people to know, like yourself. My wife and I, and our partners, invest in selected special individuals. Some people invest in oil or transportation or consumer goods, but we invest in people, those who are well-positioned to move to the next level, and would, but for lack of sufficient financial support or connections. We find it very rewarding, win-win, as the Americans say. Well, we've detained you kind folks long enough. I hope we'll meet again."

He offered his hand and everyone shook everyone's.

"Perhaps we will," Robert said. "Thanks very much for the coffees, Gunter, Maria. Lovely to meet you both."

~

Back in their room, Tim said, "What was that about Noël Coward, Rob? You had a funny look."

"Oh, just the way Maria said 'the continent' reminded me of him. Coward was wickedly clever."

Robert sat on the edge of the desk, mimed smoking a long cigarette, and sang:

> In a bar on the Piccola Marina
> Life called to Mrs. Wentworth-Brewster
> Fate beckoned her and introduced her...

"It's a hoot, and it wouldn't be considered naughty nowadays. I worked it up in my university days. A concert tour 'on the continent' would be something, though, wouldn't it?"

"Keep dreaming, maestro. Anything could happen. We'll look up their website when we get home. I've heard of Coward, but I've never heard you sing his songs. Let's feature you at a dinner-party, instead of the murder-mystery! I'll try to learn the accompaniment to your act."

Robert sat to read the newspaper review, courtesy of his admirers, while Tim checked the flashing light on the hotel phone. It was a message from Elaine.

"Hi, Tim, got your messages. Apologies for not calling you earlier. I was with the RCMP some of the time. They wanted to check details of our story before they called on Mister Bad Apple. I'm pretty sure they'll lay charges soon. Mister Bad himself has not contacted us. He's likely been planning how to blame the people he'd bullied into letting him get away with his crimes. Otherwise, everything is humming along. We'll have a full paper this week and...but...I'm sorry to have to tell you..."

Elaine's voice had begun to tremble, instantly causing Tim's heart rate to jump, long-distance.

"...to tell you that Roger and I have split. It was unlikely we would last anyway, since I'll be leaving here at the end of my contract, but still." She exhaled a shaky breath and cleared her throat. "But there it is. Leaves me more time for work, I guess. There's plenty of that. None of this should worry you, Tim, but I thought you deserved to know. You've been so supportive and encouraging of me. That's—"

The recording had timed out. Tim waited for the automated voice to tell him how to replay the message, which he did, and then erased it.

He sat back in the chair at the desk. Poor Elaine. She seemed so happy with Roger. This has probably happened to her before in other towns through her career. It's tough to grow a relationship when she's moving around the country on one-year contracts. Her man would just be settling in when she'd pull up stakes and move along, like "The Littlest Hobo", as she said.

"Are you off the phone now, Tim? Can I read this to you?"

"Uh, sure. What does it say?"

Robert read some of the review, which was well-written and full of praise. "'In fact,'" he read, "'Kirk committed no error, nothing that your reviewer could cite to show off his deep knowledge of the organ canon, leaving him to say only that all the works were played masterfully and sometimes innovatively. Further, the instrument itself bears witness to the skilled Quebec manufacturer that built it originally, installed and later dismantled it in New Brunswick, transported it across Confederation Bridge, and re-assembled it in historic Saint Mary's, which resonates to the mighty instrument as though it was purpose built. Your reviewer thought he heard a cipher during a soft passage, but realized that it was in fact an evening sparrow outside the church, lending its sweet voice to its very accurate imitator inside.' Isn't that something, Tim?"

"Congratulations, Rob! It's great! And well-deserved! Are you happy with it?"

"Very. There's more, all about my wonderful artistry. You can read it later. What was that phone message?"

"Oh, good news and bad news. The newspaper is doing fine, but Elaine, my backbone-of-steel editor, is undone."

"Oh, no! What happened?"

"She broke off with her man, or he with her. She was so happy, and now she's not. Seems it was laid low by her contract with us which terminates when the year is over."

"He might still be carrying a candle for her, and is trying to protect himself by cutting it off now before he gets in any deeper."

"Do you think?"

"I hear about it on campus all the time. University is a tilt-a-whirl, romance-wise. Eventually, all broken hearts find their way to the music studio. I have to get quite brusque with the students sometimes so we can get on with the lesson."

"I've never known you to be brusque."

"If you cry on my organ bench you'll see it. But I'd rather you didn't."

"Agreed. What's a cipher?"

"Congratulations for asking. You know that organs are simple contraptions that blow wind through pipes. The wind is held back by pallets seated over a hole at the bottom of each pipe, until you press the key for that pipe. Sometimes a pallet doesn't seat properly, and the wind will leak into the pipe, producing a little whistle called a cipher. Of course, once it happens, it sounds constantly while the organ is on. It's no wonder organists are dotty."

"Has this ever happened to you?"

"Not yet."

~

Dan reported the slightly-good news that a let-up in the rain was forecast for the evening, which wouldn't help much with the quest for outdoor activities. Interest in that was waning, anyway, especially if it involved sitting on wet sand or even playing croquet in wet grass.

"Any chance we could get tickets to the Confederation Centre tonight?"

"I'm afraid not, Mr Brown. That show is almost always sold out on the day of, and bad weather drives even more patrons to them. I'm just after pleading with them on behalf of another guest, and there are just no seats left. But may I suggest a very pleasant alternative for you and Dr Kirk? There's a sweet little semi-professional theatre in North Rustico, a quick half-hour from here, and they have just a few seats left for the matinee today. Would you be interested? Those seats will go quickly, too."

"Oh, well...what's playing?"

"A one-act romance by George Bernard Shaw, a light comedy, and just under an hour in duration. I was just a moment ago asked to cancel a reservation at a commendable Italian restaurant, also in North Rustico. I can ask for it to be ready for you following the show, if you like? I don't wish to be rude, but I'll need your decisions almost immediately."

"Hang on, Dan. Rob, no seats at "Anne" in Charlottetown, but Dan has a theatre matinee followed by an Italian dinner, both in North Rustico. He needs to know now or the seats will be snapped up."

"What do you want to do?"

"I say let's. We need to do something."

"How do we get there?"

"Good question. Dan, please reserve two matinee tickets at the theatre and a table for two in the Italian restaurant following. Thank you very much. Can you show Robert exactly how to get there and back, though? We don't have much luck navigating these roads on our own. He'll be right down. Thanks again."

~

Dan traced Route 6 all the way for them. There were only five rights and three lefts going; returning, he said, the turns "will be in the same places, but opposite."

The village of North Rustico was very attractive, postcard-like with colourful boats and traps and sheds along the harbourfront. The one-hundred-seat theatre had a small bar and an art gallery in the lobby, and the front of house staff and ushers were dressed in little black dresses or near-tuxedos.

The two-person play was entertaining enough, perhaps not the well-polished machine that the musical in Charlottetown might have been; but they weren't there, they were here.

"I wish there was something like this in South River," Tim said as the applause faded and the house lights came up.

The restaurant was small and tables were mere inches apart, so con-versation inevitably spilled over amongst the patrons, first about the weather, then about the play, which several had just seen.

Discussion ceased when the meals were served. All guests, whether they had seen the play or not, attempted to pull a cone of privacy around themselves.

Tim and Robert skipped dessert in favour of making it back to the inn in the vestiges of daylight. The rhythmic sound of scraping windshield wipers was blissfully absent for the first time since Saturday. Tim hesit-ated briefly at only one turn on the way back because he hadn't been counting, but they worked it out and soon parked properly behind the imposing inn.

"To reward us for skipping dessert," Robert said, "can we see what An-gelique can do for us?"

They gave her free rein to concoct another entertaining drink, and sa-voured the end of their first whole day of vacation.

Before turning out the lights, Tim called Elaine's office phone, said he'd received her message, was glad the newspaper building hadn't been pelted with rotten eggs; but most of all, he was sincerely sorry about her personal troubles. He said they'd just been to a one-act play about a rela-tionship, which had an unexpected happy ending. He said he knew real life didn't always go the way people wanted, but perhaps her play would have a second act.